THE LIES ARCANA

BOOK SEVENTEEN
OF THE STARSHIP'S MAGE SERIES

Faolan's Pen Publishing
22 King St. S, Suite 300
Waterloo, Ontario
N2J 1N8 Canada

For paperback sales information, visit faolanspen.com. For special events, release alerts, and more books from the author, visit glynnstewart.com.

A record of this book is available from Library and Archives Canada.

ISBN 978-1-989674-85-7 (Trade Paperback)
ISBN 978-1-989674-86-4 (Amazon Paperback)

1 2 3 4 5 6 7 8 9 10

THE LIES ARCANA

Book Seventeen
OF THE STARSHIP'S MAGE SERIES

GLYNN STEWART

FAOLAN'S PEN
PUBLISHING

faolanspen.com

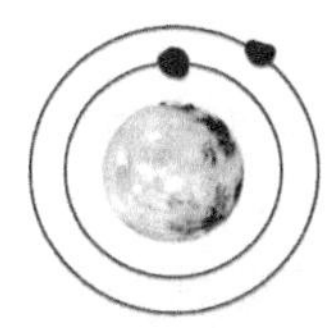

CHAPTER 1

CHIMERA LANDING WAS A BEAUTIFUL CITY. It was built out of concentric rings of towers—a mix of business, industrial, and residential—that grew shorter as one drew close to the outskirts of the city.

Those towers were glowing edifices of pale gray concrete, windows and structure alike chosen to diffuse the light from Mackenzie's star to avoid blinding observers or creating hot spots on the ground around them.

Smaller structures spread out from the towers, but even those had been built to a standardized pattern and in clearly laid-out patterns. Designed from the ground up as a metropolis for twenty million people, Chimera Landing was a monument to the skills of her architects and the tens of thousands of slave laborers who'd been forced to build the new capital of an interstellar state built by conquest.

Connor O'Hannagain figured the founder of said state, the man who had originally named Ridwan City after himself, would be horrified by its current purpose. The no-longer-slaves who had built the city were *delighted*—he knew that because he'd just come away from a meeting with the elected union representatives of the group.

Three more cities, near-perfect clones of Chimera Landing, were going up in new sites across Mackenzie's southern continent. Once uninhabited, it was now home to eighty million people.

Eighty million refugees. An unimaginable number, really, but they were also the only ones that Connor O'Hannagain and the Protectorate of the Mage-Queen of Mars had rescued out of Chimera's two billion.

The friends, family and neighbors of those eighty million had remained behind on a world now occupied by the Reezh Kazh, an alien theocracy that hadn't even talked to their lost colony before invading Chimera.

The last evacuation flight had landed a couple of days after Christmas Day. There were still decorations around the city a week later, though there was no snow there.

None of the beauty of the city or the hope inherent in the successful evacuation and rehousing of so many people—human and reezh alike— could break Connor's mood.

There was a bone-deep weariness he couldn't shake. Over half of the Royal Martian Navy's Second Fleet had died in the Chimera System—over sixty thousand human beings. Hundreds of thousands of Marines had remained behind, buried in bunkers concealed around the star system.

Yet all of the resources Mars had mustered and the sacrifices humanity had made had achieved... this. Eighty million saved from a world they'd abandoned to invasion and conquest.

"Ambassador."

Connor turned to find his bodyguard had emerged onto the balcony with him. They were in one of the tallest buildings in the city, once intended to serve as the new center of government for Ridwan Muhammad's little empire. Now it housed the city government along with the government-in-exile of the Dual Republics of Chimera.

And one Ambassador of the Protectorate of Mars.

"Agent Ansel," he greeted his Protectorate Secret Service bodyguard. Sarvesh Ansel had been on Chimera with him. He'd also accompanied Connor up onto the dreadnought *Mjolnir* for a planning session with Mage-Admiral Jane Alexander—a trip that had left them trapped on the warship when the Kazh invaded.

"You have a call scheduled with the Mage-Admiral in an hour," Ansel told him. "You should probably head back inside."

Ansel was once again acting as Connor's secretary because his *actual* secretary had been left behind on Chimera. The Secret Service man didn't seem to mind, but that was potentially because he realized Connor was in no shape to pick a replacement.

Or do much of anything, he felt. He'd been the one to promise Chimera that Mars would do everything they could… and while he was certain that the Navy *had* done just that, they had failed nonetheless.

"Thank you, Sarvesh," Connor said quietly. He didn't move.

Connor was a big man, little bothered by the wind sweeping the heights of the tower. Broad-shouldered and copper-haired with the Irish descent common to the people of the Tara System, he realized he should probably head to a gym before talking to Alexander.

Even that was difficult to find appeal in.

"Sitting out here isn't good for you, boss," Ansel finally said. "You should eat. Or work out. Or *something*."

Connor chuckled bitterly.

"All right, Agent. I will permit myself to be mothered, since I *know* I'm not in a great space right now. Lead the way to food."

It spoke volumes to the degree to which Connor had needed the mothering that he hadn't realized his meeting with Alexander was in person until about a minute before one of the Marines assigned to Ansel's team opened the door to let two women into his office.

Connor rose immediately. Etiquette might not have required it for a civilian when an Admiral entered the room, but Her Highness, Mage-Admiral Jane Michelle Alexander, was not only the commander of Second Fleet—whose remaining capital ships stood guard over Mackenzie at that moment—but was *also* aunt to the Mage-Queen of Mars and Crown Princess of the entire Protectorate.

He knew the tall gray-haired woman well, stepping around his desk to offer her his hand. Unlike his own pale coloring, Alexander had the mixed-brown skin tones of the scions of Project Olympus, the forced-breeding project that had created the modern Mage.

Their skins were a study in contrast, though the second woman looked more like Connor himself. He hadn't met her before, but as he offered his hand, he realized he knew exactly who she was.

There were very few living people in the galaxy who wore a golden hand on a chain around their neck, after all. She was half Connor's size, but shared his Irish coloring—though the copper red in her hair was streaked with gray.

"My Lady Hand," he greeted Shea Riley, Hand of the Mage-Queen of Mars. "I was not even aware that you were on the planet yet."

The last he'd heard she'd been in Pharaoh, dealing with the collapse of the caste-based Kemetic theocracy that had run that planet prior to the arrival of first, the First Legion invasion, and second, the Protectorate driving out the Legion.

"My movements around the region are kept as covert as possible, Ambassador," Riley told him with a bright smile. "I haven't left the area since the capture of Mackenzie, which I believe you knew?"

He nodded. Riley had spent several years bouncing between the various colonies conquered by the Legion, helping build new governments and structures to replace those the Legion had destroyed—and making sure those new governments were acceptable to the Protectorate.

The colonies had all fled beyond the borders of humanity's main nation-state to set up governments the Charter and Constitution wouldn't tolerate. There was an explicit requirement for certain freedoms and rights in the Protectorate, after all.

"Someone had to be saddled with the hat of effective regional governor," Alexander noted. With a gesture, the Mage-Admiral magically rearranged the chairs in the room, setting up a triangle around the decorative rug in front of Connor's desk.

Like everything else in the room, the rug had been made on Mackenzie to a faux-Celtic style quite familiar to any child of Tara. Recreationist urges were apparently near-universal in colony founders.

"And I understand that Admiral Medici declined a Hand to avoid the mission," Riley said with a wry chuckle. "Whereas *I* had already let Her Majesty hang an anchor around my neck and my response to the 'request' was *ma'am, yes, ma'am.*"

Connor joined the two women in a chuckle.

"May I offer you two a drink?" he asked, then hesitated. "I... I have to admit I have a bottle of whiskey in here somewhere, but for anything else, we'd have to ask for help."

"That's fine, Ambassador," Alexander told him. "I wanted to make sure the three of us were on the same page, to put our administrative, diplomatic and military heads pointing in the same direction."

"Am I still that?" Connor asked, a moment of self-flagellation slipping out. "My embassy, after all, is now occupied."

"That's hardly in question," Riley snapped. "Your portfolio was expanded well before Chimera fell, Ambassador. You are responsible for all diplomatic contact with the Reezh, including the Primes and the Kazh itself, if they ever talk to us."

The Primes were the old core worlds of the Reezh Ida, the worlds their empire had been anchored on—until the central Church of the Nine, the Kazh itself, had unleashed antimatter fire on that empire to bring them into line.

Now the Primes were all that remained of the Ida. Some were controlled by the Kazh. They knew at least one wasn't, but they didn't know enough to even guess the status of the others.

"You're right, of course," Connor agreed. It would take him some time to rebuild the certainty he'd brought into his mission to Chimera, but he knew he *would*. One soul-shattering catastrophe wasn't going to undermine an entire lifetime of being the one in charge, leading the way.

"What do we know on that front so far?" he asked.

"Same as we knew yesterday," Alexander said with a chuckle. "That's part of why I brought Riley along, to brief you both on the blacker-than-black stuff. This room is secure, yes?"

"Ansel had it swept when he made me grab lunch half an hour ago," he confirmed. "The security systems are top-of-the-line. I doubt they are completely unbreachable, but they are as good as anything off of Mars herself."

"And we can do better," the Admiral replied. "Lady Riley, would you care to do the honors?"

With a silent nod, Riley raised her right hand in the air. Connor felt a shift in the air, something he couldn't quite identify, and several hairs on his forearms stood up.

"We are now as shielded as we can be," the Hand said. "The only person I *know* could potentially breach my shields is, well, sitting right next to me."

She gestured to Alexander. Connor was well aware of the magical power reputed to the Royal Family of Mars, though the Hands were rumored to be nearly as strong themselves.

"What *blacker-than-black* do we have going on?" Connor asked.

"As we speak, Captain Kelzin has taken the three *Rhapsodies* back to Chimera," Alexander told him.

The *Rhapsodies* were a breed of ship that Connor knew very little about. He'd only learned the stealth ships existed as part of his mission to Chimera and the planning for the mission to the Reezh Primes.

But the three of them available to Second Fleet had been a day's flight out of Chimera when the hammer finally dropped. They'd fallen back on Martian bases—and he had heard nothing further about them.

"Assuming things go according to plan, their scouting run should finish early tomorrow morning OMST," the Admiral concluded. Olympus Mons Standard Time was set to the twenty-four-hour clock of the faraway mountain where the Mage-Queen reigned.

Olympus Mons, like the rest of Mars, hadn't *had* a twenty-four-hour day until the first Mage-King had ruled the planet. As part of his magical terraforming, Desmond Michael Alexander the First had adjusted the planet's rotation.

"Much as I'm anticipating grim news, it will be good to *know* anything," Connor admitted. "Is there any chance we'll hear from the stay-behind force?"

Over half a million soldiers of the Royal Martian Marines and the Protectorate Guard had dug into buried bunkers on Garuda, Chimera's habitable planet. Combined with the local military, they'd have a decent chance of retaking the planet—assuming the Royal Martian Navy managed to regain control of the system's space.

"Almost zero," Alexander told them both. "We know they shut down their Links in case the Kazh can detect them, so they're limited to more-usual forms of communication."

"They could probably transmit *from* Garuda without being picked up, but we can't transmit *to* them," Riley noted. "We'll need to play some games testing how effective the stealth ships are against reezh scanners going forward, but today's trip isn't the time for that.

"Though if the situation were different, I'd be on the next trip for an emergency insertion."

Connor rolled that thought around his head.

"I'm not certain what purpose that would serve, my lady Hand," he pointed out. "From a morale perspective, the Hands are well known across the Protectorate. Losing one of you would be dangerous."

"Hands *are* dangerous," Riley replied drily. "And we are expendable. I *will* be going to Chimera before the Navy is ready to retake her, Ambassador, but with Chambers on the planet, it's less necessary."

Connor blinked. The only person Riley could be referring to was Mage-Captain Roslyn Chambers, the young officer who had served as his embassy's military attaché before being moved to Alexander's staff—and also the woman who'd made contact with Chimera in the first place.

Chambers was a smart and effective officer, but he wasn't sure how she made enough difference that Riley felt the other woman reduced the need to get a Hand on planet.

"I feel like I'm missing something," he finally admitted.

"That's part of this briefing, Ambassador," Alexander told him. "And the reason we're doing it in person. Even the Link isn't secure enough for this conversation, but since we're sending you into the Primes, my niece and I have decided you need to be fully read in to the Tartarus and Merlin Files."

"The *what?*" Connor asked.

"The files where we document everything we know, all secrets included, about the true nature of Olympus Mons and the Mage-Kings of Mars."

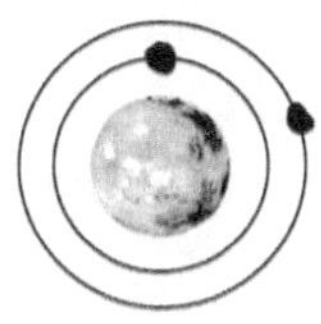

CHAPTER 2

CAPTAIN MIKE LAMONTE WU KELZIN was, in his utterly unbiased opinion, one of the luckiest men alive. Even a decade after his wedding, he wasn't entirely certain why Kelly LaMonte and Xi Wu had picked *him* to be their husband.

In his more honest days, *Rhapsody in Bohemia*'s tall blond Captain would admit that the same personality traits that had left him stunned when Xi Wu had proposed were probably the ones that somehow had kept those two incredible women in his life.

He'd also admit that *his* sense of duty to humanity and Protectorate was less ironclad than Kelly LaMonte's, but that was why his wife was the Director of Stealth Ship Operations and tapped to be the next *head* of the Martian Interstellar Security Service—and Mike was "merely" the senior stealth-ship Captain for the same service.

And, he knew, inevitably going to get dumped in the same seat as Kelly when she got saddled with responsibility for the entire intelligence apparatus of the Protectorate of Mars.

"Kelly has to miss these days," he said aloud, knowing that his *other* wife was standing behind him.

Xi Kelzin LaMonte Wu was the senior Ship's Mage and Executive Officer of *Rhapsody in Bohemia*, which meant she was the woman with her hands on *Bohemia*'s simulacrum, weaving magic to conceal them.

The silver model between Xi's palms was, in some magical sense Mike didn't try to understand, the ship. Through it, she could teleport them between the stars—the simulacrum's main purpose—or, as she was doing right now, render them invisible to any technological sensors.

"I'm sure Kelly does," Xi told him. "Which only convinces me that you're both crazy—and reminds me that neither of you have to do the magic for this part."

"Sir, could you... please not distract the woman hiding us from the multimegaton warships whose *missile range* we are hanging out in?" the only other person on *Bohemia*'s bridge asked plaintively.

Commander Columba Fischer was the senior officer of the seconded detachment of RMN spacers required to run *Rhapsody in Bohemia*'s weapons. The second generation of *Rhapsodies* were armed with the absolute latest missiles, the Wyverns the RMN was only just rolling out to their own ships.

Fischer—technically *Lieutenant* Commander Fischer, but they received the courtesy promotion because none of the civilians wanted to use the extra syllables—had come with the four missile launchers to make sure MISS didn't accidentally shoot anything Mars didn't want destroyed.

They were also, in Mike's opinion, an utterly irredeemable pessimist.

"If the Shining Shield of the Nine were going to pick us up, Fischer, they'd have seen us while our engines were burning an hour ago," he told the Navy officer. *Bohemia* and her sisters were far more visible when accelerating. There was only so much heat sinks, absorption networks and even magic could do to hide an antimatter engine.

Which was why the three stealth ships were now making their final passes with their engines offline... and why *Rhapsody in Bohemia* was far closer to the enemy fleet than her two sisters.

"An hour ago, we weren't twenty light-seconds from that monstrosity over there and closing," Fischer replied.

Mike grinned at the Commander.

"*That monstrosity* is what we're here to see," he reminded them. "And the rest of the Kazh fleet."

The Shining Shield of the Nine was a poetic name for a military force that was responsible for the greatest atrocity humanity had ever seen. The ships that orbited Garuda weren't the *same* ships that had burned the old

Reezh empire to the ground for rebellion, but they served the same masters and the same mission.

Mike didn't like seeing them in orbit of a world full of friendly people. He wouldn't have liked it even if half of Chimera's populace hadn't been human.

"Do we have a number on the fleet now?" he asked Fischer.

"Working on it," the Commander replied. "They've been reinforced, if less than I think the Admiral was afraid of. They're not up to their preferred three-to-two ratio of smaller classes, but they definitely picked up some extra dreadnoughts."

"Type Ones, you mean."

"Yeah. Dreadnoughts, like I said."

Mike chuckled. He would have expected the naval officer to stick with the official categorization of the reezh warships—but at over seventy million tons, the largest reezh starships were definitely in the same range as the mighty dreadnoughts of the Royal Martian Navy.

"And the final number?"

"Second Fleet burned the bastards down to somewhere between five and seven Type Ones; we didn't have a solid number," Fischer told him. "There are eight now, so they definitely picked up at least one more.

"They've got eleven Type Twos, so one fewer than their usual org structure, but, again, more than we thought they had left. Sixteen Threes, twenty Fours, thirty Fives that I can see from here."

"Probably more Fives and Fours scattered through the system," Mike concluded. Those were the smaller classes of enemy ships, one and five megatons apiece. "Keeping an eye on the rest of the system."

"Meaning that *Armor* and *Blue* could run right into them," Fischer agreed. "Though, of course, *they* aren't falling toward six hundred million–odd tons of capital ships *right in freaking front of us.*"

"They are not right in front of us, Commander," Mike countered. If there had been junior people on the bridge, he'd probably have had to work out how to yank the Navy officer up short for that.

On the other hand, he suspected that Fischer was clear enough on protocol that they wouldn't *be* quite as alarmist in front of junior crew.

"We are going to pass the closest escorts—*escorts*, Commander, not the big guys—at fifteen light-seconds," he continued. "With engines down and every heat-sinking system on this ship running at maximum, plus Mage Xi concealing us, the Navy couldn't pick us up at more than twelve.

"And the Navy knows our girls exist. These guys don't."

"Which would be a great theory, Captain, if we don't know that they looked right through the same stealth shielding on *Rose* before Mage-Captain Chambers caught up to her."

"I agreed with you on that point when we talked about it earlier," Mike said. "Command says they know what's going on there, but that's why we're only bringing one ship close to Garuda."

"Everything from *Thorn* suggests that *Rose* was detected immediately upon arrival too," Xi pointed out, her focus still on the simulacrum. "We're *fine*, Fischer.

"And the closer we get, the more we know—and the more we know, the sooner Alexander can get back here and kick these people out."

Fischer grumbled but fell silent, their focus on their work.

"Orbital forts are gone, we knew that," they noted. "Looks like most of the orbital industry is intact. The only new thing is… Yeah. I *knew* you had to be here somewhere, you buggers."

Mike waited patiently.

"All I was seeing was warships," Fischer explained. "We knew there had to be a logistics contingent, and they had to have an invasion fleet, too. I was picking up warships but not freighters, which I thought was odd."

"And?"

"They're using lower orbits than we would and have them tucked in underneath the warships and industrial platforms," Fischer told Mike. "There… still aren't enough of them, though. I'm picking up maybe a dozen ships, fifty megatons each."

"How did they *hide* that?" Mike asked.

"They're almost entirely powered down. No engines, nothing. Weird place to stick your logistics ships."

Mike studied the positions as Fischer put them on the display, then grimaced.

"Those aren't the logistics ships," he said. "Those are the *invasion* ships, and they're positioned like that to provide ground fire."

As if to confirm his words, a new energy signature blossomed on the screen. One of the transports had just fired a proton beam at the surface. The pulse of energy was catastrophic enough when it hit a starship, but hitting a planetary target, it wouldn't just obliterate what it hit—it would also mess up weather for weeks afterward.

And, in doing so, lose much of the energy that would hurt the target. There was a *reason* the RMN used precision kinetics for the same mission—and controlled the supply of the things even more than they controlled ship-to-ship missiles.

The latter, after all, were designed and hard-coded to fail if they hit an atmosphere.

"Hopefully, Harmon or Truong has eyes on the support train," Mike said quietly. "They've got to be somewhere in this system. It's not likely they dropped off their cargo and just left."

"That... depends, actually," Fischer admitted. "They might have, given what we know about the enemy's limits.

"They only have so many murdered Mages to go around, right?"

Mike swallowed an angry response as he glanced at his wife. Xi was ignoring Fischer at this point, which was a damn good thing.

The Prometheus Interface was one of the worst atrocities humanity had inflicted on themselves, a machine that could take the brain of a Mage, keep that brain alive and force them to jump a ship as if they were just a machine.

The reezh used something similar for most of their ships. Even if the Burning and the Fall of Chimera hadn't happened, Mike—and anyone else who knew a Mage!—would have hated them for that alone.

Bohemia's sensors drank in the light around them thirstily. The level of information they needed meant that Xi was doing almost twice as much work as usual too. Just concealing the ship while letting enough light reach them for navigation was difficult enough, but Mike's partner was hiding them from the reezh *and* letting enough radiation and light in for them to get real data from the planet.

"What are we seeing on the surface?" Mike finally asked, unable to really engage with the question of how many murdered innocents the Reezh Kazh had to fuel their starships. "They shot at something. What was it?"

"No idea," Fischer admitted. "We didn't have enough detail to see what was there before the beam hit and, well, now it's ground zero for a thunderstorm."

Mike grimaced.

"The drones might have something?" he asked. There were over a dozen drones making their own ballistic courses through Garuda orbit at the same time as *Bohemia*. None were on an exact parallel to her vector, but they might have got a glimpse at the planet at the right time.

"We'll find out when we download them all in a few hours," his Tactical Officer said fatalistically. "Assuming we don't lose them all, of course."

"You helped write this plan," Mike pointed out. "If you thought it wasn't going to work, you should have said something then." He snorted. "Well, *more* then."

"It's more likely to work than any other plan we came up with," Fischer replied. "I figure we'll get *Bohemia* out, but the drones don't have Mages aboard to hide them. They're smaller targets but more visible than us.

"Of course, because the Kazh haven't seen *us*, they'll be looking for launches and pickups far further away." They paused thoughtfully. "Probably."

Despite the doomsaying, all of the probes were at the rendezvous three hours later. *Rhapsody in Armor*, on the other hand, wasn't.

"Truong, did you even get a blip from Harmon?" Mike asked Captain Truong Truong, the Mage in command of *Rhapsody in Blue*.

"Nothing," the Alpha Centauri–born officer replied grimly. "They were going a lot farther than either of us, though. I thought you gave him permission to meet us at the out-system rendezvous if he had any concerns?"

Rhapsody in Armor had been heading to Ifrit, the inner gas giant of the Chimera System. The Dual Republics of Chimera had built an immense megastructure there: an orbital accelerator that used the vast amounts of fuel available from the gas giant to produce antimatter. Without Mages, it was the only way to produce the volatile substance in quantity—and even the relatively small *Rhapsodies* had fuel-burn rates measured in hundreds of kilos of the stuff per day.

Captain Elias Harmon had needed to jump back from Ifrit to make the rendezvous with the other scout ships. Jumping out of the system made just as much sense.

"I forgot I'd told him that," Mike admitted. "It's been a stressful couple of days."

"Tell me about it," Truong agreed. "And we were just skimming the unoccupied zones. I have some good news, even if it's going to be a mighty pain in the ass."

"There are people out there."

"There are people out there," Truong confirmed. "It looks like the Kazh have ignored Leviathan completely so far. It's not like there's *much* out there—there's a reason Admiral Wang managed to hide his Sanctuary from everyone out there."

Mike nodded grimly. Admiral Wang had arrived in Chimera as a deserter from the Republic Interstellar Navy, with his ships equipped with Prometheus Interfaces and murdered Mages. While some of his Prometheans had chosen to remain aboard those ships and help defend their new homes, over a dozen hadn't.

They'd been hidden, even from the Chimerans, in a secret base on the ninth moon of Leviathan. There had been *just* enough activity around Leviathan to cover the supply runs, and not enough for anyone to realize their Navy was running a secret facility protecting a bunch of traumatized innocents trapped in machines.

"We could carry... maybe two hundred people between the three of us," Mike said, doing a quick mental calculation. Even with their boarding teams of special-forces cyborgs, the *Rhapsodies* had crews of barely fifty souls. They could hot-bunk and overcharge the life support to get people to Fleet Base Deveraux or maybe even Mackenzie, but it wouldn't be comfortable or safe.

"The people I spoke to weren't even willing to give me *names*, Kelzin," Truong replied. "Let alone how many of them there are or enough to coordinate any kind of evac plan. They agreed to give me what passive sensor data they had from the last month, but they are determined to keep their heads down."

"Okay, so they didn't tell you anything," Mike conceded. "But you're flying a covert scout ship that they probably didn't even *see*. What are we looking at?"

"About twelve thousand people, give or take a thousand," his subordinate said instantly. "I'm guessing it's everyone who was in the outer system, pulling together to maximize shared resources.

"They've got a trio of cloudscoops running in low orbit and a dome settlement on the first moon. Leviathan One is the size of Mars, so they've got a lot of ground to hide in."

"Okay. So, depending on how the *rest* of the data looks, we might end up trading a ride out of here for a whole bunch of passive-listening gear," Mike said. "We can make use of a preexisting base at Leviathan, I think."

That part might even be his call. Or, more accurately, if Alexander *didn't* want to take advantage of it, he'd be the one to decide if MISS did want to use it.

Whose brilliant idea had it been to put *him* in charge?

"We'll wait here for an hour, picking up all of our drones, then jump to the out-system rendezvous," he told Truong and his bridge crew at the same time. "Per the plan, Harmon will either be here by then or waiting for us at the rendezvous."

And then they would put together all of their data and see just what hell they'd abandoned the Chimerans to.

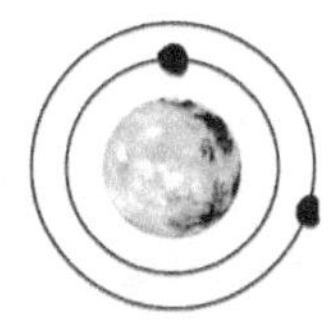

CHAPTER 3

WHAT CONNOR HAD EXPECTED to be a short briefing, a meeting of minds before Alexander took most of her capital ships back to the fleet base in Exeter to watch for reezh scouts, had turned into a five-hour briefing on some of the deepest secrets of the Protectorate.

The Mage-Admiral and the Hand had both come prepared to demonstrate the easiest example of the art of the Rune Wright. Both had stripped down to black tank tops to show the runes that marked their flesh.

A single Rune of Power curled around Shea Riley's left arm, covering most of her forearm and with a few spirals reaching up onto her bicep. The Runes that marked Jane Alexander were clearly related to Riley's tattoo, but both of Alexander's arms were covered, and the runes continued up onto her shoulders and under the tank top.

"You have *five* of these Runes of Power?" Connor finally asked.

There were parts of what he'd been told that were no surprise. The Olympus Mons Amplifier was an open secret, with aspects of even its origins revealed publicly as part of the campaign to convince the Protectorate's Parliament to support Chimera. That the Mage-Queen of Mars and her predecessors commanded magic no other Mage could match was well known, as was the fact that the Hands were lent a portion of that power.

It was still a shock to see the polymerized silver inlay carved into the two women's skin and recognize it as the source of that power.

"Only a Rune Wright can create the Runes," Alexander told him. "And we can't read someone else's magic well enough to put two or more Runes of Power on another Mage. We can give a Mage, such as Shea here, a single Rune but no more.

"On ourselves, five seems to be the safe limit." She shrugged. "Montgomery only has three these days, a consequence of his injuries."

Connor blinked as the answers to several other questions fell into place. Prince-Chancellor Damien Montgomery, formerly the Prince Regent during Mage-Queen Kiera's minority, had been posthumously adopted by Mage-King Desmond the Third, Kiera's father.

Many people had questioned it, though the man's humility and calm competence had eased fears quite quickly—and the fact that they'd still been fighting the Republic at the time had silenced most of the doubters who'd remained.

"That's why he was adopted, I take it," Connor noted.

"Exactly. The Olympus Mons Amplifier can only be used by a Rune Wright, one able to see the flows of magic," Alexander told him. "We now know, with some certainty, that the reason is because the Amplifier was built by reezh and was never supposed to be *used* as an amplifier by humans."

Connor was going to have a great deal of reading to do. Even the hours of briefing he'd just gone through could only be high-level information, and the Tartarus and Merlin Files themselves would give him the details.

He would rely on other people's analysis for most things, but something told him he needed to know as much about this particular topic as possible.

"Which brings me to the question you've danced around for several hours," he said quietly. "Why do I need to know this *now*?"

"First, because Mage-Captain Roslyn Chambers has a Rune of Power," Riley told him. "That means one of our strongest magical assets is already on the surface of Garuda, which opens options we might not otherwise have."

"Wait, Roslyn is a *Hand*?" Connor asked. Hands didn't serve as starship Captains or embassy military attachés. They were the direct representatives of the Mage-Queen. The only reason Shea Riley wasn't the most powerful person in the *star system* was because even Hands tended to defer to the Mage-Queen's aunt and official heir.

"Roslyn's situation is… complex," Riley admitted. "During the Tau Ceti Incident, Prince Montgomery needed magical fire support. He had two Mages with him that he trusted completely: his bodyguard commander, Guard-Captain Denis Romanov; and Mage-Captain Roslyn Chambers.

"Denis Romanov accepted a Hand from Her Majesty shortly afterward. Captain Chambers left in pursuit of *Rose* and the remnants of Nemesis." The Hand shrugged. "I don't know whether she was ever offered a Hand, but she has remained in her role in the Navy so far."

"Kiera's immediate circle has discussed elevating Roslyn to a Hand at least since the mess in Sorprendidas in 'sixty-three," Alexander said. "The general consensus is that she is more valuable where she is, serving as Her Majesty's friend and confidante without carrying the burden of a Hand.

"Damien giving her the Rune of Power changed that math surprisingly little," she concluded. "There may come a time where Kiera decides that Roslyn is worth more to her as a Hand than as her eyes and ears in the Navy, but I'm not sure we're there yet.

"For the moment, it is critical that the key decision-makers know about her abilities… and that those abilities remain classified. We would prefer not to explain *why* a Mage-Captain, distinguished only by her personal relationship with the Queen and the Chancellor, possesses the powers more usually attributed to Hands."

Connor nodded as he slotted the information into the picture he had in his brain. Whatever went down with Chimera now wasn't going to be his problem, not directly. He suspected that reminding people of the promises and treaties made was going to fall on him, but the real mission for him at this point was to deal with the Primes.

"While that is important, it doesn't seem enough to brief me in on all of this," he said, waving at the two black high-security cases holding the datachips for the Tartarus and Merlin Files.

"It's not. The main reason we're briefing you on all of this is because the nature of the planetary amplifiers is key to the existence and balance between the Primes and the Nine," Alexander said grimly.

Olympus Mons had been built by reezh. The conclusion was obvious and answered some of the questions he'd had about how the ten early colonies had survived the Burning and the fall of the Reezh Ida. There had been eleven Primes once, the closest colonies to the reezh home system: the Nine, named for their pantheon of gods. They knew one was gone and at least three survived.

"The Primes have planetary amplifiers," he guessed.

"*Mountains of Astral Might*, they are called in the files we have from the Chimerans," Alexander confirmed. "How, exactly, one got built on Mars is a question we will likely never answer, but we know all eleven Primes and the Nine itself have one.

"We have every reason to believe that they require special training even for a reezh to use, but they will not be *impossible* to use as they are for a non-Rune-Wright human Mage," she concluded.

"Against the power of a planetary amplifier, no fleet we can assemble could possibly succeed in assaulting the Reezh Primes. We *need* more information—and boots on the ground, and allies. All of that, Ambassador, is going to fall into your court."

"So it is," he agreed. Somewhere in the briefing, the fog of depression and grief he'd been dealing with since leaving Chimera had fallen away. There was a goal in front of him, one he could achieve—and few others could even *attempt*.

"I'm going to have to review all I can of these files," he continued. "I've already gone over what information we have on the Primes, and it isn't much. We know what the next step is, of course."

"We do, but there are a *lot* of complicating factors," Alexander agreed. "Once we have Kelzin's report from Chimera, we'll begin to assess our next steps."

"We also need to know where *Barracuda* is," Connor said. "The last thing we need is for the last warship of the CSN to sail into a waiting Kazh fleet and betray whatever deal Ordin agreed to."

The Chimera Space Navy had sent one of their limited number of jump-capable warships to make a diplomatic mission to the Ordin System, the only Prime they didn't know was still connected to the Kazh. Slower than a Martian ship, she'd still been expected back before the final attack on Chimera.

If she was coming back and was merely late...

"I know," Alexander said with a grimace. "On the other hand, you know the state Second Fleet is in."

He'd been aboard the flagship *Mjolnir* during the battle. Only forty warships had left Chimera in the end, and many of them were badly damaged.

"The plan Captain Chambers' Operations team put together called for the stealth ships to sweep the Prime Systems to learn all we could before making contact," Connor pointed out. "That required moving a logistics force forward, including an escort.

"We could knock multiple objectives off if we set the courses correctly and attach the right assets," he noted. "We can route via Chimera—avoiding the system, of course—and invert the course *Barracuda* would take back from Ordin."

"*We*, Ambassador?" Alexander asked with an arched eyebrow.

"The other objective, of course, would be beginning diplomatic contact," he told her. "If we pick a ship to use as a consular vessel from the convoy's escorts and send myself and whatever staff I can pull together aboard her, that will minimize the number of ships you have to spare."

His office was very quiet, and then Alexander began putting her jacket back on.

"You may not be wrong, Connor," she said quietly, "but right now, I'm feeling *extremely* twitchy about the forces available to me. In a few more weeks, Second Fleet will start receiving reinforcements in the cruiser and destroyer types. At that point, I will be ready to deploy the kind of force you're thinking of.

"Until we have those reinforcements, I think we simply don't have the forces to spare. We may need to accept whatever consequences the loss of *Barracuda* entails."

"Admiral—"

She held up a hand to cut him off.

"I am *not* ruling out your suggestion, Connor," she said. "I need to go over the idea and the options with my staff, and, sadly, lacking Roslyn, that's going to take longer than I'd like.

"I'm not going to make any decisions on *anything* until we've heard from Kelzin. I don't like making plans in the dark, Ambassador—and given that it will be a week before the *Rhapsodies* can reach Exeter or Mackenzie, there is only so much rushing that's worthwhile!"

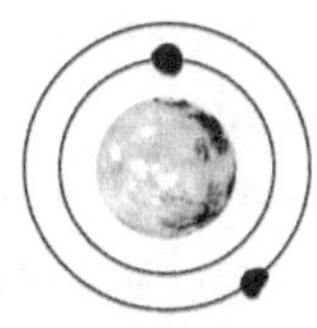

CHAPTER 4

XI SQUEEZED MIKE'S HAND as the holoconference assembled around them. Command of a starship—at least as small as a *Rhapsody*—was something he could handle, but public speaking and presentation was still a struggle.

He wasn't sure at what point *he'd* realized that his bravado covered a degree of introversion, but consciously utilizing it had helped find a balance he enjoyed.

Plus, well, both of his wives knew him inside and out, so they knew when to prop him up and when to cut him off at the knees.

His other wife had a momentary warm smile for him as she appeared in the crowd of faces. Kelly LaMonte's hair was currently a dark burgundy and he wondered if she'd changed it ahead of a call she knew he was on.

It was his favorite of her many colors.

The sad truth, however, was that the Director of Stealth Ship Operations, MISS, was one of the least important people in the meeting. Mage-Admiral Jane Alexander was probably the most important, though there were several members of the current Protectorate High Command present via Link, including the Chair, Mage-Admiral James Medici.

The Link, the quantum-entanglement communication system the Protectorate had taken from the defeated Republic, allowed everyone to appear present on Mike's ship in real-time. The holographic software in his office expanded it around him and Xi, creating the illusion of a chamber large enough to contain the thirty-odd people present.

"Thank you for coming, everyone," Mike told them. "I understand that this is the first news we've had out of Chimera since December thirteenth, and there are a lot of questions.

"My people and Director LaMonte's people in Sol have gone over the data enough for initial assessments, but I remind you all that the information we have available is preliminary. While we got in closer than anyone else could, our data is still being analyzed."

"From what I've seen, Captain, a certain one of your ships got in closer than is wise, even for one of your *Rhapsodies*," Medici observed. The Black Admiral was still slim and muscular, even as age and stress had turned his hair pure white.

"We needed to know *everything* about the situation on and around Garuda, Admiral," Mike replied, putting on his best shit-eating grin. His risk-reward assessment had been on a knife's edge, but the sheer necessity of exactly that knowledge had tipped it over.

"And because *Bohemia* took the risks we did, we now know quite a bit about what's happening on Garuda's surface," he noted.

None of it was *good*, of course.

"The key data, of course, is force levels," he continued. The illusory conference room acquired an equally illusory holographic map of the Chimera System.

By now, the layout of the system was probably burned in to all of their brains. Ifrit, an inner gas giant half the radius of Jupiter, forever scorched by the harsh-burning star. The asteroid belt was next out, a critical source of resources for a star system that had survived on its own for centuries.

Chimera II was a burnt ball of rock with almost no value. If it was named, Mike didn't know it. The same was true of the frozen ball of Chimera IV.

Chimera III was Garuda, a chilly windswept world home to two billion people, half human and half reezh. The centerpoint of everything that had gone on, including the evacuation of eighty million souls.

Chimera V was Leviathan, larger than Ifrit but enough farther from Garuda to have been mostly ignored by the systems industry. Three more frozen balls of dirt and a third gas giant, so far away from everything that even its size hadn't earned it a name, made up the outer system.

New icons appeared on the display, red icons gleaming with sanguinary warning.

"As our data analysis continues, we expect to pick out more of the smaller warships, but the current count of Kazh warships in the system sits at eighty-five," Mike told them all. "Headed up by eight Type Ones, we see clear signs of reinforcement since Second Fleet withdrew from the system—and estimate the total weight of the enemy fleet in excess of one-point-five billion tons."

Three times what was left to Second Fleet, per his briefings.

"We have also confirmed fourteen of what appear to be planetary-assault ships," he continued, adding those icons above Garuda and Ifrit. The Type Twos escorting the two invasion ships at the gas giant had been the reason for *Armor* missing the original rendezvous—there'd been more warships than they'd allowed for, forcing Captain Harmon to delay his jump.

"While we can't say for certain how many ground troops each carried, they appear to be about halfway between our *Bushido*-class ships and the former Republic's *Saladin*-class ships. Our initial estimate is that each vessel likely carries the equivalent of a Marine or Guard heavy armored corps: eighty to a hundred thousand soldiers with full air/ground/water combat capability."

The *Saladin*s that had been reactivated for the evacuation effort had been built to deliver a quarter-million troops in a single assault wave. The Republic had suffered from similar limitations in their FTL capabilities to the Kazh—identical, really, since both were anchored on murdered Mages. The reezh ships were smaller, but there was a value to not keeping the entire landing force on a single ship, however well protected.

"Based on that, we believe the Kazh have landed approximately one million troops on Garuda and have at least a hundred thousand troops in the facilities and colonies at Ifrit and the Chimera Inner Belt."

"What about the Accelerator Ring?" Medici asked. "From what we've seen, the reezh appear to have limited antimatter production. If they captured that..."

"Our only data for the time period between the departure of Second Fleet and our own arrival comes from a small group of satellites in high orbit of Leviathan, sir," Mike noted carefully. "That said, the Ifrit Accelerator Ring is gone. Based off the data from Leviathan, we believe the charges placed by the local troops were detonated thirty-six hours after the evacuation.

"As of *Rhapsody in Armor*'s sweep of the Ifrit planetary system, there were seventeen fragments totaling approximately four percent of the Accelerator Ring's mass and volume remaining in orbit. We can't be sure if the reezh were in possession of the station for any length of time."

He figured they could see the danger as well as he could. Based off the records they had of the old Reezh Ida, the Kazh had not significantly advanced their technology in the centuries since the Burning—but they remained an advanced civilization with immense resources.

If they realized what the accelerator had been doing, that alone might be enough to duplicate it. Any close examination or records they retrieved would only make the process easier.

"It would take them a decade or more to duplicate the platform from scratch," Alexander noted, the Mage-Admiral looking at the datacodes around Ifrit—codes that clearly meant something to her if not Connor.

"Both the ring at Chrysanthemum and the ring at Ifrit benefited from having full access to the schematics and construction plans from the original at Legatus, and they *still* took most of a decade to build.

"We can hope to have this mess resolved before they can possibly get such a structure online."

Mike wasn't entirely sure *how*. He wasn't fully briefed on the construction plans of the Royal Martian Navy, but he knew they weren't expecting massive reinforcements anytime soon—and the reezh fleet assembled in Chimera was only weak in comparison to the forces that had overwhelmed Second Fleet.

"We're dancing around what we all need to know," the Ambassador said flatly, O'Hannagain leaning forward as the conference focused on him.

The man might have been a troll for his size relative to Mike, and the spy-ship Captain tried not to quail. Like his wife and the commandos his ship carried for special actions, Mike had cybernetics that made him more dangerous than he looked, but O'Hannagain's breadth and muscle were clear even through the conference call.

"And that is, Ambassador?" he asked the man carefully.

"Garuda. We left two billion people on that planet, Captain Kelzin, and I think we all need to know how bad it's getting."

Mike didn't argue. He'd had a few other notes to brief on—mostly about the refuge at Leviathan—but that was the biggest piece after the enemy fleet strength.

"Even diving as close as *Rhapsody in Bohemia* did, we can only learn so much from space," he warned quietly. "That said..."

The central display shifted, zooming in on the planet itself.

"None of Garuda's orbital defenses remain," he noted. "We have no way of knowing if any of them were boarded or evacuated, but the scan data from Second Fleet suggests they were all vaporized as soon as the enemy forces made orbit.

"The majority of the orbital *infrastructure*, however, is intact. We detected energy signatures consistent with ongoing operation, as well as a level of orbital traffic that would, just barely, support that operation."

He highlighted the small craft they'd detected.

"All of the small craft we saw in the orbital traffic were local," Mike said. "We didn't detect any military traffic or, for that matter, any traffic we would associate with the invasion force.

"In terms of civilian traffic, the numbers and movement were on the light side but appeared almost normal—with one glaring exception." He highlighted it, an entire area of space above the planet flashing slightly to show its complete emptiness.

"Not one shuttle was seen going from orbit to the surface or vice versa," Mike explained. "While orbital traffic is continuing, the occupiers appear to have isolated the orbitals from the planetary population."

"And the surface?" O'Hannagain asked.

"Unsurprisingly, the fighting is mostly over." No one had expected there to be ongoing resistance. The orders to the military forces on Chimera had come in two varieties: surrender or hide. The surrendering forces should have laid down their arms almost immediately, and the hidden forces weren't supposed to reveal themselves before the Navy returned.

"We saw signs of light guerilla action in several areas we have visuals on, but we didn't see any signs of major formations from either side. The problem..."

He swallowed, and then highlighted the situation.

"The problem is that we also saw signs of ongoing orbital bombardment, including two heavy-proton-beam strikes on the surface while we passed by. We expected an initial strike around Twin Sphinxes and the Dual Republic leadership there—the decoy military bases set up to cover the concealment of the local military were expected to be hit, for example—but our models suggest that the worst of the storms should only last a week at most.

"We are not certain what the Shield are shooting at," Mike admitted. "That's one of the things the analysis teams on Mars are digging in to. But they *are* continuing to bombard planetary targets, with devastating levels of collateral damage."

He put the next visual onto the display without announcing or explaining it. Everyone in the holographic conference had seen Twin Sphinxes before—several of them had even walked the streets and spoken with people.

It was recognizable, he knew, which was part of what drove the horrific stunned silence as they looked at the devastated metropolis.

Twin Sphinxes had been a city of two halves, with clear dividing lines between human architecture and reezh architecture—but those halves hadn't been a neat split. They'd been on a neighborhood or, often, building-by-building basis.

Now many of the outer neighborhoods were ruins, burnt or obliterated by firestorms. A massive chunk of one of the inner areas was just *gone*, where the military headquarters at the Triangle had clearly been ground zero for a strike.

"We don't have good visuals on most of the major cities," Mike said quietly. "Unfortunately, that suggests that the Kazh have been engaging in bombardments near to, if not directly on, those cities.

"We do have overhead of Twin Sphinxes, as you see, and the city is..." He had to pause to think through his next words very carefully. "...Mostly intact," he finally allowed.

"The damage we see, while dramatic, appears to be incidental to the destruction of the Triangle and bombardments of the military bases in the region. Collateral-damage estimates around the destruction of those facilities appear to have been low."

He had to pause and take a drink of water. There was no good news to really give about the state of the Dual Republics' capital. Twin Sphinxes still *existed* and the presence of Kazh troops suggested that most of its people remained, but it had been cruelly battered.

"We chose to risk the decoys there," Alexander said, her voice sounding ill. "We... assumed that they would use kinetic weapons for the bombardment. Why wouldn't they? They're cheap and effective."

"But it appears that their proton-beam weapons are capable of such bombardment as well," Medici told her, the Protectorate's senior military officer speaking very levelly, as if every syllable were being measured and weighed. "They are already to hand, which can make them more immediately useful... if one is prepared to accept the collateral damage."

"The amount of energy transferred into the atmosphere is sufficient to start fires across large areas and trigger localized hurricanes," Mike said.

"And you're still trying to work out what they're shooting at now," O'Hannagain said grimly.

"This is a nightmare."

No one argued with the Crown Princess. Her words hung in the air and on everyone's minds.

After a few seconds, Mike cleared his throat.

"While we're still interlacing the footage from the ships and drones, it *does* appear that most of the cities are intact," he assured his audience. "Twin Sphinxes seems to be the worst off, though none of them are untouched."

"What about the bunkers?"

General Akuchi Kamau was a broad-shouldered Black man, possibly the only person in the room to rival the Ambassador's width—and he'd been silent up to that point.

He was the commanding officer of the Royal Martian Marine Corps, which meant there were tens of thousands of his people in the bunkers he'd just asked about.

"Even MISS did not have final locations for all of the Chimeran facilities," Mike noted. "However, the facilities I do have coordinates for appear to be untouched so far—and our scans do not suggest any locations with sufficient damage to mark an underground facility having been blasted out from orbit.

"I *believe*, though I can make no guarantees, that the underground network concealing the liberation forces remains untouched."

"If we can get to them," Kamau growled. "Mage-Admirals?"

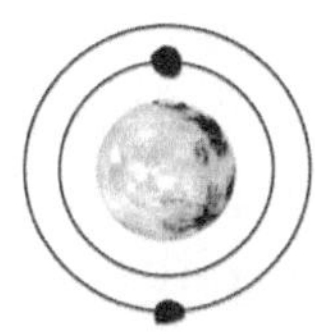

CHAPTER 5

IN ALMOST EVERY MEETING that had taken place between Connor and the administration of the Dual Republics of Chimera, there had been both a human and a reezh official present. There had been exceptions, of course, but the Chimeran government had been headed up by the Dyad, an executive minister from each species, and the pattern had continued down much of the structure.

He was unsurprised to be met by a matching set of human and reezh officials when he was escorted into the office of the Mayor of Chimera Landing.

Mayors now, he supposed. Though the two meeting him were officially the government-in-exile for the Dual Republics, they also served as the heads of Landing's municipal authority.

"Ambassador, we appreciate you taking the time to meet with us," Jessica Lang told him. The ivory-skinned younger woman had been a Director in the Republic's "Department of the Stars," responsible for astronomy, regional surveys and—theoretically, before the Protectorate had arrived in the region with all the grace of a drunk elephant—diplomacy.

Her counterpart was named Jozha, a reezh of indeterminate age and gender to human eyes who had served in the same role for the Western Department of Stars. That was, the reezh half of the organization. Like all of their people, Jozha was tall and gangly to human eyes, with double-jointed arms and legs, and a face with four eyes divided by an armored shield reminiscent of a man-sized triceratops—though thankfully without horns.

"My authority and role were given to me for the negotiations with Chimera, Director Lang," he pointed out gently. "I retain some responsibility toward your government-in-exile."

"Such as we are," Jozha noted. They waved Connor to a seat.

The office was impressive, a corner unit at the top of the tallest tower. Floored in marble tile and with the windows divided by carved pillars of black stone, it was an elegantly beautiful space. A pale shadow of the immense throne room that had been intended to occupy this floor for Ridwan Muhammad, but there had been many retrofits to the city, even before the Chimerans had arrived.

There were few decorations in the space and Connor realized there weren't even desks. It had been set up as an informal conference area, with multiple sets of holographic-projection equipment. The two Chimeran leaders were clearly going for a structure quite different from even the one in place in Chimera.

"*Director* is still the correct title," Lang told him with a sad smile. "Jozha and I are certainly not the new Dyad Ministers. We are, for this moment, merely the Dyad Directors of Chimera Landing—and, as the senior Dyad, responsible for Hopefall, New Maki, and New Sphinxes."

Maki was a reezh word meaning *Sanctuary*—and the city of Maki on Garuda had been the single citadel of the reezh colony that had maintained an advanced technological civilization until a lost and distressed human colony expedition had arrived.

Four cities had been built on Mackenzie's southern continent—or were still *being* built, in the case of New Sphinxes—to the pattern of Chimera Landing. A dictator's ego project had proven the saving grace of the immense evacuation.

They'd had somewhere to *put* eighty million people, though Connor wasn't going to give Ridwan Muhammad much of the credit for that. The real work had been done by the work crews the First Legion commander had kidnapped and pressed into service—people who had volunteered to work for the Protectorate doing rebuilding projects across the region.

"How can I assist the Directors of Chimera Landing?" Connor asked. There was a small table, surfaced in the same black stone as the wall pillars, between the chairs the three of them had taken. As he spoke, the door opened to admit a gentleman in a plain suit—a man whose movements said *bodyguard* but whose tray of water glasses said *butler*.

The glasses went on the table and the man swept out of the room, leaving Connor to pick up a glass and level a questioning look on his hosts.

"We have heard that a scouting mission was completed through the Chimera System," Lang finally said. "We were hoping that you would be able to provide us an update on what is going on back home... and how long it may be before the Protectorate is able to free our people."

That was what Connor had expected, and he removed a datachip from inside his suit jacket, laying it on the table.

"I discussed the possibility with Admiral Alexander," he told them. "The chip contains the information she and her staff feel they can release safely. There is a section on there that we would prefer was restricted to yourself and other government members, but most has been cleared for public distribution.

"If..." He considered the two officials, then shrugged. "If you feel it will not cause panic. There is little good news, my friends. Your planet has been invaded, bombarded and occupied. While there do not appear to have been massive atrocities against the civilian population, the Kazh have clearly been far more willing to accept collateral damage than we anticipated."

As had been pointed out several times in the lead-up to the battle, the Kazh were the heirs of the Reezh Ida—a state that had burned *hundreds* of worlds and killed trillions of their own people to end a rebellion.

The Protectorate had *known* that and tried to incorporate it into their planning, but it was clear now that their best efforts had drastically underestimated the enemy's willingness to destroy.

"We will review it," Jozha promised in the gravelly tones of a reezh. "We do not wish to cause a panic, but there are many questions. We... need to know the fate of our home."

"I understand. As for a relief force..." Connor shook his head. "There are eight Type One warships in the Chimera System, backed by over a billion tons of lesser warships.

"While the Navy has hesitated to commit to anything, I would not expect them to risk a counterattack until they had a force of eight dreadnoughts of their own.

"A force that, right now, simply does not exist."

There had been eight *Mjolnir*-class dreadnoughts in commission. As it had been explained to Connor, only six would ever actually be deployable, with two in repair and refit.

One had been lost at Chimera, bringing their deployable strength down to five.

A new class was being built, but even Connor wasn't cleared to know how many there were or how far they were from completion.

"I would expect a minimum of six months, more likely a year, before the Protectorate will be able to do more than survey Chimera from a distance," he warned gently. "If the Kazh draws down their forces, that may change, but... we cannot rely on them doing that."

"No." Lang looked tired suddenly, slumping in a way that added ten years to her visible age. "But what do we *do*, Ambassador?"

"Live," he suggested. "Keep the faith while helping your people adapt to their new homes. We will not be able to return as quickly as any of us would like, but we *will* return to Chimera, I promise you."

"That does not feel like enough," Jozha replied. "And yet you are not wrong. These are dark times we have entered, and many among our people blame the Protectorate—and yet those of us here in Mackenzie owe our freedom to you."

"I understand," Connor conceded. "Even if we were not bound by honor and treaty to retake Chimera, though, I do not believe the Reezh Kazh would leave us alone."

If he hadn't been as certain of that, he would have had to argue *against* continuing the war. Every argument that had been made against helping Chimera against the Kazh was still true, after all. They were at the end of their logistics train, facing an enemy of still mostly unknown strength.

But Connor's read of the people who had repeatedly attacked Chimera—without even demanding surrender, let alone *talking*—was that they would hunt the Protectorate to the far reaches of the galaxy.

For humanity to be free, they would have to stop the Kazh.

"I do have a request for the two of you," he continued. "Two, actually. One professional... one personal."

The two officials looked back at him. Lang attempted to conceal her surprise, but she wasn't as good at it as she thought she was. Jozha had the advantage of being reezh, and Connor was far from an expert at reading them.

"A personal request, Ambassador?" Lang finally asked.

"Nothing major," he assured them. Connor had a long-standing reputation in the Protectorate of being unbribable and incorruptible—one he valued more than any bribe or favor anyone could offer him!

"I know that a Christine Aukema and her children were on the final evacuation list," he continued. "With the chaos, I haven't been able to track down where she ended up, and I want to make sure they're settled and as all right as they can be.

"She's a friend's sister and I promised that I'd check in on her."

Except that he hadn't been supposed to leave Chimera, so Ombeline Aukema—who had been his lover while he was there—hadn't asked any such thing. Since he was in Mackenzie, though, he felt obliged.

"The confusion has left a lot of people trying to find each other," Jozha told him. "We have an entire office dedicated to fielding such requests. I will make certain yours is put in the queue."

"There is no need for priority, in that case," Connor said with a chuckle. *Of course* the request he had been torn over making was normal and similar to hundreds—thousands, probably!—of similar ones being made of the municipal governments of the refuge cities.

"And the professional request, Ambassador?" Lang asked.

"I need a reezh diplomat, Ministers," he told them. "We're putting together a plan to scout the Primes and make contact with any potential friends among the old reezh worlds. If we get lucky, we'll find *Barracuda* and I'll be able to work with the embassy that was sent to Ordin, but we are unfortunately unsure of what happened to her and her people.

"Computer translation will only go so far in converting from English to Reezh, and I'm not even going to pretend I have enough understanding of reezh culture to handle whatever oddities will arise from dealing with the old Primes."

There was a silence as the two ministers traded glances and the kind of silent communication born out of a long and close working relationship.

"We don't have many people I can say are qualified for that," Lang warned. "Most of the people who studied diplomacy, even in theory, were on *Barracuda*."

"The best-qualified candidates for your request would be the two of us, in fact," Jozha said. "That isn't an option, unfortunately. There are a few candidates I can speak to and see if they are interested."

"We cannot promise more than that," Lang concluded. "How soon will you need this person?"

"I'm not certain of the timing yet," Connor admitted. "No sooner than a week, but hopefully not much longer than that. The faster the diplomatic mission gets moving, the sooner we are likely to achieve anything."

And the sooner they achieved something, the sooner they might be able to retake Chimera from the enemy.

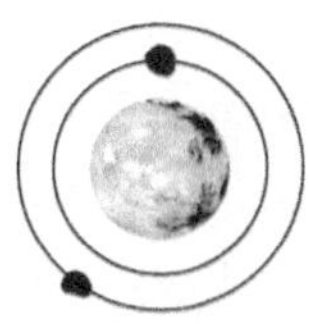

CHAPTER 6

CONNOR HAD SPENT HIS CAREER moving at the highest levels of the Protectorate. He'd served as a Member of the Dáil Taran, Tara's legislative assembly, while in his twenties—as a hand-picked candidate of an outgoing planetary governor. After that, he'd moved on to the Protectorate Arbitration Commission, acting as a neutral third party in discussions between star systems and interstellar megacorporations.

He understood the need for security, even in the presumed safest of locations. His patience was still strained as he worked through the series of security checks required to link him into the latest conference with Mage-Admiral Alexander.

They were using the Link, which was theoretically absolutely secure so long as no one had captured a terminal, but he still had to activate several layers of encryption and then submit to both automatic and live verification of his identity by a stone-faced Marine officer before he was finally linked in to the call.

Most of it was normal enough that he'd barely registered the extra—not until the images of Mage-Queen Kiera Alexander and Prince-Chancellor Damien Montgomery popped up above his desk, opposite that of Mage-Admiral Jane Alexander.

"Your Majesty," he said, surprised. "I see that your aunt continues to add extra guests into our catch-up meetings."

"I added myself to this one," the Mage-Queen told him. She was still terrifyingly young to Connor's eyes, but he knew better than to misjudge her.

Kiera Alexander might be a slim and gorgeous redhead in her late twenties, but she'd ruled the Protectorate in her own right for six years—and the man who had ruled it for three years before that still sat at her right hand.

"Jane invited *me* after that," Montgomery said with a chuckle. "She appears to be under the illusion that, even as Chancellor of the Protectorate and the theoretical head of Kiera's government, I have some modicum of control over our Queen."

"I have some idea, Your... Highnesses, of what our Queen looks like uncontrolled," Connor pointed out. It was exactly that kind of mess that had led to his own appointment as Ambassador, as Kiera's attempts to handle the Chimeran crisis without fully engaging her Parliament had rubbed enough people the wrong way to nearly precipitate a constitutional crisis.

A crisis a constitution that was less than ten years old didn't need, even if the young Mage-Queen had been entirely within the letter of the document!

"I am learning," Kiera told them all. "But while I have agreed to delegate and leave the day-to-day management of this situation in the hands of professionals like my aunt, it remains our most dangerous and critical ongoing matter.

"I am staying informed, and there are times I'm going to stick my overly aristocratic nose in."

Connor had to admit that Kiera did not have what anyone would regard as an *aristocratic* nose. She had more of an adorable button going on, which was a thought that nearly touched on lese majesty.

"By which Her Impetuous Majesty means she's found something she's going to overrule her field commander on," Jane Alexander noted. The Admiral's tone was disapproving but not quite as sharp as Connor would have expected.

That, plus the fact that he was in the meeting, told him what was going down.

"We're launching the diplomatic mission," he said.

"I would not lean as heavily were it not you in command, Jane," Kiera admitted. "I would convince Damien or you, in fact, and have *you* do the leaning for me."

The young woman's frankness was endearing—and questionable. Connor hoped he had made it clear that while Kiera Alexander *ruled* the Protectorate of Mars, Connor's first loyalty was to the people and the nation, *not* the monarch.

"I am not certain you should be so frank on these matters, Your Majesty," he murmured. "Their Highnesses are family, but I am not."

"No, you are not, Connor O'Hannagain," she agreed. Suddenly her green gaze was locked on to him, and any vestige of adorableness fled as he met eyes carved from frozen jade.

"You are not even, I am quite certain, *my man* as some people would use the term," she continued. "Am I wrong?"

"No, Your Majesty," he said. "I serve humanity, then the people of the Protectorate, then the Protectorate itself. You are... farther down that list."

She was *on* the list now, he had to admit, which was more than she had been when he'd accepted the appointment to Chimera.

"And *that*, Connor, is why everyone in this room trusts you to speak for Mars, to wield a type of authority my father and the Kings before him only gave to their Hands and Voices," the Mage-Queen said. "I do not trust you to put my interests first. I trust you to put the *Protectorate* first—and to have the spine necessary to tell me if I'm wrong, a skill I can reliably locate in frustratingly few people."

"Even I, Your Majesty, might quail at that task," Connor admitted.

"I doubt it." Damien Montgomery didn't raise his voice or even stress his words, but there was something in the man's calm tone that carried surprising weight. Barely a decade older than his Queen, it was easy to forget that the slim man seated next to Kiera Alexander had once stopped an orbital bombardment with his magic.

The Merlin File included details of Montgomery's achievements that remained secret. Connor had thought the man's reputation was overblown—and certainly, much of what *was* public knowledge had been expounded upon by media looking for a hero—but much of it remained silent.

"Now that we're finished talking up each other's characters and patting our egos, the task before us?" Mage-Admiral Alexander said. "The *problem*—that I have raised repeatedly—is that I am drastically short of strength and I don't want to send our only ambassador plenipotentiary off without a proper escort!"

"Your heaviest losses were in your capital ships, Jane," Kiera pointed out. "Which is why they're currently split between Mackenzie and Exeter, getting shoved into every repair slip the two systems have.

"Ambassador, in your opinion, would a battleship serve for your embassy? Put aside the question of what resources *might* be available. What type of ship would you *prefer* for a consular vessel?"

Connor had to stop and think about that for a moment.

"There would be an argument, I suppose, for using a ship that is larger and more powerful than anything the Reezh Kazh are known to possess," he said. "However, even with your instruction, I already know that the dreadnoughts are not an option."

He had seen Jane Alexander start to open her mouth. The only dreadnought available was *Mjolnir,* and there was no way the damaged dreadnought was even capable of the long flight to the Primes, let alone that anyone was going to move her away from Mackenzie until Second Fleet was far stronger.

"Honestly, without the ability to deploy something that could truly awe anyone we interact with, we want to use something more... humble," he concluded, then chuckled. "*Humble* in this case being quite relative. We will want a vessel with a powerful degree of self-protection—while the plan calls for heavier backup forces to be on hand, there is a high likelihood that the consular ship will be placed in vulnerable positions where she is alone and surrounded by potential hostiles."

He didn't have a list of ships in front of him, but at this point, he knew at least the rough types the Royal Navy operated: destroyers, cruisers, battleships, and dreadnoughts. He'd just ruled out the largest and smallest types, which only left one option.

"I would guess, given what I know of our Navy, that my best option would be a cruiser," he concluded. "Given the mixed nature of the mission, I would presume we would need at least one other cruiser for support, plus an escort for both the cruisers and the logistics vessels we will be taking with us?"

"I think you might have spent too much time around Mage-Captain Chambers, Ambassador," Jane told him with a chuckle. "Unless you are directly quoting from the ops plan she drafted based on your proposal?"

"I... was not consciously doing so," Connor replied. "But I did go over many of the components of the plan and had reviewed her team's executive summary, so I may have been recalling pieces of it."

"And the more-limited request does put the situation into perspective, I hope," Kiera said. "We don't need a battle squadron to take Ambassador O'Hannagain into the Primes. This time around, we're not looking for a fight—quite the opposite.

"With the amplifiers in play, any of the Primes is effectively immune to any force we can deploy at them," the Queen reminded them. "Even once we have an entire deployable squadron of the new *Lancelot* dreadnoughts, we will need to learn far more about the nature of our enemy before we could risk a hostile approach to any of their systems.

"That is going to fall mostly on you, Ambassador. We need friends among the old reezh worlds and we need information. Scouting ships, ancient records and long-range optics can only tell us so much. We need to talk to people on the ground, to learn what they think is going on."

"You don't want much, do you?" he asked. But he grinned as he said it. "I don't think we have anyone better qualified for this, Your Majesty. I'll have to rely on MISS for as much initial information as those optics can get me, but I think I can get them to talk to me.

"And once we're talking, we have a chance."

Of course, he hadn't managed to get the *Kazh* to talk to him, but Connor figured that the Kazh were going to be the main thing opening doors for him with their old core worlds. Mars, through Connor, was the only counterbalance the Primes would ever have to the Nine and its imperialist church.

"We're still talking about detaching a lot of ships I'm not convinced I can spare," the Mage-Admiral warned. "The minimum I'd want to send to escort the scouting ships alone is three cruisers and a dozen destroyers—which is over *half* my remaining escorts."

"Half your remaining escorts at this moment," Montgomery corrected. "With the support of the militias, we've got a lot of lighter RMN units moving in your direction. You know the numbers and ETAs better than I do, Jane, but...?"

"I have been promised six battleships, twelve cruisers, and twenty destroyers," the Admiral admitted. "But the closest of those is still a month away. Any *further* reinforcements..."

"... we need to build," Kiera Alexander said grimly. "But those reinforcements mean you *can* spare the ships right now, Jane—and I honestly don't think we can afford for *Barracuda* to wander into Chimera and reveal that the Ordin government is talking to us."

That had been Connor's point before, but he waited silently now. The Mage-Queen could theoretically give orders to her aunt, but Connor suspected that if Jane Alexander put her foot down today, that was the end of it.

But the lack of real fire to her complaint earlier in the meeting told him that she'd already been wavering.

"You're not wrong," the Admiral finally conceded. "We know that the Reezh Kazh are going to start surveying out in our direction. With the capture of Chimera, they're going to have a decent idea of where we are, which means I need escorts and capital ships in position to cut off scouting squadrons—*especially* escorts.

"A full-strength escort for the consular and scouting mission will take up every modern destroyer we've got back to operational status."

"I know, Jane," Kiera said. "But if we hold this to our own devices, we won't even be able to *attempt* to relieve Chimera for over a year—and I don't think we'll *ever* be able to actually threaten the Kazh.

"We need friends. Just as Chimera needed us, we need the Primes."

The Mage-Admiral looked over at Connor and spread her hands in a shrug.

"Then you'll get your consular mission, Ambassador," she told him. "I'll pass the orders and we'll concentrate the ships here, probably by the time Kelzin gets back.

"Try not to lead them back to us, all right? Right now, Exeter and Mackenzie are the most fortified systems out here, and neither of them could stand against what's left at Chimera."

"I'm going out to try and make new friends, Admiral, but I know the risks," Connor assured her. "We'll keep our tracks covered."

As much as they could, anyway. Fortunately, *that* part wasn't Connor's job. He just needed to not tell the Navy to deliver him into a trap that caught them all.

When the people setting the trap didn't look or think like humans.

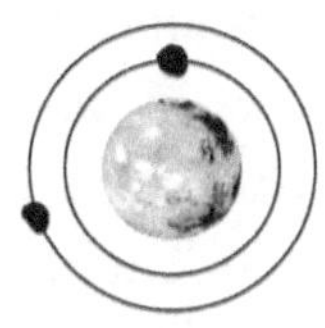

CHAPTER 7

MIKE WAS STUNNED BY HOW MUCH datawork a small ship with a crew of fifty-odd souls could create. *Rhapsody in Armor* created a surprisingly large amount of forms and reports for him to fill out and review, but as the senior Captain he also ended up with plenty of work from the other two ships.

Clearing them took more of each day than he wanted, but the only person he could have offloaded them onto was Xi, and he wasn't going to do that to his wife. She'd complain to his other wife, and then he'd be outnumbered as well as having been an ass.

The main reports he'd been filling out that evening, though, were both unusual and promising. Someone in RMN logistics had wanted a detailed estimate of the *Rhapsodies'* burn rates for fuel, food, water and any other consumable he could think of.

Given that each of his ships carried a twenty-trooper detachment from the elite Bionic Commando Regiment, there were some unusual pieces among their consumables. Mike's own cybernetics, for example, were entirely powered by his own body—but that process required him to both eat roughly a thousand calories a day more than most humans *and* intake some unusual vitamins and minerals.

The BCR troopers had those needs *plus* replaceable power packs for running their systems at high levels. None of it was particularly difficult to manage, so long as the supplies were in stock.

The request told him that they were going to be restocking quickly when they arrived in Exeter, which raised all kinds of possibilities.

"You know you are supposed to work a shift of only so many hours, right?" Xi said, walking through his office door without bothering to knock.

"Eight hours on watch, six hours on other duties," he told her. Two hours for meals and showers, eight hours to sleep. The non-officer members of the crew only had two hours of non-watch duties, but *Armor* was a tight ship.

They only had so many people.

"You were on watch eight hours ago and you haven't left your office," she said. With a gesture, she turned his console display off with a touch of magic and then slid into his lap.

"So, what keeps the big bad Captain oh so busy?" she asked as his brain completely failed to recalibrate.

"Consumable stocking list requests," he told her. "Which you know, being the not-quite-so-bad executive officer."

"We *could* have divided and conquered on that," Xi pointed out. "Or even asked Kelly if we have a standard document. For all that we don't have very many of our ships, they are pretty standardized."

"I… didn't think of that," he admitted. "I didn't want to dump work on you, and the burn rate for each ship is sufficiently different, I didn't think of any kind of standard load."

Xi sighed and kissed his forehead.

"It's a good thing you're pretty, Mike."

He was reasonably sure he was more than just *pretty* at this stage of his life, but he definitely had his moments.

"So, other than going over my shift by two hours and eating a BCR ration bar instead of a proper meal, what else did I miss?" he asked.

"Well, I *was* planning on jumping you when you got back to our quarters, but that was an hour ago," she told him. "And it turns out the timing might not have been great anyway. We got a ping on the Link. Kelly wants to talk."

"Work or personal?"

"Well, she signed the request as *Director* and scheduled a call thirty-five minutes in advance, so I'm guessing work." Xi sighed. "Which means that while I know Kelly would be happy to see me in your lap, there may be other people on the call and I should pull up a chair."

Xi's guess that there would be others on the call was correct. It was fewer than Mike had feared, but the presence of the First Commissioner of the Martian Interstellar Security Service, Elidi Borysov, was definitely enough to keep things professional.

Mike didn't know the other two faces on the call personally, but he recognized the members of the Oversight Board by sight. He didn't know what Dilshod Cortez or Alex M'Bogo had done before they'd taken their seats on the organization that organized and watched the Protectorate intelligence service.

For the MISS, the question *who watches the watchmen* had a specific answer: the Oversight Board. The First Commissioner was the only MISS agent who actually knew who all the members of the Board were or even how many of them there were.

Mike knew the half dozen Board Commissioners, like Cortez and M'Bogo, who chose to be more active in the management of the Service, but the rest were intentionally obfuscated from the working members of the service.

"Commissioners, Director," he greeted them. "I have to admit that even a relatively senior field agent gets worried when three members of the Oversight Board are suddenly on his Link.

"What do you need from *Rhapsody in Bohemia?*"

"By preference, not to get hit by a meteorite on your way to your destination," Borysov said. There was a rumble to the older woman's voice, a certain type of not-quite-hoarse tenor that had served the woman well as an agent.

Only someone who knew Kelly as well as Mike did would have noticed her wince at the boss's pointed comment. The scout ship that had been *supposed* to be assigned to Second Fleet at Chimera had suffered exactly that issue, hit by a fluke of in-system navigation that had rendered her incapable of deployment.

They didn't have enough *Rhapsodies* in play to absorb an unexpected loss, which had resulted in Mike and his three ships—*Bohemia* newly built and the other two with barely completed refits—failing to make it to Chimera in time to help against the Kazh invasion.

"At this moment, Commissioner, all three of my ships are in deep space," Mike noted. "We are about a day's travel from Exeter."

Even over the Link and talking to the leadership of his service, Mike wasn't going to give them the exact location of his ships. That had been drilled in to him and the other stealth ship commanders.

"You're being redirected, Mike," Kelly told him, the first thing his wife had said in this meeting.

"To where?" Xi asked immediately. As XO and senior Ship's Mage, Xi was responsible for *Bohemia*'s navigation.

"You're going to Mackenzie, Captain Kelzin," Borysov said firmly. "Mage-Admiral Alexander has activated a modified version of the plan we were planning to follow prior to the Fall of Chimera."

"We're scouting the Primes?" Mike hoped he concealed his delight. There was no other real point to having his ships out on the frontier like they were. It was *useful* to be able to take a vessel right into Chimera orbit, but a lot of the real work could be accomplished by a destroyer in Leviathan orbit with her engines shut down. A few sacrificial drones here and there, and ninety-plus percent of what his ships could do could be handled by the Navy.

Penetrating the amplifier-defended star systems that remained of the Reezh Ida was a task that truly called for the capabilities of his ship and the skills of his crew.

"That is half of the mission, yes," Kelly agreed. "You'll be working with a logistics squadron out of Second Fleet to carry out preliminary surveys of the Prime Systems prior to Ambassador O'Hannagain making contact."

Oh. That was going to be an interesting mess—and Mike suddenly understood why three of the Oversight Commissioners were on this call.

"I believe I understand, sirs," he told them. "That does put a great deal more immediacy on our scouting work if the Protectorate is going to be following up in a matter of days, not weeks or months."

"Exactly." M'Bogo leaned forward as the Black man bit off the single word. "Given what we know of the systems from Captain Chambers' scout runs, do you believe your ships can do this without excessive risks?"

Mike had to think about that one. Chambers had been flying an unusual ship when she'd visited the Primes, a Navy cruiser custom-built with the same stealth systems as a *Rhapsody* but on a far vaster scale. For all the magic and technology built in to shielding the vessel, she'd been detected in the Nine and in at least one of the Primes.

"It will not be without risk, Commissioners, Director," he said finally. "We know that the Ordin System, for example, did manage to detect *Thorn* when Captain Chambers was in the system. We believe we know how and I can take countermeasures to that, but the combination of magic and technology used there is a quite-effective augment to the visibility given by the planetary amplifier itself."

The current best guess was that the heliopause of the Ordin System was seeded with passive sensor platforms linked to a command-and-control center by FTL coms of some kind.

"It is also difficult to detect, which will make risk assessment more difficult as well. That said..." He grinned confidently. "A *Rhapsody* is less than two percent of the size of a *Thorn*-class explorer cruiser. If Mage-Captain Chambers' ship was invisible, we simply do not *exist*."

"Good." Something in how Borysov said the single word drew everyone's attention, but it was Mike's gaze that the First Commissioner clearly locked on to.

"Your open and official orders are to scout the Primes for Second Fleet while keeping close to the consular fleet to share logistics capability," the older spy told him. "While your missions are connected and you won't be able to significantly precede the consular mission, there is no official need for you to stick around while the Ambassador is talking to strangers."

Mike placed his hands on the desk in front of him and leaned slightly forward, not only focusing his attention on what Borysov was saying but making it clear to everyone *else* he was doing it.

There was going to be a second shoe.

"The second, unofficial part of your orders is that we want the *Rhapsodies* to stick around and keep a very careful eye on the consular mission, until you are absolutely certain that they are safe in a given system. Only then are you authorized to send two of your ships to begin the next phase of the mission."

Which meant they wanted Mike to tie one of his ships up watching over the Ambassador whenever he was in a Prime star system. That made an annoying amount of sense, even if it was going to impede the survey op.

"The Oversight Board has discussed the current situation with the reezh, both the Chimeran refugees on Mackenzie and the Reezh Kazh and the Primes," M'Bogo said quietly. "The blunt truth of the matter is that we have exactly *one* experienced diplomat, a man we will need to apprentice and train up the first new generation of true diplomats we've needed in two centuries.

"Ambassador O'Hannagain's value is in him talking to these aliens and laying the groundwork for new relationships; we cannot tie him up teaching students... but he is also effectively irreplaceable."

"If the situation in a star system appears to be going sideways and the consular escort seems unlikely to be able to escape, your orders are to extract Connor O'Hannagain at all costs," Borysov said flatly, still holding Mike's gaze like she could look into the pilot's soul.

"You do not have the space, the weapons, or the capacity to salvage the entire expedition—but you can penetrate a blockade, retrieve a single individual, and take him to safety."

"That may require us to abandon an entire squadron of warships to their fate," Mike noted. It wasn't an objection. He didn't *like* the order, but it was only a contingency plan, one he saw the value of.

"We trust your discretion and judgment, Captain," M'Bogo told him. "Your partner, Director LaMonte, speaks highly of both your and Mage Wu's ability to think on your feet and react as needed.

"If the situation becomes such that you need to activate that contingency plan, I doubt that even all three of your stealth ships would suffice to change the fate of the consular escort."

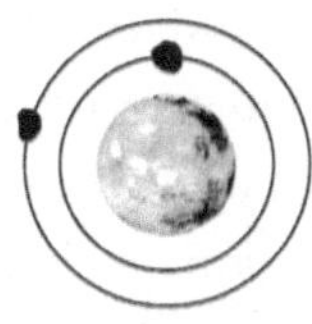

CHAPTER 8

IT WAS ONE THING TO HEAR THE PLAN of *keep building cities to the preexisting plan to save time* and agree with the logic. It was something else entirely for Connor to look out the windows of the car carrying him through New Maki and realize that he couldn't tell he'd left Chimera Landing.

If the plane that had brought him to the third of the four new cities had turned around completely and landed back where it had started, he wouldn't have been able to tell without looking at the street signs and business names.

Fortunately, his driver—a reezh security officer named Rozh—seemed to know his way around and the location of the apartment address he'd been given.

Government and municipal services in the new cities were still a rough mix, from what Connor had heard, though the Evacuation Commission had made sure that there were enough positions filled in advance that things weren't complete chaos.

Even so, Ansel had brought two other agents with him, making it a good thing that Rozh had brought a vehicle large enough for them all. The big ground car was a pure passenger vehicle: if it had storage, it was underneath their feet and Connor hadn't seen it.

There were plenty of other vehicles on New Maki's roads, running people and supplies between homes and new businesses. There was a frenetic chaos to the city that reassured Connor in many ways.

The evacuation had to be a shock to the system for the people who'd come there, but the Protectorate and the Evacuation Commission had set up a lot of structures to get people working and living again. Since the entire city had come together in a matter of weeks—modern technology and half a million determined, motivated and well-paid experts made the impossible possible—every business he saw was brand-new.

The delicatessen on the ground floor of Christine Aukema's building was being run by a pair of reezh, with signs in both English and Reezh above the door declaring a specialty in some form of meat dish that Connor had vaguely heard of on Chimera.

Everything about the fifteen-story building—part of the outermost ring of towers in the concentric design shared by the four cities—screamed *brand-new*.

Including the sign on one of three elevators noting that it was out of order, and they expected a warranty team by to fix it on the eighth. Depending on when the sign had gone up, that was impressively fast!

All three of his bodyguards escorted him up to the seventh floor, and Connor gave them a side-eye as he approached the door.

"Let's not panic the poor woman, shall we?" he suggested. "I'm here to check if Miz Aukema needs anything, not make her life harder!"

"Of course." Ansel didn't say anything more, but the other two agents drifted away to hover by the elevator—and Ansel shifted his outfit so that his weapon was concealed behind his back.

Connor couldn't complain about that, he supposed, since he was also wearing a concealed pistol. He raised his hand to knock—and the door slid open before he even touched it, revealing a woman whose familiarity punched him in the guts.

Christine Aukema was *definitely* Ombeline Aukema's sister. They were of a height and build, though the younger sister had her hair cropped into a short and presumably maintainable bob.

"Mr. O'Hannagain," she greeted him. "I appreciate your attempt at easing my fears, but I was expecting you to come with guards. Ombeline was torn between snark and understanding when it came to your escort."

He inclined his head.

"I appreciate your understanding, Miz Aukema," he told her. "I regret that we weren't able to meet under less-difficult circumstances, but I wanted to be certain that you were settling in and had everything you need."

"Come in" was all she said. "Your... agents, yes? They can come in too. I have a pot of tea on."

One advantage of having an entire city built in advance was that the Evacuation Commission had been able to make certain that every family group heading to Mackenzie would have a space that was sized to their needs.

The apartment the Aukemas had moved into was a solid example. Connor wasn't sure how many bedrooms it had, but it had a seating area by the kitchen and dining space and clearly had a *second* seating area tucked away in back, as he could hear a pair of children chattering away.

He took a seat and watched, amused, as Ansel and the other two agents found spots to sit or lean out of the way. Miz Aukema clearly guessed the pattern and gave them a somewhat-reproving smile as she passed out cups of tea.

"I am glad to get to meet you, Mr. O'Hannagain," she told him. "Ombeline and I were both busy in the time you were on Chimera, but you had become quite important to her. My sister's taste in men swings from *terrible* to *mercenary*, so I was curious as to which end of her particular spectrum you fell on."

"*Mercenary*, I'm quite certain," Connor allowed with a smile. The tea was quite good. "The tea is excellent, Miz Aukema."

"Thank you. The Mackenzies have done everything in their power to make sure we have all that we need, but I'm not used to their tea," she admitted, looking down at the cup. "I'm not sure if it's the plant is somehow different, or the other inclusions or... what, honestly. It's *fine*, but it doesn't taste quite right."

"Moving between worlds always comes with things like that," he said. "When I first left Tara, nothing tasted right. My home's atmospheric pressure is higher than most human-inhabited planets, which made everything taste noticeably different!"

She chuckled, then looked down at the tea again, her eyes unfocusing slightly.

"It's... hard," she admitted. "I didn't expect that I would deserve a personal check-in from anyone. There are a lot of people here."

"There are," he agreed. "And the new Directors running the cities are doing everything they can, with the full backing of the Protectorate and Mackenzie. But I know that if I had planned on being here, Ombeline would have asked me to check in for her."

"I was wondering," she said. "The news said you were staying on Chimera, right up to the end."

There was no real accusation there, but it was a question.

"I was supposed to stay. I'd *promised* I would stay," he confirmed. "But I was on *Mjolnir* for a meeting when the enemy arrived, and there was no time to move people down to the surface or vice versa.

"I got pulled away and people who were supposed to leave stayed behind." He shook his head. "It was messier than we'd hoped."

"I was aboard one of the *Saladins*," she told him. "It was... unpleasant. My younger child—"

She cut herself off, taking a sip of the tea.

"That would be Jeremy, yes?" he asked. Ombeline had said she had a niece, Rowan, and a nephew, Jeremy.

"Yes. He was injured in the maneuvers," she admitted. "We got medical care, but he has been... quiet since. We're getting counseling visits, but so is everyone else."

It was only as Christine mentioned the boy's quiet that Connor realized the two voices he could vaguely hear from deeper in the apartment were both definitely girls. Rowan had a friend over, he supposed, and her brother was sitting quietly.

There was little warmth to that thought in his mind, but there was only so much he could do.

"School will start soon," Christine said. "That will help all three of us."

"That's right; you're a teacher," he remembered. "Do the schools have the supplies they need? There is… There are a lot of plans and hopes in play, Miz Aukema, but the impression of someone on the ground is valuable."

She pursed her lips thoughtfully, looking for a moment completely unlike her intentionally and vociferously cheerful sister.

"We have the physical resources we need," she finally told him. "The schools, the tablets, the materials—even our own teaching materials, brought with us in the ships' memory banks without many of us knowing.

"What we lack is the breadth of skills most of us would prefer. I'm a science teacher, primarily, focused on students in the final fifth and sixth divisions. Fifteen- to eighteen-year olds, by standard Terran chronology.

"Quantum states, astrophysics, thaumic theory, those sorts of things."

He nodded.

"And?"

"I will be teaching my normal load of two of those classes," she said. "I will *also* be teaching an English communication class, a Reezh language class and handling two physical education periods per week.

"Looking at what we do have, I suspect there were more thumbs on the scale for the evacuation lottery than anyone wanted to talk about," she noted grimly. "We have twenty-nine teachers for a student body that should have thirty-two. That's close enough that I think someone was making sure we had enough teachers… but if so, they were treating all teachers as interchangeable."

It was the kind of thing where if someone had told Connor *We're making sure we have enough teachers,* he would have agreed and signed off on it without further thought or detail—but as soon as Christina Aukema pointed out the problem, it was blatantly obvious.

"We have a random mix of specialties and skills among the available teachers, with no real records of who has done what to work from. My old director was on the first evacuation flight, so he was beginning to see the problem, and I've been helping with that since I landed."

She shivered slightly.

"I worry I've done too much. I haven't spent as much time with my children as I should, with my husband... back on Garuda."

Connor knew she almost just said her husband was dead. There was no hope in her voice at that moment.

"Your husband would still have been in training when the Kazh fleet arrived, Miz Aukema," he reminded her gently. "Without breaking confidences, I can assure you that he would *not* have been anywhere near a battlefield unless something went very wrong."

There might not have been enough time to move the training battalions underground, but the facilities had been spread out across the planet, well away from any of the decoy bases that had been set up to be detected from space.

Her husband, Dave Thwaite, would have been moved underground with the rest of the trainees. The plan had *always* been for the forces being recruited and trained to be used for the stay-behind force rather than trying to hold the planet against an enemy with orbital superiority.

"I..." She swallowed. "I don't know if I can dare hope, Mr. O'Hannagain. I know Ombeline said something similar, but I *know* she was trying to make me feel better."

The moment of darkness was broken by a peal of laughter from the other room, loud enough to fill the entire apartment with the sound of teen joy.

"That's Ashley," Christine said wryly. "The school director's daughter. She's too old to be hanging out with either of my kids, but she knew them both before and has decided to *be* their friend. I think it's her way of coping... and I think it helps."

"It's hard," Connor told her, repeating his earlier words. "I left Tara of my own choice, pursuing ambitions and duty. None of you had a choice, not really."

"Everything is different," she murmured. "I grew up on Garuda. I could never have told you how much of our architecture, food, even our *language* had incorporated things from the reezh we shared our world with.

"And then we are here, in a city built for us but built to a style so very different. Even the lines of the buildings just... remind me that we aren't home."

"I wish there was more we could do," he told her.

She laughed at him. It was a bitter sound, far less joyful than the giggling teenagers a few moments earlier.

"Your Protectorate built entire cities from the ground up in a matter of weeks," she pointed out. "I have only the vaguest idea of how much effort it took to gather the ships that brought us here—but I spoke to the Prometheans flying our evacuation transport.

"Their sacrifice on our behalf... There are no words, Mr. O'Hannagain. What was done to get those of us here to safety was incredible."

The *Saladin*-class ships had been invasion transports for the armies of the Republic, the antimagic secessionists who had nearly toppled the Protectorate. And like the warships of their new enemy, those ships had been powered by the extracted brains of murdered Mages.

Many of those murdered Mages had survived, removed from their old ships and given a refuge in a Protectorate that, wracked by guilt, had no way to restore them to their bodies. Faced with an urgent need for ships that needed Prometheus Drive Units, the Mage-Queen herself had asked those victims, now calling themselves *Prometheans*, if they were prepared to volunteer to fly ships for the evacuation of Chimera.

Dozens had agreed, enough to pull tens of millions out of Chimera who would have been trapped without them.

"The courage of the Prometheans who flew those *Saladins* is..." He trailed off himself. "You're right, Ms. Aukema. There *are* no words. We owe it to them to make certain that you are all taken care of—and I owe it to Ombeline to make sure that you and your children are okay."

"I appreciate that, Mr. O'Hannagain," she told him. "I believe we are... as okay as anyone can be right now. My only real ask would be..."

She trailed off and he smiled broadly at her.

"Miz Aukema, by the random chance of your sister's boyfriend being one of the highest-ranked officials of the Protectorate in this star system, you have a chance to speak to power," he told her. "As I told your sister, when she asked things of me, I can do few favors—but I *can* pass on requests and information."

The only favor Ombeline Aukema had ever asked of him had been impossible: for him to get Christine and her children onto an evac ship. Dave had removed that problem by volunteering for Chimera's defenders, trapping himself but seeing his family safe.

For the sake of the men and women like Dave Thwaite, if for nothing else, Connor was already doing everything he could think of to do.

"As I said, we have a random mix of specialties among our teachers, one that isn't necessarily going to wash out, even across the four cities," she said slowly. "But part of the problem is that, because of the way our researchers and academics got evacuated first, we actually have more specialists than generalists and first-division teachers."

The first division was the first two years of schooling, the youngest of children in education.

"I suspect, though I don't *know*, that the Mackenzie schools could make better use of our specialists than we can—and I hope that they have generalists they can send us in trade. We all want our children to get the best education possible.

"If we work with our hosts, I think we might manage to get a better education for *all* of Mackenzie's children."

"As I said, I can make no promises," Connor said, but he smiled. "Even so, I will definitely speak to Governor Kerekes. I believe that concept will be welcomed."

It made enough sense to him that he might even bend some of his usual rules and make sure that even-higher authority heard about it. Connor didn't think he'd need to put any real weight behind the idea to make sure it happened.

He figured the moment Kiera Alexander heard about it, it was going to be a done deal.

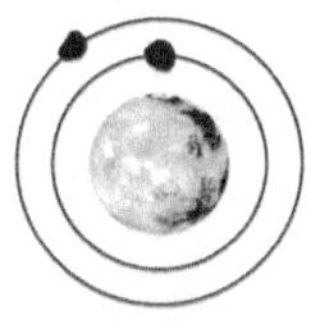

CHAPTER 9

AS MIKE HAD EXPECTED, there were tenders waiting for his three ships when they arrived in Mackenzie. Any of the three tenders was twenty times bigger than all three of the scout ships combined, but it was easier for them to restock and refuel his ships one-on-one.

Less than six hours after his ships entered orbit of the inhabited planet and tucked up to the logistics ships, he was on his way down to the surface. A beacon guided his shuttle onto the roof of one of the massive towers at the heart of Chimera Landing, where a trio of Marines met him and Xi.

It had been a while since he'd seen the level of efficiency and security the Navy put into this meeting. The last time he'd seen it, Kelly had been the Captain and he'd been the Executive Officer—during the war with the Republic.

Even the conflict against the First Legion around Mackenzie hadn't seen the type of care and precautions involved as they followed the Marines deeper into the tower. Even their implants were interrogated, forced to give up their serial numbers to confirm Mike and Xi were who they said they were.

Finally cleared through, the Marines brought them to a set of double doors and stood back.

"Herself is waiting for you," the Sergeant in charge of the detail told them.

Mike swallowed. That meant the Marine thought he knew who he was meeting—and there was only one person out in Mackenzie who would meet every marker for *that* form of address.

"Thank you, Sergeant," he replied, then opened the door for Xi to step through.

Neither of them were going to mistake the graying old officer on the other side of the room for anyone except Mage-Admiral Alexander, after all.

"I believe you've spoken with Ambassador O'Hannagain at various points in the last few weeks," Alexander introduced him a minute or so later, gesturing to the massive red-haired man in the perfectly tailored suit.

"I don't think you've met Mage-Captain Ketil Rantala," she continued, waving to the other officer in the room.

Rantala was a dark-haired and skinned man with a shaven head and an average build. He didn't have the near-standard ethnic blend of the descendants of the Project Olympus victims, and he wore a blue-dyed sash made from some kind of animal skin Mike wasn't familiar with.

"I have not had the honor," Mike agreed, offering the other man a firm nod.

"My wife, Ship's Mage and Executive Officer, Xi Wu," he introduced his partner. "I take it that Mage-Captain Rantala is being assigned to our little operation?"

"Exactly." Alexander smiled thinly. "Coffee will arrive momentarily, and then we can get to work. We've established many details already, but there are points you'll all need to be clear on."

As if summoned by her words—unlikely, if only because Mike's implants told him the room was so sealed against intrusion, he was reasonably sure oxygen molecules were getting IDed in the air vents—a pair of RMN stewards stepped into the room with trays of food and coffee.

Mike was sufficiently unsure of the protocol that he waited for Rantala to grab a cup of coffee and a sandwich before he followed suit. Alexander waited until everyone had eaten at least a few bites before leaning in and tapping commands on a tablet tossed onto the conference table.

He'd missed the tablet—something Xi would tease him about later, if she'd noticed, since he was *supposed* to be a well-trained spy as well as a starship captain—since it blended in to the mottled black surface of the space.

Everything else in the room was a pale gray speckled with black, an odd eggshell-like pattern that managed to dim the room without overwhelming. It was a calm space, buried well away from the outer walls of the skyscraper and probably armored, if he judged correctly.

It also definitely had high-end holoprojection equipment, as a map of the Nine and Primes appeared above the table. Two extra dots appeared off to one side, marking Mackenzie and Chimera.

"People, this is our problem," Alexander told him. "We are one hundred and fifteen light-years from Chimera here—and then Chimera is a further one hundred and seventy light-years from the nearest of the Primes."

The reezh had possessed eleven core colonies, systems with enough power to survive the Burning. Mike had reviewed every scrap of data Mage-Captain Chambers' sweep of the region had gained them and knew that one of the eleven was gone, scorched to ashes sometime between the Burning of the Reezh Ida and humanity bumbling into the region.

That left ten major colonies, each mustering populations and industry on par with Sol itself.

"Two hundred ninety-five light-years from here to the Nine," he noted aloud. "Two weeks, if we push the Mages on the scout ships."

While only six of the fifteen Mages aboard Mike's ships were officially fully trained Royal Martian Navy Mages—a much-sought title that confirmed the Mage was trained in both jumping starships and a number of other combative magics—all of them had been given the same training and could match the same six hours per jump.

And while Mike wasn't able to follow everything his wife had learned, he knew Xi had trained to a level *beyond* that of the RMN's Mages. Much like Mike was expected to do many things a non-Mage Captain in the RMN wouldn't have to do, Xi Wu was trained to do many things an RMN Mage wouldn't know how to.

"The one thing that has been decided is that every vessel assigned to this mission will have five Mages capable of six-hour jumps aboard," Alexander told him. "Speed and flexibility are going to be the key to this.

"We're sending you in for information primarily," she continued. "That will fall almost entirely on Captain Kelzin and his stealth ships."

"As I understand, the reezh Primes have demonstrated the ability to detect our stealth vessels," Rantala noted. "Is it safe to rely so much on them?"

"They've demonstrated the ability to detect the *explorer cruisers*," Mike corrected calmly. "The *Thorn*-class ships are far larger than the true scout ships, with all of the detriments involved in that from a stealth perspective."

"And we are aware of how *Thorn* was detected in each case," Xi added. "There are preliminary sweeps we can engage in to avoid both planetary amplifiers and outer-system surveillance networks."

"We are cautious by default, Captain," Mike assured Rantala. "There *is* a risk, but we will watch the path ahead of ourselves, to make certain we are taking careful steps. We know Ordin, for example, has an outer-system surveillance network that appears to have some kind of faster-than-light communication set up to their active fleet.

"So, when we reach that system, we will spend time to make sure we have located that network and assessed its capabilities before we enter the key parts of the system."

"There are also many things we can learn from a distance," the RMN officer said. "My only comment, Captain, is that long-range scans do not require stealth ships. *Last Stand at Alamo* has sensors almost as good as yours and a flotilla of recon drones. We can do quite a bit from a safe distance… if we can identify what that distance is."

"And that is what will fall on my people," Mike promised with a broad smile. Rantala was being reasonable, after all.

"It will," Alexander agreed. "I want to be clear right now, gentlemen, Miz Wu: the scouting-and-surveillance mission is the absolute priority here. We're deploying resources we can't truly afford to risk, from the cruisers to the stealth ships themselves."

To Ambassador O'Hannagain, Mike knew as well. He doubted the diplomat knew about the secret orders the MISS ships had to ensure his safety.

"The diplomatic mission ties in to both halves of that if I succeed," O'Hannagain said. "Give me time to talk to any of the Primes that aren't automatically our enemy, and I can get both intelligence and safe harbor for our ships—but I need to *know* that we can safely enter the system.

"Which falls on Captain Kelzin," he confirmed with a nod to Mike.

"Agreed." The room was silent after Alexander's last word as she surveyed them and the map. "Your mission is quite straightforward: survey the Primes. You are *not* authorized to approach the Nine itself. That's a risk we can't take."

Mike would have done it if the order had been given, but he was a touch relieved that it hadn't been.

"What about *Barracuda*?" O'Hannagain asked. "We still don't know her fate, and that is... concerning."

"We may never know the fate of the Chimeran delegation to Ordin," the Admiral said grimly. "But that said, while your course and even order of scouting missions are entirely at your discretion, I *suggest* taking a path past Chimera and visiting Ordin first. We have the course that *Barracuda* should have taken to get home."

"If we have that, my people will find her if she's there," Mike said firmly. He had to agree with the Mage-Admiral, though: *Barracuda* was probably gone and they would never know what had happened to her.

"Ordin seems like the best place to start for diplomacy as well," O'Hannagain agreed. "But without knowing what happened to the Chimeran delegation, I lean toward skipping them. We'll see what the scouting missions turn up, I suppose."

"I am content to start there," Mike said. "We can move on afterward. We will be spending quite some time in each system before I'll be comfortable declaring one safe for your diplomacy, Ambassador."

"You and I can discuss what qualifies as *safe* on our way, I'm sure," the big Ambassador told him with a confident smile.

Somehow, Mike doubted they were going to come to an agreement, but hopefully, the other man would listen to him.

"You'll have *Last Stand at Alamo* for your consular ship, Ambassador," Alexander told him. "Rantala?"

"Sir?"

"You're a Commodore as of the start of this meeting," she said with the grin of a grandmother revealing a candy bar they'd hidden from the kids. "You'll remain in command of *Last Stand*, but you'll also command Task Group Twenty-Eight, the force assigned to this."

"My staff are still arm-wrestling for how many and which destroyers you'll get, but you're definitely getting *Prince of Frogs* and *Eye of Newt*. *Salamander*-class cruisers, for the three of you who wouldn't know," she explained.

Three cruisers plus some number of destroyers was a decent-sized force. More than enough to protect the logistics ships Mike needed, though...

"What about logistics support?" Xi asked, clearly living comfortably in his head.

"We're pulling Mages together to have four tankers and four tender/colliers with five apiece," the Admiral confirmed. "Most of TG Twenty-Eight's time will be spent escorting them, so they'll consume food and supplies faster than fuel. Overall, you should have supplies for an eight-month mission."

That was hopefully overkill, but Mike could see the point. The more time they had to do this job right, the better off everyone was going to be—and it wasn't like the RMN would be ready to fight a real war for at least that long.

"That should serve, sir," he told her. "When do we depart?"

"Second Fleet is still sorting out exactly what you'll have, but as of this moment, TG Twenty-Eight formally exists and is seconded to MISS, Captain Kelzin," Alexander told him. "We will have the last units assigned to Mage-Commodore Rantala's command within forty-eight hours."

"Then we leave as soon as those ships are assigned and prepped," Mike replied. "The sooner we're in space, the sooner we're in the AO—and the more likely we are to find *Barracuda* alive."

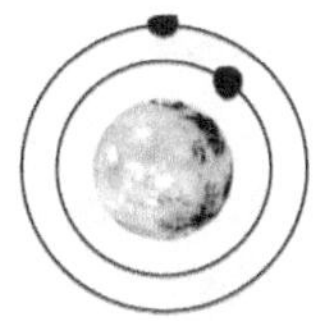

CHAPTER 10

CONNOR WAS CONSIDERING if there was anything in his glorified hotel room that he needed enough to pack onto a starship when there came a knock at the door. It wasn't a familiar knock, and that was unusual.

Only a handful of people would knock on the door to his quarters without prior notice, and almost all of them were trapped on Garuda. The only person likely to show up at his door was Sarvesh Ansel, and the Secret Service Agent had a very particular knock—*tap-tap-tap*, a quick rhythm with minimum force, just enough to be heard.

This was a heavier, slower, sound—*crack*-beat-*crack*—that Connor didn't know.

Despite himself, he reached inside his jacket and put his hand on his gun. Zahid Kootenay had made sure he had concealable holsters for all of the weapons he'd brought with him, including what his aide had called *that monster hand cannon*—a custom-smithed revolver firing the same rounds as a Marine's anti-exosuit penetrator rifle.

Today he was carrying a more-regular caseless six-millimeter, the Royal military's standard Macy-Six.

"Enter," he commanded.

The door to the luxury suite swung open to reveal an unfamiliar reezh. She wore the toga-like garment common to both species in Twin Sphinxes—and now Chimera Landing—and blinked carefully at Connor over the top of her armored frill.

She did not step into the room, only spreading her hands slightly and bowing.

"Ambassador O'Hannagain?" the stranger asked, her voice the usual gravel-truck-containment-failure of a reezh.

"Yes. And you are?" Connor demanded. "I am unused to unscheduled arrivals."

"My… apologies, sir," the reezh said, her English clear but hesitant. "I spoke to your bodyguard. I was told you knew."

"Very well. And who are you?" Connor repeated. Someone might have sent a message. He hadn't checked his wrist-comp and he wasn't going to yield enough control of the situation to look at it now.

"I am Adazh Komarazhi," the reezh introduced herself. "Daughter of Sozha Komarazhi. Student and teacher in the Western Department of Stars, as the humans call such things."

The name meant nothing to him, but the *Department of Stars* answered his question.

"You are the diplomat I requested?" he asked.

"I am… a translator," Komarazhi said carefully. "I have studied diplomacy. Human-reezh relations. My mother was closer to what you name. She is aboard *Barracuda*."

Connor released the gun and took the moment to check his wrist-comp messages. There was nothing there with regards to Komarazhi, which meant she was either very dangerous or someone had forgot to send a message.

He triggered a call.

"Sarvesh," he greeted the senior agent. "Your people cleared someone through to my quarters without telling me. I *think* she's legit, but can you check?"

It was probably a good sign that Komarazhi neither objected to his making the call while they were mid-conversation nor to waiting.

"They should not have done that," Ansel agreed grimly. "But we have a chaotic mess of Marines and my people right now, and no one is really sure what the protocols should be. Give me thirty seconds."

An icon on the display told Connor his bodyguard had put him on hold, and he gave the reezh woman a small smile.

"I believe you," he told her. "But we have grounds to be very, very careful."

The computer pinged at him and Ansel was back.

"Yeah, she's legit. Agent Cole and Sergeant Harn both thought the other was sending you a notice," the man told Connor. "Forwarding you Adazh Komarazhi's file. Her mother was the closest thing to a diplomat the Republics had—and her other parent was Captain Joto, *Barracuda*'s commanding officer."

Even across the species barrier, Connor could read Komarazhi's wince as Ansel laid out her parents' fate. No one knew for certain, of course, that *Barracuda* was lost—but even so, the younger Komarazhi had to know her parents were likely dead.

The wrist-comp popped up a holographic image of the reezh. The colors were always slightly washed out with the translucent images, which in Adazh Komarazhi's case managed to highlight a red mottling to her stone-gray skin that wasn't immediately visible in the hotel corridor's lighting.

Looking back at her, though, Connor was certain she was the same person.

"Thank you, Agent. Sort out the coms issues with your people, please," he requested. "Our reezh diplomat and I will have an initial brief."

Not least to see whether the young woman was willing to follow her parents into the dark, knowing that they could all share *Barracuda*'s fate.

Adazh Komarazhi took a seat and a drink—it was easy to get reezh-compatible drinks in Chimera Landing these days, with the entire population being from Chimera—with calm grace.

Connor wasn't sure how old she was, let alone how that would translate into an equivalent biological or cultural age for a human, but he could tell she was nervous. Determined, but nervous.

"I asked the Dyad Directors of the city for a diplomat," he told her. "I presume they're the ones who sent you to me?"

"Yes, Ambassador," she confirmed. "Our world is captive. You have warned us that the Protectorate will not soon be able to free Garuda, so your mission seems the only hope for the friends and families we left behind.

"Any help we can give to your mission serves our own cause, but not many of the Departments of Stars made it to Mackenzie. Most who would fit your need were sent on *Barracuda*. I... remain."

Connor nodded.

"And you want to find your parents," he guessed.

"That is part of why I *wish* to go," Komarazhi agreed. "But the Directors asked me to go because I am the best we have. I have learned from my mother and studied what little of diplomacy we can teach.

"As I said, I am a translator. I have studied human-reezh relations and the languages of both species," she continued. "I speak the main Korazhi dialect, what you call the reezh language, as well as two other languages that have limited usage on Garuda.

"I speak your English, though not as well as I like, and can read German, Spanish and Mandarin. I cannot..." She paused. "Hear? No. Understand those three spoken."

Connor gave her a reassuring smile.

"If those three are somehow required, I am perfectly capable of speaking and understanding them all," he told her. Along with Gaelic and several other languages. "My reezh Korazhi is barely present, however, which is part of why I asked for a diplomat.

"There is only so much that a translator can carry for me—and a computer translation program cannot even manage *that*. A qualified diplomat can both translate for me, when needed, and *speak* for us all when I cannot."

"I understand, Ambassador."

"Do you?" Connor studied her. She seemed clever enough and brave enough, but he had to worry.

"I will need you to stand at my side as we negotiate with people who could have destroyed your homeworld at any point in the last few centuries," he said quietly. "You'll need to tell me, subtly, if I'm making mistakes—and I may well need you to carry on secondary negotiations while I rely on more-automated translators for my own talks.

"That last will require me to decide I can fully trust you, but I believe we share enough goals that I expect to get there," he noted. "But you will speak for Chimera on this mission, Komarazhi. I will speak for Mars, but I cannot speak for the government-in-exile of your people."

"I understand this," she confirmed. "The directors made it clear. I am *their* diplomat, not the Protectorate's—not that the difference is large."

"That may change," Connor said. "I... would appreciate a warning if that happens, but for now, we are aligned in our goals."

The Kazh needed to be defeated. Chimera needed to be liberated. Some structure for relations between the reezh star systems and the Protectorate of Mars needed to be built.

"I believe so," Komarazhi said. "I must ask, Ambassador. Do we intend to find *Barracuda?*"

"We cannot divert significantly from our mission to do so," he warned. "We have shaped our course to maximize the chance that we find your parent's ship, but I cannot promise anything. As much as we can do without risking the scouting operations and our embassy, we will do."

"That is more than I would dare ask, Ambassador," she replied. "We must stand together, speak together, to find a path forward.

"Or all that my people ever was will be lost to a nightmare we had forgotten."

Brave enough. Clever enough. Plus, if she was the one that Jozha and Lang had sent, she was almost certainly the best they had. He had that much faith in the Dyad Directors.

"The first thing I'll need you to do, Komarazhi, is make sure we have reezh translators for the trip," he told her. "I have a contact with the Task Group's logistics team. We've made arrangements for some reezh personnel to be aboard each ship, but we had no idea how many we'd be able to get."

"I will speak to my colleagues," she promised. "How many translators would you need, Ambassador?"

"As many as we can get," he admitted. "I'd like at least five, not including you, aboard the consular ship *Last Stand at Alamo*, plus one on each of the other warships. If you can recruit... twenty, I think they will serve.

"We will need support staff for them, of course, so we'll need to make sure Commodore Rantala's people know how many to expect."

"I will begin immediately," she promised. "How long do I have?"

Connor made a show of checking the time on his wrist-comp.

"The Task Group is currently scheduled to leave in thirty-two hours."

"Then I will also work quickly."

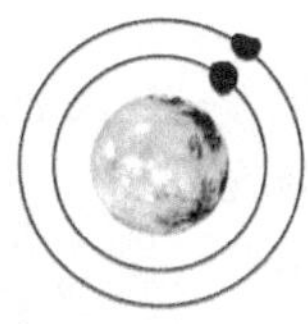

CHAPTER 11

TASK GROUP TWENTY-EIGHT was an impressive collection of metal, even to Connor's relatively uneducated gaze. Thanks to his former military attaché, Roslyn Chambers, he could easily distinguish between the three cruisers, the dozen destroyers, and the eight freighters making up the flotilla.

The image he was looking at was an illusion generated by the shuttle's computers, showing each of the twenty-three ships at a disproportionate scale to the space between them. At the level of zoom he was using, the ships wouldn't have all fit on the display, after all.

It still took him a minute to locate the MISS stealth ships. They were predatory things, smooth lines and shadowy edges that blended into the background of deep space—quite unlike the near-even pyramids of the destroyers or the tall spikes of the cruisers.

The destroyers all looked the same to him, but he could at least tell that there *were* two types of ship among the freighters and that one of the cruisers was different from the other two.

The different cruiser was their destination. Longer and narrower than the other two, she also had a distinct inverted "skirt"—a shorter pyramid between her widest point and her engine. Connor had no idea why *Last Stand at Alamo* had that rear section when the other two cruisers lacked it, but all of the destroyers had it.

"These are Martian warships, are they not?" Komarazhi asked.

"They are," he agreed. "I believe that one"—he tapped the screen—"is *Last Stand at Alamo*."

The reezh diplomat sat next to his right with Ansel just past her. Another dozen or so reezh—his requested translators and support staff—were scattered through the shuttle.

Even with Connor's Marine-augmented security detail, the shuttle felt empty. He'd never worked with a lot of staff, but the staff he *did* have had been left behind on Garuda.

He could only hope that Zahid Kootenay—his secretary who was *also* an MISS counter-espionage agent—was keeping them safe. There was nothing he could do for them except make sure the planet was liberated sooner rather than later.

"They are quite different from those of the Chimera Space Navy," Komarazhi noted, glancing to a window that was showing a more-accurate view of the void around them. On that view, *Last Stand at Alamo* was visible as a slowly-growing white triangle, still small enough to be blotted out with a finger.

"I thought the CSN's ships were also built by humans," she said.

She didn't phrase it as a question, but Connor recognized one when he heard it.

"Different human nations," he told her. "The ships Admiral Wang brought to Chimera were deserters from a nation that waged war on the Protectorate. Like the Reezh Kazh, their ships were powered by murdered Mages.

"Admiral Wang deserted when he learned this truth," Connor added quickly, before Komarazhi could question the involvement of Chimera's national hero—and martyr, he reflected grimly—in the horror of something like the Prometheus Drives. "That was what brought him to your people.

"But his ships were built in a system that did not *officially* use magic. They have rotational cylinders inside their armor to provide working gravity to the crew."

Connor suspected that explanation was simplified, but it was the only one *he'd* ever needed.

"And your ships do not?" she asked. "The vessel I traveled to Mackenzie on was a... *Saladin*, I believe? It had such a cylinder inside it."

"The *Saladins* were Republic-built ships, operated by volunteers from the victims of the Republic's drive construction," Connors said quietly. "Like the ships you were used to, they used rotational gravity.

"Our ships"—he gestured to *Last Stand*, now more visibly a spike in space over twice as tall as it was wide—"do not. They have multiple Mages aboard, serving as key members of their crew, and are able to maintain magical gravity throughout the vessel."

"*Magical* gravity?" she asked, her rocky voice still carrying soft awe. "You speak of this like it is ordinary, Ambassador."

Connor paused at her comment, then had to laugh.

"A strange thought, but you're right," he admitted. "I am a citizen of the Protectorate and have spent most of my time in our government. It is a rare day where I do not spend time in conversation with at least one Mage, and I have spent a lot of time on our starships, all of which are carried between the stars by Mages.

"Their skills and gifts are commonplace to me, I suppose." He waved around them, where they were all belted in to their seats for safety and to keep them in place in microgravity. "But not quite so commonplace, of course, as to allow a shuttle like this to have gravity.

"I can ask one of the Ship's Mages to tell you more of the gravity runes, if you like," he offered. "I have to admit I know very little of the structure and nature of magic. I know what it can do where it is relevant to my own work, but I am not a Mage, so I have learned almost no theory."

And what theory every Protectorate citizen learned in school, well... that had been over twenty years past.

A few moments before the shuttle touched down on the deck of the flight bay, Connor felt a sudden sensation of *down* as it dropped into the magical field above the metal floor. Komarazhi's exclamation of surprise helped him see the magical trick for the wonder it was.

Not only did the Mages aboard *Last Stand at Alamo* weave a magic that gave everyone aboard the ship a sense of gravity identical to being on a planet, they manipulated its exact extent to make the process of landing shuttles on the big ship easier.

"We will have to wait a few moments until the decking is safe to travel," Ansel told the reezh. The less-experienced part of the contingent, like Komarazhi, were starting to move with alacrity. The rest, including about a third of the reezh who clearly had space travel experience, knew that rushing would just increase their wait.

Connor took a few seconds to rise and stretch. He had a quick routine that went through most of the key muscle groups, and after over an hour strapped into the chair, he could feel it release tension across his body.

"We've got your luggage, sir," Ansel murmured. "You should probably be the first off; I suspect the Commodore will be waiting."

"Of course. Thank you."

That would be the usual courtesies for a senior official, Connor knew. He'd got out of the habit of expecting them, with how often he'd bounced up and down from *Mjolnir* since she'd arrived at Chimera.

The light next to the shuttle hatch flicked to green thirty seconds after he reached it. It slid open smoothly with a ramp extending to the deck, allowing him to duck out of the spacecraft and enter *Last Stand at Alamo*.

There was an astringent tone to the air he hadn't encountered before on spaceships, though it was almost overwhelmed by the sauna-esque feeling of the air immediately around the shuttle.

Technicians in full-body safety gear were still working on the shuttle, attaching various pipes, hoses and harnesses. Connor gave them an acknowledging nod he doubted they even noticed, and then set off toward the cluster of black dress uniforms he saw waiting at the safety barriers.

Rantala had changed his uniform since their last meeting, with different insignia at his collar and a few extra touches of gold braid. Despite the changes, he still wore the blue-dyed sash.

"Welcome aboard *Last Stand at Alamo*, Ambassador O'Hannagain," the man greeted Connor. "May I present my Executive Officer, Mage-Commander Tonya Bourgeois, and my Ship's Bosun, Master Chief, Luca Sinagra."

Bourgeois was a small curvaceous blonde woman. Her eyes were a sharp cold blue and Connor suspected she would be able to tell, to the millisecond, how long he spent noticing her chest.

Luca Sinagra, on the other hand, was a willowy man with short-cropped graying hair and dark Mediterranean coloring. He was clearly measuring Connor in his own way—and Connor had the suspicion that falling short on *either* of Rantala's companions' measurement would be a concern going forward.

"Thank you for having us aboard, Mage-Commodore," Connor said, offering his hand to Rantala and nodding to the other two officers.

Or was Sinagra not an officer? Connor wasn't clear on how that worked.

"Mage-Captain," Bourgeois corrected gently. Connor blinked at her in confusion. "Aboard *Last Stand at the Alamo*, Mage-Commodore Rantala is still her Captain, a title that tradition says holds precedence over his exact rank.

"I believe I understand; thank you, Mage-Commander," Connor said cheerfully. It was exactly the kind of minutiae he would have looked up if he was dealing with a new organization, but he thought he'd known the Royal Martian Navy.

"And if you're going to hypercorrect our guest, Mage-Commander, I must remind you that our ship is *Last Stand at Alamo*, not *the Alamo*," Rantala told her. There was a lilt to his tone that suggested this was an ongoing discussion.

"There is no such place as Alamo," Bourgeois replied with a small smile. "And it is the Battle of *the* Alamo, as in *the* Alamo Mission. Whoever dropped that definite article wasn't doing their job."

"Wartime experience said we wanted shorter ship names," Sinagra told the XO. The bosun's voice was melodic, almost calming. "I'm sure someone thought it was an excellent compromise to save a syllable."

"Not to a Texan," Bourgeois replied in a slow drawl that Connor instantly knew was her natural accent.

"A continuing discussion of merit and great weight, I understand," he told them as Adazh Komarazhi caught up to him. Survesh Ansel was with her, though Connor knew the Agent had kept him in sight the whole time.

"As for my own companions, this is Senior Agent Sarvesh Ansel of the Protectorate Secret Service, responsible for my personal security, and Ambassador Adazh Komarazhi, a diplomat of the Chimeran government-in-exile that will be acting as their representative in these discussions."

From the quadruple blink Komarazhi gave in response to that, the reality of her position hadn't quite sunk in. She wasn't just *a diplomat*; she was *the* Ambassador from Chimera. In the discussions he was hoping to have with the Primes, she would be present in all of them. As the junior partner in their alliance and representative of an occupied power, there was a limit to what her Ambassador status was worth, but it was still important and very real.

And he'd be *damned* if he'd let the Royal Martian Navy treat her with one drop less of respect than it deserved.

"Of course, Ambassador Komarazhi," Rantala said without missing a beat, giving the reezh woman a sweeping bow. "You are most welcome aboard *Last Stand*. We were advised that there would be a number of reezh accompanying Ambassador O'Hannagain, including yourself.

"If you and Ambassador O'Hannagain will allow, Mage-Commander Bourgeois will show you to your quarters and answer any question you have. I would be honored if you both joined me for dinner this evening in the Flag Mess."

He smiled brightly.

"All of the Task Group's Captains will be joining us, for a chance to get to know each other before we all sail off into the deep dark together."

"I would be delighted," Komarazhi confirmed, throwing a side glance at Connor from one of her lower eyes.

"As would I," Connor agreed. "We will all want to know the names and faces of the people we'll be working with."

He'd like more than that, if he was honest, but it seemed that Mage-Commodore Rantala hadn't drawn enough attention from his old friends in the Arbitration Commission for them to have a file on him.

The only information Connor had on Rantala was the man's Navy dossier, which was sadly lacking in the kind of personal information Connor preferred to have on people.

He'd learn it the old-fashioned way, he supposed: by getting the other man drunk and listening to him talk.

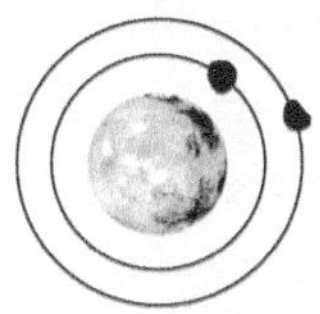

CHAPTER 12

MIKE KELZIN GENERALLY INSISTED on flying himself and Xi around, if he had any choice in the matter. He'd been gently overruled this time by his XO and his ground-force commander, one Major Britta Rennell of the Protectorate Bionic Combat Regiment.

Given that Rennell, the senior BCR officer for this operation and in charge of all three BCR squads present, had probably outweighed Mike and Xi combined *before* the Protectorate had added a hundred kilos of combat cybernetics to the woman, he respected her opinion when she decided to raise it.

That put Rennell and another BCR commando in the shuttle with him and Xi as escort, and a pair of pilots from *Rhapsody in Bohemia's* shuttle pool flying the spacecraft over to *Last Stand.*

No one had even blinked at the two soldiers, though, and they'd been given seating for dinner. The pilots hadn't been so lucky, and he hoped that they were getting fed on the flight deck.

Mike checked on the MISS people and realized they were all together, clustered against one side of the room as they waited for the dinner to actually start. He met Xi's eyes with a swallowed sigh.

There were four very clear groups in the room, he realized. The MISS crews—Captains, XOs, and BCR officers—were a total of ten with the extra commando Rennell had insisted on.

The freighter captains had come on their own. They were all RMN officers, but the Logistics branch was always prickly in Mike's experience.

Most RMN line officers respected the crews that kept them fueled and armed, but enough *didn't* to justify the chip.

That put eight BuLog—Bureau of Logistics—Mage-Commanders against the opposite bulkhead from the MISS officers, with three dozen line officers milling around in between—and a small number of civilians, probably from the Ambassador's people, circling through.

"We're not going to make friends holding up the bulkhead, people," Mike told his officers quietly. "Let's get circulating. We need these people to watch our backs and haul our fuel, after all."

The mental gear-shift that ran through his officers was almost visible. They were Agency operatives, after all, even if their current job put them on the command decks of starships. They all knew how to mingle, how to make friends.

They just *also* knew how to protect information and watch each other's backs, and it sometimes took a kick in said back to recognize which skillset was needed in a given situation.

There was only so long before the meal was likely to start, so Mike made a beeline for the most important person in the room he hadn't met yet: Captain Mage-Commander Aslan Descoteaux of the Armed Auxiliary Fast Heavy Freighter *A Dancing of Ravens*.

At one point, the RMN had closed down the AAFHF program and sold off most of the ships. When the number of Mages aboard a ship determined its speed between systems, they'd decided they didn't really need a ship with both fusion and antimatter engines, capable of keeping up with the battle fleet at ten gravities for days on end.

Mike had flown aboard one of the first generation of the big ships, *Red Falcon*, which had ended up being given to his old Captain in trade for a ship that a Hand had been forced to destroy for reasons Mike still didn't understand.

That first generation were all long gone now, but war had seen the designs brushed off. The *Bushido*-class transports now used for troop transport were an evolution of the old design—and so was an entirely new generation of the concept.

"Mage-Commander," Mike greeted Descoteaux as he stepped into the tall man's circle of conversation. "I'm—"

"Captain Mike Kelzin, of our spy ships," the Navy officer finished for him, offering his hand. "I've heard stories about you, Captain."

"You have?" Given how covert most of Mike's work had been the last decade or so—and the fact that he'd followed in Kelly's shadow for most of that time—that was actually concerning.

"I presume you remember the name James Kellers?" Descoteaux said.

"I do," Mike agreed. "Chief Engineer on a pair of ships that got into a lot more trouble than we ever should have."

Kellers had been Chief Engineer on *Blue Jay* when they'd found themselves in the early stages of Damien Montgomery's meteoric rise. He'd been Chief Engineer on *Red Falcon* afterward, though Mike didn't know much about what Kellers had done after that.

"I last saw him at his wedding," Mike admitted. "We've fallen out of touch. It's been a busy few years."

And prior to the Link, the stealth ships had been off any kind of communications loop for months at a time. It had been hard to keep up correspondence with anyone.

"Well, I don't know what he was doing between his wedding and the war," Descoteaux told him, "but from what I hear, he and his wife found themselves offered voluntary reactivation at *her* discharge rank. *Commodore* James Kellers and Mage-Commodore Maria Soprano work for BuShips these days—and the first job they were put on, as I'm told, was the new AAFHFs.

"I was just a test pilot back in those days, but Kellers had *stories* about his old ships. I helped on the new girls and now I fly one—and the Commodore had quite the chuckle when I told him that!"

"I imagine he did." Mike smiled. "It's good to know he's doing okay. Even at his wedding, well."

Kellers had been one of the worst injured on *Red Falcon*'s last flight. Soprano hadn't given the man much chance to feel sorry for himself, Mike suspected, but he'd needed a lot of life-supporting cybernetics—including replacement eyes—to even be able to stand up and say *I do*.

"He doesn't give details about much of what his last ship did," Descoteaux said. "I can tell when something's above my clearance, Captain Kelzin—*and* when someone's hurting over it. He still had extensive and obvious cybernetics when we first met, though the Navy has been slowly upgrading them on him."

"That is *also* good to hear." Mike shook his head. "I didn't know you knew Kellers. I was going to ask you about *A Dancing of Ravens* and see how she stacked up to *Red Falcon*."

"She's a fine ship, though there are days I'd love a cruiser," Descoteaux told him. "Only one of the tankers and two of the colliers are built to the standard, but each of us has the missile defense of one of the new-build destroyers and two-thirds of the missile launchers."

"That's a *lot* to keep hidden." The old ships hadn't really *hidden* their guns, Mike supposed, but they had been low-key enough that *Red Falcon* had been able to pretend she'd been disarmed.

"That's our big advantage over the first-gen ships," the BuLog officer replied. "There was no point in hiding the weapons on the explicitly military ships. We're especially not low-profile about the RFLAM turrets. The launchers and heavy beams, well." Descoteaux shrugged. "Those are harder to see in the first place."

Rapid-Fire Laser Anti-Missile turrets were gatling-style defensive weapons used in one variation or another on every armed human vessel built in Mike's lifetime. The Republic hadn't even changed the acronym when they'd used the same concept on their own ships.

"She can keep pace with the fleet?" Mike asked.

"So long as I and the other Mages keep the runes up to date, we can run up to the same fifteen gravities as everyone else," the other man confirmed. "It's a pain, but I'd rather have to spend thirty minutes of every watch wandering into strange corners of my ship than *not* be able to stick with the cruisers if we're actually under threat."

"Though the cruisers aren't going to leave *A Dancing of Ravens* far behind," Mike pointed out. "You're the ship with all of the spare explosives."

The other three colliers all had missiles aboard, but each of the three ships had a specialty. *A Dancing of Ravens* carried seventy percent of the missile reserves for the entire task group.

"Three different types," the Logistics officer grouched, though there was a sparkle in his eyes as he did it. "Phoenixes, Samurais and the new Wyverns. Each a different size, each with slightly different storage requirements. They don't even all take the same warheads!"

"The *Rhapsodies* all carry Wyverns, so we'll only be bothering you for one type of missile," Mike promised, then snorted. "Not that we're likely to be bothering you for missiles at all. If we have to fire *anything*, we've done something very wrong."

"I knew that about your ships, but you weren't even factored into our load allotments. *Last Stand* might be the only warship carrying the new birds, but she still has a hundred and twenty launchers. I have over ten *thousand* Wyverns aboard, with twenty-four hundred on the other three ships." Descoteaux echoed the snort.

"I think I'll have missiles to spare for your ships."

"Your attention, please, everyone."

Rantala had a fascinating ability to pitch his voice so that it cut through the soft conversation around the dining table without sounding like he was raising his voice.

Mike would have shouted, then made a joke about it. He took mental notes as the RMN Mage-Commodore managed to get the attention of the thirty-plus people in the room without needing to do either.

"As I hope everyone knows, our final list of vessels was completed four hours ago with the assignment of the destroyer *Iago il Pappagallo*," Rantala told them. "Mage-Commander Elise Nikolaev was the last person to get invited to this dinner and made it with roughly three and a half minutes to spare."

He raised his glass to the Slavic-colored woman near the end of the table, who threw him a salute only marred by her being seated.

"While we are hoping to avoid combat, I would prefer to get some combat drills under our belts before we deploy," the Commodore continued. "Orders from Second Fleet are clear, however, and our warships have all worked together in large formations. I hope that will smooth over some of the rough edges, but we will be carrying out exercises on our way."

Mike knew everyone in the room was asking the same questions in their head. Mike knew where they were going first, but *when* was still at Rantala's discretion.

"All of our ships have final supplies to load, and *Pride of Liberty* has a Mage down to a nasty bout of flu. Mage-Commander Galilahi Waya, I understand a replacement has been arranged?"

A broad-featured woman seated at the same end of the table as Mage-Commander Nikolaev looked up and nodded firmly before saying anything.

"Yes, sir," she confirmed. "I'm informed I should have Mage-Lieutenant Telford aboard by oh two hundred OMT. Mage-Lieutenant Quattrocchi is already on the surface in the hands of civilian doctors—and complaining bitterly about being sidelined."

Likely between fits of vomiting, given what Mike understood it took to sideline a Navy officer that completely.

"That's the timeline Mage-Commander Miyajima from Ops gave me," Rantala confirmed. "Assuming there are no issues with Mage-Lieutenant Telford's arrival, we should have every vessel in Task Group Twenty-Eight fully stocked and crewed by oh two hundred Olympus Mons Time."

When the first Mage-King had used the power of the Olympus Mons Amplifier to complete the terraforming process on Mars, he'd also decided to adjust the planet's rotation to give it the same twenty-four-hour day as Earth. That left Olympus Mons itself as the standard time for the Protectorate, the shared clock that everyone could refer to.

Except occasionally for warships that went a bit too fast, Mike supposed, but their computers were supposed to adjust for that.

"We'll give ourselves a grace period, because something *always* happens," Rantala told them, "but formal orders will be going out shortly. We will depart Mackenzie orbit at oh four hundred hours OMT, accelerating for jump space at fifteen gravities."

Mike saw several of the freighter officers open their mouths to object and swallowed his grin. He could guess exactly what Rantala was thinking.

"Several of our ships are not used to pulling full military acceleration, but all of us should have both the engines and the gravity runes to handle it," the Mage-Commodore reminded them all. "If there is a *problem* with either on any ship in this task group, I want to know now, here in Mackenzie with search-and-rescue units on hand and no hostiles in sight rather than in enemy space with a hostile fleet in pursuit.

"Assuming no such problems, we will jump at approximately ten hundred hours along the Mackenzie-Chimera jump route," he concluded. "We will stop one jump short of Chimera in five days."

Rantala surveyed the room.

"Any questions?"

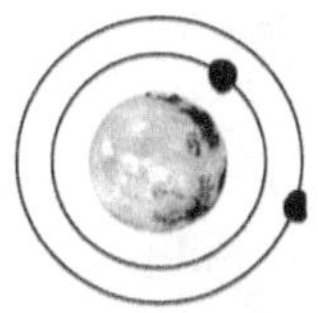

CHAPTER 13

IT WAS IMPULSE AS MUCH as anything else that led Connor to decide he wanted to be on one of the observation decks when they left Mackenzie orbit. The decision to invite Komarazhi was more thought-out, recognizing that she both had likely never seen a planet from orbit *and* might not realize she could just... go to the observation deck.

The deck was a decent-sized space, too, twelve meters long and three deep, with one entire wall given over to a section of armor transmuted to transparency by magic. Connor didn't know if that process cost the armor any function or effectiveness, but he still hoped there were shutters to cover the window when the ship went into battle.

"It's..." Komarazhi trailed off into a stream of soft reezh words that Connor couldn't follow, walking as close to the wall as she could and staring at the planet below.

"I have seen pictures of Garuda and Mackenzie, but... it is not the same."

"It isn't," Connor agreed. "My home made a point of sending all the newly elected politicians up into orbit, so we'd sit in a space like this and look down at our home. It helped put a lot of the little conflicts we made such a big deal of in perspective."

It didn't really *stop* those conflicts, but it helped put them in perspective. The Dáil Taran was notoriously loud and boisterous compared to the parliaments and assemblies of other Protectorate worlds—and yet they had a better record than most of being able to find compromise legislation that could actually pass and *work*.

"I can see that working for my people as well," she murmured. "Though our government always... worked well enough, for all the secrets we now know were hidden away."

"Some things needed to be protected," Connor assured her. The secrets the Dual Republics had hidden away about the reezh had been dangerous and powerful ones—and in the main, they'd hidden them from the humans, not from the reezh.

And, unlike the equivalent organizations in the Protectorate, the Reezh Ida Lachai had recognized that their job was to keep secrets for a reason—and that there was a time to reveal all they'd concealed.

The archives of the Reezh Ida Lachai—along with the Lachai herself, the last reezh Mage on Chimera—were on their way to Mars to help found the new Institute of Interspecies Thaumaturgy.

"But we see what your Nemesis did, and I wonder how close Garuda came to similar dangers," Komarazhi said, her thoughts clearly following a similar track to his own. "Those were people who had seen views like this." She gestured at the window. "How could they do all that they did?"

Connor just shook his head.

Nemesis had grown out of the Keepers, the human equivalent to the Reezh Ida Lachai—an order of Mages and officials put together by the first Mage-King. Sometime between that man and his grandson, Desmond the Third, the Keepers had gone completely off the rails.

They'd operated in complete secrecy and gone so far as to kill researchers and bury archeological sites that proved the past existence of the reezh—but their worst crime, in Connor's opinion, had been to act as the incubator for Nemesis.

Nemesis, in ways Connor wasn't cleared for, had been involved in starting the secession of the Republic of Faith and Reason and their acquisition of the Prometheus Drives. They'd assassinated the Mage-King of Mars, a mistake that had led Damien Montgomery and Kiera Alexander to track down their leadership.

But enough had survived to create a new problem, when Nemesis had stolen one of the new explorer cruisers and gone hunting for proof of the enemy they'd committed their crimes to face.

They'd found Chimera. But Chimera had been harmless, no justification for their atrocities.

So, Nemesis had turned their magic and weapons on Chimera, stealing an ancient computer core kept barely operational by the Lachai. That core had led them to the Nine and alerted the last remnants of the Reezh Ida to the existence of both their lost colony and of the Protectorate.

"Because they believed they were right," Connor finally told Komarazhi. "Because they believed that everything they did would be justified by the truth of the war they wanted to fight.

"And because the ends were so great, no means was unacceptable."

There was a long silence, which broke when the task group started moving. Engines rumbled beneath their feet as *Last Stand at Alamo* came alive, the massive power of engines waking at the command of the tiny mortals who controlled her—and the same power offset within her hull by the magic of those same mortals.

White sparks lit up the darkness in the window, other vessels of the task group bringing their own engines online and haloing Mackenzie in the fire of matter-antimatter annihilation.

"A friend's sister was in the archives under the museum," Komarazhi finally said. "One of the murderers killed her."

Connor said nothing. There was nothing to say—the Protectorate hadn't sent Nemesis out to Chimera or done anything to enable their attack on Twin Sphinxes, but the Mage-Queen herself had taken responsibility for not doing more to stop them.

"Our Lachai could have turned the same way, couldn't they?"

Connor forced a chuckle.

"Have you *met* Razhkah?" he asked. "It took multiple attempts to convince her to accept leadership of a multinational institute investigating all of the files she never had a chance to read and comparing them to everything humanity knew about magic.

"There are souls that can fall into corruption, and there are people who are just too stubborn. Razhkah would never have permitted something like Nemesis to flourish."

He shook his head.

"I wish we'd had someone like her."

Connor looked out at Mackenzie, a world that had been invaded by leftovers of the Republic. All of the systems in the region had suffered at the hands of the First Legion, but the First Legion had been born of the Republic—and the Republic had been a creature of Nemesis.

"Will we return to Chimera?" Komarazhi asked.

"No. You heard the Commodore," he said. "We stop one jump short. Then we'll jump onto the route *Barracuda* was supposed to take home and follow that to Ordin."

"We're looking for my parents?"

"We are," he agreed. "We had to go somewhere first, and there's a real risk to everyone if *Barracuda* falls into Kazh hands."

"Why? There is nothing they would know that the Kazh hasn't learned from my world already."

Connor was still learning reezh voices, but he suspected if Komarazhi was human, she'd be on the edge of tears.

"We *believe* that all evidence of voyages to the Primes other than Captain Chambers' pursuit of *Rose* was destroyed," he said quietly. "If we succeeded, and I have no reason to believe your government failed, the Kazh don't know there has been any contact between Chimera and the Primes—let alone the Protectorate and the Primes.

"Alliances with the Kazh's old enemies are our best chance for making this work. The less information they have about our efforts to make those alliances, the better."

"And we may save a ship and people who don't know they're in danger," she whispered.

"We may."

Connor had to agree with the Navy's assessment: something had gone very wrong in *Barracuda*'s mission. They might find the ship crippled or wrecked somewhere along her route home, or they might never find her.

Either way, he doubted they were going to rescue Komarazhi's parents. So long as the chance existed, though, he wasn't going to steal her hope.

"You can stay here if you want, but I'm heading back to bed," he told her. They weren't the only ones on the observation deck, though everyone else had given them and their conversation privacy.

"I will," she said. "It won't be a problem?"

"Your wrist-comp is loaded with the areas of the ship you're cleared for," he told her. He figured someone on *Last Stand*'s crew had explained the same, but she was a first-time diplomat on a strange warship.

"It'll guide you back to your quarters by a safe route and warn you if you're going somewhere you shouldn't. From the lecture they gave me, you should be clear for most of the non-combat spaces."

Connor was cleared for places like the bridge and Flag Deck, but he was the *Protectorate*'s Ambassador—and had, it seemed, proved he knew when to put his hands in his pockets and shut up.

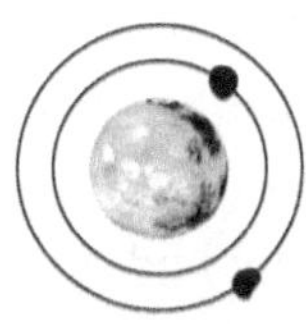

CHAPTER 14

MIKE HAD LEARNED, shortly after getting his implants, that it was best for him to exercise either alone or with people who were *very* comfortable with the cybernetics. Since Xi was asleep after jumping *Rhapsody in Bohemia* a few hours earlier, that meant alone at that moment.

Full speed was hard on the Jump Mages. Each of the five of them aboard *Bohemia*—and every other ship in the task group—was jumping every six hours. It left them perpetually exhausted and struggling to get other tasks done.

After this jump, Xi would take a nap for a few hours, then try and get other light tasks done before she was next up.

Like most non-Mages in the Protectorate, Mike often wished he shared their gifts. Watching his Jump Mage wife walk the edge of permanent exhaustion to do her job, though, left him all too aware of the costs.

Not that his own choices didn't have costs, but he'd at least *chosen* to have his arms detached, rebuilt and reattached with joints that could rotate three hundred and sixty degrees. It wasn't really his *exercises* that he needed to do away from unfamiliar eyes.

It was his stretches. While large chunks of his body were no longer original parts, the new pieces had been integrated with his existing ligaments, tendons and bones—which meant that he had to stretch and exercise, just like someone without his hardware.

And Mike had made a few people vomit over the years putting his limbs through their upgraded paces. Only the first couple had been by accident—after that, it had taken someone being obnoxious to either him, his wives or the Bionic Commandos serving on his ships to get him to show off the inhuman flex of his upgraded limbs.

The augments had multiple uses. Even sticking to things he'd talk about outside his marriage; Kelly had once used that flexibility to throw a surprised Legatan agent to his death. Mike had used it to escape hand-cuffs and other bonds on multiple occasions.

"Captain."

He looked up as the door opened and Major Rennell stepped into the gym. It was the smallest of the three exercise spaces on his ship and he was quite certain he'd locked the door, but he had no illusions about what Rennell could do to any lock on the ship.

For one thing, while she was a combat cyborg, she was assigned to MISS, which meant she had intrusion hardware—and for another, she was in charge of security on *Rhapsody in Bohemia*.

"Major," he said. "I was just finishing up."

His left arm and right leg were currently knotted into each other in a way Xi, for example, couldn't do without breaking limbs. He held the stretch for a few seconds longer than he might normally have, both to make a point to Rennell and knowing that it wouldn't *bother* Rennell.

Her left arm held a single-use fifty-kilowatt pulse laser, after all, and was designed to allow her to easily replace most of her forearm after firing the weapon.

She waited in silence until he released the pose. Something in his back popped loose as he stabilized and turned to his BCR commander.

"How can I help you?" he asked.

"How long until we're expecting to see any action, sir?" she said.

He shrugged.

"Two days still to Chimera, then nine or so to Ordin. If we find *Barracuda* along the way, it'll be a flip of a coin whether we send you or Rantala's Marines," he admitted. "Honestly, Major, I'm afraid this is the same as our usual ops. A lot of sneaking and peeking, not much landing commandos."

She grunted.

"Landing commandos usually means I don't get some of my people back," she pointed out. "Quiet isn't bad. But my people are being twitchier than usual—I think it's because this is a new team *and* we're sailing in company with other teams. And, well, Marines."

The only reason there wasn't a massive rivalry between the Royal Martian Marine Corps and the Bionic Combat Regiment was because most of the Marines didn't even know the BCR *existed*. There were millions of Marines in the Protectorate, and the BCR was only about five thousand strong in total.

"In my opinion, Major, your people's sense of inferiority with regards to Her Majesty's Marines is actively dangerous," Mike warned her. "You serve very different roles—they are the Protectorate's shield and sword. You are our scalpel."

He smiled as a thought hit him.

"But if you want me to talk to Mage-Commodore Rantala and put you in touch with the senior Marine, I could see cross-training your units being valuable," he continued. "I know that Rantala is training his ships hard"—a process that the *Rhapsodies* were observing from a distance rather than participating in—"and I imagine he'd *love* to put his Marines through a real challenge."

Rennell gave him a predatory grin.

"If my people can't give his Marines a real challenge, then that will be a wake-up call we need," she noted. "You're not wrong about the sense of inferiority. It's not that we don't expect ourselves to be better—it's that it bothers many of my troops that the Marines don't even know we *exist*."

"Which is to everyone's benefit," Mike replied. "But for this mission, if the shit hits the rocket hard enough that I'm sending you in to do anything, I can *guarantee* you that you'll be working with Marines.

"So. Cross-training. I'll talk to Rantala."

"Thank you, Captain. I think it will help."

Mage-Commodore Rantala had taken a solid minute or so to process just what kind of troops were aboard Mike's ships—but once he had, the wicked grin he'd had at the thought of cross-training had mirrored Rennell's own at the thought.

That handled, Mike had checked the time. Xi had overslept on her nap and was about to miss their scheduled call. He considered *not* bothering her, but that seemed rude. He pinged her wrist-comp.

"Love, Kelly's due to call us in five," he said when she finally answered with a sleepy voice.

"Ach. The last jump took too much out of me," Xi told him. "I'll... be there in a few."

"Shower and brush your hair, or whatever you need, first," he replied. "Kelly won't mind if you're a few minutes late. She'll be glad to see you."

"I'll be there," Xi promised.

He dropped the call and glanced at his desk. There wasn't much he could get done in the couple of minutes before the call came in. He chuckled at himself—since when had *he* been dutiful enough to try to find work to do in a five-minute break?

Instead, Mike pulled two beers from his fridge and opened one for himself, waiting for the Link call to come through. There had been a time in his life when he'd have told anyone who asked that he didn't think he could do long-distance relationships. That Mike Kelzin might not have been able to, but the older and wiser man who'd somehow lucked into a marriage he wouldn't have dared *dream* of had discovered that it wasn't as bad as it could be.

Though instant communication certainly helped. The three of them hadn't been separated for any real length of time prior to MISS having the Link set up on their ships, after all.

A gentle chime echoed from his desk, a cheerful sound quite unlike any of the usual notifications his systems were set up for. With a wide grin, he tapped Accept on the call and waited for the hologram of the Director of MISS Stealth Ship Operations to appear above his desk.

"Hey, Mike," Kelly greeted him. She was clearly off duty, wearing a dark blue tank top that went perfectly with her current burgundy hair. "No Xi?"

"She'll be here in a few minutes," he promised. "She's jumping like everyone else aboard and her nap ran long."

They shared a long look.

"Keep an eye on her for me, eh, love?" Kelly asked. "We both know she's not as able to run this pace as the Navy would ask for."

"I know and I will. I promise."

Most Jump Mages powerful enough to jump four times a day were snapped up by the Navy after their training. Xi Wu hadn't met that criterion at twenty-four, when she'd finished her university training.

Their wife was generally an above-average Mage, though, so Mike hadn't been entirely surprised when MISS testing said that she *could* make those jumps with the right preparation and rest. But, unlike the Mages the RMN employed, she really did need to *rest*.

As the XO of the ship, in charge of two other Mages who were in the same razor edge of ability as her and two fully trained Navy Mages, Mike knew she felt pressured to keep up her admin work even under this pace.

"I know, we've been through all of this before, but this is the first time you're taking a ship out without me," Kelly admitted. "I worry."

"We're just in a war zone facing mysterious aliens," Mike told her. "I can handle all of that, no problem. You have to deal with"—he shivered theatrically—"*politicians*."

His confidence got him a smile from Kelly, which had been his aim. If she'd shown any hesitation to share his confidence, he would have happily run her through contingency and safety planning, too.

"I can't say I like being behind a desk with you two in the field," she admitted. "Deimos isn't nearly far enough away from Mars to keep my head truly down, but it's way too far away from you two."

"You kept Mike behind a desk for almost four years, love," Xi Wu said, stepping into the room. She wore a burgundy bathrobe that set off her skin and hair beautifully, and Mike took a moment to just revel in his luck as he looked at her.

"Four years. And it almost drove our dear husband off a cliff," Kelly said. She was *also* eating the eye candy, Mike realized, and he shared a knowing smile with both of his spouses.

"I wasn't that bad," he protested. "Though I will admit that working on the second-generation *Rhapsody* design and construction project was more to my taste than some of the other work we were doing."

He raised a hand before either of them said anything else.

"You also shouldn't say where you are, Kelly," he reminded her. "The Link is secure, but you're one of those folks whose address should be kept quiet."

There was no one aboard *Rhapsody in Bohemia* that Mike wouldn't trust with Kelly's location, but there were definitely people on the stealth ship who weren't *cleared* for it.

Mostly because one of the more covert hats his wife wore was Director of Communications Surveillance. The Link was anchored on a two-point communication link: each entangled particle was only linked to one other.

To make a galaxy-wide communication network available to everyone, that meant that every Link terminal had links to a mix of other terminals and central switching hubs. There were over a dozen such hubs, with more slated to come online regularly.

And every one of them had an MISS listening facility attached. What the old Charter and new Constitution allowed MISS to *do* with said facilities was quite limited, but it was enough to keep a lot of analysts employed.

"I know, I know." Kelly made a sad waving gesture. "I mean, this Link is on *our* network, which means you're linking directly to... here. It's as secure as we can get, and I'd love to put *some* of the double-think aside when it's just the three of us."

"And we should," Xi agreed. She pulled a chair up next to Mike and rotated to put one shapely leg across his knees—making it clear to him and probably Kelly that she wasn't wearing anything under the robe.

"These calls are to keep you sane," she continued, "since there was no way we could justify *you* getting back onto a stealth ship—and Mike and I aren't nearly as valuable behind desks."

She smirked.

"Except when Mike is designing starships. *That* was a delight."

Both of Mike's wives turned benevolently indulgent smiles on him, and he flushed for a moment. All of his confidence failed in the face of these two women, as it always had.

"It was an interesting challenge," he said quietly. "A new application of old skills. It was fascinating… and fun."

"And a delight for *us*," Kelly said, repeating Xi's word with clear intent. "You loved it, and we loved seeing you dive into it. But I don't even need to ask Xi how you've been doing to know that you took to the command deck like you were born in the big chair, didn't you?"

He had to return their smiles and didn't even try to argue.

"Turns out part of why I flew shuttles was I didn't like other people deciding what I did," he said. "I trusted my first few squadron heads—and I *definitely* trusted you as Captain—but being in charge just feels… *right*."

"Don't worry; if his head gets too big, I just take my shirt off and he starts panicking while he tries to explain why we love him," Xi told his other wife with a giggle. "I swear, we're going to be having our fiftieth anniversary, and this man is still going to be wondering if we are really in love with him or if there's a trick just waiting to be sprung."

Mike shrugged helplessly. He couldn't argue the point.

"That's okay, Mike; it's cute," Kelly assured him. "Most of the time."

He snorted.

"Sure it is. How's the cloak-and-dagger back home?"

Kelly sighed. "Messy," she admitted quietly. "We all knew Chimera was going to fall, but I think a lot of people convinced themselves it wasn't *really* going to happen. Second Fleet's losses… didn't help."

Over sixty thousand Navy spacers had lost their lives in the desperate running battle to get the last evacuation flotilla out. There'd been twenty-eight *million* people on the evac ships, which meant no one had blinked at the cost, but it was the worst single battle loss the Royal Martian Navy had suffered.

Ever.

"Politics are flying back and forth, and we're doing everything we can to keep Her Majesty informed while staying well on the right side of the Constitution," Kelly concluded. "It's falling down in the directions we need, but I wish we didn't need things to go this way."

There was a long pause and a flash of something darker in her eyes.

"And there's at least one Senator that makes me regret that the Constitution makes it pretty clear I'm not allowed to assassinate our citizens, regardless of how large of a self-centered piece of shit they are."

Mike winced. Officially, MISS had never and would never engage in such an action—but he'd been part of several task forces working to roll up Nemesis before they'd stolen *Rose* and poked a sleeping empire.

There had definitely been a few operations where the objective had been to *kill*, not *capture* key Nemesis people, when MISS couldn't put together enough evidence for MI-single-S—the Martian Investigatory Service, the Protectorate's interstellar police force—to make an arrest.

"Even if I could guess who you mean, which I most definitely can't," Xi said virtuously, "I would have to discourage that line of thinking, love. There is one very easy way to get rid of a Senator, after all. Wait them out."

Any sitting Senator of the Parliament of the Protectorate had just finished the sixth year of their ten-year term—and they weren't allowed to serve a second.

Mike supposed that Senator Gareth MacClery could run for election as a Member of Parliament, but one of Tara's twenty-seven MPs wielded significantly less influence than their sole Senator.

Not that he knew exactly which particular elected official his wife was angry at. He could just guess.

"If nothing else, my loves," he said quietly, "having a mix of loyal and *disloyal* opposition serves the long-term interests of the Protectorate.

"The former will rally behind the Mage-Queen when we need them— but the rest will be sufficiently vocally contrary that no one thinks Kiera *is* having her political opposition assassinated."

"Oh, believe me, I know," Kelly conceded. "The entire Oversight Board and I got locked in a room with Damien Montgomery and Governor-Emeritus Robert Christoffsen for a full-day lecture on it a week ago."

Mike swallowed any comment as part of the weight of that sank in. While the reality was that it was almost impossible to keep knowledge of the Oversight Board's membership restricted to just the First Commissioner, given that they ran an organization of *spies*, it was still the intention that the Commissioner was the only active MISS operative or bureaucrat who knew the entire Board.

If they'd pulled Kelly into a meeting like that with the Board, he had to wonder how long they thought it was going to be before she became First Commissioner herself.

"That was probably more comfortable for you than half the Board," Xi pointed out, following a different train of thought than Mike. "You at least know Damien."

"If the words *in a biblical sense* leave either of your mouths, I will find out if I can dock your pay from here," their wife threatened, but there was a hitch of a giggle in her voice.

A long time ago, Mike had thought he was in competition with Damien Montgomery for Kelly's affection. As it turned out, Kelly hadn't even *noticed* him in that sense at the time—and since he'd always regarded *a good friend* as a hell of a consolation prize, he'd left it there for a long time.

The now-Prince-Chancellor of the Protectorate, on the other hand, with his passionate focus, dark eyes—and literal magic—had been very noticeable to the engineer, and they'd been lovers for several high-intensity months while their ship and lives were in danger.

They were still friends now, over a decade later, which Mike knew had helped smooth Kelly's path through MISS a few times—and his and Xi's with it.

He'd be jealous, except that he *knew* Damien and would calmly kill or die for the man if necessary himself.

"But yes, being comfortable with the Prince-Chancellor helped, even as he and Christoffsen hammered home the long-term goals of Her Majesty's government."

She snorted.

"Goals that would probably accept seeing Montgomery replaced as Chancellor over somehow breaking Parliament to Her Majesty's will at this point."

"Because *that* is going to happen," Xi Wu said. "Has anyone told him which planet he's going to be Senator of once his term limit as an MP runs out?"

The political discussion was harmless—for them, at least, as all three were unquestionably hitched to both Damien Montgomery and Kiera Alexander.

"No, though I don't look forward to the person who has to tell him and Kiera about the latest fallout from the *Saladin* deployment," Kelly said, her eyes sparking with wicked amusement as she looked at them.

"Oh, gods," Mike muttered. "What now?"

The *Saladins* had required Prometheans and Prometheans had volunteered to jump them. Except that most of the Prometheans the Republic had murdered had been teenagers—Mages by Right identified by Royal Testers but left in the hands of the UnArcana Worlds to be trained properly.

No one had anticipated that those carefully supported and nurtured academies would be taken over by the conspiracy that had birthed the Republic, and those *children* killed in job lots to fuel the Republic Navy.

The entire Protectorate, both the parts of it that had *been* the Republic and the parts that hadn't, suffered from a near-infinite amount of guilt over the whole mess. An infinity of guilt focused on the several hundred known survivors.

"This one is at least coming from the Prometheans themselves," Kelly told them. "I got the update from Jane earlier today. *She's* still thinking how to pitch it to Kiera and Damien, but the Prometheans have thrown us not just one but *two* curve balls now."

"Good for them," Xi said. "They deserve to surprise us. I would expect nothing less from smart young Mages, regardless of their disability."

"Well, several of them want to formally petition for ownership of the *Saladin* hulls they're installed in," Kelly said. "I imagine the ships would have to go in for a good deal of refit before they'd be usable as standard cargo ships, but some of the Prometheans realized that, given *control* of the hulls, they're actually okay with being Jump Mages of their own ships."

"Good for them," Mike echoed Xi. That made perfect sense to him. It meant the Protectorate wouldn't have to build Prometheus Drive ships, the massive planetary-invasion transports would become far less threatening to anyone, and the Prometheans would gain some measure of autonomy. "That will give them control of their own lives; it's a good idea."

"I think they'll get it," Kelly admitted. "But it'll be a political football—only dwarfed by the *other* curve ball, which I think is going to be a political bomb."

"What did they do?" he asked—but her mix of amusement and concern told him, he suspected.

"At least a dozen of them want to volunteer for the Navy."

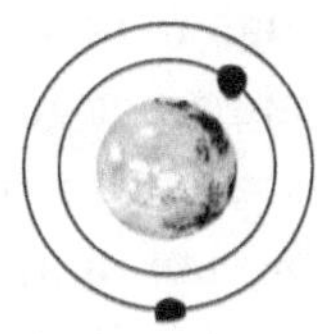

CHAPTER 15

CONNOR HAD BEEN SURPRISED by the invitation to breakfast, of all things, with Mage-Commodore Rantala. A polite senior Steward greeted him at the location he'd been directed to, sweeping him into a much smaller and more intimate dining room than the Flag Mess of the formal meal he'd shared with the task group's commanders.

"The Commodore will be here in just a moment, Ambassador," the noncommissioned officer told him. She was an older woman, at least a decade older than Rantala—or Connor himself, for that matter—with short-cropped graying hair and a demeanor that suggested that if it came to a clash between her and the cruiser's armor, the armor would come off worse.

"Thank you, Chief...?"

She hadn't introduced herself and his ability to read RMN insignia was limited to the senior officer ranks. He'd be lost trying to distinguish between Lieutenants and Lieutenant Commanders, let alone the various gradations of "Chief Petty Officer."

"Senior Chief Steward Mariya Pavlenko," she said with a firm nod. "I'm the Mage-Commodore's personal steward."

Pavlenko gestured him toward an uncomfortable-looking seat at the table. She followed up the silent instruction with the delivery of a large mug of coffee to the same seat, which hurried Connor into the chair.

Everything in the room had the appearance of plain wood, polished to gleam under the ship's lights, but the chair still smoothly adjusted underneath him to handle his height and breadth. Connor took a small sip of the coffee and made the appropriate pleased sounds when he realized Pavlenko was hovering *just* enough to be watching for his reaction.

It was truly excellent coffee, almost as good as Mage-Admiral Alexander served—and the Crown Princess owned her own coffee plantations.

There was a very quiet vibration, and Pavlenko checked her wrist-comp. The gesture was smooth and well practiced, and Connor might not have noticed it if he hadn't been expecting it.

"The jump is complete. Commodore Rantala is on his way here," she told him. "I will go check on the meal."

She stepped out of the room, leaving Connor alone in what he guessed was the Captain's private dining room. Where Rantala needed more space, he was clearly willing to use the Flag Deck spaces on the ship, but so long as he remained *Last Stand at Alamo*'s Captain, the man presumably had seen no reason to move.

Beyond the deceptively simple-looking wood table and chairs, there was surprisingly little decoration in the room. A side hutch in the same style as the table was set against one bulkhead, but the other walls were unoccupied and plain.

The answer to that was made obvious the moment Ketil Rantala walked into the room, a command entered on the officer's wrist-comp waking the wallscreens that surrounded them.

There wasn't much to *see* on the screens, given that the Task Group was in deep space, but the sudden feeling of being suspended in the void was eerie.

"Captain," Connor greeted Rantala, rising to offer his hand. "Thank you for the invitation. I wasn't sure what to expect, but I'll admit I figured there would be more guests."

Rantala chuckled and took the proffered hand.

"There are a lot of moving pieces to this mission, Ambassador, and the truth is that Captain Kelzin's is probably more important—but Captain Kelzin isn't on my ship, and I have almost no ability to assist in his mission.

"Whereas you, my ship and I will be present throughout your entire time in the Primes. I want to be certain I understand what you're thinking and planning. My job is to make certain that you complete your mission and survive, Ambassador."

"I appreciate that." Connor retook his seat. He thought he understood why he'd been the only one invited now, if it was going to just be the two of them.

"Have you been keeping in contact with Captain Kelzin, Ambassador?" Rantala asked as Pavlenko brought him his own mug of coffee. "Thank you, Mariya," he told her. "It smells incredible as always."

"I spoke with the Captain at the general meeting, but I haven't had any contact with him since," Connor admitted. "His mission here is a precursor to mine—I can't provide him any useful information until I've made contact in at least one place, and he needs to complete his sweeps before I can do that."

"I knew you had spoken before the mission; I wasn't sure if the two of you were friends," Rantala admitted. "The structure of this operation and my Task Group is... uncomfortable for me, Ambassador. Chains of command and org charts are near and dear to the military heart for a reason, but I find myself in a situation where I have command of all of the ships and Navy personnel of my Task Group... and not only am I not in command of the mission, but I also arguably have *two* civilian superiors."

Connor took a moment to process that and make certain he understood what Rantala was thinking. Often, saying the correct diplomatic thing just required those extra few seconds of thought, after all.

"From my perspective, of course, I don't see Captain Kelzin as a civilian," he admitted. "I suppose he is an MISS officer, isn't he?"

"Much as a civilian freighter Captain is a merchant-service officer, even as an owner-operator," Rantala confirmed. "I am not certain what the Captain's official title is when he isn't on a starship, of course. A great deal about the Agency is classified or concealed. It has served us well, but I find myself lacking in protocol or doctrine to handle the situation."

Because, of course, while Kelzin was a civilian, he wasn't someone that Rantala could give instructions to the way he might a civilian ship. While Connor hadn't even considered *who was in charge* to be an important thing to sort out, that was because he'd recognized that each of the three of them had their own areas and would be in charge in their area.

The arrival of two plates of waffles delayed his response, and he nodded his own thanks to the younger steward delivering the food.

"My question, I suppose, is what is the immediate concern," he told Rantala. "Our mission has three different components, each under the authority of the person in charge of that component. Neither Kelzin nor I are going to ignore your command of the military component of the expedition, which limits the potential problems, doesn't it?"

"To a degree," the Commodore conceded. "But, for example, we are currently point-six-five light-years outside the Chimera System. My plan and our course call for us to make two jumps around the perimeter to align with *Barracuda*'s expected course home—however, I have no idea if Captain Kelzin is planning on doing a sweep of the Chimera System as we go through.

"Depending on what would be needed for that, it may work best for us to delay here or at the final expected *Barracuda* jump point. But I do not know what his intentions are."

Connor swallowed his initial reply. The solution seemed obvious to him, but he was a diplomat these days—and had been a negotiator before that.

Rantala was a naval officer and Connor suspected this was the first time he'd been in command of a force with any civilian component that wasn't clearly subordinate. The man was senior enough that Alexander hadn't blinked in bumping him to Mage-Commodore, which Connor presumed meant he'd commanded more than an individual ship before, but this was still a different situation.

"I would hope, I admit, that Captain Kelzin would have informed you if he was planning on anything that would require us to detour from our plan," Connor finally said, after finishing the first waffle.

He wasn't sure who was doing the actual cooking—he presumed Pavlenko was supervising rather than making food herself, but he could be wrong—but the food didn't rise to the standard of the coffee. Nothing in the meal was bad, but it was comparable to what Connor would have been fed in the officers' mess he'd eaten in the last five days.

"That would be my hope as well," Rantala said. "But I don't know Kelzin, and protocols for working with MISS scout ships have, well, generally been entirely ad hoc."

"Well, then, Captain, there's one solution to all of your problems and a few of mine." A solution that had probably been Rantala's responsibility to figure out, but Connor could also argue that *he* should have started the wheels rolling on it.

"There are three components to this mission and there's someone in charge of each component. We really need to get the three of us on a call and sort out just what we're all planning."

"That seems... obvious, I suppose," Rantala said slowly. "But—"

"You haven't been the man in command for close interactions with civilians before, have you, Captain?" Connor asked.

"No," the Mage admitted. "I made Captain during the campaign against the First Legion, a battlefield promotion to command a destroyer squadron when our flagship—and squadron CO—were lost.

"I don't know how well you know the Navy operations, Ambassador, but while *destroyers* do a lot of work on their own, destroyer *squadrons* tend to stick with bigger ships. *Last Stand* is my second cruiser, but my independent operations haven't needed anything like this."

Rantala shook his head.

"And there are some horror stories about people getting smacked down for trying to exert authority over MISS ships," he admitted. "I may be a bit out of my depth on this one, though, let's be clear, I am *entirely* confident in my ability to command the naval component of our mission."

Connor hadn't doubted that for a second, but it was good to hear the Mage-Commodore say it. Even if Rantala didn't fully believe it, he had to *say* he did or he would lose all credibility.

And if that was true in negotiations over nickel shipments, he imagined it was even more true of command.

"We're both right here," he told the Mage-Commodore. "This room appears to have all the equipment we'd need for the conference. Why don't we finish eating and then see if we can loop Kelzin in?"

Whatever the MISS leader had going on in his own morning, it wasn't important enough that he couldn't make time for Connor and Rantala. Pavlenko barely had time to refill their coffees before one wall lit up with the rotating Seal of the Protectorate—a star-encircled crowned mountain on a red planet—marking an establishing connection.

The entire wall then faded into a high-fidelity feed of an office so blandly perfect and standard that it *had* to be intentional. The desk, filing cabinet, the lighting... everything in Mike Kelzin's office appeared to have been designed to be some platonic average of "boring starship office."

"Commodore, Ambassador," the man in the middle of that blandness said cheerfully. "I hope I can help you."

"The biggest thing we realized over breakfast this morning, Captain, is that the three of us really need to make sure we're not thinking past each other," Connor told the spy. "Commodore Rantala was concerned that you were planning on scouting Chimera and wasn't sure how that might impact the flight plan.

"From that, *I* realized that I should have made sure that we were talking things over on a regular basis," he continued, unhesitatingly taking any responsibility for the misstep off the other two men. He needed them to work together and with him far more than he needed them to think he was perfect.

"I'd like to set up a daily meeting, just the three of us to start, to go over where we're at in terms of our plans," Connor concluded. "There are a few people we may want to bring in later, but right now, I think *we* need to be absolutely certain we're on the same page."

There was a moment of sheepishness on Mike Kelzin's face, gone as fast as it appeared.

"That makes sense to me," he offered. "As far as scouting Chimera goes, I was planning on detouring on the next jump. We would have let the Commodore know shortly, but since my intent was to rendezvous at the first Chimera–Ordin jump point on time, I didn't worry about letting anyone know in advance.

"We weren't going to change the schedule."

"Assuming you didn't get caught, Captain," Rantala pointed out, his tone soft.

"Were we going into a system we didn't know with enemy positions completely mysterious, I would make allowances for that," Kelzin replied. "But we know *exactly* where the reezh forces in Chimera are positioned. We will be jumping into separate points in Leviathan's orbit, to download information from the scanning platforms we put in place.

"We aren't even going to bring our engines online, Commodore," the spy assured him. "Even without magic, we'd be invisible at the distance and energy levels we're using. The risk is as close to zero as it possibly can be—and even if we are *detected*, there is no way they can catch us."

"We will still want to have the task group standing by when we arrive at that jump point," Rantala said. "The drill will serve my people well, as will the preparation if the Kazh somehow *do* manage to follow you through a jump.

"Remember, Captain Kelzin, we know nothing about the capabilities of our enemy. Just because they haven't shown the ability to track jumps yet doesn't mean they lack it. Consider how limited our own ability to do that is!"

Connor wasn't even sure what the limits were on Trackers, the specialist officers the RMN occasionally used to follow jump spells. He knew there weren't many of them, which seemed strange to him but was outside his area of expertise.

"Fair enough, Mage-Commodore," Kelzin said respectfully. "I don't expect us to really need backstopping until Ordin at the earliest."

"And what if we find *Barracuda*?" Connor asked.

"That's not going to be a scout-ship job, Ambassador," the spy replied. "My commando teams would be *delighted* to be involved in the boarding actions, if they become necessary, but approaching and handling a derelict is definitely a Marine Corps task."

"We'll manage that part, as the Captain says," Rantala agreed. "Though now that the thought is on my mind, there are a few uses I can think of for your ships in that situation. Since I have you on the call..."

Connor leaned back and sipped his coffee as the meeting became more technical. The two starship Captains weren't going to be fast friends anytime soon, he judged, but they were both professional and willing to work together.

It just hadn't occurred to either of them to open the desperately needed line of communication.

He'd find it hard to believe—except that easily two-thirds of the crises the Arbitration Commission had been called in to fix wouldn't have required him if the two sides had been willing to come entirely clean to each other.

Of course, there had been reasons they were willing to tell a neutral third party things they hadn't told their competition or government. That was the reality that had paid his salary for over a decade.

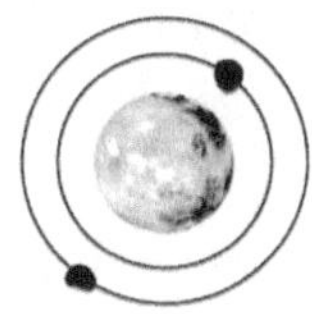

CHAPTER 16

MIKE WATCHED THE GAS GIANT swing in its eternal orbit and wished he could do more for the people trapped there. That was on Alexander at this point—small as the population of the Leviathan One refuge was, it was still tens of thousands of people, far more than they could fit into all of Task Group Twenty-Eight's ships.

Going this way, at least. They might have the space on the way back if they needed to, but the truth was that a single ex-Republic *Saladin* or even one of the Protectorate's own *Bushido* assault transports could easily get everyone out of the glorified refugee camp at Leviathan.

Getting those transport ships into and out of Chimera without fighting the Kazh was a very different task from sneaking three almost-invisible scout ships in.

"We've got a full download from the satellites," Fischer told him, the Navy officer studying the map even more intently than Mike was. "Do we have any good news to tell these people?"

"I'm not sure we can even tell them that the Admiral is working on a plan," Mike admitted. "She *is*, but anything we tell these people might end up in the Kazh's hands before we can actually get out here to rescue them."

"Most likely," Fischer agreed. "They don't have any defenses, either. The only thing keeping them safe is that the boneheads haven't really poked around out here, I'm guessing."

"Which is plenty, really," he told the Navy officer. "Hell, the CSN hid their *Prometheans* out here without the Chimerans ever realizing they'd done it—and that was when no one was really trying to hide.

"Star systems are big places."

"Yeah. And sensors can see ships from a long, long, *long* way away," Fischer pointed out.

Mike snorted.

"And if the Kazh haven't taken over yet, I'd say the refugees have a good handle on when they can fly around out here," he countered their pessimism. "The refuge's info last time said they had the fuel and hydroponics to keep going for a long time. They just need to keep their heads down."

Which wasn't helped by his people installing a surveillance satellite in the wreckage of the Promethean Sanctuary. The CSN had decided to destroy the station once they'd sent the Prometheans to Mackenzie, and the debris field was helping hide the drone.

"Anything useful in the downloads?" he asked.

"Won't know for sure until we put everything together after the jump," Fischer said. "First glance says that they haven't been reinforced but haven't reduced their numbers, either. Still a lot of firepower watching this system, boss."

"We're not doing anything with it ourselves," Mike admitted. "Once we bring the Links back up, put together a package and fire it back to Mars and Second Fleet. Maybe someone will see something we don't."

It wasn't up to his three *Rhapsodies* to retake Chimera themselves, after all. With more information, Alexander would be able to send *Rhapsody of Creation* to make careful contact with the stay-behind force when the fourth stealth ship arrived in a few more weeks.

Maybe. The data that Mike was seeing suggested that a close pass of Garuda would be unwise. *Bohemia* had done it on their last sweep because they'd needed the information, and his ship had locked down *everything.*

To make contact with the stay-behind forces, one of the stealth ships was going to have to get close to the alien-occupied world and actively transmit. The thought was intimidating, even for Mike.

Though he'd far rather do it *himself* than leave it to another Captain.

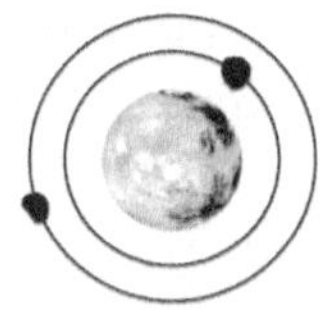

CHAPTER 17

CONNOR FIGURED THAT THE OFFICERS and Mages flying *Last Stand at Alamo* and the rest of the task group's ships had some way to tell the difference between the various empty pieces of blackness they moved between.

There was a vague memory in his head of star positions and constellations, but he was fine leaving that to the experts. He was spending the week-plus of the journey to Ordin immersing himself in the limited information they had on the star system.

Mage-Captain Chambers' survey gave him the basic geography: a bright yellow dwarf star with a mere five planets, including a massive gas giant as the fourth planet and an unusually dense asteroid belt between planet three and four.

Planet three was habitable, home to billions of reezh. An equatorial ring had been assembled around the planet from asteroids hauled into place over the centuries. Many of those the Navy had judged to be fortifications. Some were probably mobile, but most were probably simple enough, though heavily armed.

The reason for presuming some of the orbitals above Three had to be mobile was because there had been at least a hundred other asteroid monitors scattered through the system that the explorer cruiser *Thorn* had seen moving.

The gas giant and asteroid belt were both home to massive infrastructure and presumably large populations. The mobile monitors were concentrated around those two, representing powerful defensive forces.

All of that was background that Connor wasn't particularly focused on. There were other pieces in the military-focused brief that were relevant, but the outer-system surveillance network was going to be Kelzin's problem, not his.

Connor needed to talk to the Ordin reezh, which meant he immersed himself in the electronic intercepts from *Thorn*'s visit to the system. Analysts back in the Protectorate had spent months cleaning up and translating that handful of hours of radio transmissions.

Those analysts had drawn their own conclusions about what he was flying into, but he'd listened to or read transcripts of key pieces himself. Connor trusted the analysts backing him up, but to negotiate with another state, he needed to *know*, not just be *told*, what he was dealing with.

The analysts judged that Ordin was basically a constitutional dictatorship—a similar structure to the Protectorate itself, at first brush, but with an appointed leader rather than a hereditary one.

The Cadatch—the reports liked the translation of *Primary* but Connor had already decided to use the reezh title himself—appeared to be a lifetime appointment, but there was no information in their limited slice as to how the Cadatch was appointed.

There were no less than *four* governing bodies that had shown up in their intercepts. The Shola Utch, the Shola Reezh, the Shola Koth and the Aha Kadak. The House of Dawn, the House of the People, the House of Sunset, and the Voice of Power, respectively.

None of the names had come with enough context for Connor to feel comfortable using the admittedly rough guesses from his analysts. The only solid information they really had was a mention in one transmission of a Shola Reezh election, confirming that at least one of the four bodies was elected.

The diagrams the analysts back on Mars had put together of potential organizations of the Ordin government were an exercise in fiction, so far as Connor could tell. The only thing he was truly certain of was the Cadatch was able to use the "Mountain of Astral Might."

Part of that was because Ordin was still independent—but most of it was because images of the capital in the intercepts were almost always shown with an immense artificial mountain in the background. A reezh-made pyramid that rose at least three kilometers in the air, the analysts agreed that it was almost certainly the planetary amplifier.

And, like Olympus Mons, it appeared to anchor the capital city around it.

Connor sighed at the image on his screen and blanked it with a tapped command. Staring at the pyramid whose owner he hoped to speak to wasn't going to gain him much. He *knew* he'd get more valuable insight out of watching the handful of media shows they'd caught up in the intercepts, but he had only so much tolerance for lowbrow comedy in his *own* language.

Slapstick, it turned out, had some level of universality. It was no less irritating to him when the performers had extra joints and the dialog sounded like a broken gravel truck.

At least *Last Stand*'s computers were up to turning transcripts into subtitles that followed the speakers. He couldn't say there was a *story*, except in that a young reezh man kept wandering into ridiculous situations and making them worse.

Despite his distaste for the particular media form, it made for extraordinarily useful insights into Ordin's culture. After all, learning *what* they found ridiculous was extremely valuable.

A soft chime interrupted his attempt to convince himself to watch the shows again. It was something he'd programmed into his wrist-comp, to notify him when the task group jumped.

If he'd kept track accurately, this would put them barely two lightyears from their destination. It would still be just another chunk of empty space, he supposed, and duty warred with his search for an excuse.

Then his wrist-comp chimed again as Mage-Commodore Rantala called him.

"O'Hannagain. What's happening?"

"Ambassador, we've found *Barracuda*."

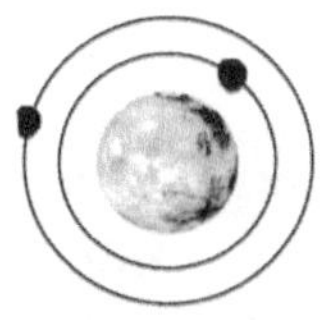

CHAPTER 18

BY THE TIME CONNOR REACHED *Last Stand at Alamo's* bridge, Rantala's people already had answers for most of the questions he'd think to ask. *Barracuda's* image was suspended in front of the Captain's seat, laid over the uncountable fiberoptic diodes that brought exterior light to the center of the ship.

Jump Mages told him that without that direct flow of light, a Mage trying to use the simulacrum at the heart of any starship was blind. The transparent computer screens over those diodes didn't seem to interrupt it much, though, and allowed every member of Rantala's command crew to study the CSN warship.

"She's intact, Ambassador," Rantala told Connor as he crossed the room.

Moving across a simulacrum chamber was an exercise in caution and practice. Connor had seen the crew pass from transparent platform to platform at a full run, but *he* still needed to watch his step and make sure he hadn't reached the end of a walkway.

The cruiser's bridge was also her simulacrum chamber, after all, and that meant it was a perfect sphere around the one-to-two-hundred-scale silver model of the ship that let Mages do their work. To fit a useful bridge crew in, consoles were positioned at odd angles and spots throughout the room, linked by pathways and platforms that each had their own gravity.

The good news was that if Connor walked *off* a platform by accident, the bridge's gravity had been designed with that possibility in mind.

Reaching the platform holding Rantala's seat—and the two-and-a-half-meter-tall simulacrum itself—Connor joined the crew in examining their hopeful ally.

"Is she under power?" he asked. "Any communication?"

"We're a good ten light-minutes from her right now," Bourgeois told him. "She'll only be seeing the light of our emergence about now. We won't receive any response from her for another ten minutes."

"As for *under power*, she seems to be," Rantala continued, taking over from his XO smoothly. "Her engines are offline, but she's radiating heat and we're picking up active scans of the area. They look like missile-defense radar, frankly, so she's intact but twitchy."

"*Twitchy* sounds dangerous," Connor said. "If... if she attacks us, how much trouble is that going to be?"

"*Last Stand* alone outmatches her," the Commodore told him. "With the rest of the task group, the problem would be trying to disable her without seriously damaging her. We could *obliterate* her, but we don't want to do that."

"Right now, Captain, this remains your area of expertise," Connor replied carefully. "But I do have a suggestion."

"We're waiting to see what she does or says, Ambassador; I'm open to all kinds of options." Rantala's gaze kept flickering around the chamber, and Connor realized that the screens surrounding the Mage-Commodore were giving the man a lot of information on his task group and his own ship.

"Have *we* tried to contact her?" he asked the Captain.

"We're scanning to be certain we're alone out here," Rantala told him. "We sent a standard data-handshake on arrival, with our identity beacons and so forth. Captain Joto's people should be able to interpret that, but any Kazh vessels will be more confused."

"As will Ordin vessels," Connor agreed. "That said, Captain, there is a reason *Barracuda* is here instead of in Ordin or back in Chimera. Something has gone very wrong and... well, *twitchy* is probably the right word.

"Being very upfront about who we are could help—but beyond that, our reezh Ambassador is Captain Joto's daughter, Rantala. I think she deserves the chance to try to talk to them, and if anything is going to make sure we get the chance to find out what happened here, seeing their daughter on the coms is probably it."

There was a moment of silence and then the Navy officer nodded sharply.

"I'll send a recorded message immediately," he told Connor. "Can you get Adazh Komarazhi up to the bridge?"

"Sir, I'm obliged to note that she's not cleared for the bridge," one of the junior officers that Connor didn't know spoke up.

"And I will happily trade someone with zero technical education getting a look at our bridge consoles for a chance to avoid any problems here," Rantala said drily. "I'm clearing her. O'Hannagain, get her up here. Coms, get me a camera."

After Rantala sent his message off to *Barracuda*, someone threw a pair of timers up on the display: how long until they'd see the Chimeran cruiser's reaction to their arrival and how long until they saw any response to the Commodore's message.

The first timer hit zero and there was a moment where Connor thought everyone on the bridge was holding their breath. There was no visible reaction on the part of the ship on the screen, and the calmly organized discussions and movement resumed after a few seconds.

Connor brought up the information he had on *Barracuda* on his wrist-comp. *Benjamin*-class cruiser, commissioned by the Republic six months before the final battle of the Siege of Legatus. Had deserted the Republic Interstellar Navy with Admiral Wang during that battle, after Damien Montgomery had revealed the true nature of the Prometheus Drives to the RIN crews.

Twenty million tons, one hundred and thirty missile launchers, a cylinder half a kilometer long. Crew of just over two thousand normally, but *Barracuda* had been stripped down to the minimum they could run her with to minimize the human crew.

She'd left for Ordin with seventeen hundred and eighty souls aboard, including a hundred and sixteen human technicians without trained reezh replacements and a diplomatic delegation seventy strong.

"I'm here," Komarazhi announced as she stepped onto the bridge, one of Connor's Secret Service agents keeping pace a step behind her.

That was a *good* idea on Ansel's part, Connor realized, and made a note to thank the man later. It avoided the question of whether she should be on the bridge unescorted while making the escort a protective detail or honor guard—and, since the PSS didn't report to Rantala, inserted a neutral arbiter into any problems people had with her.

"Thank you for coming, Ambassador," Rantala told her before Connor could say anything. "Please join me and Ambassador O'Hannagain here at the simulacrum.

"As you see, we have located your parent's ship," he continued, gesturing to where *Barracuda* hung on the screen. "They would have seen us about five minutes ago, but we have seen no sign of reaction from them.

"I would like you to take over initial communications with *Barracuda*, in the hope both that Captain Joto is still in command and that a reezh face may calm worried nerves even if he isn't."

The last part of Rantala's request hit Komarazhi like a blow, but she stepped up onto the platform as quickly as she could.

"I will do what I can," she promised.

"Coms, get the reezh Ambassador a pickup," Rantala ordered. "We'll send her signal straight to *Barracuda* and hope they're listening."

The lack of apparent reaction on the part of the other ship was clearly starting to bother people. Connor could read tactical displays—neither swiftly nor well, but Roslyn Chambers had instilled a basic skill in him while she'd been his military attaché—and he could tell that Task Group Twenty-Eight was quietly shifting into defensive formations.

They weren't going to start a fight, but the freighters were tucking in behind the defensive perimeters of the destroyers and cruisers. If something went wrong, TG 28 was ready to protect themselves.

A noncommissioned officer—a Chief Petty Officer, if Connor was getting better at the insignia—stepped onto the platform with them. She gave Komarazhi a measuring look and seemed to recognize the reezh's confusion.

"Ambassador?" the Chief asked. "I'm Chief Amala Misra, from our Coms team. Have you used our coms systems before?"

"Not at this level, I'm afraid," Komarazhi admitted.

"Okay." Misra poked at her wrist-comp for a second. "Look at the orange light on the side of the Captain's console, please."

Connor saw the same light. His experience with Navy communications was enough for him to judge the likely angle of the pickup and step out of it, leaving Komarazhi to face the camera alone.

Misra was clearly looking at the feed on her wrist-comp as she gave Komarazhi a reassuring smile. "Turn just a touch to the left," she instructed. "There you go. Let me know when you're ready to start recording—the message is going to take ten minutes to arrive; there's no point in rushing or trying to transmit live."

It would still be a few minutes before Rantala's message arrived, for that matter.

"I'm ready," the reezh Ambassador declared.

"When the light turns green, you are recording," Misra told her. "Three. Two. One. Go."

The light turned green and Komarazhi did not, as Connor had feared, freeze. She adjusted her head to face the camera with her lower eyes, the ones usually concealed by her armored ridge.

By human standards, those eyes were short-sighted. Looking at someone with them was generally considered a sign of intimacy or vulnerability.

She spoke in reezh, of course. Connor's ability to follow the language was weak, but he got the gist of it: she was the Ambassador of the Chimera government-in-exile, she was with the Ambassador of the Protectorate, was Captain Joto still in command and did *Barracuda* need assistance?

"Recorded and sent," Misra reported.

"Thank you, Chief," Komarazhi told the Navy woman, switching languages with a fluidity that impressed Connor. Outside of German, Taran Gaelic and English, he couldn't switch that smoothly.

Though he supposed English and Reezh were Komarazhi's equivalent of English and Gaelic for him.

"Task Group has completed reorganization into formation Lambda, sir," Bourgeois reported. "Should we bring up active sensors for missile defense? There may be a reason *Barracuda* has her defensive radar live."

That wasn't Connor's call, though he wasn't sure how firing beams of theoretically harmless radiation into space would be interpreted if Captain Joto was feeling twit—

"CONTACT!" Someone bellowed. "Major jump signature at one million kilometers!"

"All ships to battle stations," Rantala snapped. "Defensive radar online, RFLAMs free—amplifier use *denied*, I repeat, *denied*. Take *no* offensive action!"

Connor's opinion of the Mage-Commodore moved up a notch. For a horror-filled moment, he thought he'd have to tell the senior Navy officer to hold fire and try to make that stick.

"Contact has not fired," the XO said after a few moments. "Twenty million tons... yeah. That's *Barracuda*, sir. She is at full battle stations and has all weapons armed, but she has *not* fired."

"Chief Misra, please resend Ambassador Komarazhi's message," Connor suggested softly.

"Indeed," Rantala confirmed. "All ships, maintain defensive posture. We *know* Prometheans like the Picard Maneuver—but the only Prometheans here today are friends, yes?"

Connor hoped, at least. He knew what the Picard Maneuver—jumping through a lightspeed battle to allow either surprise or even stacking lightspeed laser fire—was from watching Second Fleet unleash it on the Kazh's invasion fleet at Chimera.

He'd heard in those conversations that fully awakened Prometheans were better at that kind of precision jump than any human, though *he* wasn't going to pretend he understood.

"Incoming coms channel, standard CSN protocols," Misra announced.

"Ambassadors, I think we're all up," Rantala told them. He gestured to spots on either side of his chair as the seat adjusted slightly farther away from the simulacrum.

"Connect *Barracuda*, Chief."

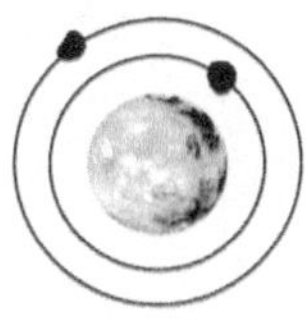

CHAPTER 19

CONNOR COULD HEAR the smothered grunt of emotion from Komarazhi when the reezh on the screen wasn't Captain Joto. His insignia marked him as a Commander, which meant he'd been a department head or something similar, but he *wasn't* the cruiser's commander.

Or the reezh Ambassador's parent.

"Ambassador," he greeted Komarazhi in English, tilting his head back to match her gesture of looking with the lower eyes, even as he clearly eyed the humans askance. "It seems that we are dramatically out of date in our information, as we feared."

Barracuda had left on her mission as Connor had been arriving in Chimera. Everything from the alliance between the two states to the fall of their home system was unknown to them—it had been judged unwise to send a Link with them.

"Much has occurred since you left," Komarazhi told her. "Where is Captain Joto? Is Ambassador So Komarazhi still aboard?"

The reezh Commander closed all four eyes and bowed his head.

"Much happened to us as well," he said slowly. "I and the other survivors of the crew owe our lives to our human crew—and to Lisa and Trevor. Ambassador Komarazhi... the elder Ambassador Komarazhi," he corrected, "is not aboard and I do not know her fate.

"Captain Joto is aboard but they are badly wounded. We have been... uncertain of our course of action for some time now."

Connor could translate the careful choice of words without even asking for the opinion of the military officer beside him. To pull together a crew of reezh, the CSN had put people aboard *Barracuda* who were inexperienced for their roles. The CSN had existed for less than a decade in its final form, after all.

Without their commanding officer or the civilians in charge of the actual mission, the crew had fallen into arguing and been unable to make a decision.

"Forgive me, Commander, but who *are* you?" he asked, interrupting while Komarazhi was taking in the news of her parents' fates.

"Apologies... I am Commander Lazho Moran," Moran introduced himself. "I was Tactical Officer before... everything."

"I think we are going to need a full and complete briefing, Commander," Rantala said quietly. "Do you have wounded other than Captain Joto?"

"Many," Moran confirmed, all four of his eyes closing again. "Our medical staff is either among them, dead or missing."

"Then I think the next step is obvious. My medical team is fully up to speed on treatment for reezh, Commander. If you are willing, I and the Ambassadors will accompany them over to your ship and we can debrief in person—including Lisa and Trevor, of course."

Lisa and Trevor were the cruiser's two Prometheans, Connor realized.

Which meant that, along with all of the other bad news they had to deliver, Connor was going to have to tell two of Admiral Emerson Wang's adoptive children that the ex-Republic Admiral was dead, along with too many of their siblings in the Chimeran Navy.

"We... would be grateful for the assistance, Mage-Commodore," Moran admitted. "We have managed to keep people alive we thought we would lose, but we are running out of fresh winds."

CHAPTER 20

CONNOR AND HIS COMPANIONS WAITED calmly for the initial rush of medical staff to clear the shuttle before exiting. That had the advantage of warning Komarazhi that the shuttle bay on a CSN cruiser didn't have gravity—gravity on this vessel was only available in the massive rotating drum at the ship's heart.

Moving in zero gee was a careful exercise, one that Connor had made certain to master a long time before. With help from Ansel, he got Komarazhi out of the shuttle and into the shuttle bay.

Commander Moran was waiting for them, standing off to one side to avoid getting in the way of the medical teams. He wore magnetic boots and gave Rantala a crisp salute as the Protectorate party approached.

"Welcome aboard *Barracuda*," he greeted them. "She's not in the shape we'd like her to be, but we are still here."

"A question of luck, timing and paranoia, that, I'm afraid," a new voice interjected.

The voice was feminine and human, and it took Connor a moment to pick out that it was emerging from Moran's wrist-comp.

"Lisa, I presume?" he asked.

"Exactly," the Promethean confirmed. "Relaying through the Commander's wrist-comp seemed the simplest way to join the conversation while you made your way to the medbay."

"We presumed that Ambassador Komarazhi would want to see Captain Joto," Moran said. "Lisa and Trevor are keeping an eye on the injured, but I don't believe the Captain is going in for any treatment immediately?"

The questioning tone told Connor at least half of the problem with the warship. Moran was almost certainly the senior officer standing, and no one seemed to be arguing with his being in command—except *him*.

And if the acting Captain was unwilling to command, it would throw even more complications into whatever situation they'd found themselves in.

"Joto is among the more stable of our induced coma patients," Lisa said gently. "Given proper treatment, he should make a full recovery. Proper treatment for his injuries was beyond the handful of remaining medical personnel."

"Let's go see the Captain," Connor suggested. "And then, perhaps, Lisa and Commander Moran can tell us exactly what happened in the Ordin System.

"We're heading there ourselves from here."

"Then you will need to know everything we do," Lisa said from the speaker. "If only so you know that you will be shot at."

Connor had been starting to worry about that.

"We *will* be shot at?" Komarazhi asked. "How can you be so certain?"

"Because," Moran said grimly, "for reasons we are not certain of, the Ordin System has dissolved into civil war."

Visiting Captain Joto was depressing. From the file photo Connor had seen, the Captain usually shared with their daughter the pale gray pebbled skin most common among reezh, but they were so pale on their hospital bed, they were nearly white.

An oxygen mask was wrapped around their face, and several different sensors and tubes were connected to ports on their arms. The only way Connor was even certain Joto was alive was that the scanner screens were still showing a pulse and the bag attached to the oxygen mask kept inflating and deflating.

Komarazhi knelt at her parent's side, taking their hand in hers and whispering something Connor didn't even try to hear.

"The Captain is on the list for surgery in approximately three and a half hours," a male human voice said from the walls. "The timing is dependent on how the other surgeries proceed, of course. The medics from Mage-Commodore Rantala's ship are triaging the cases as quickly as they can."

"Thank you, Trevor," Connor told the Promethean, using the man's name to make sure none of the other guests had any clear moments of confusion.

"Moran, Commodore," he continued quietly. "I think we can leave Ambassador Komarazhi with her parent for now and proceed somewhere for a debriefing?"

She started to rise, and Connor laid his hand on her shoulder. He didn't try to hold her down, but he had a massive weight advantage over the slightly built reezh.

"Adazh, we are going to take time to process everything they tell us before we go *anywhere*," he assured her. "Whatever the initial debrief gives us, I'll make sure you know. You haven't seen Joto in months, and he is injured.

"You can stay. I won't *insist*," he finished with a gentle smile, "but I think you should."

Komarazhi was silent, then made a small assenting gesture with her left hand.

"Thank you," she whispered.

Moran led them to a conference room near the bridge. Like most of the CSN ships Connor had been on, it was aggressively plain, with a folding metal table and chairs of a similar style.

Unlike the chairs in Rantala's space on *Last Stand*, the standard prefabricated seats were exactly as uncomfortable as they looked. Connor had a real moment of concern as he sat down and the chair—mass-produced for the *Republic* Navy years earlier—creaked under his weight.

"You have a lot of wounded for a ship with limited exterior damage," Rantala said quietly. "What happened?"

"A lot." Moran clearly wasn't certain where to even begin.

Connor sympathized with the reezh officer, but it was more and more clear that *Barracuda*'s paralysis had a lot to do with her current acting commander.

"Start at the beginning, I suppose," he told Moran.

"Our mission was, from our initial parameters, a rousing success," Lisa said from the room's coms systems. A moment later, a holoprojector hummed to life and a new figure joined the room, taking a seat at Moran's right hand.

Connor suspected Lisa had shaped her avatar off of whatever photos and videos she'd been able to source of herself before her murder. She was an adorably button-nosed blonde girl, maybe thirteen, who came up to maybe the middle of Connor's chest. She'd been tall for her age and had the gangly awkwardness of a growth spurt.

She clearly hadn't yet encountered the complex culture the Prometheans in the Protectorate were creating, which included a great deal of complex self-expression in their visual avatars. On the other hand, her chosen avatar was also a twist of the knife at any member of *Barracuda*'s original crew.

"Mage Lisa," Connor said respectfully. "I take it you made contact with the Ordin?"

"We were making no attempt to be subtle or sneaky about anything when we arrived," she told them. "We arrived one light-minute clear of Orandar, the habitable planet, and sent our messages ahead.

"We had an unusual ship, which drew attention, but Captain Joto and Ambassador Komarazhi refused to engage in any aggressive action. The Ordin Cadatch ozh Ahadan were more used to Kazh raiding forces, so they were suspicious to begin with, but it only took a few days to get an agreement on allowing us into orbit for discussions."

"The... primary and voices?" Connor questioned the reezh phrase. Lisa didn't need to worry about the vocal cord damage that came with humans trying to properly pronounce reezh—or Korazhi, as Komarazhi had pointed out the dialect was called—words.

"The Ordin government, yes," Lisa confirmed. "The Cadatch is a monarch, similar in role to the Protectorate Mage-Queen, and the Ahadan are the six assemblies that serve as the rest of the government. They do not have a clear division between legislative, judicial, and executive powers as we would see it, with the Cadatch ozh Ahadan sharing all of that between all seven components."

"I'll want every detail you have on that," Connor told her. "For now, my apologies for the interruption."

"I will attempt to explain the complexities as I go, if they are relevant," the Promethean promised. "It took Ambassador Komarazhi some time to grasp them herself, brilliant as she is. If her daughter is half the politician the elder is, perhaps you can find a route through the mess."

Everyone was silent for a moment. Connor glanced at Moran, but the reezh officer seemed happy for the Promethean to continue the briefing.

"There was some debate on the planet as to who should manage the negotiations," Lisa finally said. "The only contact Ordin has had with other systems for a long time is violence from the Shining Shield of the Nine. The Shola Dahn—the House of the Shield, the representatives elected by the Ordin military—felt that they should manage everything, but the Cadatch had enough power to claim it had to be him and make it stick.

"His name is Izhom," the Promethean noted. "He had our delegation brought to the capital, where he met with them in the shade of the Mountain of Astral Might—the seat of the Cadatch's power.

"As we'd guessed based on Captain Chambers' visit to the system, the Cadatch is the designated wielder of the Mountain of Astral Might, the system's final line of defense. That power is what makes him the final arbiter amongst the six Ahadan, the Voices and Houses."

"If everything was going according to plan, wasn't Captain Joto supposed to leave the delegation here and return to Chimera?" Rantala asked.

"That was the plan, but the compromise we made to buy some trust was that *Barracuda* would remain in the system," Lisa replied. "It was a forty-day flight each way for us, after all. Joto and So Komarazhi didn't believe that the negotiations would last long enough for us to make it home and return."

The Promethean paused to consider her next words. It was a reminder that while she spoke through a computer and could do many things that would otherwise be limited to computers, she wasn't an AI and there was an organic brain tucked away in *Barracuda*'s engineering sections.

"They were wrong," she finally said. "They underestimated, I believe, how little trust a nation that had been in a cold war for multiple centuries would have for strangers. A week became three, then five. Then ten."

Connor had to do the mental math, then shared a grim look with Rantala.

"What?" Lisa asked.

He had to remember that the Promethean was watching the room through the surveillance systems, not through the eyes of her teenage avatar.

"Chimera fell to the Reezh Kazh on December eleventh," Connor explained. "If my math is correct, that would have been about ten weeks after you arrived in Ordin."

He might as well have cut every tendon in Moran's body. The extra joins in a reezh's limbs allowed for an astonishing degree of deflation when they completely collapsed in on themselves.

"How?" Moran whispered. "You were supposed to save us!"

"We tried," Rantala answered instantly. It took a solid four or five seconds before the Commodore continued, obviously forcing himself to control his breathing.

"The Kazh possess some form of faster-than-light communication," he told Moran. "They attacked on a shorter cycle than our worst fears, and we could only move so many ships in time.

"We evacuated over eighty million people—and sixty thousand Martian spacers died in Chimera, trying to hold the system. We did everything we could, but the Kazh..."

"The Kazh have spent centuries waging cold war and plotting for a total war to retake their wayward Primes," Lisa said flatly. "The Protectorate has spent the same time believing they are alone in the galaxy. There are no massed reserve fleets in the Protectorate, no armadas ready to strike out at a sign of weakness among their enemies."

"We are accelerating construction and launching new recruitment campaigns," Connor said quietly. "But it will take at least a year, probably more, before the Protectorate is ready to try to liberate Chimera.

"That is why we are here, to seek allies among the Primes."

"As were we," Lisa reminded everyone. "Which went... poorly."

"Ten weeks of negotiations went nowhere?" Rantala asked.

"No." That was Moran, though the reezh officer was now simply staring at the table. "I did not hear what the Promethean heard. But Joto heard more. I listened to him. The negotiations went well until..."

"Until what?" Connor asked into the silence.

"Until something we said appeared to blow up the entire star system," Lisa told him. "After ten weeks, Ambassador Komarazhi believed she was close to a deal. Our alert levels had been lowered—we even had people on shore leave.

"Everything was very warm, and progress was clear. *Very* clear, Ambassador, Commodore—there are Ordin-built missiles in *Barracuda*'s magazines. The reezh weapons are a bit bigger than ours, but since we only had a single salvo for our launchers aboard, it seemed worth squeezing them in."

"Then what happened?" Connor asked.

"Trevor and I were watching everything," the Promethean said. "We saw it first, though not in time to realize what was happening. The combination of a human mind with computer processing allows us to be very, very good at pattern recognition.

"We didn't realize that the pattern we were looking at was someone moving soldiers loyal to them into the capital and onto the station many of our people were moving through for shore leave," she said grimly. "It was a coordinated attack, when it came. The capital fell in a day. The station our people were aboard was attacked by one of the in-system corvettes.

"Captain Joto was aboard the station. The officers remaining on *Barracuda* hesitated—and then one of the stations fired on us. Commander Moran took command and engaged the corvette attacking the station, trying to evacuate as many people as we could.

"The corvette was badly undergunned for the target it was attacking, but none of the orbital platforms appeared to be shooting at it. *We* were under heavy fire, but we managed to dock with the station and take aboard our crew and several thousand other passengers before one of the orbital forts hit the station with a nuclear weapon.

"We jumped clear of the planet," Lisa continued, though Connor suspected that even many of the things she was giving Moran credit for had been *her* decisions and commands. "We managed to rendezvous with a station at the gas giant, long enough to offload our passengers and get some more information on what was going on—but then a fleet of local ships appeared.

"We fled the system. We didn't know enough about the sides to want to get involved, and, well…"

Moran sighed into the silence Lisa left.

"We are not certain how many of our crew were on the surface versus on the station," he admitted. "But only half of our crew are aboard *Barracuda*, and a third of those are wounded."

"You said this ship was under fire," Rantala noted. "We saw no sign of exterior damage."

"Wide-aperture gamma ray pulses," Lisa said flatly. "A close-range weapon but quite effective if you want to capture a starship intact. Our armor couldn't stop it, and we can only harden systems, not people."

Connor wasn't sure what that meant, but the wince on Rantala's face told him it was bad.

"How many are dead?" the Commodore asked.

"Two hundred and thirty-seven," Moran whispered. "We're missing almost eight hundred people as well. Eight hundred and fifteen hands alive, two hundred and sixty-two of them in medical care."

Those numbers were clearly burned into Moran's brain.

"How long ago did you leave Ordin?" Connor asked.

"Sixteen days," Lisa told him. "We jumped twice along our planned route to make sure we evaded any pursuit, then we had to engage in what repairs we could. After that… there was no consensus on what we needed to do next."

"I have no authority over you, Commander Moran," Rantala pointed out, before anyone even said anything. "The Ambassador and I will need all of the information you can provide us on Ordin and what the civil war looked like when you left. Who are the sides, who might be allies to us—"

"Who controls the amplifier," Connor cut in.

"We are unsure. That is part of why we fled so precipitously," Lisa admitted. "As the situation had not resolved itself and major forces were in motion, I am inclined to believe that no one is in control of the amplifier.

"We did learn one key thing when we dropped off our rescuees, Ambassador, Commodore. We know the force behind at least the initial coup.

"The Aha Kadak, the Voice of Power." The alien name hung in the air, heavy with a meaning Connor knew he didn't understand.

"The Mages," Lisa explained. "And while they may not use the Priest-Mage title of the old Ida, they are definitely still a closed system of a small group of families. If anyone in the Ordin System still has ties to the Reezh Kazh and the Nine, it would be the Aha Kadak and the Mage lineages they speak for."

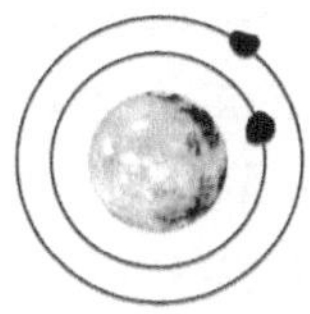

CHAPTER 21

MIKE LISTENED TO THE SUMMARY from Rantala and O'Hannagain and made his decision on the spot.

"You're going to need to stay here while you sort out what's going on with *Barracuda*," he told the other two men. "And we're going to need as much data about the situation in Ordin as possible."

"You can't charge ahead on your own, Captain," Rantala objected.

Mike grinned at the Mage-Commodore's image on top of his desk.

"If you mean just *Bohemia*, no, I don't plan on it," he agreed. "I'm taking all three *Rhapsodies*. We've been at this jump point for four hours already, just getting aboard *Barracuda* and beginning to triage the mess over there.

"I'm going to give my Mages another four hours to breathe, then we're going to double-hop right on in. Thanks to *Barracuda*'s scan data, I now know where the eyes I need to avoid are, and I can get into position to get data that's only a day old instead of two weeks or more."

Possibly less, but he wasn't going to tell Rantala that. The Commodore couldn't really put a leash on the stealth ships, but Mike didn't really want to piss him off, either.

"We know nothing about what's happening there right now," O'Hannagain said. It was a warning to both of them, Mike suspected.

"And that's why my people need to go in," Mike said. "We're not going in to kick up a hornet's nest. We'll keep the Links silent, even. We'll have Mages ready to pull us right back out the moment anyone twitches in our direction.

"It won't be perfectly safe. Nothing is. But we'll be as safe as it's possible to be—and we'll get the information we need."

The other two men were silent as Mike waited for them to cave to the inevitable. It was his call, but the Task Group's two-part mission, three-part command structure really called for consensus between the three of them.

"He's right, Commodore," O'Hannagain finally said. "We need information, and we need it soon."

"We do." The Mage-Commodore nodded. "But I'm not comfortable sending you in with no support. *Prince of Frogs* will accompany you on the first jump. Fall back on her if you need support—and *she'll* have her Links online.

"If anyone comes after you, well, the rest of the Task Group will have something to say about it."

That was a better addition than Mike had expected. Maybe he was doing Rantala a disservice.

"I won't complain about having Mage-Captain Schrijnemakers along for backup," Mike told the other two men. If nothing else, there was only so much Mage-Captain Cyriaque Schrijnemakers could do to interfere once Mike left the battlecruiser behind.

"You don't need our permission," Rantala told him. "But you have our approval. Be our eyes, Captain. We're hoping to talk to these people, so we absolutely *cannot* walk in blind."

The call closed down and Mike shut his eyes for a moment. Then, grinning, he walked out of his office onto *Rhapsody in Bohemia*'s bridge.

"All right, people," he told his tiny staff. "We're sending the Mages to bed for four hours and prepping for an incursion op into Ordin.

"And that means we need to go over the data from *Barracuda* with a fine-toothed comb. They sat in orbit of Orandar for over ten weeks. If we can't find the platforms the Ordin found *Thorn* with from that data, we are *not* nearly as good at our jobs as I think we are."

If he had to go into Ordin without knowing exactly where the outer-system sensor platforms were, he would. But he'd told O'Hannagain and Rantala that he *did* know where those sensors were, and he'd be embarrassed to admit that he'd lied.

It took three of the four hours to pull it off, which was an easy half hour less than Mike had allowed for it in a worst-case scenario.

The end result was fascinating.

"That's a *lot* of sensor platforms," Fischer said.

"Somewhere in the region of half a billion," Mike agreed. Mind-boggling as the number was, the sensor network was laid out twenty-eight light-hours from Ordin's star. Even a single ring of platforms at that distance would leave the individual sensors over a light-second apart—and the network appeared to be arranged in a staggered herringbone pattern. The pattern was three deep at any given point but created an effective depth equal to six platforms.

"Assuming we're missing at least ten percent of the platforms in the areas *Barracuda* had sensor data on, we're looking at a network covering a band about two and a half million kilometers high and only a single platform thick," he continued. "I hesitate to assume that all of them have FTL communicators, though Chambers was right to presume that *some* form of faster-than-light detection was in play."

"We don't have enough detail on any individual platform to say much of *anything*, Captain," Fischer pointed out. "All we really know for sure is that there is a repeating occlusion pattern that follows a loop around the ecliptic plane of the system."

"Agreed. So, let's worst-case it," Mike told them. "Every platform is capable of FTL transmission to a central processing center that is in the hands of a faction that is hostile to us. Full interpolation of information in real-time at a facility with the hardware to handle it."

"Even for *me*, that might be an unusually bad worst case," the RMN officer said thoughtfully after a second. "Except that we know they detected *Thorn* clearly enough and early enough to put a starship into position to get a better view of her last survey point."

"Exactly. And we know the planetary amplifier provides them clear detection in roughly *this* zone." Mike tapped a command, adding a red section spilling out from the star. That was only about a light-hour deep, though they'd learned the hard way that the reezh were more effective with it than the Martian Mage-Monarchs had ever been.

"Add in conventional sensors around Orandar, the gas giant and the asteroid belt…" New red spheres materialized around each planet as Fischer spoke. Time delay was a factor on all of the scanners except the amplifier.

"The innermost two light-hours of the system, maybe even three, aren't practical," Mike said as he studied the chart. "There are definite signs of a smaller sensor network closer in. This outer-system net…" He shook his head. "It tells us something and I don't like it."

"*Thorn* wasn't the first ship to buzz Ordin," Fischer said.

"Exactly. The Kazh are regularly passing through this place to keep an eye on things, and the Ordin have been pushing their scanner networks farther and farther out to make sure they stop the Shining Shield doing more than just stopping by."

There was a lot of red and orange on the map. They weren't as certain about the inner-system sensor networks, but Mike was sure they existed. There was no point in making the massive investment of the outer-system network unless the space closer to your home was already locked down.

"Here." He tapped a portion of the hologram. "Against a defender without an amplifier, staying out of the ecliptic makes us harder to see, but we *know* the reezh picked *Rose* up when they followed that doctrine.

"But twelve light-hours from the star, perpendicular to the ecliptic and the likely location of the scanner arrays, buys us a lot of space. We're not coming in close enough to be an immediate threat, and lightspeed is still a thing for their sensors.

"We'll come in with an extended triangle dispersal, here, here and here." Three green markers appeared on the display. One ship would come in directly "above" the star, the other two on the opposite side of the ecliptic and offset by half a light-hour.

Keeping them well out of the locals' sensor reach was the main priority. Nothing they would see was going to be real-time, but that was the nature of the game.

"I'd say we should drop buoys, but it's probably a waste of time," Fischer said, tracing their fingers across the display and clearly mentally estimating time. "There's no way the Ambassador is going to want to visit these people from twelve light-hours out, so we won't have much of a chance to pick them up. And they're not big enough for Links."

The buoys were stealthier, if significantly less mobile, versions of the sensor probes the Navy liked to use. And like those probes, they couldn't justify the cost in size or money to fit Link communicators into them.

Mike had been fully briefed on the extent of the Republic's penetration of the RMN at the start of the war. The Republic Intelligence Director had positioned agents on almost every ship in the Navy, and those agents had been equipped with Link communicators—a cost that had vastly exceeded the training and recruitment of those agents in the first place.

Links were becoming ubiquitous even in civilian life, but that was because their value far outweighed their cost, not because they were any-thing resembling *cheap*.

"We drop in dark as dark can be," Mike told Fischer. "We'll be far enough out that I'm prepared to risk a drone web for better information—but that's with the understanding that the moment it looks like someone is hunting us, we blow the drones and get out.

"Visitors might be from groups that are arguably friendly, but that is *not* a risk we are taking."

"This almost sounds like a plan *I* would draft," the Navy officer replied. "Where's the hard-riding rocket job they gave me as a commander?"

"You'll see him the moment someone has to fly this ship into a firestorm," Mike said. "But for this kind of operation? I'll remind you of an old adage:

"There are old pilots and bold pilots, but there aren't many old bold pilots."

He grinned.

"I'm aiming to be the exception that proves the rule, of course, or we wouldn't be pulling this stunt at all!"

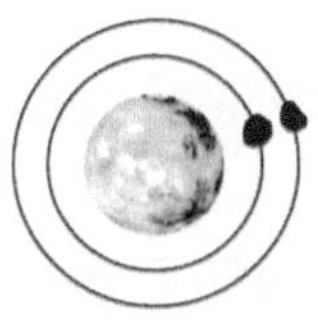

CHAPTER 22

RHAPSODY IN BOHEMIA and her three companions hung in space for a few moments as the Mages swapped seats. Mike took a single glance at the seat next to the simulacrum to confirm who was swapping in—Mage Vitaliy David, one of his MISS Mages, was being replaced by Mage-Lieutenant Ziya ad-Din Prinz, the only RMN Mage on the ship—and then turned his attention to the main display.

He couldn't jump his ship, but he was in command and often at her helm. The setup wasn't uncommon on the stealth ships, which meant their bridges were a strange mixture of civilian and military practice.

Civilian ships would split the bridge and the simulacrum chamber, making the magical heart of the ship almost purely the domain of the Ship's Mages. A warship, which usually had a Mage as a commander, put the bridge in the simulacrum chamber, resulting in a more crowded space— but also put the primary command station right at the simulacrum.

Rhapsody in Bohemia had Mike's station two meters back and a meter up from the dais around the simulacrum itself. That let him both keep an eye on the Mages where necessary and put his focus elsewhere when necessary.

His main focus was *Prince of Frogs*, the massive battlecruiser acting as their backstop for this mission. If something went wrong, the *Salamander-*class ship would have to cover his trio of stealth ships long enough for the rest of the Task Group to arrive.

Though the reezh *shouldn't* be able to follow his people through a jump. So far, at least, the aliens hadn't demonstrated that particular trick—

though the RMN hadn't shown their Trackers off to the Kazh, either, now that he thought about it.

"*Rhapsody in Armor* is ready to jump," Captain Harmon reported on his screens.

"*Rhapsody in Blue* is ready to jump," Captain Truong echoed a moment later.

"Thank you, gentlemen," he told them. Prinz had been in position before either spoke, and though no one on *Bohemia*'s bridge had audibly confirmed readiness, Mike knew his ship was ready to go.

Xi was sitting right next to Prinz, after all, and she'd have told him if there was a problem.

"Mage-Captain Schrijnemakers, we are ready to go," he told *Prince of Frogs'* CO. "Links will shut down ten seconds before Jump. We'll see you on the other side."

"We'll keep the campfires burning, Captain Kelzin," Schrijnemakers confirmed. "I'd say be careful, but I read your mission brief. I'll leave it at *don't die.*"

Mike laughed and gave the other man a sketchy salute.

"*Rhapsodies*, jump in fifteen from... mark."

Mike was not one of the non-Mages who could sense a jump. Not even every *Mage* could sense them, he was told, but magic was a funny thing.

Even without any sensation, the moment was obvious. His sensor screens blanked for a moment as *Bohemia* recognized that it was no longer in deep space, but the computers hadn't updated with the new information yet.

"Stealth protocols active," he ordered aloud. It was a redundant order, something neither Mike nor MISS generally went in for—but there were times that he had to agree with the Navy about redundancy.

"We are at full emissions control," Fischer reported. "Heat-sink protocols are active, and the wraps are deployed. We are as much of a hole in space as mere technology can make us."

"And I have the rest of it," Xi said. Prinz had slipped aside and she'd taken over the simulacrum, her hands on the liquid silver soul of the ship.

Mike leaned back and forced himself to relax. If Fischer said the EmCon and heat-sink protocols were online and Xi said she was making them invisible, they were *invisible*. Nothing in space was as stealthy as a *Rhapsody*-class ship.

"Bringing up cold thrusters," he told everyone. "I'm going to put some distance between us and our jump flare, just to be sure."

Cold thrust was a misnomer. The ion engines used for that purpose still put out measurable quantities of heat. It was simply so much less than their main antimatter engines that it could be concealed inside the magical bubble Xi was creating.

It was also much, *much* slower and measurably less efficient than those antimatter engines. Still, Mike had his ship moving away from the jump flare—the most noticeable part of their emergence into the system, a pulse of Chernenkov radiation that shouldn't be recognizable from more than a light-minute away—at a full gravity.

"Our eyes are wide and we're drinking deep," Fischer reported as they drifted. "We have a top view of the entire system. It almost feels like a strategy game. Double-tap that cruiser there to move it there."

They highlighted the ship they were speaking about, and then a random section of space.

Of course, the ship was a reezh Type Three, not an RMN cruiser. Fifteen million tons of alien technology that humanity could *understand* but not necessarily *duplicate*.

"I didn't think there were any Type Threes in the system," Xi noted. "But we're seeing them now?"

"Scan data from the Nine suggests that the reezh like a standard two-hundred-ship fleet grouping anchored on sixteen Type Ones," Mike pointed out, running through the data as it populated around him.

"Despite *Thorn* not seeing most of them, it looks like Ordin might have had the full package tucked away somewhere." He grunted. "*Had* being the operative word, of course."

There were more Type Ones in the star system than Mage-Captain Chambers' survey had detected hidden in Ordin Four. *Thorn* and her crew had picked up eight of the massive ships, but they'd been *inside* the gas giant and hard to pick out. Everyone had assumed Ordin had more ships than that, but they hadn't known how many.

Rhapsody in Bohemia's passive scanners were picking up a lot of active engines, and no one appeared to be hiding capital ships anymore. There were ten Type Ones visible in the system, though Mike's initial survey suggested they were all in singletons.

And, as he'd pointed out, there were the other four known reezh ship classes out there, from fifteen-hundred-meter Type Twos down to Type Fives of a mere thirty meters' height.

All of them, like the fleets in the Kazh and Chimera, universally two hundred meters in diameter. Mike had to wonder what the reason for that was.

"Let's nail down our numbers as well as we can," he told his people. "Nothing seems to be moving in our direction, so let's get the drones out. Expand our telescope, increase our resolution.

"The number of ships I'm seeing out there suggests that the civil war *Barracuda*'s people saw is still ongoing. Let's see if we can sort out who's winning—or, at the very least, where all the damn ships are!"

After thirty minutes, Mike gave the okay for Xi to drop the magical shield.

"At this point, if someone saw us via something FTL, they'd be here," he told the bridge crew. "That means we have a few hours before anyone will check anything out, so let's not exhaust our exit strategy."

That got him chuckles and a mock glare from his wife.

"Drone web is getting us decent imagery across the system now," Fischer reported. "It isn't pretty, boss."

"I'm seeing the high-level, but you have a quartet of smart guys in uniform in a back room running over the same data," Mike conceded. "Lay it out for me and Xi, Fischer."

"Ordin's fucked," the Navy officer said grimly. "Orandar is triple-fucked, but the whole system has descended into an epic shitstorm."

"I got that much. I was hoping for details from the uniformed analysts who are supposed to keep the spy from getting into too much trouble." Even for Fischer, the summary sounded grim and pessimistic, but something in the Navy officer's face suggested that they might even be understating.

"Biggest mess is around Orandar, of course," Fischer told them, highlighting the planet on the main displays. "Remember the imagery from *Thorn* and *Barracuda*? Orandar had a significant artificial ring of captured asteroids, almost five thousand klicks deep with the middle at geostationary.

"That had to be one *hell* of a traffic-control problem, and then all the forts started shooting at each other."

Mike shivered. There were nightmare words that described the situation he suspected Fischer was getting toward.

"The *smart* people with orbital platforms built in escape systems," they continued. "It looks like about sixty percent of the stations in the ring have blown clear of Orandar orbit and are now drifting free in what looks like the universe's biggest garden pinwheel."

Now that Fischer highlighted the streams of platforms in question, Mike saw their point. It wasn't quite as neat as "four lines of stations hurtling off into space" but there was a clear pattern of where the stations had triggered emergency thrusters that had hurled them out of planetary orbit.

They'd all settle down into new orbits eventually. Without more delta-*v* that Mike doubted any of the platforms had, they'd probably end up in a rough cloud along the path of Orandar's orbit.

But none of them were still in orbit of the planet, which meant that the icons marking orbital traffic were... a problem.

"My estimate is that probably three-quarters of the civilian platforms managed to get clear—but it looks like the military forts, with some help from the various warships and monitors, did a clean sweep of each other. There's no way to tell if the remaining civ platforms managed to evacuate in time, but it doesn't matter anymore now."

"Kessler syndrome."

Xi said it a moment before Mike could, but they'd both been thinking it. Fischer nodded grimly.

"Whatever was still intact in orbit got hit by the debris from the forts," they confirmed. "I'm not seeing any coherent energy signatures in there, but the pattern is pretty clear. Orandar orbit is impassable without major intervention at this point. Even most warships wouldn't survive trying to pass through that debris cascade."

"How long for it to clear up?" Mike asked.

"Years, possibly decades, if no one does anything," the Tactical Officer said. "A lot of it is in stable-ish orbits now. I'd need a lot more data to even make an estimate."

"A planetary amplifier should have been able to clear that up in an afternoon," Xi noted. "That suggests that either whoever is on the planet is using the cascade as a defense measure or..."

"Or no one is in control of the amplifier," Mike finished. "Which would make sense, given that no one can really fly fleets around in a star system with an amplifier. Not without permission, anyway."

"Which leads me back to my initial conclusion," Fischer said. "Ordin is fucked. We already know the Kazh is scouting the system regularly enough that they've invested massively in trying to intercept those flights.

"The cascade not only shows that the civil war is happening, it shows that the amplifier is uncontrolled. As soon as the Kazh see that..."

"There'll be an invasion fleet on its way." Mike looked for the warships on the display. Even from this distance, his ship could confirm they were all much the same—suggesting the Shining Shield hadn't arrived *yet*.

"Assuming they have one to spare," Xi said quietly. "They might need to pull ships and troops back from Chimera for that. It could... create an opportunity for us."

Mike felt guilty at the thought, but she was right. Except there were other moving pieces as well.

"Not if one side of the civil war is prepared to just hand over the keys," he pointed out. "According to Commander Moran, the rebels are aligned with the old Priest-Mage families, which suggests that they may well be willing to play along with the Kazh. If the war is over in the Kazh's favor, Ordin wouldn't be a distraction. They'd be a *reinforcement*."

"Right now, I don't think *anyone* is winning," Fischer said. "We don't have enough information to distinguish sides here, but I'm seeing a lot of different flotillas swanning around, most of them chasing or being chased by somebody."

"Each of the Type Ones appears to be anchoring a task group of what are, at least theoretically, starships," Mike noted. "From what Moran and Lisa said, the rebels were mostly using sublight ships, right?"

"From the data they provided, the initial conflict was *entirely* fought with sublight ships, corvettes and monitors," Fischer countered. "None of the starships had been brought out of Ordin Four before *Barracuda* fled the system."

"We need more information." That was why there were three scout ships, of course. They'd consolidated everything back at the fleet and even run their raw data and analysis by the far-larger analysis teams on Mars.

"How many different groups are we looking at, Fischer?" he asked.

"Seven with Type Ones, as you noted," they replied. "Five that are anchored on one or two Type Twos. And another sixteen that appear to be made up of mostly sublight ships, with a few smaller starships in play."

"But we have no way of knowing if any of the starships actually have Mages aboard, living or dead."

Mike nodded grimly, then sighed.

"The plan was for an hour, so let's see what we can scoop up data-wise in the rest of that time," he told them. "Then we flicker back off to meet with *Prince of Frogs* and go home."

Fischer nodded and turned back to their sensor screens. Mike focused on his own displays, wishing that a clear division between the various forces in play would magically appear.

The Kessler syndrome over the planet was bad enough. It was possible that the space infrastructure throughout the Ordin System was set up to be self-sufficient and not need food or other supplies from the planet... but he doubted it.

Unless someone did something dramatic, a lot of people were going to start dying in a matter of weeks—and the only vessels that *might* be able to do something about the cascade were chasing each other around the star system like a lethal game of tag.

"What are you thinking, Mike?"

He hadn't even noticed Xi crossing to his station until she leaned down next to him and murmured in his ear.

"I'm thinking this is above my pay grade, love," he admitted. "But I'm also thinking we can't leave this alone, either. We need to make sure this comes down in our favor, whatever that looks like."

"That's not something three scout ships can do," she said. "Maybe not even something the whole task group could do."

"Maybe the task group, if we're careful and apply it perfectly," he told her. "Which means the next decision is political.

"And *way* above our pay grade."

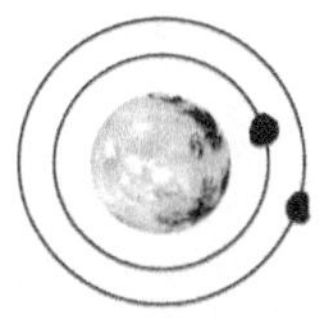

CHAPTER 23

INFORMATION DID NOT MAKE DECISIONS for Connor. Data informed his decisions, but there were so many factors in any given discussion or choice that no single piece of data could make up his mind for him.

There were probably scenarios where there was only one acceptable way forward, but he'd encountered surprisingly few of them in his career as a politician and an Arbitrator.

The mess in Ordin was no different. They had a lot more information than they'd had before Captain Kelzin had launched his scouting mission, but that didn't make the decision of what to do next any simpler.

The entire scouting op, from the three scout ships and their cruiser escort jumping away from the task group to all four of them decelerating back into formation and hooking up to the tenders for fuel, had taken under three hours.

Captain Joto was still in surgery when they returned, which left Connor alone in the meeting room. Adazh Komarazhi was with her parent, and Connor refused to begrudge that.

Plus, he wasn't entirely sure Komarazhi was ready for the meeting he was about to have. The rotating Seal of the Protectorate on the screen felt a bit sharper than it often did, because he wasn't calling *a* government official.

He was calling *the* Government, for all intents and purposes.

That thought faded with the seal itself, the screen turning dark as the room's holographic systems came online. Suddenly, the meeting table had two new occupants. Both were probably sitting at desks or possibly even in a room with each other; the software would adjust their images to fit into the room he was in.

"Your Majesty. Chancellor," he greeted the two people who ran the Protectorate. "I appreciate you taking the time to check in. I hope you are both well?"

Kiera Michelle Alexander, fourth monarch and first Mage-Queen of Mars, smiled thinly. She was a slim woman with carefully simple red hair wrapped around a gold coronet, almost young enough to be Connor's daughter.

Connor was still far from convinced of the value of the monarchy that ruled humanity, even though he now knew the power of the Olympus Mons Amplifier and that the Royal Family carried the rare gift needed to use it.

"I've had better days," the Queen said calmly. "Everything is fine, but Barry is on Earth and there was an... incident."

"Which has been handled," Montgomery noted. "By *him*."

The Prince-Chancellor of the Protectorate wore a platinum chain around his neck, which somehow only made him appear even smaller than his hundred and fifty centimeters of height. Maybe it was because Connor knew that simple chain marked Montgomery's authority as second only to the Queen herself—or because, like anyone fully aware of the last decade of history, he expected to see a platinum hand on that chain.

It was an open question whether the soft-spoken and dark-haired man in front of him had given up his status as First Hand of the Mage-King when he'd become Kiera's Lord Regent—or when Desmond the Third's will had adopted him into the royal family.

Generally, everyone assumed by the time Prince Montgomery had become *Prince-Chancellor* Montgomery, he'd given up the authority to speak with the full power of the Mage-Queen and to act as judge and jury over worlds and other Hands... but Connor had to wonder.

"Your... paramour is uninjured?" he asked.

"From what I have heard, Barry was more worried about making sure the idiots holding him hostage lived than his own safety," Kiera told him. "The Royal Guard was *right there*, after all."

"That is a story I may ask him for," Connor said, then chuckled. "Or perhaps I shall take his *Guards* out for drinks to get the real one."

Every member of the Royal Guard was a powerful and veteran Marine Corps Combat Mage, wrapped in specialty red exosuit combat armor that included runic enchantments woven by the Mage-Queen herself to augment their power.

As the Mage-Queen's boyfriend—a term Connor felt was far too immature for the man who stood at the Queen's left hand—young Barry Carpentier had a trio of those red-armored guardians with him at all times.

Whoever had taken him hostage had made a serious mistake!

"Regardless, as I said, Barry is fine," Montgomery repeated, though his smile suggested he might help Connor track down those Guards and a good source of beer later.

"We cannot say the same about the Ordin," Connor conceded. The mood of the room inevitably darkened.

"Analysis teams from the RMN, MISS and three civilian departments are grinding through the data *Barracuda* and the stealth ships brought back," the Prince-Chancellor said. "Initial conclusions are... messy.

"Kelzin's conclusion that Orandar is undergoing a full Kessler cascade is correct. From my own experience, I wouldn't want to take *anything* into that mess. Personally, I'd teleport down, but that's not an option available to the Task Group."

Connor gave the Chancellor a questioning look.

"Without an amplifier, a Jump Mage that has expanded their study beyond the most basic version of the teleport spell can move themselves and maybe two other people up to ten thousand kilometers through clear space," Kiera explained. "Not all Jump Mages can even manage that. A Rune of Power extends that range, but it would take a Hand or a Rune Wright to transport down to a planet from outside the Kessler cascade."

"It's not just the distance, either," Montgomery said, the certainty in his voice reminding Connor that the Prince-Chancellor had *been* a Jump Mage once. And was rumored to be one of *the* best practical experts on non-starship teleportation magic these days.

His injuries in the Mage-King's service prevented him from jumping a starship himself.

"For all that a jump spell never truly occupies the intervening space, anything in the way is a complicating factor. Not normally an issue in space, but with a Kessler cascade... I'm not certain even Riley could safely get to the planet. Orandar is sealed until someone can open a path."

"Something most easily achieved with the planetary amplifier," Connor said.

"It could be done with regular amplifiers, patience and skilled Mages," Kiera replied. "But yes. It would take a squadron of warships with Navy Mages weeks to clear the orbitals of a world. The planetary amplifier could do it in hours."

"And lacking the planetary amplifier, our potential ally is vulnerable." He hadn't disagreed with that part of the assessment. "There is argument for allowing that vulnerability to act as a distraction for the Kazh. There are no humans in that system, after all, and it is unfortunately likely that even our friendly Chimeran reezh are dead."

It was probably for the best that Komarazhi hadn't made this meeting, Connor realized.

"I can tell you that Parliament would not be overly enthused with us getting into another war," Montgomery said. "If Ordin were under attack from the Kazh, there would be no question. We are at war with the Church of the Nine, and them attacking another system would represent a clear strategic opportunity for us to deal them a blow.

"While it is purely a civil war in Ordin, it's harder to justify. Especially with our resources already stretched *past* the breaking point."

The call was silent.

"I have heard little about pushback from Parliament on the continuation of the war," he finally said.

"Outside of a few individuals, some of whom manage to be vocal out of all proportion to their importance, Our Senators and Representatives recognize the threat," Kiera told him. "I am attempting to be in closer contact with all factions, though..."

She trailed off and Connor coughed delicately.

"Senator MacClery continues to show his ass on my homeworld's behalf, I take it?" he asked.

"I will..." Montgomery searched for the words, then snorted. "I will give Gareth MacClery the truth of his convictions. He is not, so far as I can tell, being vocally contrary because he is being paid or managed.

"He truly believes that the Constitution as we have written and interpreted it is dangerous, and that the Protectorate should change it before it does major damage."

"The Constitution is barely older than his Senate seat," Kiera growled. "I miss Montague."

"I'm sure the Governor's heart would be warmed by that admission, Your Majesty," Connor told her. Catherine Montague had been part of the Council of the Protectorate, the theoretically advisory representative body of the Protectorate's systems before the Constitution.

She'd declined to run for any of the new Parliament's seats and instead gone home. Connor hoped she'd been *planning* to run for planetary Governor, given how quickly it had happened.

"The politics back home are a major component of what we do next, Chancellor, Your Majesty," Connor warned. "I was sent here to make an alliance, but I am not certain that mission extends to involving ourselves in a civil war and tipping the balance."

"TG Twenty-Eight has three cruisers, Ambassador," Montgomery said calmly. "I would suggest talking to Mage-Commodore Rantala before you charge in to try to win a war for the Ordin."

"There are a lot more people who'd need to sign off on that than just Rantala, Chancellor," Connor said with a chuckle. His plenipotentiary authority was probably enough for him to sail into Ordin and conclude an alliance, but since he had live coms with the capital, it seemed unwise.

"You're the man on site," Kiera told him. "Mike, quite reasonably, refuses to make a recommendation on something well above his pay grade. This *is* your pay level, I'm afraid, and I want your opinion."

"I would want more information before committing to any military endeavors," Connor said slowly. The bits fell into place as he spoke, and the rise of his usual confidence brought a smile to his face.

"But there's only one way we're going to *get* that information, Your Majesty. If we are going to do anything in Ordin, we need to go there and talk to them. I suggest we jump into the system and attempt to make contact with both sides—or however many there are, frankly.

"I don't want to make commitments until we have more information about what's going on here and what kicked off this civil war, but we're not going to get that information by eavesdropping on their radio transmissions.

"We need to talk to the Ordin. And then, depending on what we learn, we can either make an alliance with one side or another—or we can extract whatever remains of the Chimera delegation and leave."

"They may not let you leave at that point," Montgomery warned.

"My Lord Chancellor, was there ever a point in your career where you would have let that stop *you*?"

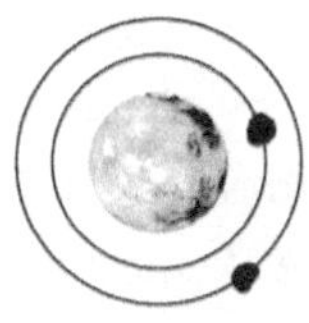

CHAPTER 24

THEY NEEDED MORE INFORMATION. That was the main point of Connor's planned entrance into the Ordin System, of course, but even for *that*, he was going to need more data than he already had.

It wasn't information that was going to be extracted from intercepts and long-range observations, he suspected, and that left him with a limited number of sources. Connor could contribute to the process of tearing through *Barracuda*'s sensor data and the records of their meetings, but that wasn't his primary skillset—and the advantage of the Link was that there was an entire legion of the best analysts available doing just that back on Mars.

No, his time was better spent on more old-fashioned types of information-gathering and alliance-building.

Last Stand at Alamo's sickbay was as large as many planetside hospitals, though it was split into three sections across the cruiser's volume. A handful of Chimeran Army troops stood guard just inside the door, their attention pose different from humans'—the extra joint in each limb didn't lend itself to standing perfectly straight—but still perfectly clear.

Matching the reezh soldiers was a team of Marines, but they were letting the Chimerans take the lead on security for the part of the ship handling their wounded. It was a subtle gesture of respect but one that Connor knew would be meaningful to *Barracuda*'s battered survivors.

"Lieutenant," he greeted the reezh in charge of the detail. "I'm here to see Captain Joto and Ambassador Komarazhi."

Joto had been moved onto the flagship because while they were *stable*, their injury was complex—and while the human surgeons were trained in reezh traumatic brain injuries, it was the type of thing where they wanted to be working in their space with their tools.

Since Joto was reportedly awake and coherent, Connor figured no one was going to argue with moving many of the complex-but-stable patients over to the RMN flagship.

"Room at the end," the reezh officer told him, gesturing. "Doctor is floating."

Hovering, Connor translated after a second. He gave the reezh a firm nod and stepped forward past her. The reezh was trying for idiom, but her mastery of English wasn't *quite* there.

Surgeon-Commander Qurbon Saidova wasn't being quite as bad as the soldier implied, but he did intercept Connor before he reached the door at the far end of sickbay. Saidova was a tall man in light blue scrubs over the black shipsuit of an RMN officer, with what appeared to be long black hair tied up in a hairnet at the back of his head.

"While I appreciate Lieutenant Shizhilo's responsibility for security, these are my patients," the Chief Surgeon said pointedly. "What's going on... Ambassador?"

"I'm here to see Captain Joto and their daughter," Connor told Saidova. "Adazh isn't your patient, and I understand that Joto is receiving visitors?"

"I have allowed the Captain's *daughter* in to see them," Saidova replied. "You understand that family is a different scenario entirely from regular visitors."

Connor smiled.

"I do," he allowed. "And if you tell me that Captain Joto is not up to receiving visitors, I will leave them be. The last thing I want is to cause any risk to them."

He might, depending on what exactly Dr. Saidova said, send his questions via the younger Komarazhi. At the moment, he wasn't entirely convinced that Saidova was actually protecting his patients so much as his turf.

"I presume you don't know Captain Joto?" the doctor asked.

"I don't," Connor conceded. "I want to talk to him about the Ordin System, Doctor, before we take this ship into a civil war. I believe the Captain will know more about the negotiations and the conflict than their junior officers. His knowledge could save lives."

Including the one belonging to Dr. Saidova.

The surgeon studied him, and he wondered if he was being a touch too manipulative. Then Saidova sighed and nodded.

"If they ask you to leave, you're done," he told Connor. "I have a watch on the Captain's vitals, and they've been solid through their conversation with their daughter, so I think they're up to a heavier discussion."

Given that Joto had potentially just had to tell Adazh that her mother was dead, Connor wasn't certain that his questions counted as *a heavier discussion*!

"Ambassador!" Komarazhi started to scramble up from her seat. A reezh scrambling was still a disconcerting sight to Connor—the extra joints added flexibility that looked *wrong* to his eyes still.

"You don't need to get up, *Ambassador*," Connor insisted. He turned his attention to the reezh in the bed and gave Joto a measured bow.

"Captain Joto, it's a pleasure to see you awake," he told *Barracuda*'s commander. "I understand that you've had a rough time, so if you need me to come back later, I'm fine to do so."

"That is not necessary," Joto told him, their voice slow and their English precise. "I know who you are, Ambassador O'Hannagain. Adazh has been telling me what has happened in our absence. Little is good news."

"I know." Connor unfolded a second seat from the room's white walls. Most medical spaces in the Protectorate were very, *very* standardized— part of how the Protectorate helped the system governments to upkeep the health systems they mandated was by using the mass purchasing power of humanity's largest-ever government to keep down the price of medical equipment.

Everything from the scanners to the chairs to the layout and walls of the room would be identical or nearly identical in any medical facility across over a hundred worlds.

Connor knew *exactly* where the chairs were recessed into the wall.

"Is there anything about the last few months you would like me to speak to, Captain?" he offered. "I have been involved in the Protectorate's effort at the highest levels. Only timing and ill luck put me on a ship rather than on Garuda's surface when the enemy struck.

"There is little you can ask that I cannot answer."

Joto chuckled, sounding like a small rockslide.

"How did you move *so many* people?" they asked. "I see the need for the evacuation, but the scale…"

"I can barely comprehend it myself," Connor admitted. "We had almost a thousand starships moving people out of Chimera by the end. Had the Kazh given us more time, there would have been hundreds more in the next wave.

"Even so, we got lucky." He shrugged. "We had six colony ships that were ready to go but not committed, and we had the old Republic ships— ships Prometheans volunteered to fly to save lives."

"I need to speak to Lisa and Trevor as soon as it's possible," Joto murmured. "We owe them everything. I was knocked unconscious very early, from what I understand, but it was our Prometheans who saved my ship and my people."

"That's up to your doctor, I'm afraid," Connor warned. "That said, I can't see any reason why you couldn't talk to them right away. I know they were worried about you."

Joto closed all of their eyes.

"I will have to tell them that Admiral Wang is dead," they murmured.

"They know, Captain," Connor said gently. "We told them. They know—and they know that Admiral Wang transferred the remaining Prometheans of the CSN to the ships being evacuated. We got all of them out, Captain—though it's easier to evacuate dozens than millions."

"And your people got millions out," Joto said. "It would be a miracle if the result was…"

"Any significant change to how many remained," he conceded, looking over at Komarazhi. "We thought we had more time. The Kazh… disabused us of that notion."

"And so, you are here, looking for allies, as we were," the Captain told him. "What do *you* need to know, Ambassador?"

"Ambassadors," Connor corrected gently. "Adazh is here as the representative of the Dual Republics in exile. She will go into Ordin with me."

And the junior partner was still a full Ambassador, with the ancient rights and protections thereof—protections that the reezh had similar traditions around. Whether the battered remnants of the Reezh Ida and the centuries-long conflict following its fall still honored those protections, well...

That was why Connor had brought cruisers.

"A small encouragement to give you everything I can, of course," Joto recognized. "But I need little more, Ambassador O'Hannagain. So was on the surface when the Kadak launched their attack."

"Commander Moran was unsure who had been where," Connor noted.

"Moran is a loyal officer who had risen to the limits of his competence and experience," the reezh said harshly. "As a Tactical Officer, he is good, but he needed *far* more experience and mentorship to be ready to hold an independent command.

"I would have done all that I could to keep the burden that fell on him from doing so, but our winds were not so kind. It was possible he would surprise me, but... it does not sound as if he did."

"He got your ship and many of your people out," Connor murmured, suddenly feeling the urge to protect the reezh officer who'd ended up as Acting Captain of *Barracuda*.

"Including me," Joto said after a moment's pause. A few more seconds of silence passed, the reezh leaning back against his pillow and closing his eyes again.

"I do him a disservice," Joto finally conceded. "He did not carry the burden in the way I would have preferred, but he carried it farther than I would have expected of him. It seems he carried it far enough."

"He feels responsible," Komarazhi told her parent. "He got everyone out and *then* panicked."

"And he didn't deliver your ship into the hands of the Kazh—who already controlled Chimera by the time he had to retreat from Ordin," Connor noted. "We are all here because of how much Moran *succeeded.*

"But he didn't know how the delegation was distributed or where the people So was talking to might have gone."

"Our entire delegation and roughly three hundred crew members were on the surface," Joto told him. "Six hundred on the station we were using for short-term leave. Only half my crew was on my ship—So was confident that she would have a treaty soon, and every conversation I had with their military officers suggested that we were *safe*.

"I was wrong."

Those three words were hard to get out of anyone in Connor's experience, and poisonously painful to say as well.

"Only half of the people on the station were rescued," Komarazhi murmured. "I'd thought they got more out."

Joto seemed to age between breaths.

"How many?"

"Eight hundred and fifteen souls aboard *Barracuda*, with two hundred and thirty-seven confirmed dead," Connor told them.

The silence dragged on for a while. Connor didn't want to push the reezh, and not just because he still needed information from them.

"There were less than eight hundred people on the ship, including the humans we couldn't send on shore leave," the Captain finally said. "Moran *did* get half of the people on the station to safety, which might have been a miracle. The others... might not have been able to escape at all, from what I remember."

"*Barracuda* evacuated a number of civilians, but the station was destroyed," Connor confirmed. "Moran offloaded those civilians before leaving the system, but my impression is that he did so in neutral territory, or as close as he could find.

"Which means I don't know where to go to negotiate with anyone when I get there," he admitted. "I was hoping you could give me a location."

"Orandar," Joto replied. "Whoever is in control at Ushola, the capital city."

"And not just because that's where So is." Connor knew Joto's type. The officer would move worlds to get their wife back, but they wouldn't undermine the operation for it.

"If Cadatch Izhom is still alive, he is the man you want to speak to," Joto said grimly. "And So was making good progress with him. She believed he was a reezh we could work with."

"Unless the Cadatch made it off-world early on, I can't reach him," Connor warned. "Orandar's orbitals are a mess of debris, basically impenetrable. All evidence we have is that no one is in control of the planetary amplifier—which suggests that Izhom is dead."

"It does. From what they said, the Cadatch rarely leaves Ushola, let alone Orandar," the Captain confirmed. "I don't know where his people would rally if he's gone. I'm... not sure they would. The Aha Kadak might be one of several Voices and Houses, but they are regarded as second only to the Cadatch."

"And Cadatch isn't hereditary, so there's no clear successor," Connor guessed.

"Exactly."

"Someone is fighting on," he told the reezh officer. "There are multiple fronts, and we can't even identify sides, let alone where to make contact with anyone. Any information you can give me, Captain, gives me a better chance to find out what's going on."

He shook his head, leaning forward to meet Joto's lower eyes.

"Right now, there is no way we can authorize a mission to retrieve the delegation from the surface," he admitted. "It would take this entire task group weeks to clear a wide-enough gap to get shuttles through for an extraction.

"Knowing that the delegation was intact on the ground with some level of security when things collapsed, we'll attempt to make contact with So Komarazhi once we arrive, but so long as the Kessler cascade remains... we need some level of stability in the system before we can attempt to clear a path."

Joto grunted, a pained sound like a rock breaking.

"We didn't discuss their emergency civil-war plans," they noted. "But there was something So mentioned, a place that was linked to the Cadatch's personal pet project. She said he'd asked her not to mention many details, but he felt it was the most critical thing he was working on."

"What was it?" Connor asked.

"She didn't say. I know it was an off-world training facility of some kind—something to do with the 'lie about the Channelers.'" Joto was starting to sound exhausted. It didn't make what they were saying add up for Connor, though it sounded familiar somehow.

"So, it's somewhere they might defend, somewhere they might fall back on," Connor concluded. "Somewhere where whoever is standing against the Aha Kadak might have leadership."

"Yeah. I just... I don't know where it is or even *what* it is," Joto admitted.

"That's more than I had a few minutes ago, Captain, and if your doctor isn't about to throw me out, he should be," Connor told Joto, rising to his feet. "Rest, Captain. We're going back into Ordin.

"We're going to save So and everyone else we possibly can. You have my word."

Even if *possibly* was carrying a lot more weight in the promise than Connor really liked.

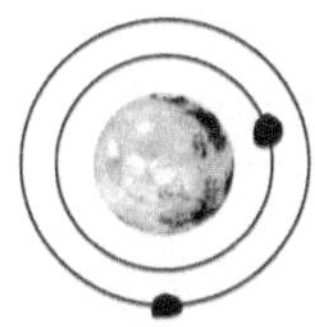

CHAPTER 25

"'THE LIE ABOUT the Channelers'? You're sure that was the quote?"

Mike watched O'Hannagain's response to Mage-Admiral Alexander's question. The task group's leadership was Linked in with the commander of Second Fleet as they tried to sort through everything they knew.

His own attention was split, *mostly* focused on the meeting but also keeping an eye on a shared data channel where Xi was connecting with a group of MISS analysts on Mars.

"That is what Captain Joto told me," the Ambassador confirmed. "I can't say for certain that was what So Komarazhi *said*, as it was in an off-the-record conversation. The Cadatch apparently asked her to keep this training facility concealed, even from her own people."

"Do you understand what she meant?" Alexander asked.

Mike had no idea himself. He wasn't even sure what *Channelers* were, let alone what lie a reezh head of state would want to disprove. He had a far-better understanding of the breakdown going on in the analysis channel, but it was his job to participate in the meeting and speak for the spy ships if something came up.

"I have heard the term *Channeler* before," O'Hannagain said, "with regards to reezh Mages, I believe. I think it's a rough English translation of an old reezh word for them."

"It's not." Something in Alexander's tone pulled the last of Mike's attention away from the analysis. He didn't know the Crown Princess well, but he hadn't heard that level of anger before.

"*Channeler*, Ambassador—or Channeler of the Astral, in full—is what the Reezh Ida called the people they killed so they could put their brains in the Engines of Sacred Sacrifice, their equivalent to the Prometheus Drive," the Admiral explained. "They have systems, a mix of technology and runes, to identify them."

"So, Mages," O'Hannagain repeated. "Like the Mages by Right our Royal Testers find."

Even *Mike* knew that distinction. Mages by Blood were born to Mage parents, tested early and trained thoroughly to take their place as wielders of magic supporting the Protectorate.

Mages by Right—like Xi Wu—were identified by the Royal Testers around age thirteen. Every kid had to undergo it, but the vast majority had the same reaction to the test as Mike had—boredom. Those who pinged the test were immediately moved into new schools and new paths, training them up to make certain they, too, would be able to wield magic to serve mankind.

"The test is similar, yes," Alexander confirmed. "Thanks to the Reezh Ida Lachai, we've had a chance to study the device's use, and it's a touch more effective than our own processes.

"But to the reezh, that test isn't identifying a Mage. It's identifying a *Channeler*—someone who *isn't* a Mage but someone that the Engine of Sacred Sacrifice can enable to cast the jump spell. Only people born to the bloodlines of the priest caste and trained from birth are Mages."

"Mages, after all, have rights and privileges. Channelers are a *resource*." Rantala sounded vaguely ill, though this didn't appear to be news to him.

"The lie that the Cadatch was attempting to disprove was... that Channelers weren't Mages?" O'Hannagain suggested. "I can see how that would cause him difficulties. Potentially even trigger this civil war, if the Aha Kadak realized what he was doing and decided that protecting their privilege was more important than not killing people."

"Do we know that the Ordin were still doing that?" Mike asked. "It's not something that would show up in the scans my people were doing."

"No mention of anything in either direction was included in the notes Ambassador Komarazhi's delegation sent back to *Barracuda*,"

O'Hannagain said. "I suspect that So had an answer, one way or another, but she seemed to be managing how much information was being recorded.

"To her detriment now," he concluded grimly. "We have no idea if she's alive, and if she is, she's underneath a debris cloud we can't breach."

"If there is a training facility in the star system that is teaching Channelers to be Mages, we have a moral obligation to see if we can protect it," Alexander told them. "Though we hardly have the forces to do much."

"The first step is to make contact with people," O'Hannagain said. "My preference is definitely the Cadatch's people, if he's still alive, and the people who don't want to kill kids for their brains, no matter what.

"But we can't even define sides until we've talked to *somebody*. Captain Kelzin, is there any clear pattern that would suggest a division of the system down any kind of physical line?"

"No," Mike told the Ambassador. "What we're seeing so far suggests that most individual stations or asteroid colonies have picked one side or another, but the boundaries are being drawn at the individual-settlement level, not even by regional clusters, let alone planetary systems.

"When we scouted the system, there was no active fighting going on, but my impression is that we were seeing maneuvers for the upper hand. The gas giant's system appears to be a mess of conflicting loyalties, and several of our flotilla groupings were either there or heading there.

"The only thing keeping that area quiet at the time, I think, was that everyone was already in each other's weapon range. When the shooting starts, it's going to be a mess, and no one wants to throw the match."

"And the rest of the system?" Rantala asked.

"We're still isolating sides and trying to identify what each of the fleet groups we're looking at is attached to. Our initial impression is that we're seeing a lot of flotillas that have paired off—i.e., one force is defending something, and the other is positioning to contain the first and potentially attack what they're protecting."

We've found it. The text message floated across Mike's eyes, and he smiled at his audience.

"If everyone can excuse me a moment, I believe our analysis teams may have some kind of answer for us," he told the others. "I'll check in with them and return in a few seconds."

Switching over to the analysis channel was a touch of a button, though Xi was the only person who appeared to replace the conference.

"You have a location for the Cadatch's training facility?" he asked.

"We didn't have a lot to go with, but I think so," she told him. "Honestly, that was part of what we *did* go with—we found a place that appears to be guarded by a Type One that doesn't seem worth it.

"It's a cluster of asteroids that are home to a decently intense extraction-and-refinery operation, plus a couple of rotating cylinder habitats. Maybe a million people, tops, but there's a seventy-five-million-ton warship and her escorts standing guard over the cluster—*and* a second Type One with escorts shadowing the first, waiting for a misstep.

"A fifth of the Type Ones in the entire star system are hanging out around a backwater mining outpost? There's a reason for that—and it's that something *other* than a mining outpost is in that cluster."

"That's as good a logic as anything we're going to find," Mike agreed. "Swap over to my conference channel. Unless there's someone else we should be crediting for the win?"

"It was a group effort, but MISS analysis cells aren't *supposed* to be identified," Xi told him. "You're a brat, husband of mine."

"And I'm giving credit where credit is due, wife of mine," he replied. "Linking us over."

If she'd been one iota ruffled or had a single black hair out of place, he might have given her time to clean up, but she was as perfectly turned out and gorgeous as ever.

They both popped up in the video conference at the same moment. Alexander was speaking, but she paused when she saw his return.

"You said you might have them?" she asked.

Mike quickly laid out the analysis Xi had given him a moment earlier.

"I agree with the assessment," he concluded, "but it was Mage Wu and the analysis cell that put it together."

"Well done, Mage Wu," Alexander told her. "Did you or the analysis cell have a suggestion on approach?"

"Everyone in the system has to be on edge," Xi said quickly. "There are a lot of ready trigger fingers over there. If we come in too close, we'll draw fire before we even introduce ourselves—and potentially give away advantages we could use later.

"Suspecting that we're looking at the Cadatch's pet project gives us a reason to pay attention to that cluster, but it's a strategic and political question whether we want to make it *obvious* that we know something is there.

"I would suggest that we keep our cards in our hand and arrive a significant distance away from any of the flotilla locations, at what looks like a regular safe-arrival point. We know we want to talk to the people at the training facility, so we position ourselves closest to them, and then we see how things play out."

"Thank you, Mage Wu," Rantala said. The Mage-Commodore looked around the conference. "I have to agree with that suggestion," he continued. "If you see a diplomatic or political reason to do something different, Ambassador, lay it out."

"I can talk to everybody from wherever we arrive," O'Hannagain said confidently. "Moving in close to the facility cuts the lag for that conversation down, but we'll be pitching to the whole system from the moment we jump.

"That part is my job, and I'll handle it. Keeping us all safe is yours, Commodore."

"For which purpose we're going to keep a solid distance between us and everyone with a missile launcher," the officer said fervently.

"I can take *Bohemia* into the system ahead of the task group and make sure there's nothing waiting for you," Mike offered. "It seems worth keeping our options open.

"That said, I think I do want to send *Rhapsody in Armor* and *Rhapsody in Blue* on to Kutchan," he continued. "*Thorn* only visited three Primes— we know Cozhan and Azha are in the hands of the Kazh, and the sooner we can see which of the other seven are potential allies, the busier we can keep Mr. O'Hannagain."

His own orders said that he needed to keep a stealth ship around to haul the Ambassador out if things went spectacularly sideways, but the survey mission needed to keep moving too.

"We'll want to send both firepower and fuel to support them, Commodore, though how much is clearly a military decision…"

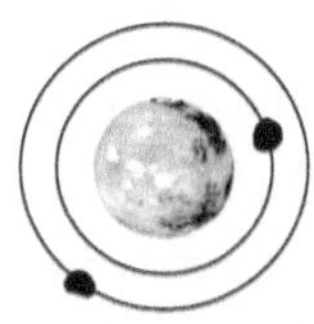

CHAPTER 26

RHAPSODY IN BOHEMIA DIDN'T JUMP into the far corners of the system this time. That meant her jump flare was almost certainly going to be detected, but their mission was different.

"Jump complete," Mage Maiella reported, stepping back from the simulacrum and tripping.

Fischer was there as she did so, the Navy officer stepping into her fall and catching her in their left arm. There was a moment of silence on the bridge, then Commander Fischer calmly set Maiella back on her feet and gave her a broad grin.

"Watch your step, Parvati," they told her. "There are too many gaps and stairs on a bridge."

"That there are, sir," she agreed.

"Go rest, Parvati," Mike ordered. He glanced at her long enough to see Xi put a hand comfortingly on the younger woman's shoulder.

"Stealth spell is up," Mage-Lieutenant Prinz reported, his own focus on the task in front of him.

"Heat sinks are also online. We are good to—"

There was the tiniest of jolts as Mike brought *Bohemia*'s cold thrusters to life. Two gravities was as much as the ion thrusters could move the ship, but it was even more necessary than before that they leave their emergence point behind.

"How are our assorted friends around the system?" he asked.

"The flotillas we identified last time have definitely been consolidating... and blowing each other up," Fischer said, the last few words grim. "It looks like one side has secured control of the largest asteroid-settlement cluster. There's a Type One falling back toward the gas giant that looks like someone has kicked the *shit* out of her, and she has a lot fewer escorts than she should have."

"Falling back sublight?" Mike asked. "Interesting choice there. Presuming, of course, that she *has* a Mage or Promethean aboard."

"At her current acceleration and vector, I'd say there was a battle at that settlement cluster about thirty-six hours ago," Fischer said. "There's another Type One at the cluster, plus a half dozen of the biggest monitors."

"What about the gas giant?"

"Still looks like a pair of cowboys with nuclear pistols in each other's mouths," the Tactical Officer told him. "There are three Type Ones there right now, with two more—including our cripple—on their way. Two Type Ones at our target, as before, but it looks like both groups have been reinforced by smaller ships.

"Two more Type Ones above Orandar... and my count is coming up one short versus last time."

"They've been busy over the last few days," Mike said. They'd left the system three days earlier, though the time lag on the sensor data they'd collected meant that it had basically been four days since their last information.

"I'd say we're looking at two of the flotillas we identified last time having been completely destroyed," the RMN officer told him. "Other groups have consolidated, and I'd say there's been at least four battles. There's still twelve fleet groups of significant size, with the largest two being at the gas giant— with the next-largest being the one at Orandar, the one at the settlement cluster in the asteroid belt and the two around our target."

"All right. Any sign that anyone has noticed us?"

The closest reezh force was over a light-minute away, which meant there was a decent chance that *Bohemia*'s arrival had gone completely unnoticed.

"Nothing yet. We've been in space long enough for four of the fleet groups to pick up our jump flare," Fischer confirmed. "I would expect everyone to be wired up, looking for jumps, personally, but they might think they have everyone pinned in place."

"Not an assumption *I'd* want to make, even in an in-system civil war," Mike said. After almost twelve minutes, they'd only put a few thousand kilometers between themselves and their emergence point. Even with it looking like the locals hadn't picked them up, he wanted more.

"Prinz, do you think you can cover an antimatter burn with this much distance?" he asked the Mage on the simulacrum.

"For a few minutes, sure," the Mage-Lieutenant confirmed. "Assuming full thrust, anyway. If we slow down the pulse, I can cover for longer."

"I want us well away from this point before it turns out someone is just calculating their microjump," Mike replied. He ran a series of numbers on his chair's computers.

"I need twenty-two minutes at full power, Lieutenant," he told Prinz. "That will get us to half a light-second away and moving at over two hundred KPS. Can you do it?"

Against the Republic of Faith and Reason, the answer would have been *yes*, without question. The problem was that MISS had known *exactly* what the RIN had been equipped with for sensors, allowing them to calibrate their invisibility nearly perfectly.

Against the reezh, they *didn't* know and needed to err on something as close to true invisibility as possible.

"Give us thirty seconds to identify a safe venting vector," Prinz suggested. "If we can keep even a half-degree vent open, I can make it work."

"Fischer, get Prinz a safe vector," Mike ordered. "We have a sixty-minute window to nail down a jump point for the task group, but we need to make sure *we* don't get seen, either."

"On it."

A busy silence reigned on *Rhapsody in Bohemia*'s bridge as his people got to work. They didn't have a lot of time, and they had some key work to do, but Mike knew his people.

He kept his hands on the controls, guiding his ship ever farther away from their point of emergence. It seemed likely that no one had seen them, but he didn't want to take any risks. He had a pretty solid idea what at least one side of the civil war in Ordin would do to his wife if they captured her.

"We have the vent vector, sir," Prinz reported. "Ready to shield on your mark."

"Understood. Mark in thirty," he ordered.

The seconds ticked away as various systems on his ship thrummed to life at his command. The count hit zero and Mike hit the ignition command.

The ship shivered under his feet, the magic Xi and the other Mages kept up to date absorbing the acceleration with only that shiver to show. Fifteen gravities had been the Navy standard since the War, starting as what the ships could manage with the runes only letting a couple of gravities of thrust through.

By the time the Republic had surrendered, a new gravity-rune pattern had been installed across the Navy—and the MISS stealth ships had started with it. The magical gravity that his ship maintained every day could offset fifteen gravities easily.

It required more maintenance and fell off in efficiency with surprising sharpness after passing that line, but the ability to maneuver at almost one hundred fifty meters per second squared without impeding the crew at all was considered worth it.

"Everything looks clear for us to be invisible," Fischer reported. "Of course, there's a non-zero chance the outer perimeter network will see this in a day or so."

"Hard to avoid that," Mike conceded. He tapped a point on the folding screens. A submenu opened up, allowing him to rotate it in three dimensions and set an exact set of coordinates.

"Flipping you a dot, Fischer, Xi," he told the others. "I make it clear of gravity interference and targeted as a one-light-minute standard emergence for Orandar. If the TG comes out there, the ships in Orandar orbit will see them first, but the next group—at only eighty light-seconds—will be the ships at the Cadatch's facility."

The Cadatch's *school*, unless Mike had misunderstood the discussions the previous day. The place where the Cadatch had taken the equivalent of Mages by Right and was teaching them to *be* Mages instead of simply being people with the potential to be killed and shoved into a ship.

If the school was what Mage-Admiral Alexander thought it was, it seemed pretty clear which side of this civil war Mars belonged on.

"It makes sense to me," Fischer agreed. "I make it three light-minutes minimum to any other forces in play, and the main fleets at the gas giant are ten light-minutes.

"No matter who comes after them, they'll have time to talk."

"Making sure they have that time is our job. *Talking* is the Ambassador's." Mike studied the map. Too many moving pieces—and at that, the reduction in moving pieces spoke to thousands already dead.

"Once O'Hannagain boots up the transmitters, *our* job becomes making sure no one sneaks up behind him."

Mike's ship didn't have a great many weapons, but he knew her eyes were second to none. No one was sneaking past his people.

Unless, of course, the Ordin had more techno-magical tricks up their collective sleeve. They still weren't entirely sure how the outer-system sensor network actually *worked*, after all.

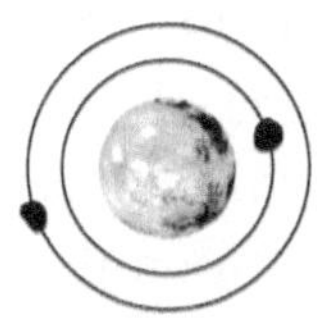

CHAPTER 27

"I HAVE TO ADMIT, while I would have been perfectly happy to see Joto and their people heading back to Exeter to rejoin the rest of the CSN, *Barracuda* sticking with us did provide options."

Connor looked over at Mage-Commodore Rantala. The RMN officer's attention seemed fixed on the countdown to their jump into Ordin, but he was reasonably sure the words had been addressed to him.

"Joto is the senior officer of an independent, allied military," he said genially. "It's not like any of us had the authority to order him to go home."

"Oh, we could have managed it," Rantala said. "The government-in-exile did formally promote Captain Atwood to Admiral and put him in command of what remains of the CSN. We could have relayed a Link conversation between him and Joto, and *Atwood* can give Joto orders."

Connor considered that scenario silently for a moment, then snorted.

"Orders Joto would have disobeyed," he pointed out. "Their *wife* is in Ordin somewhere, living or dead."

"Exactly. Never give an order you know won't be obeyed, Ambassador," Rantala said calmly. "We could have managed to get orders for Joto to report in, but that would have just created trouble. By *not* doing so, we can convince them to stay in deep space and watch over the logistics ships, which spares *Eye of Newt* to come into Ordin with us. And two cruisers are more intimidating than one."

Prince of Frogs, accompanied by the *Bard of Winter*–class destroyers *Wolfgang* and *Mikado*, had followed the two *Rhapsodies* when they left for their next scouting operation, along with two of the support ships.

The rest of the support ships were remaining one jump short of Ordin, guarded by *Barracuda* with the destroyers *Sondheim* and *Miserables*.

Last Stand at Alamo was flanked by *Eye of Newt*, and the two cruisers were surrounded by a sphere of the other eight destroyers of the task group. The countdown continued on the screen, into the final minute before they leapt into an alien system to make what, from Ordin's perspective, would be First Contact.

"Let us hope it's enough," Connor said. "We know they've still got nine Type Ones and a pile of Type Twos, any one of which outweighs the entire consular squadron two-to-one."

"The goal, Connor, is not to fight anyone," Rantala replied. "If I think we can't avoid a fight, I am jumping the entire task group out."

That was the first time the Mage-Commodore had laid out that decision quite so frankly, and Connor was silent for a moment in surprise.

"We are trying to make allies here, Commodore," he finally said, pitching his voice so only Rantala could hear him. "Running away won't help."

"Nor will dying pointlessly," the other man replied. "I'm here to back up your diplomacy, but I'm also responsible for your safety and the safety of everyone on these ships. Show me a critical point where a mere forty-odd million tons of warships can make a difference, and we'll talk about doing something, but until then? I will *gleefully* run rather than stand and fight against either side in a civil war that has nothing to do with us."

That pointed statement carried Connor through the jump into Ordin.

Last Stand's bridge had been receiving full data updates from *Rhapsody in Bohemia* via the Link, a small test of whether or not the reezh could detect the technology in action. Her screens barely flickered as they moved from using the spy ship's sensor data to feeding from their own.

A Mage-Lieutenant stiffly walked back from the simulacrum, giving the Mage replacing her a crisp salute before leaving the bridge.

Connor knew her stiff-backed posture and suspected the young woman had collapsed against a wall as soon as she was out of sight.

"We are in the Ordin System, Ambassador," Rantala told him calmly. "The next step is yours."

"I'm waiting on—"

The bridge door slid open barely a second after it had closed behind the Mage-Lieutenant. A PSS agent escorted Adazh Komarazhi through.

Under the bridge lighting, the slight red mottling to Komarazhi's gray skin was more visible than in most places.

"With your permission, Captain, I'd like to record our first message from here," Connor told Rantala. "I presume you have software that can edit out any information that we can't risk being transmitted? I want them to see that I am in a simulacrum chamber and therefore *not* on a ship using a Prometheus Drive or equivalent."

The explanation appeared to cut off a complaint before Rantala could finish opening his mouth. Connor should have told him in advance, but that would have given the Mage-Commodore time to marshal arguments.

As it was...

"I see your point," Rantala conceded. "Commander Bourgeois, can we sanitize a video from the Ambassadors to cover anything we're worried about?"

"We need to transfer any recording we make into reezh formats anyway, sir," she replied instantly. "I think we can do a security cleanup. I can also think of at least one spot I can put the two of them that serves the Ambassador's purpose while avoiding any real screens, so we don't need to do anything."

Connor gave the XO a small bow.

"That sounds like a brilliant compromise, Mage-Commander," he told her. "If you'd care to show us where to park our feet?"

From the momentary spark of amusement in Rantala's gaze, the Mage-Commodore had heard the word Connor had *almost* ended that sentence with.

Bourgeois fussed over Connor and Komarazhi for a good thirty seconds, getting them aligned on a set of clear steps. An orange light marked the pickup, and once they were facing toward it, it didn't look like any of the screens in the bridge would be visible in the video feed.

Enough of the simulacrum chamber would be visible for anyone aware of the concept to recognize it, Connor judged, which made the Mage-Commander's selection perfect for his needs.

"Are you all right to translate as I speak and introduce yourself?" Connor asked Komarazhi. "You are more than just a translator, of course, but—"

"But we don't want to involve anyone else. I came along to translate, Ambassador, I will be fine."

Her eyes were bright and her words fierce. Since Connor preferred her to translate, he wasn't going to push at all—but he'd held up her status as the Chimeran Ambassador all along, and he wasn't going to change that now.

"We can record when you're ready," the Lieutenant Commander seated at the console with the pick told them.

"Let's see what this star system has to say for itself," Connor replied. "Record in five."

The officer held up the fingers on one hand and folded them down as the countdown proceeded. Connor didn't need the five seconds to prepare himself, but he knew the count in was easier for the tech side.

The orange light on the pickup turned green, telling him that it had gone active, and he leveled a calm look on it, knowing that he was going to be the first human the recipients of his message ever saw.

"Greetings to the people of the Ordin System," he said brightly. "I am Ambassador Connor O'Hannagain of the Protectorate of the Mage-Queen of Mars."

Komarazhi spoke when he fell silent, repeating his words in reezh Korazhi and adding her own credentials. He understood enough of the language to know roughly what she was saying, if not enough to fully follow everything she said.

"Through our allies in the Chimeran government, we learned of your system and have reached out to make contact ourselves," he continued as Komarazhi finished. "We have come a long way to make contact with the Cadatch ozh Ahadan, to speak of the past and future and dangers that threaten us all."

A momentary pause to let Komarazhi translate. He wished he could see any of the people he was speaking to. It was easier to judge how a spiel was landing when he could see his audience—but this was hardly the first recorded speech he'd given.

"Thanks to the Chimerans who came before us, we know that the Cadatch Izhom leads this system wisely and well. We send our greetings to him and to the Ahadan of his people. We await your response and hope for positive discussions."

Once Komarazhi had finished her translation, the pickup light flicked back to orange, and she turned to him.

"You did not wish to address the civil war we see?" she asked.

"Let them think we only see what the consular squadron sees right now," Connor said. "For two reasons, Adazh. First, because it will lead our potential enemies to underestimate us; and second, because their reaction to our apparent innocence will tell us a great deal about *who* our potential enemies are."

He turned to Mage-Commodore Rantala.

"If I may make a suggestion, I think we should proceed toward Orandar at a moderate acceleration, Captain," he told the commander of the task group. "I can't speak to what the safest course is, of course, but I understand that if we proceed forward at one gravity, we can return to a safe area to jump with ease?"

He knew the basics of interplanetary maneuvering better than he was pretending and he suspected Rantala knew it, but he was going to let Rantala run his part of the mission until and unless the Commodore actually got in the way.

"Agreed. Helm, set up a course for all ships to approach Orandar at a standard zero-zero, one gravity. How long for turnover?" Rantala asked.

"Just under twelve hours, sir," a junior officer replied in a few seconds. "We'll enter a high orbit at a zero relative velocity in twenty-three hours, forty-five minutes."

"Pass it to all ships and execute sixty seconds from now," the Commodore ordered. "All ships will maintain a Mage at ready status until further notice. We will, at all times, be ready to jump out of this system."

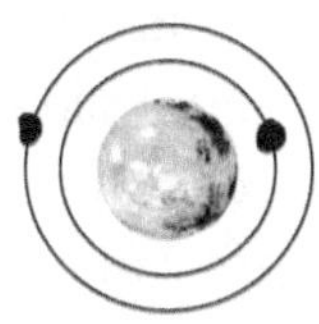

CHAPTER 28

AS THE SHIPS BEGAN TO MOVE, Rantala gestured for Connor to return to his station.

"The forces around the Cadatch's training facility and above Orandar have already seen us," he noted. "They'll receive your message shortly. What kind of response are you expecting?"

"I'm not sure," Connor admitted with a smile. "There are a lot of unknowns here. That's part of why I left my message so vague. It leaves the ball in their court for how they respond. We're friendly, so what do they do?"

"Sir!"

Every eye turned to the Tactical Officer who'd just spoken.

"Profile change on Orandar Flotilla," the young woman reported. "All ships are accelerating in our direction at eighteen-point-six MPS-squared. No active sensors directed at us yet."

"Two point two reezh gravities," Bourgeois noted. "They could push harder, but they're still putting on quite a clip for ships without magical gravity."

"I see we have drawn attention," Connor said. "What now?"

"We wait and see who talks to us," Rantala replied. "Even assuming our friends have the same missiles the modern Shining Shield has, we're still almost four hours from range. We can be long gone before they reach us."

"Profile change on Flotilla Alpha and Bravo, by the target cluster," the Tactical Officer. "I think Bravo started moving first; they're pushing up to twenty-five MPS-squared. Alpha is only pushing to twenty, but their vector isn't a direct intercept for us."

"Plot them all on the chart," Rantala ordered calmly.

New icons popped up on the display, each accompanied by vector information that Connor didn't quite follow.

He had seen enough tactical displays at this point to know that there was a pattern to what was going on, but he couldn't see it.

"Interesting," the Commodore murmured. "What do you see, XO?"

Connor wanted to shake Rantala and make the man explain what was going on to *him*, but he supposed that it was still part of the man's job to make sure that Tonya Bourgeois was ready to take over his job if something happened.

"Flotilla Orandar is headed directly for us, clear intercept course," Bourgeois replied. "Flotilla Bravo is pushing hard, aiming to get into powered-missile range of us at around the same time as them. Bravo and Alpha are just about evenly matched, though the comparison against Orandar is a bit more... complex."

Connor could see that much. All three groups of ships were anchored on a seventy-five-megaton behemoth that was theoretically FTL-capable—though they hadn't seen any sign of any Ordin ships jumping since *Thorn*'s original visit.

Alpha had four Type Twos and twenty-plus lighter starship combatants, plus a dozen sublight monitors of assorted weights. Bravo only had two Type Twos, the battleship-equivalents, and a dozen Threes and Fours, but had almost thirty asteroid monitors.

Orandar had *two* Type Ones but only a single Type Two, backed by twenty asteroid monitors.

The division didn't really matter to Rantala's squadron—each of the Type Ones alone outmassed and outgunned the human ships—but it suggested that Flotilla Orandar wanted to avoid whichever of Alpha or Bravo was their enemy.

Assuming they weren't *both* Flotilla Orandar's enemy.

"The synchronization between Bravo and Orandar suggests that they are working together," Bourgeois continued. "The position of Alpha, however, is just about solid proof that they and Bravo are *not*—unsurprisingly, since they were both maneuvering around our target cluster and shadowing each other.

"What their positioning and lower acceleration *also* suggest is that they're prioritizing defending the target cluster over anything else. The two forces were both outside of missile range of each other before Bravo started moving, and Alpha's course and lower acceleration keeps them between that cluster and Bravo."

"*And* keeps them in position to maneuver between the target cluster and Flotilla Charlie, over at the main asteroid settlement," Rantala noted. "Alpha has more starships than any of the other flotillas in our immediate area, with enough tonnage to offset even Flotilla Orandar's pair of Type Ones, but they're in the middle position between at least two enemies."

"They're still vectoring toward us, which suggests they aren't entirely sold the odds are against them," Bourgeois replied.

"Or they recognize that we represent a new player, one that can completely tip the balance of power here," Connor told them both. "TG Twenty-Eight might not be enough to take on any of the flotillas, but our presence suggests a greater power that could intervene."

"Not quickly," Rantala said grimly. "If Mage-Admiral Alexander left Exeter tomorrow, she wouldn't be here for three weeks. The twenty-fourth, at the earliest. Their entire *war* hasn't lasted much longer than that, and I have the distinct feeling the balance of power is clear."

"We can guess which of the four Flotillas around *here* are on the opposite sides," Connor countered. "The rest of the forces are still question marks without more data."

He shook his head.

"I was expecting *somebody* to talk before anyone started throwing fleets around," he admitted. "Any incoming transmissions?"

Last Stand was capable of receiving and translating any messages the locals sent. They'd converted the message he and Komarazhi had recorded into the local formats, based on data *Barracuda* had provided.

It was the best they could do, but Connor was frustrated. The Ordin *had* received his message—everyone in the *system* would have, soon enough—and somebody had to think there was a point to answering it.

But he couldn't *make* anyone answer.

"Nothing yet," the Communications Officer said, then held up a hand as one of her people passed her a headset.

"That looks promising," Connor told her. He took a moment to surreptitiously check her name on his wrist-comp. He should probably have known Lieutenant Commander Flavia Senft's name, but he'd done most of his coordinating with the ship's crew through Bourgeois.

"We have incoming from Flotilla Orandar," Senft confirmed. "Just running translation protocols now. Can someone pass Ambassador Komarazhi a headset? *She* doesn't need the translation."

A dark-uniformed Petty Officer seemed to appear from nowhere, offering Komarazhi a set of headphones clearly designed for a reezh skull. With a nod, the Chimeran put the set on.

A moment later, the screen in front of them switched to a recorded video message. There were subtle distortions in the feed, marking the translation between completely different computing and compression protocols.

Centered in the display was a single reezh with unusually smooth skin, almost pure white with odd striations of gray. Connor was trying *not* to lean on stone metaphors for reezh, but the stranger's skin could have been carved and polished from marble.

"Greetings to Connor, Ambassador of Mars," the stranger said. The words were a computer-generated translation, with the reezh's actual speech muted to avoid confusion.

"I am Forward Commandant Sujam," they introduced himself. "In the name of my Cadatch, Izhom, I welcome you to our system. I am afraid I must also warn you that rebels have raised banners and fleets against the righteous rule of the Cadatch ozh Ahadan.

"I am bringing my own squadron forward to provide security to your vessels. I recommend you maintain your current course until I can bring you inside our defenses. Once we are closer, a more-regular conversation can be held."

The message ended and Connor *hrm*ed to himself.

"Ambassador?" Rantala said. "I am not certain that it is wise to place ourselves inside close weapons range of a force of that power and unknown allegiances."

"Oh, I don't believe the Forward Commandant's allegiances are unknown at this point," Connor told the Mage-Commodore. "Adazh? Your opinion?"

The reezh woman looked at him, lifting her chin to study him with her lower eyes.

"It is a trap."

"I thought the same," Connor agreed. He glanced back to Rantala. "No one is going to expect us to blithely sail up to a group of unknown aliens and tuck inside their missile-defense net, are they, Captain?"

"If they know anything about how an amplifier can be used offensively, it would be ridiculously dangerous for them to allow it," the Mage-Commodore agreed. "I am not sure what the diplomatic protocol would be in this situation, however."

"Ambassador So Komarazhi approached Orandar in a single shuttle while *Barracuda* remained *thirty light-seconds away*," Connor told him. Rantala had probably seen that part but hadn't registered it as important.

"They'd been in the system and talking for almost three weeks before *Barracuda* was permitted into an actual orbit of the planet, and even then, she was under the guns of several fortresses.

"Trust for that kind of situation goes both ways, Captain Rantala, and I do not believe Forward Commandant Sujam trusts us or believes we will trust him. But if we will happily trot up to his guns, he's not going to turn down the opportunity."

"Ambassador, we have another transmission. It *looks* like it's coming from Force Alpha, but the report from *Rhapsody in Bohemia* suggests they're only relaying it."

"Any idea where it's actually coming from, Commander Senft?" Connor asked.

"They're doing a decent job of concealing the transmission, but I don't think they expected *Bohemia* to be where she is or for an invisible ship to have sensors as good as hers," Senft said. "It's not certain, but I'd put money that it's coming from our target cluster—and that it's from our *target*.

"Audio-only," she continued. "Translation on main speakers, original to Ambassador Komarazhi's headset again."

The translated voice told them nothing about the speaker—and Connor would guess that the original transmission hadn't contained anything identifying either.

"Ambassador Connor O'Hannagain of the Protectorate of Mars. Ambassador Adazh Komarazhi of Chimera. In the name of Cadatch Izhom, I bid you welcome. And in the name of Cadatch Izhom, I bid you warning.

"The Cadatch ozh Ahadan has turned upon itself. Fleets long concealed against the ancient enemy have been awakened and turned their weapons upon each other. You will find no allies here, for we are too weak and too divided to look to an outer universe we have only reason to fear.

"The vessels approaching you from Orandar are unlikely to be your friends. Their leaders may try to deceive you, to learn what they can from you before they remove you as a factor from our politics, but they will only see you as a threat.

"For your own safety, and for the sake of So Komarazhi, I beg you to leave this system and never return."

The message ended and Connor reached over to place his hand on Adazh Komarazhi's shoulder. Reezh shoulders were heavier than human ones, but Connor had massive hands and Komarazhi was slight for her people. His hand was large against her and strong enough to hold her as she slumped against him.

"And *that*, Captain Rantala," he said quietly, "is what honesty looks like in this mess. Our speaker warns they can't protect us, warns us against their enemy—inevitably—urges us to leave... and then they reference someone they met, someone we might not have known, but whose name Adazh shares."

"So, less of a trap but just as much of a problem."

"Exactly."

Silence fell over the warship bridge, and Connor realized that the Mage-Commodore was waiting for him to make a suggestion.

"What is your assessment, Captain, of the situation for the Cadatch's people, assuming they're Flotilla Alpha?" he asked.

"Not good," Rantala said slowly, turning to look at the display. "It looks like both Flotilla Orandar and, I'm going to guess, Flotilla Charlie are allied with Bravo, which puts them on the opposite side from Alpha.

"That also leads to Delta, the force that got kicked out of the main settlement cluster by Bravo, being the Cadatch's people. They're falling back toward Four, so in a lot of ways, the real question is which of the fleets at the gas giant belongs to the Cadatch."

"If you had to guess?" Connor knew he didn't have the skills to assess the military balance in the system. That was why he had needed a military attaché in Chimera and part of why Rantala was with him.

"Based off the three we're reasonably certain on, it looks like the majority of the starships have stayed loyal to the original government," Rantala said slowly. "That would lead me to guess that Flotilla Gamma-Two, which has two Type Ones and half a dozen Type Twos, is the loyalist force there.

"Which would make the balance a bit more even, depending on what the other flotillas scattered through the system are thinking," he admitted. "But the problem is that the vast majority of the big sublight monitors seem to be with the Aha Kadak, by almost three to one. If the starships can actually jump, they should have the strategic mobility to circumvent that weight of metal, but... if they can jump, why is Delta running in open space?"

Connor nodded. That added up, even if he didn't like the conclusion. "How bad does it look?"

"We don't have solid numbers on the mass or volume of the monitors—and what's *useful* tonnage on something built out of an asteroid is always a big question mark," Rantala warned. "And our numbers on the smaller corvettes are an estimate at best."

"But?" Connor prodded.

"I'd guess that this system probably had about ten billion tons of starships, monitors, and corvettes before this went to shit," the Mage-Commodore said. "There's about *eight* billion tons left, which means a *lot* of dead ships—but given the shit storm that apparently went down above Orandar and the battle I can see happened at the asteroid settlements, I might even be underestimating their losses.

"Right now, counting corvettes and monitors, I'd guess the rebels probably have fifty to a hundred ships more than the loyalists—but the advantage is mostly in monitors, which are easily twenty or thirty million tons apiece."

"And the rebels have five Type Ones and the Loyalists only have four," Connor guessed.

"Exactly. Once Flotilla Delta reaches the gas giant, they almost certainly will push to remove the rebels there, which might begin to tip the balance, but Flotilla Alpha can't hold that mining cluster on their own."

"Which means they *stayed* in that cluster for a reason."

"Yes."

Connor was no strategist, but he could see the pattern. He didn't like it.

"So, the Cadatch—or, at least, his off-world leadership—is in the cluster Flotilla Alpha is defending," he said. "Between Orandar, Bravo, and Charlie, the rebels have the forces to take his defenders, but Orandar and Charlie were tied up in other missions.

"Except now we've pulled Orandar, Bravo and Alpha out of position. Now that Orandar is moving, is there any reason to stop *without* rendezvousing with Bravo and moving on the Cadatch's HQ?"

"I don't see one," Rantala admitted. "But we're not certain what they were doing above the Kessler cascade, anyway—potentially, they were trying to cut a path through for their own people. It's not certain that the spaceborne infrastructure of the system is self-sufficient, after all."

Or vice versa, Connor realized. Few heavily spread-out systems in the Protectorate were, after all. Heavy industry and fuel refining took place in orbit or off-world, with agriculture and administration on the planets.

Critically, the off-world stations, colonies and outposts were likely dependent on Orandar for food—but Orandar's population, including the agriculture that produced said food, was probably dependent on the off-world infrastructure for fuel.

"We can't even remove ourselves from the equation now," Connor admitted. "Just by showing up, we've moved key pieces out of position."

"We also don't have the missiles to change anything," Rantala warned. "Assuming their weaponry matches the Kazh's, we can outrange them with *Last Stand*'s Wyverns and *Eye of Newt*'s Samurais, but that's only a fraction of our armament.

"We could play enough games to give any of the flotillas we can see a bad day, but probably not enough to take one out. A Horatio-style stunt might be enough for us to functionally cripple *one* flotilla, but that wouldn't even save Alpha."

Horatio had been the series of knowingly reckless and intentionally provocative sequenced jump attacks Second Fleet had used to level the playing field against the invasion fleet at Chimera. It hadn't been enough to *win* the battle, but it had been enough to leave the attack fleet incapable of intercepting the last evacuation fleet and investing the planet.

The Reezh Kazh's commanders had chosen the system over the evacuation convoy and Second Fleet—a choice that had spared the lives of everyone currently in Task Group Twenty-Eight.

Connor didn't know how to put something like Horatio together, but he'd been thinking about it—and he was glad to know that Rantala was doing the same.

"We have enough firepower to tip an even fight but not a four-to-one fight," he concluded. "I..." He considered the situation.

"I need to talk to *somebody*," he finally decided aloud. "We're still at, what, two minutes turnaround for coms with Forward Commandant Sujam?"

"Basically. The range will drop more quickly as we proceed toward each other and build velocity, but we've only cut a couple of light-seconds off so far."

"How fast could you get us to a jump without revealing anything we don't want to?" Connor asked. "I think we've got as much value out of this particular visit as we're going to get. We know the sides a bit better now, which means we need to start making calls—and I'd rather not make decisions with fleets flying my way!"

That got him a few chuckles from the peanut gallery of officers pretending not to listen in too closely.

"If we flip and go to three gees of acceleration, we can be back at the area we jumped into in forty minutes," Rantala said after a few seconds. "As long as it took us to get here, basically."

"Let's get moving," Connor said. "Adazh, Commander Senft, let's send some answers to our new friends."

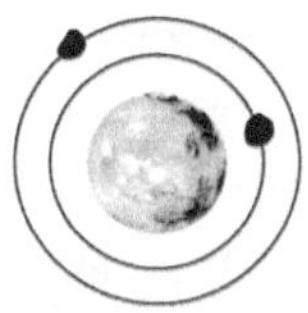

CHAPTER 29

"I NEED YOU TO GET INTO THAT CLUSTER, Captain, and see if you can tell us where and *what* Flotilla Alpha is defending."

Rantala's request was about what Mike had expected. He wasn't, Mike noted, trying to give the MISS crew orders. Like Rantala, Mike used *Captain* on a day-to-day basis as commander of a ship—but like Mage-Commodore Rantala, his actual credentials were different. The bland title of *agent* covered a lot of sins in the Agency, though the only people who needed to know he was the boss already did.

If he decided that Rantala was giving orders he didn't like, he had a few options—including the fact that while his military rank was a courtesy, it was a courtesy intended to avoid those problems.

According to RMN rank lists, Commodore Mike Kelzin was almost a year senior to Mage-Commodore Ketil Rantala by date of rank. Neither of them, he suspected, would regard that rank as *real*, but it was enough that he could use it to avoid orders.

So, Rantala made polite requests for things Mike was planning on doing anyway.

"I was thinking much the same thing, Commodore," he told Rantala. "Once we're in position, I might even be able to act as a relay for the Ambassador to talk to whoever's in charge."

There was a pause.

"How close do you think you can get?"

"In open space, against an enemy who is only barely aware something like the *Rhapsodies* exists?" Mike shrugged. "Laser range, probably.

Possibly even amplifier range. But this isn't going to be open space. Asteroid clusters aren't walkable, but there's still going to be plenty of things for us to hide behind or vent heat into.

"I'm not aiming to be able to give O'Hannagain real-time chats with people, but I can get a lot closer than anyone is going to be comfortable with," he concluded. "Give me a few hours."

"The Ambassador is telling everyone thanks but no thanks and then we're jumping out," Rantala told him. "We'll be gone in half an hour, no more. You're our eyes. I don't get the impression we're done here, though the risks are... uncomfortable."

"I'll be happier with you all out of the system," Mike admitted. He wasn't a fan of his orders regarding O'Hannagain. There was no way *Bohemia* could evacuate more than a tiny fraction of the Task Group's people, but he didn't like the cold-blooded assessment of *who* was worth saving.

"Believe me, Captain Kelzin, sitting in a fifteen-megaton cruiser watching four dreadnought equivalents head in my direction is *not* on my list of how I want to spend my day," Rantala said wryly. "We're only one jump away and you have the rendezvous coordinates. If anything goes wrong, get the *fuck* out of Dodge, Captain. MISS doesn't give medals for heroism."

"We're scouting and scooting, Commodore," Mike replied. "We've got eyes on your back; don't worry."

He dropped the channel and checked his course. The entire time since the consular squadron had arrived in the system, *Rhapsody in Bohemia* had been accelerating toward the "target cluster." Somewhere in that cluster of rocks being chewed up by miners and refiners was something unusual, something strange.

Something that Flotilla Alpha clearly thought was worth dying for.

The problem was that *Rhapsody in Bohemia* was still twenty-eight hours from reaching the cluster. They'd emerged two light-minutes away.

The only *good* news was that the target cluster was three light-minutes from Orandar. Flotilla Bravo's position had been on the Orandar side of whatever Alpha was protecting and outside of missile range from Alpha.

So many moving parts that Mike could count. If Bravo and Orandar changed their courses to head toward the same destination as he was, they could get there ahead of him—assuming they blew past at high velocity, anyway.

To make zero-zero... that depended on their pace. Right now, two of the flotillas he could track were making high acceleration, but they wouldn't want to sustain that once TG 28 was gone.

If they cut to one reezh gravity, it would take Flotilla Orandar eleven hours more to reach the target than it would take *Bohemia*. They'd just be in *missile range* by the time he arrived, which meant the battle with Alpha would probably already be over.

Mike needed better options.

"Xi, Fischer, I'm open to clever plans," he told his wife and senior subordinate. "Right now, we're not going to get to the cluster in time."

There was a silence, then Fischer made a grumbling noise.

"I have to say what I'm about to say," they noted. "Not because I agree with it, because *someone* has to: if we can't safely intervene, why are we getting involved? We might be better off just leaving the system with the rest of the task group."

"Well, first, because the Ambassador and Mage-Commodore asked us to find out what Flotilla Alpha was guarding," Mike replied. "And second, because we think there's a school of some kind involved, one for training the reezh equivalent of Mages by Right. That's something I have to feel is worth trying to protect."

He met Xi's eyes and nodded to her. His Mage by Right wife nodded back.

"There are two simple options, Mike," she told him. "First, we go to full acceleration and hope that their sensors aren't any better than the Republic's. With a bit of wiggling on the course and trading off Mages on the invisibility spell, we could get there in eight hours."

"More like thirteen or fourteen," Mike countered. "Because you wouldn't be able to shield us all the way in to the cluster, even against Republic sensors. We kept a twenty-light-second safety margin in place on those ops."

"We can still cut five, six hours off the time, enough to give us a bit of time to poke around," she said. "But you're right. If we can't get there with guaranteed quiet, why risk it at all? Second option is to jump.

"It's less than three light-minutes and our velocity is still under a thousand KPS. Any of the five of us can make that jump, and it will be less visible because of the limited distance."

Mike sighed. That was the conclusion he'd been trying to avoid. *Rhapsody in Bohemia* could leave the Ordin System invisibly. Their initial arrival had gone unnoticed, which suggested that either the outer-system network were the only scanners looking for jump flares or that the people usually keeping watch were distracted by the civil war.

Neither scenario would help *Bohemia* if they jumped right into what they knew the loyalists were treating as one of their key security zones. They'd be lucky to avoid getting immediately shot, even if Xi and the others were able to hide them once they'd arrived.

"They're going to be watching for the Aha Kadak's ships to pull a stunt just like that," he said. "Jumping would be the *fastest* option, but it ends up being a hostile act to the people we want to talk to."

"Do we want to talk to them?" Fischer asked. "Us, specifically, I mean. We're considering the possibility of acting as a relay for the Ambassador, but our job is primarily to scout the place and see if there's anything there that makes it morally or militarily worthwhile to intervene, right?"

Morally or militarily worthwhile was a mouthful, but it covered the scenarios. There were things that no RMN officer could stand by and watch happen. Mike was supposed to have more moral flexibility, but there was a reason he was a stealth-ship captain and not another type of agent.

"And if it turns out that we misinterpreted the Cadatch's words to So Komarazhi and the facility is actually where they're producing Prometheans?" he asked.

"Then that is morally worth intervening," Fischer replied. "Just... in the opposite direction."

"Flotilla Alpha is out of position, though not as far off as Bravo," Xi noted. "I think I can pick a jump position where we're out of their line of fire, if not necessarily blocked from their ability to detect us."

"Which means we're risking the survival of this ship on whether or not the Cadatch's people left defenses behind when they went off to see what the hell the strangers in the system were doing," he said drily. "A bet I don't exactly want to take."

But time was a tyrant without mercy.

"Fischer, show me every rock big enough to put us in a sensor shadow from the cluster that's between three and six light-seconds of those rocks," he ordered. "What options do we have?"

Highlights appeared on the screens surrounding them. A tapped command zoomed in on the target area, and Mike steepled his hands against his chin.

"There are a few options. But this one looks interesting, doesn't it?" He highlighted a particular rock, just over a million kilometers from the cluster—on the opposite side from both Flotilla Alpha and Flotilla Bravo, which meant it was almost five million kilometers from the theoretically friendly fleet.

"That's a weird shape," Fischer said slowly. "And the sensor return is even weirder. How has something that large gone unexploited?"

The rock in question was irregularly shaped and almost a thousand kilometers long. The scan suggested it was almost entirely carbon-based minerals, with limited metal content. Irregular as the shape was, it also clearly resembled a turd.

"The region around it was already exploited," Xi explained to the RMN officer. "We're looking at what's left of a billion or so tons' worth of asteroids. This would have slowly spun out from one of the big refinery stations over twenty or thirty years—probably two or three of them from the size."

"It's low metal content, so it's not as good a hiding place as a solid nickel-iron rock, but there is a lot to be said for sheer size," Mike agreed. "Xi, can you put us in its shadow? Get us in close without being seen?"

"In my sleep, love. Shall we?"

Another display showed a new set of icons as TG 28 jumped out of the system at last.

"Let's do it before I get nervous about being alone in an alien system," Mike told her. "Fischer, keep sensors wholly passive, but I want the missile-defense suite fully online. No risks."

"No risks," the officer confirmed. "We need data, not medals, right?"

"As Commodore Rantala observed, Commander, the Agency doesn't give medals."

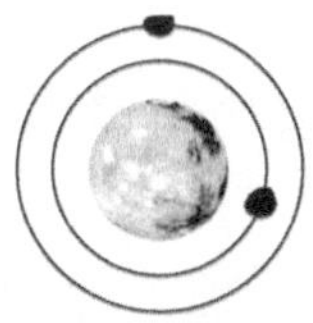

CHAPTER 30

MIKE DIDN'T NEED TO HOLD HIS BREATH. With the technology and magic wrapped around him and his people, they could have a disco party in the mess at maximum volume and it wouldn't have an impact on their stealth.

Unless they distracted whichever Mage was at the amplifier, of course.

Xi jumped them, stumbling slightly afterward as she passed the simulacrum over to Mage Manel Siegel. The younger man did everything except salute Xi as he took over, vibrating with the enthusiasm of a spy still on their first mission.

It would soon catch up to Siegel that he was a Mage and even the Agency was unlikely to ever use him as an actual spy. His role aboard *Rhapsody in Bohemia* was only slightly different than it would have been above an RMN warship—and while Siegel was borderline on his qualification for that job, he *did* qualify on the measure where Xi hadn't at his age.

"The cloak is up," he reported. "I have our visible light signature wrapped up and feeding back into our heat sinks."

"As is everything the technological side of the setup can catch," Fischer added. "Heat sinks are at forty percent capacity. It wouldn't hurt to find something to discharge into, but we have plenty of time if we don't bring up the antimatter engines."

"The good news is that if we need the main drives now, we're probably not going to be trying to hide them," Mike replied. "The bad news is that if we need the main drives now, your antimissile systems are going to get a workout."

He checked the fuel levels versus the cold-thrusters usage. They had plenty of delta-*v* left, though he was definitely glad they had the tankers just outside the system. Using the antimatter engines, the fuel he had would be enough for a week of maneuver and operation.

Using the cold thrusters, it was... less. A lot less. *Bohemia* would still have *antimatter* left after running out of hydrogen, which was better than the alternative in a lot of ways but highlighted the problem of the ion thrusters.

But he'd been in on the meeting where they'd compared using the main engines at low thrust versus the cold-ion thrusters. The byproducts of a matter-antimatter reaction were highly energized and highly radioactive. The colder ions were much harder to detect for a given level of thrust, even if they were actually putting more mass out into space.

As *Rhapsody in Bohemia* did at his command that moment. The thrusters began to push the ship toward the nearest edge of their asteroid shield, and Mike watched a tiny and all-too-close horizon approach.

"No sign that anyone picked us up," Fischer replied. "I'm surprised. I was expecting that we'd create uncertainty and avoid being localized, not really avoid being detected at all."

"Everyone is very distracted," Mike said. "If I turn out to like any of them, I'm going to have words about this. Nobody's sensor doctrine in this system is up to standard."

"For the level of effort that they've put into building the networks, that seems odd," Xi noted. She hadn't left the bridge, taking a seat next to him. Mike could see the signs of strain on her face and wondered if he should kick her off the bridge.

Except he needed her brain as well as her magic.

"I know. Which makes me wonder if their field forces are too used to relying on fixed sensor installations and analysis centers for this kind of detection," Mike said. Now that he'd mentioned it, the hypothesis fit the data.

"We know the outer-system net was using FTL coms of some kind," he continued. "That *had* to have a single source, with an around-the-clock staff. There were probably other networks in place, too. If everything was feeding to a single facility, maybe with one backup..."

"Or even more than one backup, but they were all either on Orandar or in orbit," Fischer continued as he trailed off. "We know that most of their fleet was concealed to the point where *Thorn* didn't see it.

"I can't imagine they carried out many exercises on jump-flare tracking and interception while they had the fleet tucked away inside a gas giant."

Mike nodded and shivered as an uncomfortable thought hit.

"Fischer, get a buoy spread out as we move around," he ordered. "And reconcile the passive data we have from here against the data we had from our previous location—and our *original* data.

"Right now, we're roughly where the rebels would expect the loyalists to be looking from. They know what each other's sensors look like. Is there something they're trying to hide that our data might reveal?

"Because I swear, there has to be a reason they haven't moved on Alpha."

"On it."

His Tactical Officer set to work just as they finally passed over the horizon. They had an analyst team elsewhere on the ship that Mike presumed would be doing the work of brushing their three datasets together, as his own gaze was on the set of asteroids they'd been heading toward since the beginning.

The central point was a dwarf planet, a not-quite-spherical asteroid eight hundred kilometers across at its widest point. Still dense with heavy metals, and the passive scanners could pick up the energy signatures of heavy extraction work going on across the rock.

Orbiting it, using the dwarf planet's minor-but-real gravity as an anchor, were a trio of massive smelters. Each of them was a ten-kilometer-high array of piping and machinery that, if they were anything like the human version, had crews of a quarter-million apiece.

Trailing the refineries were the habitat platforms, eternally spinning in space to provide one reezh gravity to their inhabitants.

The dwarf planet was the largest object in the cluster, but there were easily a thousand other major asteroids within half a million kilometers of it. All told, it didn't even add up to the mass of a small moon, but clusters like this were far easier to break down for resources than even a dwarf planet. Dozens of mining ships roved the area, with more locked on to promising pieces of rock they were processing.

"Okay, so, that's what a heavily industrialized mining cluster looks like," Mike said cheerfully. "Now, how do we find the secret training facility the system's monarch tucked away in here?"

"Well, I'm going to guess it's either in a station above the dwarf or on the dwarf itself," Fischer replied. "Given that *most* refinery centers like that don't have quite so many missile launchers seeded into the satellite traffic."

Orange icons—potential but not definite hostiles—began to speckle Mike's view of the complex above the big asteroid. They weren't massive weapons platforms—not the heavy orbital forts that had guarded Orander, for example—but each of those icons marked a platform with something the system IDed as a weapon.

"How many?" he asked.

"I've got solid IDs on a hundred-sixty of them and probables on at least twice that," Fischer told him. "They might be new—but this is probably one of the places they source the asteroids they build into monitors. I don't think they're all crewed, but I could be wrong. It looks like two missile launchers and two defensive lasers per unit. Could easily have zero crew... or anything from ten to twenty hands."

Almost five hundred platforms as definites or probables. A thousand missile launchers—and if the satellites weren't big enough to be real battle stations, they were big enough that they weren't one-shot platforms.

It was more firepower than the RMN was estimating an Ordin Type One fielded, though it was probably light on antimissile fire and the ion cannons that made Kazh warships so terrifying at close range. There was a reason that Flotilla Alpha had been willing to leave the cluster temporarily undefended.

Except that the launchers also explained why Flotillas Bravo and Orandar hadn't come for Alpha yet. The rebels probably knew the dwarf planet was defended but weren't certain how heavily.

"Fuck."

"Captain?" Fischer asked. The Tactical Officer wasn't the only one looking at Mike questioningly, but they were the one who spoke first.

"What are Bravo and Orandar doing now that the TG is gone?" he asked. "I can guess, but we need to know."

Fischer turned to their displays, checking the data flowing in to *Bohemia*'s scanners and computers. Their focus had been on their target, not the fleets they'd left behind, but now that was looking like it might have been a mistake.

"That... has got to suck," the Tactical Officer said slowly. "Both flotillas are up to five reezh gravities, roughly forty-two MPS-squared. Alpha and Bravo have both flipped, they're heading back for the cluster, but Alpha is still only pulling roughly twenty MPS-squared, two and a half reezh gees."

Half the acceleration of the people coming after them. They had to know that wasn't enough. Mike could run the results in his head, though the exact timing was more complicated.

The rebel flotilla would bring Alpha into missile range before the loyalists could return to the cluster. They'd commit themselves to entering the range of the missile platforms around the dwarf planet, but they'd be able to engage Alpha in isolation.

And then Flotilla Orandar was coming up behind to finish the job if Bravo failed. They would still be over half a day behind, but even if Alpha pulled out a win against Bravo—and Mike couldn't see how they *could*—they wouldn't win against the pair of undamaged Type Ones leading Flotilla Orandar.

"Xi?" he asked quietly.

"Mike?" She could see the same pattern he could.

"Please tell me that the asteroid is just a refining colony," he told her. "That we're not looking at some life-changing endeavor that could change the fate of all reezh or something like that."

"I can't say one way or another, not without getting onto the planet," she replied. "Manel, are you getting anything through the amplifier?"

Mike knew that most Mages could detect magic to some degree, but it was more on the order of a vague buzzing that magic was *happening* than anything useful. With them still a million kilometers distant from the dwarf, Xi wouldn't be able to feel anything.

Siegel, holding the simulacrum and operating on a different scale through his link to the ship, might be able to sense more.

"There's something there," he said. "I'm... not sure what—it's not like anything I've ever felt before—but it's big enough for me to feel from this far away, and even through the amplifier, that's not nothing."

"Planetary amplifier?" Mike asked. That would be a hell of a trump card for the Cadatch to have hidden, if he'd built a second one of those. Of course, if there was a planetary amplifier at the dwarf planet, the war would probably already be over.

"No. I know what Olympus Mons feels like, and this is something else," Siegel said. "It could be..."

He snorted.

"No, who am I kidding?" the young Mage asked rhetorically. "I have *no* freaking clue what I'm picking up here, Captain. Might be a lack of experience, but..."

"Manel, if you're picking up more than *there's magic somewhere nearby*, you're doing better than most of us can," Xi told the youth firmly. "I know it's not much to go on, Mike, but I wonder... The only working version of the runic artefact the reezh use to detect Channelers went to Mars with the Lachai. It could be one of those.

"Or just a bunch of Mages doing practice spells at once, preparing for a desperate defense. I can't tell you for sure."

"But everything we're seeing lines up with our assumption, that the Cadatch had a Mage school for people the Kadak wouldn't train," Mike said with a sigh. "All right."

"All right?" his wife asked.

"Yeah." He smiled. He suspected it was a pained expression, but that would only reveal his inner conflict. "It's not my call, I suppose. I'm just a spy.

"Fischer, get those buoys out wider if you can," he continued. "I'm going to keep us drifting toward the planetoid for the moment, but we need every piece of data we can get on all three flotillas heading our way—but Bravo as priority."

"We're getting decent visual on them now," Fischer confirmed. "We couldn't find anything they were trying to hide from the loyalists, but there's a degree of *why bother* going on. The loyalists have more starships, but there are a *lot* of asteroid monitors.

"The odds are very much in the favor of the assholes, I'm afraid."

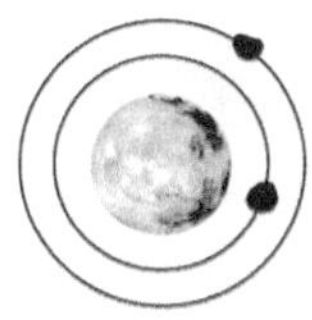

CHAPTER 31

"I WOULD LOVE TO BE CERTAIN," Connor growled, glaring at the report from *Bohemia.* "If we know that's a school for Mages by Right, then I suspect Her Majesty would feel we have a moral responsibility to protect and rescue them.

"But when all we have is a balance of probabilities…"

He trailed off. He and Komarazhi had joined Rantala in the Commodore's office. The officer had put Kelzin's report up on a wallscreen and was busy at something on his desk Connor couldn't see. Like the man's dining room, Rantala's office was equipped with furnishings and wall panels that *looked* like wood but clearly still had all of the functions of the more-utilitarian pieces they'd replaced.

"I am torn," Komarazhi admitted. "These are my people, and I would see them at peace. I would suggest we support the side *against* the Kazh and its castes, but I know we lack the numbers to make a difference here.

"And my mother is somewhere down there, a prisoner or dead. I *want* to act, but I am but one voice." She shrugged, hands up in the reezh way. "I have no authority here; I know this. But I also feel that these ships may better my own people by surviving to join the relief of Chimera."

With a different senior officer, Connor would have been more concerned about restraining the Royal Navy than convincing them to fight. For a painful moment, he missed Roslyn Chambers. The Mage-Captain was somewhere on Garuda right then, either dead or fighting for her life. There had been no plan to get her to safety with the government and the stay-behind forces, and he worried for her fate.

Rantala looked up at them and his face was a mask of iron. Connor had never seen the Mage-Commodore look quite so harsh and determined.

"You two can be as conflicted as you want," he told them, his voice somehow both gentle and iron-hard. "*I* am the commanding officer of a deployed Task Group of the Royal Martian Navy, responsible for twelve thousand lives and over two hundred Mages.

"I am sworn to honor Her Majesty's oaths and protectorates, and I am sworn to honor the Compact between Mage and Mundane. It is the oath of every Mage that magic will serve humanity, not damn it."

There was a long pause and Connor wondered just what Rantala had been looking at on his own screen.

"I may not be a Mage by Right," Rantala concluded. "But seventeen of my Jump Mages and fifteen of my Combat Mages *are*, Ambassadors. Necessity meant that I had to bite my tongue and swallow my rage for this mission, even as we entered, and you treated with systems we *knew* murdered innocents to fuel their starships.

"But this? People given a chance to find the truth of their heritage and gifts threatened because they will not simply lie down and die to leave the status quo?

"No, Ambassadors. The Royal Martian Navy will *not* stand by and permit this to happen. If Mage-Queen Kiera herself ordered me to stand down, I would defy that order. Politics and constitution be *fucked*.

"Task Group Twenty-Eight is going to war. While I breathe, those children will *not be harmed*."

Connor met Rantala's flint-hard eyes and bowed his head. He had misunderstood, he realized. He had mistaken a self-control so iron that it had *hurt* for caution and potentially even cowardice.

He had been so very wrong.

"I am tasked by Her Majesty and the Parliament of the Protectorate to speak with their voice and to negotiate on their behalf," he told Rantala. "It is not in my remit to declare war on their behalf, but I know our Queen.

"As the senior civilian member of Her Majesty's Government present, you have my *full* support and endorsement for this effort, Mage-Commodore. And my personal gratitude."

Connor grinned.

"I believe Captain Kelzin can put me in touch with our soon-to-be allies," he continued. "In your opinion, Mage-Commodore, will that help your plan or hinder it?"

"I think surprise will be of the absolute essence," Rantala told him, a touch of the iron stiffness slipping away from his face. "I am, after all, about to attack seventy-plus warships with twelve warships."

"Thirteen, Mage-Commodore."

Connor and Rantala both looked at Komarazhi in surprise.

"Twelve means you are already leaving the supply ships undefended," the reezh Ambassador noted. "I believe we could use munitions and any technicians qualified on CSN systems that you can transfer before we jump, but I cannot ask Captain Joto to sit this one out.

"Nor, I believe, would the Prometheans aboard *Barracuda* permit it."

Connor expected Rantala to return to the bridge, but to his surprise, the man led them to *Last Stand*'s Flag Deck. There was a bare skeleton crew in the space, who scrambled to their feet as the ship's Captain and squadron Commodore entered the room.

"At ease," he ordered. "I need squadron-command links transferred here. Commander Sedona, I know we have protocols for interfacing with CSN ships. Find them—twenty minutes ago.

"I want a live all-Captains conference, including Joto, in ten minutes. We have two hours, people, before things are going to get hot in Ordin— and fate says we're playing firefighter.

"Get to it."

The half dozen officers and spacers in the room stared at Rantala for a few seconds, then turned to their consoles as one.

The Flag Deck was as different from the bridge as it could be to Connor's eyes. Where the bridge was a sphere, driven by the nature of the simulacrum chamber, the Flag Deck was a more-regular space, a box ten meters long by five wide. It was a single deck, with rows of consoles all facing toward the front.

At that front, there was enough space for several people to stand and work on a wallscreen that Connor suspected was mirroring the current tactical display. There was also enough space for the large holoprojectors he saw in the ceiling to do their work, providing the squadron CO with a three-dimensional view of his command.

"Ketil?" Connor asked, joining the Mage-Commodore in that open space.

"Sometimes, I can be a Captain and a squadron CO, but the moment I bring in an allied vessel, I have to stop pretending," Rantala told him. "*Last Stand at Alamo* was a prestige command, the second ship of a brand-new class, and I lost her within six months.

"The promotion is hardly a *bad* thing, but I barely got to know this ship. Now, though... I need to let go."

Rantala's problem was so far outside Connor's sphere of experience or expertise that all he could do was nod his understanding and sympathy. More sympathy than understanding, if he was honest, though the complaint made a surprising amount of sense overall.

Like a boxer squaring himself up to his opponent, Rantala squared his shoulders against the task ahead and opened a com link on his wrist-comp.

"Tonya," he greeted his XO quietly as a small holographic image of her appeared above his wrist. "I have to do something I should have done a bit ago."

"Sir?" Bourgeois asked, her tone at touch confused.

"You're now a brevet Mage-Captain," Rantala told her. "*Last Stand at Alamo* is yours. You've been doing the job since we left Mackenzie, while I've been pretending I had enough time left after managing the task group to also be our girl's Captain."

The tiny Bourgeois straightened to attention.

"I understand, sir," she said. "I... didn't feel that I was doing all of the work, sir, or I would have said something."

"That's because you were a better XO than I deserved and were already doing more than you should have," Rantala told her with a chuckle. "All-Captains call in seven minutes.

"We're making our plan to protect the Cadatch's school. Best guess is there's a hundred or so Mages by Right down there, doing everything they can to avoid having their brains scooped out—and some assholes who think that their brains *belong* in that scoop."

"Then *Last Stand* shall teach them the error of their ways, sir!"

The plan didn't call for Connor to contact the loyalists until they were in the system, so he followed Rantala into the all-Captains virtual meeting. The Mage-Commodore took over an empty room next to the Flag Deck that Connor realized was supposed to be the squadron CO's office.

All it had were the built-in wallscreens and holoprojectors; they had to bring in their own chairs. The equipment generated a fake table in front of them that merged with the desks of the thirteen starship commanders.

Except there were fourteen Captains, and it took Connor a moment to put a name to the last face. Mage-Commander Aslan Descoteaux was the CO of one of the auxiliaries, the tankers and freighters trailing behind TG 28 to make sure they didn't run out of fuel.

"Thank you all for coming," Rantala told them. "You know the Ambassador."

No one countered him. No one even seemed to blink at Descoteaux or Bourgeois's inclusion, either, and Connor guessed they were usual attendees, unlike him.

Joto was new, of course. Connor gave the reezh a firm nod, glad to see that they were looking significantly better than they had in the sickbay.

He supposed if they *hadn't* been doing better, they wouldn't have been back on their ship.

"Captain Joto has joined us at my invitation, as Ambassador Komarazhi has volunteered their services for the task before us," Rantala continued. "Given the odds we're looking at going up against, *Barracuda*'s firepower could make all of the difference.

"Captain, what is the status of your ship?"

"My crew is badly understrength," the reezh officer replied. "I have eight hundred personnel capable of standing their stations on a ship designed for a combat crew of over two thousand.

"I have two salvos of Excalibur Five missiles in my magazines, backed by five more of reezh missiles that we have retrofitted to fit." Joto chuckled. "Mostly by removing fuel, so we ended up with the same acceleration profile as our Excaliburs.

"All of our lasers are online and fully functioning, and we have the power supply to feed them. What I lack are the hands needed to operate the on-mount controls or perform damage control if we take hits.

"At this moment, Mage-Commodore, *Barracuda* is very much a glass falcon. We can strike, but the moment we take damage, we will lose effectiveness with no remedy."

"Thank you, Captain Joto," Rantala said. "That's more than I expected *Barracuda* to have, given the losses and damage you suffered."

"My crew who remain are dedicated and skilled. We have done all we can to make certain our vessel is combat-ready," Joto said.

"And your Prometheans? Are they capable of using the Prometheus Interface as a full amplifier?"

Connor didn't even know that was *possible*. From some of the expressions of Rantala's Captains, he wasn't alone in that lack of knowledge, either.

"Excuse me one moment," the reezh Captain replied before vanishing from the conference.

The confusion at Rantala's question was only added to by Joto's confusion. Connor was less confused by *that*, at least. He'd been at the dinner where Roslyn Chambers had pressed Admiral Emerson Wang to admit that there were surviving Prometheans in Chimera he hadn't told the Chimerans about.

People who worked with the Prometheans on a regular basis ended up quite protective of the young Mages who lived in their ships. A question like Rantala's, Joto was going to ask his Prometheans.

Not necessarily whether they *could* do what Rantala had asked—but if Joto should *tell* him if they could.

Rantala seemed to understand that and waited calmly for the thirty seconds it took Joto to return, waving away the handful of questions that were raised.

"Captain?" he asked when the reezh reappeared.

"I was not aware that such a thing was possible," Joto told Rantala. "But Lisa informs me that, yes, she is capable of using the Interface as an amplifier. She warns that she lacks full magical training, however, and has limited capabilities with it."

There was a long silence on the conference before Rantala spoke again.

"My thanks to Lisa for her courage," he said, in a tone that suggested he knew damn well the Promethean was listening.

"While the RMN was fighting the First Legion, we discovered that some of the Prometheus Interfaces had software and file libraries included that were designed to activate if the Promethean woke up," Rantala explained to the others. "One such Promethean, Sharon Deveraux, was instrumental in the liberation of the Exeter System and the rescue of the enslaved prisoners there.

"We are not certain by what logic Dr. Finley decided which Interfaces did or did not have those files, but we do know they *existed*. We are also not certain if the Interfaces can function as an amplifier if they *don't* have that software."

Connor nodded slowly. Combine that with the Protectorate's culture-wide PTSD over the mere *existence* of the former Republican Prometheans, it was no surprise that there hadn't been any testing.

"If we make it through the next twenty-four hours, Captain Joto, I will make it a personal priority that both Lisa and James receive as much magical training as we can manage," Rantala told Joto. "It seems the least we can do if they help us out today."

The Commodore now had everyone's attention, Connor noted. It was a neat trick, one he filed away in his own mental portfolio. Imply dramatic danger without specifying what was going on.

"Captains, we find ourselves in an awkward situation," Rantala told them. A tap of a command added the live feed from the Ordin System to the virtual conference.

"We know, from *Barracuda* and the notes they had from the elder Ambassador Komarazhi's mission, that there is a facility *here*, in this asteroid cluster, that the Cadatch described to So Komarazhi as meant to deal with the *lie about the Channelers*."

Connor *felt* as much as he heard the growl from the Captains. Every one of them except Joto was a Mage, and it seemed that *they* had been paying attention to the grotesque division among reezh Mages.

"We believe, from the presence of a major loyalist force here, that either the Cadatch or key members of his government fell back to the training facility," Rantala continued. "The asteroid holding it is heavily defended, enough that the rebel forces have blinked at attacking it so far."

"Until we drew the defenders out of position," Bourgeois guessed.

"Exactly. As we speak, the force that should be defending this place is shedding velocity to head back, but the rebel force that was shadowing them is pulling twice their acceleration. They will reach missile range in a bit over two hours.

"Both forces are led by a Type One, but the rebel force has twenty-seven of this system's asteroid monitors, giving them what we believe to be a significant advantage in firepower and survivability over the defenders.

"Barring any kind of intervention on our part, the force we've designated Flotilla Bravo will bring Flotilla Alpha into range and destroy them before they can reach the defensive umbrella of the school's defenses.

"They will then proceed to reduce the school's defenses. We're uncertain what will happen after that, but given the general tendency of the Kazh, I expect that either the students will be captured and *sacrificed*—or the entire facility will be destroyed by orbital fire."

Connor wasn't a Mage, and even he wasn't inclined to let either of those happen. It was clear that none of the Mages in the room were going to.

"So, what are we going to do?" Bourgeois asked.

"We are going to intervene," Rantala declared. "Let me be clear: we are badly outmassed, outgunned and outmatched. The single Type One can probably fight our entire task group to a standstill in a fair fight.

"Which means it can't be a fair fight, my friends. We have about an hour to put our heads together and come up with the nastiest knife-fight ideas we can all think of—and then we'll have another hour to put them into practice.

"Because while I am prepared to let Flotilla Alpha be a distraction, I am *not* going to let the only significant allied force in the region die because we didn't get there in time."

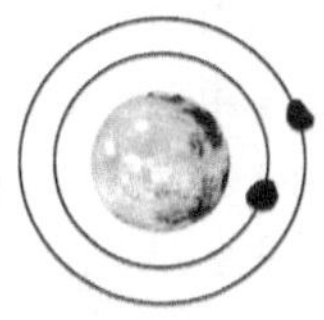

CHAPTER 32

MAGE-ADMIRAL JANE ALEXANDER WAS, in Connor's considered opinion, a bad influence.

Or possibly Roslyn Chambers was. He didn't know if she'd met Rantala at any point, but he knew that she'd drafted at least some of the skeletons Second Fleet's operations team had turned into the plans that had bought Chimera time for the last evacuation fleet to get clear.

He doubted he fully understood the level of risk that Rantala and his people were taking. All he knew for certain was that both the Commodore and Agent Ansel were insisting that he change into a shipsuit, the RMN uniform underlayer that acted as an emergency spacesuit.

While everyone else was preparing for what he hoped wasn't going to be a suicide charge, Connor obeyed that instruction.

He'd worn shipsuits before and was convinced they were one of the most uncomfortable garments ever invented by mankind—and this was coming from someone who was regularly forced into wearing a tie.

Still, after ending up in an emergency suit at the Fall of Chimera, he'd let Ansel talk him into having one custom-fitted. It was still stiff, chafing in some places, and felt like it was about to cut him in others, but it fit.

Once the underlayer was on, he looked at himself in the mirror and decided that there was *no way* he was going to be seen in the basically skintight outfit. It was clear that the RMN trained any sense of self-consciousness about bodies out of their people—a necessity for a coed working environment—but Connor was not *quite* so nonchalant.

He might work out to the point where he was perfectly confident that no one was going to *mind* seeing him in a skintight bodysuit, but he still couldn't quite bring himself to walk around in it.

The shipsuit's legs were *just* thin enough to allow him to put slacks on over it, but there was no way he was putting a regular shirt on. He was too large a man, and the shipsuit's main functions were mostly installed in the back, across his shoulder blades.

He could, however, put a suit jacket on over it and let the shipsuit act as his shirt. That seemed to work well enough... and his eyes fell on the concealed holsters.

Ansel would be pissed if he didn't wear one. Connor wasn't quite sure what kind of problem was going to result in his needing a gun on a spaceship, but...

Better to load for bear and face rats than load for rats and face bears.

He checked the speedloaders and self-test functions of his heavy revolver. It was a custom-smithed piece, with the most modern electronics matched to one of the most ancient forms of magazine. Each of its five cylinders was as large as his own thick thumbs, and the cartridges barely fit.

If *Last Stand at Alamo* was somehow boarded by hostile combat exo-suits, well, Connor O'Hannagain would have something to contribute.

More likely, though, he'd be contributing through a headset and a video pickup. He was more comfortable with that, anyway.

Connor found himself met at the Flag Bridge door by a Marine. Now that Rantala was actively using the space, there seemed to be more security.

"Ambassador? With me, please," the armored young woman greeted him. While there was another Marine standing by the armored hatch—currently open, as the cruiser prepared for action—this one appeared to have been waiting for him.

"Lead on, Corporal," Connor said, hoping he'd read her rank insignia—a single broad V, embroidered in gold—correctly.

He either got it right or she wasn't bothering to correct him. She led him through the Flag Deck to a seat that had been folded down out of the wall next to the CO's "pacing deck."

"Take a seat, sir," she told him. "The Mage-Commodore asked me to make sure you were secure and settled before things got heated."

Buried in the slew of suggestions and requests, Connor knew, was a command that even the Ambassador really shouldn't refuse. He gave the Marine a nod and took the indicated seat.

He wasn't surprised by the first safety belt the woman pulled out of the wall. The second and third *were* surprises, but by the time she was done securing him in place, he was confident that he wasn't going to be floating away if something dangerous happened.

She took the helmet from his hand and placed it on a hook within easy reach and then connected it to a small cable.

"Connect your suit umbilical here," she instructed.

It took Connor longer to find the thick cable-like tube than it had taken the Marine to belt him in and hook up his helmet, but she stood patiently while he sorted it out and slotted it into a port underneath the helmet.

"If you hit this release *here*"—she tapped just above a faintly glowing gray panel next to the umbilicals—"it will unlock and retract both the connectors and the safety belts. If it fails—it shouldn't, but it can happen—the umbilicals will release with a counterclockwise twist.

"The belt buckles have manual release levers on the bottom. Check them for me?"

Connor followed the instructions, locating the small metal protrusion on the bottom of each of the belts.

"Good. You shouldn't need any of this," she echoed. "But we're going into battle, and we would prefer not to lose the senior civilian. Sir."

"Thank you, Corporal," he told her. Despite her gruff manner, he could tell she was a bit concerned that he might take the somewhat condescending nature of the lecture the wrong way, but he understood.

The last time he'd been in a space battle, he hadn't been supposed to be aboard the warship—and *Mjolnir* was one of the largest and most powerful warships in existence, outclassing even the reezh Type Ones. There'd been a lot less thought put into keeping him safe.

He was never going to object to people trying to keep him safe. Especially since his secured seat still gave him a decent view of where Ketil Rantala was standing, watching the tactical display being relayed from *Rhapsody in Bohemia*.

"Range is fourteen million, four hundred thousand kilometers," someone reported. "Estimated missile range in forty-three seconds."

"Time lag?" Rantala asked.

This was clearly the Mage-Commodore's element, Connor realized. Rantala was calm and collected, projecting nothing but pure confidence as the clock ticked toward their engaging a vastly superior force.

"Current average range from scanners is one-point-five-four million kilometers, sir," the same man replied. "Time lag is five-point-one-three seconds."

"Thank you, Commander."

In Connor's experience, the bridge of a starship was rarely quiet. Flag Decks, on the other hand, seemed to be more-isolated spaces. Probably intentionally, he realized, to allow the officers in Rantala's position to think clearly, without the chaos of the ongoing management of a ship in conflict.

The Flag Deck was deathly silent as those seconds ticked away.

"Flotilla Bravo has fired. Exact numbers... hard to assess. Enemy jamming is less effective against the *Rhapsody* than our mainline arrays, but it's enough to confuse numbers of this magnitude. Estimate well in excess of ten thousand weapons."

"Understood. See if you can refine that prior to impact, Ops," Rantala ordered. "Break it down by launching class as well. If there's something fragile throwing above its weight, that may change our targeting plan."

"Yes, sir. Performance is as expected from *Barracuda*'s analysis, sir," the Commander continued. "Flight time approximately nine minutes."

Connor turned to see who was speaking. He didn't know the Black man standing at the front row of consoles, looking over his people's shoulders, but he could pick out two things at a distance: the man wasn't wearing the collar medallion of a Mage, and his insignia was the three wide bars of a Lieutenant Commander, not the three wide and one thin of a full Commander.

Either the man had been breveted like Mage-Captain Bourgeois or there was another of the courtesy things—like calling Rantala *Captain* aboard *Last Stand* until he'd officially given up command—the Navy had.

"No launch from Flotilla Alpha, sir," the officer continued. "They're holding their missiles to maximize effectiveness, I would guess."

"As would I, Mendelssohn," Rantala agreed. "I expect them to fire in about five minutes, depending on how rapidly Bravo decides to empty their magazines."

Connor had sat in on the planning sessions, but he hadn't followed most of it. He knew enough to know that they were going to let the battle begin and for Bravo to focus in on their enemy before engaging, but the details were beyond him.

"Bravo has fired again," Commander Mendelssohn said after what seemed like far too little time to Connor. "Ninety-second cycle. The Shining Shield could do significantly better, and the missiles are comparable, so I think they're limiting their long-range fire."

Rantala simply nodded at that, his gaze fixed on the icons marking over twenty thousand missiles hurtling toward the people they were hoping to save.

A third rebel salvo joined those icons, and even Connor was starting to feel a bit intimidated by the tsunami of red markers on the screen.

Everything they were watching was taking place over a light-year away. It couldn't impact Task Group Twenty-Eight until they chose to get involved, but that was a *lot* of missiles.

"Anything interesting popping up in the sensor feed from *Rhapsody in Bohemia*?" Rantala asked the officer standing behind him.

"The missiles are *too* similar to those the Kazh used at Chimera, sir," Mendelssohn said after a few seconds' analysis. "If I didn't have the time frame the development should have separated on, I'd have guessed they were only one or two generations away from the same source. Ten or twenty years of development—not two hundred."

"Isn't that interesting?" the Commodore murmured.

Connor was thinking the same thing. That suggested that either the former core worlds of the Reezh Ida had been passing technology back and forth more than the apparent cold war suggested—or that neither the Nine or the surrounding worlds had spared much effort for technological advancement over the centuries since the Burning.

If he knew which, that would tell him a lot about the cultures he was dealing with. He knew *reezh*, yes, but he knew *Chimeran* reezh, who had been an isolated colony under the Ida and had seen a global tech loss down to pre-nuclear levels before a human colony expedition had found them.

While there would be commonalities between the Primes and the Chimerans, their cultures could—*would*—be very different.

"Bravo has fired a fourth salvo—and Alpha has fired, sir. Estimate nine thousand missiles."

The blue icons of allied missile fire seemed paltry against the avalanche of fire coming from the rebel fleet, but Connor assumed the commander of the loyalist force had some idea what they were doing.

"Wait... new identifications. Eighteen...no. I have over *thirty* thousand missiles heading toward Flotilla Bravo," Mendelssohn said, his voice surprised.

"Oh, my," Rantala murmured, and Connor could *hear* the man's smile. "So, tell me, Commander, how many of those are missiles our friends pre-deployed into space while Bravo was firing, letting them fall back and engage their drives for time-on-target... and how many are decoys pretending to be half a dozen missiles?

"We *know* the Shining Shield had the latter, though they only triggered them at the final attack phase."

There was a surprisingly long pause.

"They couldn't possibly have the energy budget to maintain a decoy for the full nine-minute flight, sir. Could they?" Mendelssohn asked slowly.

"Our sensor data from Chimera suggested that all of the Shining Shield missiles had both full warheads and one of several ECM packages," Rantala replied. "If they removed the warhead assembly entirely and deployed a missile as a dedicated ECM platform? Would they be able to do that, Commander?"

The pause was almost as long before Mendelssohn nodded.

"From what we know of their miniaturized fusion tech, yes," he allowed. "Of course, if someone could identify the decoy missiles, they'd be able to ignore them completely. And if Alpha has those, why doesn't Bravo?"

"They probably do. But if you know you have a three-to-one advantage in launchers, you're going to go for brute-force ECM to get your missiles through," the Commodore told the man. "Because sometimes, the right answer to a problem *is* a hammer.

"In this case, though, it's believable that Alpha has stacked a salvo of missiles for every batch Bravo put into space. I bet you a fresh donut that their next salvo *doesn't* have any decoys or attempts to make it look bigger, which is part of the game."

Connor waited and watched. He had no advice to give the Commodore there. He didn't have anything to do, in fact, until about the third step of Rantala's plan.

"First missiles will impact in sixty seconds. Alpha has launched a second salvo, ninety-five-second cycle."

That seemed to mean something to Rantala, though all Connor got was that it was longer than Bravo's. He doubted that was good news.

"Size?"

"Under nine thousand missiles, but not by much. No extras," Mendelssohn confirmed. "I'll note I didn't take the donut bet, sir."

Rantala chuckled.

"No, you didn't, Ops. You might get to keep the flag-staff job after all."

The exchange was a pale attempt at humor. Connor could feel the weight on the Flag Deck as they watched the missile fire tear in on Alpha. The blue icons for allied units gleamed bright and true on the display, but three salvos would land on Alpha before their first massive salvo landed on Bravo.

"Set the clock," Rantala ordered, his voice still perfectly calm. "We will jump at T minus ten seconds from impact of Alpha's second salvo. Continue to update the arrival plot and target distribution until J minus thirty, Commander."

And then there was very little for anyone to do on *Last Stand at Alamo's* bridge but watch as missiles hammered in on the people they were trying to save.

There was a clear pattern to the display as icons moved. Each miniscule shift of blue represented millions of tons of starships and thousands of reezh moving through space at hundreds of kilometers per second.

"Interceptions commenced."

Zaur Mendelssohn's two words hung in the bridge for several seconds, the marker of the beginning of hell for people a long way away.

The definition of adventure, Connor supposed. He knew the blue icons vanishing from the screen was bad, but it looked like most of them were still there when the salvo was gone.

"Whoever is in command of Alpha is surprisingly good at their job for a fleet that I doubt has seen action in their lifetime," Rantala murmured. "Cold-blooded, too."

"Commodore?" Connor queried. He didn't want to interrupt, but he really wanted to know what was going on.

"We're still unclear on whether any of the ships that are *built* as starships actually have Mages aboard, living or dead," Rantala noted. "But we know the monitors and corvettes almost certainly don't.

"And Alpha put them in front, using them as a shield for the starships. The monitors took the brunt of the hits, but those things are built out of *asteroids*, Ambassador," he continued. "They lost six of them and the same number of corvettes—probably ten thousand dead, maybe more—but the same number of hits could probably have wiped out all four of Alpha's battleships."

From that explanation, Connor could follow how the next salvos went. The loyalist commander knew the strengths and weaknesses of their ships and was doing everything they could to preserve as much of their fleet as possible.

The big asteroid monitors, far more able to take hits than anything but the largest proper starships but carrying less firepower than the Type Twos and Ones, bore the brunt of that.

Alpha had started with twelve of them, and none of them survived the three salvos that hit the fleet before their own return fire reached the enemy.

Out of thirty corvettes, fifteen went with their larger sublight siblings, but over half of the loyalists' tonnage and firepower remained.

"And now it's Bravo's turn," Mendelssohn declared. "Even with *Bohemia*'s sensors, sir, it doesn't look like any of those missiles are decoys. I think they might have stacked everything they had into an alpha strike."

To Connor's eyes, they'd paid for that. Even at a range that he understood had to be impeding the reezh fire control, Bravo was firing *so many* missiles that Alpha's defenses just couldn't stand up to them.

But Alpha's stacked salvo was over twice as many missiles as Bravo had put in each salvo—and as Connor looked at it, the icons fuzzed out completely on the screen.

"Full terminal jamming just went online. We've lost track of them entirely." Mendelssohn paused. "We didn't have that problem with Bravo's missiles, though... *Bohemia* is closer to Alpha."

"The extra forty-odd light-seconds do make a difference," Rantala agreed. "J minus, Commander?"

"One hundred five seconds... now."

The jamming meant that no one aboard *Last Stand* could see how effective the missile strike was until after it had landed. *Well* after it landed, in fact—long enough that Connor had to wonder if they'd be able to reassess their own targeting.

"Antimatter hash is giving *Bohemia* problems, but it looks like they hit the rebels hard, sir," Mendelssohn finally reported. "All of the Threes and Fours are gone, plus the corvettes. I think they *tried* to put the monitors in the way like Alpha did, but Alpha's targeting was just better.

"Not sure of why they hit those ships, though."

"Most launchers per ton," Rantala explained. "They took out maybe a quarter more tonnage than Bravo did to them, but they took over a third again as many launchers. From their perspective, a solid win."

He snorted.

"Of course, from *our* perspective, I would have liked to be absolutely sure there's no amplifier on that Type One waiting to ruin our day, but here we are. I make it J minus thirty."

"J minus thirty... now," Mendelssohn confirmed. "All ships have checked in. Target distribution is basically unchanged from before. Only the Threes were on our list."

"Inform the Ships' Mages they are clear to jump on the mark," Rantala said. "We will execute as planned."

Connor was quite certain Flotilla Bravo never knew what hit them. *He* wasn't entirely sure what hit them, and he was in Rantala's command center!

He had the same countdown as everyone else to the moment of the jump. But despite the briefing and the experience of the Horatio maneuvers at the Fall of Chimera, he really didn't *get* what the officers and spacers of TG 28 were planning on doing.

From the isolated calm of the Flag Deck, there was a moment when all of the screens updated, and then things started happening too fast for Connor to follow. There was a twenty-five-second countdown, marking the plan for how long TG 28 would stick out in close range, and that was the only thing he followed.

Icons vanished from the display faster than he could even recognize which ones they were or what Rantala's people were hitting them with. He managed to establish where the rebel Type One was—eight hundred and fifty thousand kilometers "ahead" of *Last Stand at Alamo* on a line toward Flotilla Alpha—just in time to watch its icon flash red and vanish.

"Zero, zero. Jump, jump, jump!" Mendelssohn was suddenly shouting into his headset, a command to every ship in the Task Group—ships that had hopefully swapped Mages by now.

The screens flashed again as the Martian ships moved to a new location, and a full calm fell across the Flag Deck again.

"Report," Rantala said quietly.

"*Iago il Pappagallo* didn't make it," the breveted Operations Officer said quietly. "*Eye of Newt* and *Barracuda* are both reporting beam hits, hull breaches. Casualties unknown on either ship, but both Captain Joto and Captain Kumamoto's people report full combat capability."

"I'll hold them to that," the Commodore said grimly. "Task Group will activate Guardian-three. All ships are clear to fire missiles in counter-mode at will."

Connor shook his head, trying to clear the fog of barely thirty seconds of chaos he'd failed to follow. Thirty seconds that had apparently taken out a destroyer and killed over five hundred people.

Now, the surviving twelve ships of the Task Group rotated slightly in space and began to launch their own missiles. Connor wasn't sure whether they'd launched *any* of the antimatter-tipped weapons in the chaos of the close engagement, but now they did—a deadly stream of firepower targeted not on the survivors of Flotilla Bravo, over ten million kilometers distance, but on their *missiles.*

"Ambassador, we are sitting six million kilometers away from Flotilla Alpha and firing missiles," Rantala observed. "They should be able to tell quite quickly that we just shattered their enemy and are trying to protect them from incoming fire, but I imagine they will be happier if someone talks to them.

"If you and Miz Komarazhi could take over the squadron CO office and get in touch with them, that should help manage a problem I would prefer not to have," he concluded. "I had some work done in there."

"Am I… okay to get out of the safety gear?" Connor asked wryly, gesturing at the belts wrapped around him and suddenly aware of the gun pressing into his back.

"There were twenty-five seconds where you were in danger, Ambassador, and Flotilla Bravo wasn't ready for us," Rantala told him, then gestured at the screen. "There are maybe half a dozen monitors left out of that fleet, Connor.

"They hurt us, and I'm not going to enjoy telling the families of *Iago's* crew, but we just wiped out ten times our own tonnage and firepower. I hope that makes *your* job significantly easier!"

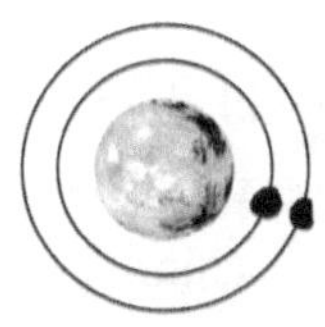

CHAPTER 33

MASTER CHIEF SINAGRA WAS WAITING just outside the office when Connor arrived, the noncommissioned officer seeming to hover as if wanting to hear that his people had done a good job.

"Where's Ambassador Komarazhi, Master Chief?" Connor asked.

"She's on her way, sir," Sinagra confirmed. "She was with the other civilians in one of the emergency safety bunkers; she shouldn't be more than a minute or two.

"Do you want to see what we set up for you two?"

"Carry on, Master Chief," Connor said with a chuckle. He was never going to stop someone from showing off, especially when said showing off was almost certainly to his advantage.

The door slid open at a touch, revealing a dramatically transformed space. It was still a plain steel utilitarian box—whatever supply of wood paneling Rantala had access to hadn't been applied to his new office yet—but it was no longer an empty box.

A table had been set up exactly one and a half meters from the back wall. Two chairs, probably among the best-looking ones on the cruiser—and probably the single best-looking *reezh* chair on the ship—had been arranged in matching spaces behind it.

Water glasses marked each spot, with small but clearly visible name tags bearing titles and the nations they represented marked who was meant for each seat, if the reezh-specific seat hadn't been enough of a clue. A carafe of fresh water sat between the two places, and both digital and physical note-taking equipment had been laid out in perfectly symmetrical patterns.

The wallscreen behind the table had been set to portray a starfield that even Connor recognized as an exterior view, focused away from the battle so as not to be interrupted by occasional explosions.

To the right of the table hung the flag of the Dual Republics of Chimera—the standard chimera of old European heraldry facing a stylized version of the equivalent reezh creature. To the left was the crowned mountain on a red planet of the Protectorate of Mars.

"Excellently done, Master Chief," Connor said. "Let your people know they did well."

Sinagra nodded gravely, but he smiled.

"I will. Do you and the reezh Ambassador need anything more?"

Connor glanced back at Adazh Komarazhi as she stepped into the room. Reezh weren't quite as obvious when they were out of breath as humans were, but she still looked like she'd pushed the pace to get there.

"Ambassador?" he asked her. "Is there anything more you think you will need?"

She took a quick glance around the room.

"No. I... did not expect this much," she admitted.

"The Master Chief wanted to put *Last Stand*'s best foot forward," Connor said. "And, Sinagra?"

"Ambassador?"

"The battle. Is it over?"

"We shot the heart out of the last few missile salvos before they reached the locals," the Master Chief told him. "There's still a few missiles in space, but the last salvo that reached them didn't manage to scratch anyone's paint."

"Good. Then let's get my part of this show on the road."

The pickup light flickered from amber to green, and Connor smiled broadly at it.

"Supporters of the Cadatch Izhom," he greeted his audience. "You advised us that we should leave your system for our own safety, to avoid getting entangled in the civil war harming your people.

"We took the time to assess what we could learn from your statements and the visit of the Chimeran cruiser *Barracuda* to your system. We were considering our next steps when my military escort realized that your maneuver to protect us against potential attack by your enemies had placed your military units in clear danger."

He paused, letting Komarazhi translate his words.

"We felt responsible for the situation we had put your defenders in, and we have chosen to intervene." He let that hang in the air. "We had other reasons, of course, some selfish and some otherwise.

"If you wish us to reintroduce ourselves, we will, but I believe we are now at a point where we would be best served by an actual conversation. I would speak with Cadatch Izhom or whoever is in charge at this facility on his behalf.

"We have some concept of what has been hidden on the asteroid ahead of us. As a token of our respect for that effort and of hope for future relations, we will not draw our forces any closer than this until we receive permission to approach."

Not mentioning, of course, that even TG 28 was in range for lasers if not the warship's amplifiers. *Rhapsody in Bohemia* went unmentioned entirely.

The light turned amber after Komarazhi was done translating, and Connor leaned back in the chair. The seat was more impressive than it was comfortable, and he was surprised that the Navy had anything aboard the cruiser that was so obviously decorative.

"These are reezh," he said to his companion. "What do you think?"

"I think that they are reezh from the Primes, from the worlds that agreed to make the rest of the colonies dependent on them for key technologies," she pointed out. "And reezh who have spent centuries keeping the Kazh from their door.

"I fear I know them no better than you. I *think* they will meet with us, but they will want more from you than they can offer us. If nothing else... they will want help to win their war."

"And we cannot provide that help," Connor conceded. "Not soon enough, even if the fleet needed were at Mackenzie or Exeter."

He thought that Second Fleet, even in its reduced state, would be more than enough. The balance of power between the two sides had been stabilized by the destruction of Flotilla Bravo.

That wasn't his call to make, though. If that was what the Ordin ended up needing, he would talk to the Alexanders—the Mage-Admiral would tell him if it was possible, and the Mage-Queen would tell him if it was going to *happen*.

Kiera, he assessed, would rather intervene if she could, but it would fall to Alexander to judge whether they actually could. In many ways, Connor's job was to say no for the Mage-Queen of Mars, because his young monarch possessed far too kind and giving a heart.

If half of what the people around Connor figured was going on in this system was true, though, he wasn't sure that *he* didn't think they should intervene.

Which left the question of could they... or, while being potentially the *right* call, whether it was a *wise* call.

There were days that Connor hated his job.

He needed more information to decide if today was turning into one of them.

"They're continuing to decelerate in to the dwarf planet, which is a response in itself," Rantala told them on the intercom five minutes later. "The last of the missiles are gone and they haven't fired anything at us, so I'd say they heard your message and someone is thinking about what to say back."

"Agreed," Connor said. "What are the bad guys doing?"

The Commodore paused for a second, then sighed.

"Flotilla Orandar broke off their approach, which is good news. Even combining our ships with Alpha, I wouldn't want to take on a pair of Type Ones."

"And bad news?" Komarazhi asked, the reezh clearly having picked up the same thing as Connor.

"Flotilla Orandar is now en route to a rendezvous point with Flotilla Charlie, which has left a small force behind at the main asteroid habitats and is now heading in our direction. Flotillas Echo and Foxtrot have also started heading our way at full speed.

"We *think* that Echo is loyalist and was making a subtle approach to this cluster to keep their shadow, Foxtrot, from jumping the gun. Now that Alpha has been kicked in the teeth, Echo is burning this way at four reezh gravities. They're over six light-minutes away, so even at a punishing pace for folks without magical grav, they're almost a day and a half away.

"Right now, Foxtrot is in pursuit, but their course is slightly off. We think they're also maneuvering to rendezvous with Charlie. Charlie, for their part, is sticking to one reezh gravity to give everyone time to catch up."

"How bad does that look when it adds up?" Connor asked.

"In about seventy hours, two *billion* tons of rebel warships are going to drop in on the loyalists like that asteroid's a pinata with candy inside," Rantala said bluntly. "And the defense is going to have less than half of that, even with us.

"Everything else is either at Four or on course to Four with too much velocity to shed and pull back," he continued. "It's possible we can punch the rebels hard enough in the nose here to tip the balance in favor of the loyalist forces there against what's left, but I'm not seeing a clear path here, Ambassador.

"I think—"

"Sir, incoming transmission from the main asteroid," Lieutenant Commander Senft interrupted. Connor suspected that the usual military protocol said she shouldn't interrupt the Commodore, but this was what they were waiting for.

"Connect it to the Ambassador, though make sure I get a copy," Rantala ordered. "Connor, this part is yours."

"I've got it, Commodore. I needed the background. Thank you."

Rantala's image gave him a nod, then vanished. A holographic screen appeared above the desk Connor shared with Komarazhi, projecting a two-dimensional video recording.

A twenty-four-second round trip was short enough that they could manage a live link, but it would be awkward enough that he was fine with recordings.

The video was of a tall reezh in a dark blue robe, with a skin pattern he'd only seen once before: on Razhkah, the Reezh Ida Lachai—the *only* Chimeran reezh Mage he'd ever met, as well as the woman charged with maintaining the archives of everything the Chimerans knew of the old Reezh Ida.

She had smooth white skin with pale, almost invisible, gray patterns, reminding Connor of fine porcelain. The stranger didn't have the various markings that told someone Razhkah was old, but her coloring was far too similar for him to believe in coincidence.

The stranger spoke in reezh. Connor had only the most basic understanding of the language, but it was enough for him to know when *Last Stand*'s computer was getting things wrong. An earbud fed him a live translation, and he hoped Komarazhi would correct anything majorly wrong.

"Greetings to Ambassador O'Hannagain of the Protectorate," the woman said. "I am Naizha, Director of the Academy on Dahnvangan. I speak for my brother, Izhom, Cadatch of the Ordin, and I lead here on Dahnvangan, so much as anyone leads."

Dahnvangan meant *Forge of Shields* or something similar, Connor knew. Presumably that was the asteroid that held the Academy—and the Academy had to be the school they were looking for.

"Your assistance in our conflict was not looked for or asked for," she continued. "But it was welcome. High Commandant Poitch is impressed with your courage and skill; she believes your attack path would be beyond her people, even if all of her ships were equipped with Guides of the Astral and the Astral Mechanisms for such an action."

Connor had no idea how the ranks for reezh militaries worked—even assuming that they all used the same ranks!—but he guessed that High Commandant Poitch outranked Forward Commandant Sujam. Quite likely, Naizha had the original top officer of Ordin's military on her side.

Shame that clearly hadn't been enough to keep all of the military on one side of the civil war.

"I have to admit that I am surprised to see a live human on a screen here in Ordin," Naizha said after a momentary pause of her own, and Connor couldn't stop himself jerking back in his chair in surprise.

There was no reezh word for *human*, so far as he knew. Naizha had used the *English* word—and as he cast his memory back to how he'd introduced himself, he didn't think he'd used the word.

The Chimerans aboard *Barracuda* might have, but the original plan had been for them to never even mention the other half of the Dual Republics. Connor hadn't heard anything from Joto to suggest they'd done so, either.

Which meant that either *Barracuda*'s electronic security had completely failed or Naizha had known what humans were before the Chimeran ship had ever reached this star system. That possibility raised *far* too many questions.

"Your presence here, Ambassador, answers several questions my brother and I had about our cousins in the Allosch System," she continued. "Questions few others might have even thought to ask, but it seems that we are not alone in keeping secrets.

"I think you and I should speak in person. Debts are owed, Ambassador, and not just the ones from today. I will have Poitch's people transmit instructions to your fleet for orbiting Dahnvangan.

"I ask that you only bring one shuttle, with an escort for both of your Ambassadors. You are welcome to bring a military observer as well, though these discussions may not intrigue them as much as the conversations I believe they will have to have with the High Commandant."

The message ended, and Connor stared at the empty screen like Naizha had reached out of it and slapped him.

"How does she know what a human is?" Komarazhi asked. "And what debt does she speak of?"

"I don't know for certain," Connor told her. "And the reasons I can guess just leave me with more questions than answers."

"So, what do we do?" the younger diplomat asked.

"We accept her kind invitation and visit her Academy with the Mage-Commodore," he replied. "And while the task group makes our way there,

I have a call to place."

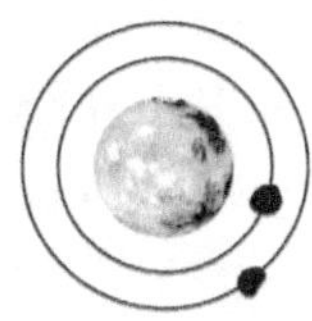

CHAPTER 34

"NO, WE WANT *Rhapsody in Bohemia* to stay dark for now,"
Rantala told Mike. "These people are friendly, but we can only extend so
much trust.

"Right now, I actually need you to move *away* from Dahnvangan,"
he continued. "I want the path the main rebel force is going to take to
get here covered by sensor platforms, whatever you can manage—while
keeping yourself cleanly out of harm's way."

"We probably have the ability to play submarine here," Mike told the
Commodore. "If we can pick out a flagship, I think we can get within
amplifier range if we go sublight and stay cold."

There was a long pause, and then O'Hannagain spoke up.

"We've had these stealth ships since, what, the middle of the war with
the Republic?" the diplomat asked. "And we knew Republic scanners
inside and out. So, why hasn't anyone done that *yet?*"

Mike grinned.

"Because it's only slightly less risky than the stunt you pulled with the
task group," he told them. "I have to cut even the cold thrust at about five
million klicks, I judge, so I'm waiting on them to overhaul *Bohemia* for
what could be hours, and I get one shot—and our only chance to survive
is to jump before they see us.

"Our massed missile and laser armament isn't going to take out anything worth the risk, so the amplifier is the only weapon we have for the
trick."

And the amplifier, in the hands of most Mages, had a range of around ten to eleven light-seconds. He was confident that Xi could wreck even a Type One if they got to about eight light-seconds, but the odds of them staying undetected without a convenient asteroid were low.

"We'll keep that trick as an option," Rantala finally said. "There may be better uses for your ship, though. It's going to depend on our conversations with the locals."

"What kind of uses are we thinking here?" Mike asked. *Rhapsody in Bohemia* was an extremely specialized vessel, and *being sneaky* wasn't a specialty that could tip the tide of a battle without something like targeted assassination.

"I'm not certain," the Commodore admitted. "But there are dozens of theoretically jump-capable ships in the rest of this star system that could make a massive difference if we got them here.

"If we can transport Mages—ours or theirs, it *shouldn't* matter too much—out to any ship with a jump matrix, that could give the defense of Dahnvangan a shot in the arm."

Mike could see that. He wasn't enthused with the idea of sticking Ordin Mages on his ship for even a single trip, but the value was there.

"But right now, you need me to provide eyes," he concluded, summarizing Rantala's first ask.

"We do," Rantala confirmed.

"And to stay on the line," O'Hannagain added, "because it's always possible that Her Majesty is going to get... excited over the latest."

Mike Kelzin wouldn't say that he knew the Mage-Queen of Mars personally. On the other hand, he'd sat down to dinner with her in a room with less than thirty people, which meant he came closer than the vast majority of her citizens.

There were advantages to your wife being the friendly ex of the man who ran the Mage-Queen's government, after all. But Mike normally left dealing with the people at Kiera Alexander's level up to Kelly, viewing his role in those meetings as being a mix of decoration and moral support.

That call, though, only had three people on it from Ordin: Mage-Commodore Rantala, Ambassador O'Hannagain and Mike Kelzin. On the Mars side, there was only Kiera Alexander.

But Mike wasn't going to admit that he didn't think he belonged in the conference. He might defer to his wives on their areas of expertise, but he was never going to *argue* with being in the room where it happened.

"She knew what a human was," O'Hannagain concluded. "And I don't think, from what she said about *debts*, that they learned it from breaking into *Barracuda*'s computers."

"From what we were promised, *Barracuda*'s computers wouldn't have had any information on the humans on Chimera, let alone us," Kiera told them. "If they broke in far enough, they would have had visuals of the human technicians still running key systems aboard, but that wouldn't have given them a name."

"I agree," O'Hannagain said. "Which leaves me only one possible conclusion, Your Majesty."

Oh.

MISS was an intelligence agency, which meant that information was tightly compartmentalized and controlled on a need-to-know basis. But Mike Kelzin had been the partner and right hand of a key MISS Director for longer than Kelly LaMonte had *been* an MISS Director.

Plus, he'd been in charge of this mission, which meant he'd been read in on the Tartarus File.

"You think the reezh from Mars came here?" Mike asked, voicing the thought before it had even fully formed in his head. "We don't know what happened to them, after all."

"We know that if there was a reezh somewhere on Mars, it was in the Keepers' vault," Kiera told him grimly. "One of the small fragments we've picked up since Nemesis decided to murder those poor idiots is that there was at least one reezh *body* stored in there.

"Before they nuked it to keep Damien out."

That wasn't information included in the official Nemesis File, Mike reflected. Somehow, he wasn't at all surprised that the nuclear detonation of the Keepers' main base and storage facility had involved Damien Montgomery in his active Hand days.

"We're thinking the reezh split? Some stayed on Mars to finish the job, and the rest tried to come home, only to find that home was gone?" Mike asked. "It would be interesting to know what they split over—or if it was a regularly scheduled swap and the new team never showed up."

"That's the kind of thing I hope you can learn from Naizha," Kiera told the Ambassador. "Preferably without committing Mage-Commodore Rantala to a suicide stand above that asteroid."

"If the Academy is what I think it is, Your Majesty, the only reason I *won't* be standing in Dahnvangan's defense will be because we have evacuated everyone involved," Rantala said firmly. "We are not leaving innocent Mages to the hands of people who will turn them into brains in jars; I don't care how many knees and elbows they have."

"I understand where you're coming from, Ketil," Kiera Alexander said gently.

Somehow, the entire atmosphere of the virtual conference changed. Mike didn't think there'd been an active change, but suddenly Kiera felt larger, almost looming as she effortlessly switched on an aura of authority he'd never seen on her before.

"I even agree with your intention and desire," she continued. "If you see a way to successfully defend or rescue those people, you have my full support to do so. But you will not sacrifice your ships and your people for nothing.

"Am I clear?"

There was a surprisingly long silence before Rantala finally nodded.

"I understand, Your Majesty. I... I understand," he repeated. "But I don't want to leave these people to this, and it feels wrong to just pull out the Mages."

"Then come up with a plan, Ketil," Kiera told him, still using his first name. "What I *want* is to see the Ordin System stabilized and brought in on our side as allies, preferably with all of their resources intact."

"The answer seems straightforward," Mike said, looking at the icon marking Orandar on his displays. "We need Naizha to tell us where

Izhom is, and then we deliver him to the amplifier, and *he* solves the problem for us."

He shook his head.

"Of course, the fact that *no one* has used the amplifier since this kicked off says that things are not that straightforward," he conceded. "Quite possibly, the amplifier has been ruined. Do we know if they can fix it?"

"We couldn't," Kiera admitted. "But we don't know how much of that knowledge the Primes and the Nine retain. That's..." She chuckled bitterly and waved vaguely toward O'Hannagain. "That's the light at the end of the tunnel, as far as some of our more cold-blooded politicians are concerned.

"The prize we get out of winning this war. We liberate Chimera, break the Nine, ally with the Primes—and in exchange, we find out where the gaps in the magical knowledge base the Eugenicists stole from the reezh are."

"We're still an hour out from orbit," Rantala finally said into the silence that followed that. "I'll go through options with my people, but I suspect that any real planning will wait until I can sit down with this High Commandant."

The conference closed down, leaving Mike in his intentionally plain office, staring at an empty coffee cup. He was close enough to a starship tactician to know that there were no easy solutions to the situation they found themselves in.

The kind of suicidal jump strike they'd pulled to take out the first of the Aha Kadak's flotillas couldn't be repeated against an enemy who knew what was coming. He'd reviewed the sensor data from the Fall of Chimera—the reezh had *very* good sensors and automatic weapon-firing algorithms.

And Mages. The fleet at Chimera had demonstrated that while many of the Kazh's ships used Prometheus Interface-style murdered Mages, they had real amplifiers and living Mages on key vessels.

Growling to himself, Mike rose and grabbed his coffee cup. The nearest coffeemaker was on the bridge, and he needed to pass on the movement and scouting orders to his people.

Everyone looked up as he stalked out of his office.

"Captain?" Fischer asked.

Mike gave them a vague acknowledging wave as he walked over to the coffeemaker. Some saint had put on a fresh pot, allowing him to fill up with new coffee and take a long swallow of the too-hot beverage.

"Give me a minute," he said after gasping against the heat. "Once I've recovered from my momentary lapse of intelligence, I'll put together a course swinging us out toward Flotilla Charlie."

"Charlie?" the Tactical Officer asked, then made a thoughtful noise. "The rebels are concentrating their forces on them, so the major assault will come on that vector line."

"Exactly. And we want eyeballs on it," Mike confirmed. "I'm regretting the lack of Link-equipped sensor buoys right now, but we work with what we've got. We set up an array to give the Navy the best possible data for identification and targeting, if it comes to the latter.

"Then we're to get clear of their approach vector and wait for further orders. There are a lot of questions in the air with the locals, and Mage-Commodore Rantala would like us to be around once he has enough answers to make plans."

He met his wife's gaze and gave her a tiny shrug he didn't think anyone else would identify.

"We're the best spy ship MISS has got, which makes us the best ship in the galaxy at sneaking and peeking, folks," he reminded everyone. "So, we'll get the Commodore his view of the incoming threat, and then we'll wrack our brains to see what clever ideas *we* can come up with."

He grinned broadly.

"Because I got shot down on *sneak into the middle of the enemy fleet and have Xi nuke the Type One sending the most radio signals*," he told them. "We might still end up doing that, depending on how the situation evolves, but everyone seems to think there are cleverer uses for us than duplicating a naval-war submarine!"

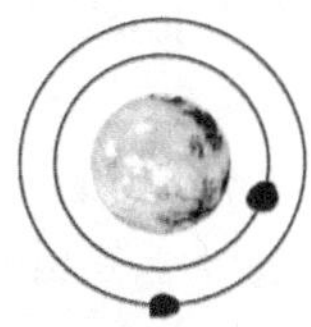

CHAPTER 35

EVEN WITH THEIR LOSSES, the warships of Flotilla Alpha made for an intimidating shield above the asteroid Dahnvangan. Task Group Twenty-Eight was positioned on the far side of the defenses and defenders alike, leaving the shuttle carrying Connor and his companions with a surprisingly long flight.

It had taken the entire task group, keeping their acceleration to a "gentle" ten gravities, just over three hours to reach orbit of the planetoid from their position twelve light-seconds away.

It took a full hour for the shuttle from *Last Stand* to cross the thirty thousand kilometers between the cruiser's final position and the asteroid itself. Komarazhi sat up in the cockpit, translating the verbal commands from the Academy's ground control, while Connor and Rantala sat in the back with the three Marines who would escort them in.

"Well, now I can see why they weren't going faster before," Rantala noted. The screens around them were showing optical feeds of the vessels around them and the Commodore was studying the ships.

"Oh?"

"That was the reason the others were able to catch up to them," Rantala explained. "They didn't accelerate as fast. And now I see why."

He pointed to a section of the wall that he'd zoomed in on the feed, highlighting the largest of the loyalist ships.

"This is their Type One," he told Connor. "It might be the biggest of them that I've seen, including the Cozhan ships that showed up at

Chimera. Hard to eyeball from here, but just comparing length to width, she's got to be nearly two and a half klicks long. Maybe as much as eighty-five million tons."

Every reezh starship they'd encountered so far, Connor was told, was built on the same basic principle: a cylinder two hundred meters across, varying in length to meet the desired size. Even the corvettes followed that form, resulting in disks little more than a dozen meters thick.

"Does her mass make her slower?" Connor asked—but even as he asked the question, he saw what Rantala was pointing out and shook his head at his own lack of understanding.

The scorch marks across the leviathan's hull were visible in the zoom. They streaked down her armor, leading to a massive gouge where her flanks met her base.

"No, but having a good third of her engines wrecked definitely did," Rantala replied, his wry tone suggesting that he'd caught Connor's recognition of the problem. "I'd guess that she got hit hard when the shield split into the two factions. That's an ion-cannon strike, I think, and I don't think whatever ship landed it lived to tell the tale."

"Because if they had, she wouldn't be here?" Connor asked.

"Exactly. The damage is too isolated to be from a sustained battle. That was a surprise attack, a traitor's backstab," Rantala said quietly. "We need to step carefully, Connor. These people have just had every certainty and expectation of their future and reasonable behavior shattered.

"I don't think reezh are different enough from us for that to not to leave a mark. They're going to be twitchy, they're going to be..."

"Wounded?" Connor suggested. "Paranoid? Suffering a level of professional and structural PTSD? I know, Commodore. I know."

He might prefer for Rantala to keep his oars out of Connor's waters, but since the Commodore was going into the Academy with him, he supposed he could forgive a level of nervousness.

"Fair, Ambassador; apologies," Rantala said, which helped with the forgiveness. "What happens now?"

"I talk to Naizha," he replied. "Until I have, I can't say anything for sure. There's too many question marks—including the fact that, as Captain

Kelzin pointed out, there's a bloody *I win* button in this star system and no one seems to have used it!"

"Any guesses as to why?"

Connor shook his head.

"Several, but I don't want to prejudice myself or you," he told Rantala. "Let Naizha tell us. It's her system, her people... and her brother who's supposed to have the big button."

Their directions brought the shuttle into a sunken hangar on the surface of Dahnvangan. When their pilot settled the spacecraft down, a large hatch slid closed above them, blocking the distant light of Ordin's star or the closer glows of the satellites, refineries and warships orbiting the planetoid.

Connor led the way off the shuttle, magnetic boots clicking as he approached the airlock. The asteroid's gravity was less than a twentieth of Earth's, and the boots would keep them grounded, assuming the Academy had metal decks.

"We've linked up with a docking collar from the locals," the pilot declared. "Air content is reezh-standard, so it'll be a bit cold and dry for the humans but perfectly breathable."

Connor nodded and opened the airlock with a tap on the control console. He cycled through the two doors and found himself in a metal-floored transparent tube that angled down toward the hangar deck.

The docking collar and boarding tube were empty, and he followed it to the side of the hangar space, where an airlock large enough for all six of them waited. The outer door was open, but there was still no one waiting for them.

"I'm not sure I like this," the senior Marine said, her hand dropping onto her slung rifle.

"Different cultures, Sergeant," Rantala told her. "And, well, they have to have expected us to bring a Mage. Everything is under control."

Sometimes, Connor forgot that the Mage-Commodore was just that. Rantala wasn't one of the Mages who demonstrated their power at every opportunity, though he wasn't wearing the same mag-boots as the rest of them were.

"We've come this far" was all Connor said before walking into the airlock, counting on them to follow him.

The Marines couldn't hang back when their charges walked right in. The airlock had plenty of space for them all—Connor suspected that it could have held the *shuttle*, let alone the passengers.

As soon as the last Marine stepped over the threshold, the airlock door slid slowly closed. Only then did Connor notice that both the airlock doors and the chamber itself were hexagons instead of the rectangular shape he'd normally expect.

The ceiling and floor were about what he'd normally see, but instead of the walls being vertical, they were made of two planes that converged at a shallow angle. It was a small difference, but one that he'd only seen once or twice even on Garuda.

Before his mind could fully fall into the rabbit hole of comparative architecture, the inner airlock door opened and there was a resounding crash of metallic boots slamming to the ground.

Sixteen reezh in gleaming white armor had come to attention in a single matched motion. Each held a sword in a reversed two-handed grip, the tip held *just* above the floor.

They formed an honor guard for Connor and his companions—in a hexagonal shape, he absently noted as he nodded an acknowledgement he hoped they understood.

He led the way forward with only a moment of hesitation. The absence of people outside the airlock hadn't prepared him for the ceremony, but this was what he *did*.

Three reezh, including the very recognizable Naizha, waited at the far end of the honor guard. The reezh to Naizha's left wore the same robe she did, though theirs was in a pale rose pink—and they had the pebbled gray skin tone that seemed to form the reezh baseline in his experience.

The reezh to her right wore what was unquestionably a military uniform. It didn't match those of the Reezh Ida from the historical files—those had been long tunics over a shipsuit equivalent—but the short carmine jacket was all sharp lines, and the purpose of the metal plate at the front of her right shoulder was obvious.

The plate held a single planet, constructed from what appeared to be emeralds and sapphires.

"Adazh," he murmured as they stepped up in front of Naizha.

"Greetings to the people of Ordin," Komarazhi began with barely a blip. The earbud in Connor's ear—linked to his wrist-comp with backup from the shuttle computer if needed—translated her reezh for him, but he was still limited to his limited fluency for *speaking* the language.

"Greetings to the Ambassadors of the Protectorate and Chimera," Naizha replied, bowing elegantly. "Be welcome to the Academy, what was once hoped to be the future of Ordin."

"It may still be," Connor said, with Komarazhi translating. "Certainly, you are gathering much here to protect it."

"You are no soldier, Ambassador, but I suspect you can do math," the reezh officer growled, her voice low and gravelly even for a reezh. "Our enemies have struck more deeply than we could have feared. Reezh I knew were true have turned on us.

"Faith, it seems, can break all bonds."

"That is a discussion for later," Naizha told the officer, placing her hand on their uniform sleeve. "Ambassadors, be known to High Commandant Poitch, the appointed leader of the Dahn Ordin. And this is Academician Troth, the proof of all of our efforts here."

Troth was the reezh in the pink robe and bowed slightly to them. Poitch simply gave them an acknowledging nod.

"Come," Naizha instructed. "We have much to discuss and, as Poitch reminds me with her every breath, little time to do it in."

"We could release Poitch and Mage-Commodore Rantala to discuss our military situation," Connor suggested.

Naizha seemed to hesitate as Komarazhi finished translating, but then made a negating gesture with her hands.

"If your military commander is also a Mage, then what we must discuss involves them as well," she declared. "Your escorts will be content, I hope, with remaining outside the door? I will bring no Paladins into the room with us."

"That will suffice," Connor agreed, without even looking at the Marines. They might object, but right now, he *needed* to know what Naizha had to say with a drive that surprised him.

CHAPTER 36

THE ACADEMY WAS SURPRISINGLY DECORATIVE in its design. Almost delicate in a way, with the initial corridors leading into a vast open cavern, probably left behind by mining work on the planetoid.

That cavern had enough lighting on the ceiling to support a garden that was a clear mix of practical and decorative, with multiple types of plants woven around the paths—and massive hydroponics arrays stacked along one wall, not quite concealed by the trees planted in front of them.

The first reezh they saw were definitely soldiers, in similar hex-cut jackets to the High Commandant, but the security quickly faded as they entered the atrium. In there, half a dozen pink-robed reezh were clearly leading classes, each of them accompanied by seven or eight reezh in brown robes.

As they were leaving the atrium to head deeper into the Academy, the delicate and decorative design continued. It was all carved from the stone, with metal plates laid on the floor for people using magnetic boots, but a clear sense of purpose and beauty had been invested in the space.

"Here." Naizha came to a stop at what Connor had initially taken for a decorative pattern on the wall. Part of the pattern turned out to be a hexagonal control panel that unlocked a door.

"There are seats here," she continued, benches emerging from the walls as she worked at the control panel. "We do not have anything designed for humans, I am afraid, but these should work for both our peoples."

"We're Marines," the Sergeant told Connor. "We'll be fine with benches designed for an extra knee."

Komarazhi giggled and translated the sentiment, if not the exact words, to Naizha.

Then Connor followed the woman into the room. It was, not entirely to his surprise, a lecture hall, its purpose obvious even to eyes raised in an entirely different culture and that had gone to entirely different schools.

It was a hexagonal space with a sunken center. The outer platform had a circle of desks that appeared to be bolted into the floor—a wise precaution in the minimal natural gravity. Like the room itself, the desks were a mix of metal and stone, but someone had put thought into their design. Simple but graceful geometric scrollwork framed each surface, with a smaller pattern in the desk marking the built-in console.

"Please, sit," Naizha instructed them all. She walked down into the central stage, probably an automatic habit, and waited for them all to take seats around her.

"Adazh Komarazhi," Naizha finally said, looking at the reezh Ambassador. "I can see her in your face. You are So's daughter."

"You met my mother?" Komarazhi asked.

"I did. There are needs and directives that keep me away from Orandar, but my brother wanted me to meet So Komarazhi and judge her. Mine was always the subtler magic of the two of us.

"Your mother was wise, if unskilled for the task before her. But who of us was prepared to speak with others of our race beyond our own stars? Since the fall of the Reezh Ida, we have been a scattered race."

"Since the Burning."

Connor hadn't been going to use the phrasing himself, but he couldn't blame Rantala for the interruption, either.

Naizha gave the Commodore a questioning look, and Komarazhi quickly translated.

"Not a term we use, but one whose meaning is clear to any who know what occurred," she told them. "An elegant summation of the atrocity the Reezh Ida committed that destroyed it. An atrocity, like so many others in our past, born of lies."

Connor let that hang.

"The story of how this war in Ordin began," Naizha said. "The story of how I know who your people are, Ambassador O'Hannagain. The story of the Burning. These are all linked, all bound together by the blood of untold innocents and a Lie that has endured far past its time."

"The lie that a Channeler is not a Mage." Komarazhi translated Connor's stark statement and the reezh leader seemed to study him.

"Yes. A Lie, I hope, that your people never suffered from."

"There are divisions among our Mages, but they are all Mages," Connor assured her.

"Then my ancestors' crimes had one righteous return." Naizha looked away from them all.

Connor's companions took their lead from him, and he could tell that she had a story she needed to tell them. He waited and the others waited with him.

"I doubt that your Mage-Queen sent you into our stars without knowing everything about our people that could be shared," the reezh teacher finally said. "So, you must have wondered why, amongst all the reezh you had met, none remembered Mars."

"In truth, it made sense that the Chimeran reezh didn't know of us," Connor told her. "But when we encountered the Kazh, it seemed clear that they knew nothing of us either."

"Because of the Burning and the Lie," Naizha replied. Even across the language barrier, he picked up the capital *L*.

"Your ancestors... were part of the expedition to Mars?" he asked as the silence dragged on.

"Yes. They made an alliance with a group of your people, a group whose motives and goals were strange but aligned with what the expedition needed. The Eugenicists."

That word, like *humans*, was English.

"Of course, so far as my ancestors knew, they were lying to your people," Naizha noted. "They told the Eugenicists the tests would allow them to breed this power back into your people, but they knew that only the bloodlines of the Priest-Mages, the Astrally Gifted, could produce *true* Mages.

"The tests and mechanisms they used to guide the Eugenicists' workings were intended to detect Channelers, not the true Gifted. They knew this. They were deceiving the Eugenicists to produce a new stock of Channelers, one whose sacrifice would reduce the burden on the Ida itself and perhaps prevent the fracture they saw coming."

Connor could *feel* Rantala's tension. The Mage-Commodore was a descendant of Project Olympus, which meant it was quite directly his ancestors who had been captive in Olympus Mons, generation after generation subjected to testing and then forced to have children at sickeningly young ages to keep the project going.

Few of even the *successes* had lived past twenty, and the Fields of Sorrow on the slopes of Olympus Mons held tens of thousands of nameless dead, the only markers monoliths listing the numbers the Eugenicists had given them—and even *those* had been raised after their creators had been thrown down.

All of it created by the reezh. To find a new *fuel source*.

"What my people did to yours cannot be excused," Naizha told them. "As I said, there is a debt owed, one beyond accounting. More than you even think, though, because it was through the lie my ancestors *thought* they had told the Eugenicists that they discovered the true Lie.

"They expected to need to fake magical capability on the part of the later generations, using their own gifts to provide some level of success to keep the project going. Instead, before the candidates reached the levels of astral connection where they planned to begin that deception, some of the students began to wield real magic."

"How did they know?" Rantala asked. Connor had to hope that Komarazhi's translation didn't carry the sharp anger in his tone—and that Naizha couldn't read it herself.

The latter was probably a lost cause. Rantala was more tightly controlled than Connor had ever seen him—but Connor could tell he was about to explode. Only the fact that no one in the room was remotely responsible for the horrors of Project Olympus was keeping him in check.

"They had to *pretend* to try to teach the candidates," Naizha said, her words carrying almost as much disgust and horror as was tied up in Rantala's tone. "And why bother to make up lessons that couldn't work when they knew that even the basic lessons were beyond mere Channelers?

"Except that the students began to learn the lessons and master the power. They were still weak, no real magical threat, but the process of forcing the next generations to become true Mages was already ongoing—and the sparks of success were enough for the Eugenicists to commit more resources. More stolen children."

Somehow, those last three words and the sick despair that filled them, even across a computer translation and a different arrangement of vocal cords, seemed to break the dam holding Rantala's rage back.

The Mage released it all in a single long exhalation, then put his face in his hands.

"Those were *my* ancestors," he whispered—and Komarazhi didn't even bother to translate.

"I am truly sorry, Commodore Rantala," Naizha told him. "What was done in that mountain was evil. My ancestors blinded themselves and told themselves that it was the Eugenicists doing all of that. That they merely provided the tools and guidance.

"But once they realized how wrong they were and what they had truly done, the expedition... shattered. There was a mutiny. Of a hundred scientists and Mages, over half were killed."

That was the part of the story Nemesis had stolen from humanity, Connor realized. By destroying the Keepers, the entire details of the interaction between the Eugenicists and the Reezh Ida had been lost.

Though, given that the misheard name *Reejit* had come from the Keepers, it was likely whatever information they had possessed had been incomplete at best.

"A handful remained, feeling obliged to finish the task and, perhaps, to limit the damage of the Eugenicists' crimes. The rest took their ship and tried to come home, to explain to the entire Reezh Ida what they had discovered, the Lie that had brought us to war."

"And they were too late," Komarazhi guessed.

"They were too late. With the support outpost abandoned, they barely made it back to our stars at all—only to find that the war had already begun. And, for dozens of worlds, *ended.*"

The chill silence that filled the room was a shared recognition of the horrors Naizha described.

"They reached Ordin. I don't know how. That's vague enough in the journals I have to suggest that they did things they were ashamed of," Naizh admitted. "They got here and decided to go no farther.

"They kept in touch as the war ended and the Ida fell forever," she continued. "The new Ordin government rejected the authority of the Kazh and the Ida. They undermined the local Kazh, but they did not suppress or destroy it.

"And, of course, they needed the Mages and the Engines of Sacred Sacrifice to maintain our security," Naizha concluded coldly. "The Aha Kadak was a necessary concession, recognizing the authority and power of the Priest-Mage bloodlines, even as we peeled them away from the Kazh itself."

And so, the caste system had endured, even as the religion justifying it had faded from prominence. Connor wasn't sure it was the choice he'd have made, but he supposed that system had benefited the people writing the new rules.

"What changed?" he asked.

"Eighteen Mages and thirty scientists and ship's crew knew the reality of the Lie," Naizha told them. "They hoped that the change in Ordin's governance would allow them to reveal that truth and begin a change.

"And then the most vocal of them, a Mage of impeccable bloodline and qualifications, was murdered. Too much, it seemed, had already changed in Ordin for something as deep and fundamental as the Lie to be undermined.

"It was more acceptable to continue murdering people to fuel the Engines than it was to accept people into the highest caste who didn't have pure-enough bloodlines," she concluded. "And the people who felt that way were perfectly prepared to kill anyone, even those of 'pure' bloodlines, to keep it that way."

"So, they went underground," Poitch said bluntly, the High Commandant speaking for the first time. "Gathering political power and money and influence until we controlled not only the Cadatch but the Shola Dahn and key members and representatives of the other Ahadan."

"We created the Academy, with Naizha and other teachers of the oldest and purest bloodlines, committing to proving the Lie. As High

Commandant, I supported it as a military necessity. We did not have enough Guides of the Astral for our dreadnoughts, and it had been a long time since we forced anyone into the Engines of Sacred Sacrifice.

"Training Channelers to be Guides represented a possibility that didn't require us to delve into things we regarded as a horror of the past," she concluded. "No High Commandant in a generation has been prepared to order the necessary murders to equip our ships with the Engines. Our fleets and defenses were secondary to the power of the Cadatch and the Mountain of Astral Might."

"How did you sell it to the Mages?" Komarazhi asked. "If they were willing to kill over it before?"

"It was an experiment," Naizha replied. "A concession by the Cadatch ozh Ahadan to the military. I do not believe many of the Kadak outside our mission thought it would work. We kept our successes quiet, allowing them to believe that we were covering failures.

"But then *Barracuda* arrived."

Connor shivered.

"Someone said her Prometheans were Mages, didn't they?" he asked.

"Yes." He didn't need a translation for that single word.

"The aide in question had no way to know the trap he had triggered," Naizha said grimly. "They knew we used an equivalent system and were more concerned, I now realize, with not admitting there were humans aboard their ship than anything else.

"The revelation that an equivalent to the Engines of Sacred Sacrifice could use Mages instead of Channelers raised concerns in many quarters. To our knowledge, no one had ever tried using a Mage in an Engine, but such an experiment would have been buried to maintain the Lie.

"The implication that Mage and Channeler might be the same after all... Suddenly, the Academy wasn't a foolish gesture on the part of the Cadatch. The visitors weren't long-lost cousins and a potential advantage to whoever solidified the treaties.

"All of these things were threats."

"Others saw hope in the implication and the realization that the Academy was a real chance," Academician Troth noted. "We were fielding more requests for information in the days after that revelation than ever before, and many—maybe even most—were positive."

"Which may have made things worse," Naizha conceded. "We realize now that at least some of these plans had to have been in place for a long time. There is no way that hundreds of ships' worth of officers and crews would turn on a dime for the Aha Kadak."

"Even once the violence began, I would have expected the Hidden Shield to obey me," Poitch said. "Our starships might have mostly lacked Mages, but they were scattered across the star system in safe hiding places. Safe hiding places that turned to slaughterhouses as the Dahnkazhla turned on us."

Kazhla was *nine. Kazh* was, from what Connor understood, a shortened form of a longer phrase that translated as *Church the Nine. Dahnkazhla* was... *the Shield of the Nine.*

"They had arranged to assemble crews aligned on religious affiliation," Rantala said, following Connor's thought. "And whatever the original trigger, you now find yourself fighting a religious war."

"Yes." Naizha turned away again. "The Kazh of Ordin, so far as we know, have no contact with the Kazh in the Nine. But they have remained a major part of our culture and society, with influence both political and moral across our system.

"Those of our Society broke from the faith early, the Lie making the Kazh's failings too obvious. Others did over time, as the Kazh lost their power of enforcement in the new system.

"But it remains our ancient faith, the one that originally united us. A religious conflict has not been seen among the reezh since before we left the Builder. We... did not expect the level of ferocity and betrayal they unleashed."

Connor was too much of a student of history not to shiver. Religious wars had been some of humanity's worst conflicts over the centuries. There had been clear religious undertones to the secession of the Republic of Faith and Reason, too, though the reality of the Republic's government and plans had undermined that quickly enough.

"I appreciate your willingness to explain that history to us, Director," Connor said respectfully. "It both answers questions about our own history and allows us to understand where things stand in the Ordin System.

"I take it from your points that the Cadatch ozh Ahadan remains opposed to the Kazh? Since the original Chimeran delegation arrived, I regret to say, their star system has fallen to Kazh's fleets.

"My people are assembling forces for a counterstrike, but both we and Chimera were hoping to find allies in Ordin. It seems, I'm afraid, that we will not find them here. The necessity of survival must occupy your attention."

"You did not intervene to save the High Commandant's First Shield because you thought we had no value to you, Ambassador," Naizha said. "I believe we still have much to offer each other, though, of course, my brother's government must survive the coming days and weeks if we are to help you.

"While I hope that I misjudge them, I fear that the Kadak will reach out to the Kazh if they are victorious, and Ordin will once more kneel to the Nine. Ordin's freedom and experiment in governance will be no more—and the Lie will continue, with all of the death and loss inherent in that."

"We intervened because we guessed what the Academy was," Connor told her. "And our own Mages by Right would not stand by while their reezh cousins were murdered. While I do not wish to abandon you to this struggle, I do not believe we can do more at this hour than evacuate the Academy's students and teachers. If we remove the supposed provocation, perhaps we can buy you some time."

The three local reezh traded long looks, and Connor saw Poitch make a negating gesture with one of her hands. Naizha simply stared her High Commandant down for a good thirty seconds, until Poitch gave a palms-up shrug.

"The Academy may be part of the reasoning given for the war, but its presence is secondary to the Kadak concentrating their forces against Dahnvangan," Naizha admitted. "We find ourselves at a curious impasse, augmented by my brother's having prepared for a scenario I did not anticipate."

Connor waited. He knew that the key to what the locals needed was about to be presented. Then he'd have to see what they could provide in turn—and hope that this was a situation where he needed the orange peel and they needed the juice, allowing them to meet in the middle and split the only orange.

"The Kadak are in control of the Mountain of Astral Might," she continued. "They made certain of that as the first step of their campaign. My brother was elsewhere, leaving him separated from the seat of his power."

There was a long pause, and it was Poitch who finally spoke.

"Cadatch Izhom is dead, Ambassadors. He led his personal guard in an attempt to breach the Mountain, to reclaim the power needed to clear Orandar's skies and end this war. The Director of the Aha Kadak expected this and met him themselves.

"The Director is now dead, but so is our Cadatch and his personal guard. While the situation on Orandar is not cleanly delineated, the capital is fully in the hands of the rebels."

"Then why have they not unleashed the Mountain on you all?" Connor asked.

"Because there were only three people in this star system fully trained in the use of the Mountain," Naizha explained. "Izhom, Cadatch and guide of us all. Okozhol Azhma, the Director of the Aha Kadak... and me."

And Izhom and Azhma had killed each other in the front plaza. Azhma hadn't been the only one anticipating the other's moves there, Connor suspected.

"Thanks to preparations my brother made, it also appears that the only copy of the training material for the Mountain left in this system is here, in the Academy," she explained. "Even *I* did not know that he'd seeded the files with a virus he could activate to destroy them. Only the copy he gave me was uninfected.

"They may possess the Mountain of Astral Might, but *I* am the only one with the key to use it," Naizha concluded.

CHAPTER 37

"BUOY DEPLOYMENT COMPLETE," Fischer reported. "We're roughly one light-minute away from the enemy fleet, so *Last Stand* will be getting close-in details for most of the trip. If they ever decide to find their gas pedal."

Mike shook his head, watching the tactical map of the star system.

"They don't *want* to step on it, Fischer," he told his friend. "They've got, what, ten hours left until turnover? A day and a half until they reach Dahnvangan?"

"About that, yeah."

"They're waiting for Flotillas Foxtrot and Orandar to rendezvous with them," Mike said. He highlighted those two fleets on the displays.

"It's some messy maneuvering, but they'll have all three groups combined into a single strike force twenty-four hours before they reach the planetoid. And our friends only get Echo..."

Mike hadn't left the bridge the entire time that they'd been laying their trail of sensor buoys. His new course now drew them away from the direct line of the Kadak fleet's approach, swinging them along a course that would bring them back to Dahnvangan well before the enemy arrived.

"There are a lot of defenses above Dahnvangan," Fischer said quietly. "We have definite numbers now. Six hundred and thirty-two platforms, each with a defensive laser system and two missile launchers."

Mike grunted and checked the status of the various flotillas again. The warships in the system were now rapidly concentrating on two points.

Everything in the inner system was either at Dahnvangan or concentrating into the fleet to attack Dahnvangan. Everything past that was heading to Delta—Shozhat, as it turned out the gas giant was called.

Which meant, so far as Mike could tell, *Fourth Home*. For these purposes, basically the same thing as Delta, which would have amused him if everything wasn't looking quite so awful.

If there was any good news, it was that the rebel forces at Shozhat were already outgunned, only saved by the fact that everyone was in energy-weapon and amplifier range of each other. Flotilla Gamma-One wouldn't survive Gamma-Two starting a fight, but the loyalists would get brutally hurt as well.

The two fleets were keeping the gas giant between them while they waited for reinforcements. Most of the rebel ships were in the inner system, though, so whoever was in command of the rebels out there was going to find themselves going from bad to worse.

In their place, Mike would have either made the suicide push around the planet, hoping to surprise the loyalist forces, or fallen back. But no one in Ordin had fought a war in living memory, and it showed.

"If we could get everyone from Shozhat here, that would tip the balance," Fischer muttered.

"I know the Ambassador was going to suggest that, but I think the problem is that only the Type Ones have real amplifiers," Mike said. "Plus, the open question of whether human Mages can teleport using reezh jump matrices."

"I would suspect so," Xi told him.

He looked back at his wife in surprise, not realizing she'd entered the bridge.

"How so, Xi?" he asked.

"You were briefed on this," she pointed out. She brushed a hand across his face gently, taking any sting out of the rebuke, as she crossed to the simulacrum.

"All of our magic is based on theirs. Not just that they built the Olympus Mons amplifier and created Project Olympus, but what little magical training the subjects got came from reezh instructors initially.

"We built our magic on a foundation of what we took from them, even when we never knew the source. One of the problems the Keepers faced was that the handful of reezh ruins in our reach had runes all over them that were *identical* to ours." Xi put her hands on their simulacrum for a moment, reaching out into space with senses Mike could never share.

"Their shipboard amplifiers are the same as ours?"

"It's still in question," she conceded. "But the possibility exists. If the first Mage-King used a reezh design for the matrix, we have no record of that. But we have no record of *anything* about the reezh, so..."

"We have no idea," Mike finished. "Which doesn't help us at all, does it?"

"I don't know what will help us, Mike," Xi told him, releasing the simulacrum and crossing back over to him. "But I know what *isn't* helping."

"Hrrm?" he half-grunted.

"How long have you been awake?"

"Umm. I don't know," Mike admitted.

"Thirty-four hours," Fischer answered for him. "Or, at least, that's how long he's been on the bridge except for bio breaks and sandwiches."

"Right. *You*, Captain, my Captain, are going to bed. If you are remotely functional, that means there are too many stims in your system and you need to sleep them out," she informed him. "Are you telling me that Kelly didn't give you instructions to make sure *I* didn't overdo things?"

"Of course she did," Mike countered. "And I was watching anyway."

"Do you think she and I didn't have a very similar conversation about you, Mike?" Xi asked sweetly. "Now, are you going to walk to our quarters under your own power or am I going to have to carry you?"

Petite as Xi Wu might be, Mike had no illusions about her ability to carry him. She'd use her magic for it and float him home, in a way that left him very few options to resist.

"No, I'll... I'll be good," he said with a chuckle. "Just promise to wake me the moment anything changes? Something has to break here, and I'm not sure what it's going to be."

"We'll wake you. But Commander Fischer and I are quite competent to run this ship for eight or twelve hours while you *sleep*, my dear Captain!"

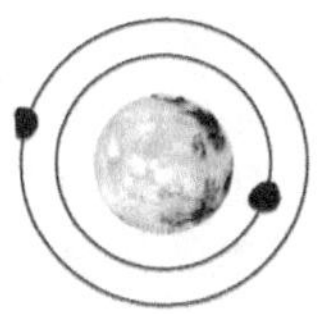

CHAPTER 38

CONNOR SAT SILENTLY in the atrium of the Academy, waiting for the military officers to finish their discussion. Time was precious, but there was nothing he could see to spend it on. He had no way to conjure reinforcements from thin air, and even the massed Mages of the entire task group wouldn't be able to get Naizha to the surface of Orandar.

He was surprised to see that the lessons continued, the rose-robed instructors leading their students through exercises he could barely perceive, let alone see the point of. Despite living in a nation defined by magic, Connor still found everything about it strange and hard to follow.

The Mages there—and he saw no reason to call them anything else— would have some ability to defend themselves when the Kadak came. Not enough, of course, which left evacuation the best route he could see.

But if they packed TG 28 to the brim, they might be able to take ten, maybe twelve thousand people with them. Enough to evacuate the Academy, but not even enough to get all of the civilians from Dahnvangan's mining facilities—let alone the crews of the warships above the dwarf planet.

"I do not know human emotions," a voice said behind him, his earbud still set to translate. "But were your astral marks those of a reezh, they would speak of determination and distress in equal measure, Ambassador."

"My astral marks?" Connor asked, turning without rising to see Academician Troth. The reezh wore the same rose robes as the instructors but did not appear to have a trail of students like them.

Troth raised his hands palm-up.

"Some among our Mages can see sparks or auras around others," he said. "Fascinatingly, while it is written of in our books and records, no Kadak has had this gift in Ordin since the Burning.

"But three of our students here at the Academy, including myself, have proven to have this power. It is not a perfect sense, Ambassador. I would not rely on my read of another of my own people, let alone my read of you, but it provides an excuse to speak to you."

Connor snorted, then realized that he didn't have anyone translating for him.

"You speak English?" he asked.

"I understand it, yes," Troth confirmed. "It is... fascinating to me. It is a language I mostly know in writing. We have few recordings from the Mars Expedition but many books and records."

Those records would probably be worth a great deal to Mars, Connor suspected. A lot of the Eugenicists' records had been destroyed in their overthrow—some accidentally at the hands of the young Mages led by the man who would become Mage-King, but most intentionally at the hands of the Eugenicists themselves.

And much of what had been preserved had been handed over to the Keepers and then destroyed in their fall.

"I would be intrigued to see those documents," Connor allowed. "We have little information on your visit to our world, for all of its consequences."

"That is not for me to allow," Troth said. "I am part of the Society, but decisions like that would fall to Naizha. Tell me, Ambassador, have you seen it? The Mountain of Astral Might the Society built on Mars?"

"Parts," he said. "There are sections that are kept secure, as I imagine there are here. There are many secrets in that mountain."

The Academician took a few moments, as if parsing what Connor had said into a form that fit his grasp of the language.

"I have never set foot in the Mountain of Astral Might here," he admitted. "No Channeler would be permitted in the structure. No non-Magi at all except for those sworn to its service, such as the Paladins.

"Those families have served the Kadak for generations. It is perhaps no surprise that they betrayed a Cadatch that challenged the traditions that define them."

"And you?" Connor asked. "What puts you here, defying those same traditions?"

"You would believe me, I suspect, if I told you the answer was that the alternative was to be sacrificed to the Engines of Sacred Sacrifice to fuel our Shield," Troth said.

If Naizha hadn't told him that the Ordin hadn't made such sacrifices in generations, Connor would have. Though he wouldn't have necessarily been surprised to discover Naizha was lying, either.

"I was not faced with that choice, though our laws require that Channelers be registered and tracked for if that becomes necessary." Troth was silent for a few moments, letting the translation catch up to his words.

"That is a harsh mountain to have hang over one's life."

"I do not think it would be easy to bear," Connor said.

"It was not. But still, I was able to live my life. I was a teacher and a historian. Enough of a scientist to realize that things that happened around me weren't quite right. That there was a pattern, one that fit some of what I'd read about the lives of Mages who'd gone undetected due to losing their families.

"When the Cadatch's people came quietly looking for volunteers to learn the Astral Gifts, I agreed. A historian must recognize the moments that changed the past... and I sensed that I faced such a moment in the now."

Troth walked in front of Connor and gestured to the Ambassador.

"Walk with me, Ambassador? I have something to show you."

Connor shrugged.

"I am waiting on the High Commandant and Mage-Commodore," he noted. "I can contribute little to the discussions of fleets and accelerations. I can see what you want to show me."

A wave brought his Marine escort from her own quiet observation, and the two of them fell in with Troth.

If nothing else, he wanted to keep the locals happy. Plus, the Academy tickled something in his mind.

He was curious.

Troth led them deeper into the asteroid. Metallic flooring allowed Connor's mag-boots to keep him grounded, though he noted that the reezh Mage was fully barefoot—presumably using magic to keep the low gravity from giving him issues.

Their path eventually led them to a spiraling corridor that dove sharply, with only a handful of exits. None of those exits were on the interior of the spiral until they reached the end, where a single hexagonal door blocked the way forward.

The Academician opened it without slowing. Whatever was down there, isolated as it was, didn't seem to have much in terms of security.

"Watch your step," Troth warned. "While there are plates for your magnetic boots, the asteroid's own gravity is magically negated here."

Connor stepped carefully, making sure that his boots locked in place. In the rest of the Academy, the boots were a necessary aid, but without any gravity, he couldn't walk without them.

With his focus on his feet, it took him a moment to realize there was a strange glow illuminating the space. He finally looked up from the plain metal plates beneath his feet and swallowed his breath.

The chamber above him rose farther than he could see. The floor was a hexagon, perfectly even, with all six walls made of natural rock polished to a gleaming finish by magic.

Suspended in the zero-gravity space were an uncountable number of glowing motes. The light was an odd silver tone, but the motes drifted in the lack of gravity like a vast swarm of fireflies.

"What is this?" he asked.

"A toy, really," Troth admitted. "But... also more than that. Watch."

The reezh gestured, and the motes—bits, Connor realized, of silver dust lit by some interior glow—moved at a silent command. Fireflies swarmed together and formed shapes. A rough spheroid at the middle. More irregular shapes orbiting around it, some small, some large.

It wasn't until the familiar spikes of the Martian warships of TG 28 took shape that Connor understood what Troth was doing.

"You can *see* with this?" he asked. "Like an amplifier?"

"It is a cousin to the Mountain of Astral Might," Troth agreed. "I could not cast through this, as a properly trained Mage in a Mountain could, but I can see quite a bit. Even things that would be concealed."

The silver suddenly shifted, the "zoom" changing as Troth pulled their view out and then refocused it, toward the approaching rebel fleet.

"The Ninth Shield," Troth observed. "Once a reserve force, a powerful squadron kept on standby to support what few active starships we had. Now the core of a rebel fleet that may destroy us."

There was a long pause.

"My cousin serves aboard one of those cruisers," he noted. "I doubt they even know where they are headed, let alone that I am here. That is the nature of the horror we have unleashed upon ourselves."

There was nothing Connor could say to that. Civil wars were horrendous things, even without the religious factor. The room they were in was an extraordinary feat of magic, quite unlike anything he'd ever seen—but it matched how the Olympus Mons Amplifier's simulacrum chamber was supposed to appear.

"What's this?"

Troth's question wasn't staged, Connor didn't think. Honest curiosity as the Mage found something he wasn't expecting—but Connor wasn't surprised when the silver shapes above them reformed, "zooming in" on a trail of small dots of silver between Dahnvangan and the Ninth Shield.

"Sensor drones. Not ours but positioned to defend the Academy," Troth concluded, his four eyes staring deeply into something only he could see. "Yours, then. Deployed by a ship we couldn't see."

Troth's gaze lost its focus, and the silver above them dispersed back into clouds of light as he turned on Connor.

"You have another ship," he accused. "A hidden one, one you didn't tell us about."

"We are strangers here," Connor replied. "Did you expect us to tell you everything until we were certain of you? Do you mean to tell me that you and your Director have no secrets you keep from us?"

As if summoned by his question, the door to the space swung open once more. Naizha stalked through the entryway, surrounded by a shimmering field of energy and accompanied by a pair of the white-armored soldiers.

Those warriors held their large swords in a manner more reminiscent of rifles than blades. Connor had no doubt there was some kind of ranged weapon in them and, for a fraction of a moment, almost went for the hand cannon holstered in the small of his back.

But he was a diplomat, and that would cause more problems than it would solve.

"Director Naizha," he greeted her. "Academician Troth was just showing me this... What do you call it?"

"This is the Astral Observatory, Ambassador," Naizha told him, confirming his suspicion that she understood English at least as well as Troth. "And you should have not shown him this, Troth."

"Perhaps not, mistress, but I have learned a great deal by doing so," Troth replied. "The Ambassador knows what a Mountain of Astral Might looks like in its heart. They have the Mountain on Mars working somehow."

"Impossible," the Director snapped. "Even with all of the knowledge available to them, the Society judged that the runes would require modification to be used by a human."

"And that, I presume, was what you intended to offer us in exchange for our help," Connor observed. He hadn't realized he'd let that slip, but thinking back... Troth had put the pieces together *very* well.

"I regret to inform you, Director, that yes, the Olympus Mons Amplifier is fully functional. We have no need of your assistance in bringing it online, nor, thanks to the archives from Chimera, are we desperately in need of your magical knowledge.

"You have very little to bargain with, I'm afraid," he said gently, "which is possibly for the best, because I think we have even *less* to offer. You should understand how long it would take us to bring ships here."

"They have another ship, mistress," Troth told her. "A vessel that even the Observatory could not detect—I saw the sensor platforms it left behind. If we cannot detect it, then neither can the Kadak's forces!"

"Why did your Commodore not mention this?" Naizha demanded.

"Because there was no point," Connor replied. "It is no superweapon, merely a scout. And we could no more reveal all of our secrets than we would expect you to expose yours, Naizha. We have been friends for what, a day?"

There was no visible signal, but the guards lowered their swords.

"I think we both have hidden things," Naizha finally said. "Our expectations not least of all."

"Trust is vital in successful negotiation, Naizha," he said carefully. "If we know all that the other desires, we can find a deal that works for us both—yet in revealing that much, we can make ourselves vulnerable."

The story of the oranges in his economics class came to mind, one of the ones he still used to justify his old job at the Arbitration Commission. A class of thirty was split into two groups of fifteen. Everyone was given an orange.

One group needed the peels from twenty-five oranges. The other needed the juice from twenty-five oranges. If there was trust and honest communication, there was an excess of resources in the room—but if everyone pushed for everything, no one would succeed.

That was the value of a trusted neutral party, in his experience. That was why the Commission had existed, to be neutral third parties who the sides *could* trust not to betray their secrets. He didn't have one of those today.

"I think... I think, Ambassador O'Hannagain, that the Ordin are as vulnerable as they can possibly be, and that revealing some of our secrets now can only help."

There was a long silence as Connor met Naizha's lower eyes, then nodded.

"Let's regather our military companions," he said. "I think we may have sent them off planning without all of the information."

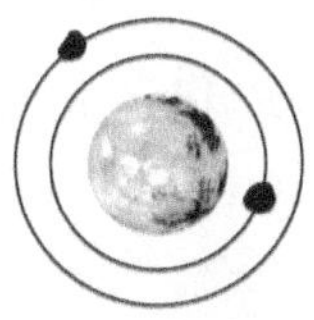

CHAPTER 39

THEY GATHERED IN THE LECTURE HALL they'd abandoned earlier to let the soldiers hash out a plan. From the expression on Mage-Commodore Rantala's face, Connor judged the planning had gone as well as it could have—the two officers had worked well together, but the reality of the situation in front of them was catastrophic.

"While we weren't getting anywhere positive, I'm not sure why we've been interrupted," Rantala told Connor quietly. "Though, if we get a chance, I need to talk to you about something I spotted here."

"This might be the chance," Connor replied. "We've both poked through each other's veils a bit here, Ketil, and the *hope* is that we're going to come a bit clean on both sides. What did you spot?"

Rantala glanced over at the reezh in the room. He even seemed to be looking askance at Komarazhi, which Connor had no intention of tolerating. He gave the Mage-Commodore a levelly impatient look.

"I knew our runic script was based on theirs," Rantala told him, his voice still a murmur, "but I didn't realize it was *incomplete*."

"What?" Connor hadn't expected that, and now the Mage had his attention.

"Martian Runic has seventy-six characters and fourteen connectors. But I glanced at some of the screens in the classes I walked by. They're teaching a runic script with over a *hundred* characters and at least twenty connectors!"

"The secondary runic cohort would not have been included in the early classes the humans were taught before anyone realized the reality of what they'd created," Naizha said.

Her clear understanding of English earned Connor a sharp look from Rantala.

"They have documents and video files and... well, a *lot*, from their Mars Expedition in English," he told the officer. "And I promised trust here, Commodore. So..."

Rantala turned to Naizha directly and spoke in a more normal voice.

"The *secondary runic cohort*, sir?" he asked.

"The Milozhari, the runic script, is divided into three cohorts, Mage-Commodore," Troth explained. That the reezh was a teacher was suddenly perfectly clear, even with the language barrier. "The first cohort is, as you said, seventy-six characters and fourteen connectors. The secondary cohort, an additional thirty-five characters and seven connectors, is usually taught around the midpoint of a Mage's training. It's required for more complex magics, including most involving any manipulation of organic matter.

"The tertiary cohort is generally only taught for specialty programs. It adds an additional ten characters and twenty-three connectors, for a total of one hundred and twenty-one characters and forty-four connectors. The tertiary cohort is only required for very specific complex magics, such as Astral Singing."

"Thank you, Academician," Rantala said slowly. "I take it that we have been building our entire magical theory on... a children's alphabet?"

"If you have constructed Astral Mechanisms without the secondary cohort, you have done wonders with that alphabet," Naizha pointed out. "I imagine, as the Ambassador has warned me, that you would have learned of the other two cohorts from the records on Chimera."

Connor realized with a small chill that there was one secret he was still going to have to keep, no matter what it cost. Nothing in this conversation suggested that the reezh had *any* concept of Rune Wrights or their ability to create unique runes not built from the runic alphabet.

The Mage-Queen and her tiny cadre of fellows might be humanity's best hope against the Kazh if that enemy shared said ignorance.

"We promised to trust," Connor told her, despite his internal realization. "So, I will answer Troth's point and question about our stealth ship. Yes, we have a single vessel in this system with both technological and magical systems designed to make her invisible.

"She isn't a warship and is almost completely lacking in weapons, but she does have an amplifier and a skilled team of Mages and crew. That is our only immediate resource that we have not already discussed, I believe."

He glanced at Rantala, who nodded grimly. The *Protectorate* had resources that he hadn't told the Ordin about, but those weren't in the system. The thirteen ships of the consular squadron were all they had.

"We have kept few secrets I think would be relevant," Naizha told them. "That I am my brother's assumed heir is obvious. If I can reach the Mountain of Astral Might... Can your ship get me there?"

"I believe Captain Kelzin could easily get you to Orandar, but his ship would not be able to penetrate the Kessler cascade," Rantala said. "You may be able to transport yourself to the surface, Director, but unless your magic can carry more with you than ours, you would be alone in a hostile city."

And exhausted, Connor knew. He doubted that would be any easier than the usual teleportation spells that transported starships.

"There are other potential ways to reach the surface," Naizha said.

"If we are lost to reason," Poitch told her leader. "It would take a dozen Mages with Astral Mechanisms a week to clear a path for even a single ship."

"And we couldn't send a dozen Mages, I know," she replied. "Any ship that leaves Dahnvangan for Orandar will be assumed to carry me. Our enemies know the threat. They will answer it, even if that requires them to abandon their fleet and jump all of their dreadnoughts to bar my way."

A thoughtful silence spread over the room.

"We can use that, honestly," Rantala said. "It's an option, one that might even the odds against the Ninth Shield. Not... enough, but removing the dreadnoughts would make a difference."

Rantala, Connor noted, had switched over to calling the Type Ones dreadnoughts—which was, he supposed, how the translator was rendering the reezh word for the immense vessels.

"I also have to ask, Naizha," Connor said, a thought striking him—a memory of a conversation on Garuda, with the late Admiral Emerson Wang. "Troth is not your only success. He is a teacher here, but if he graduated, you had other Mages who reached his level, didn't you?"

"I am the symbol, as the one most publicly known before we joined the Academy," Troth said calmly. "And I am a *very* good teacher, so I joined the Academy staff."

"The others entered specialty training, some of it of use to us now, some of it not," Naizha continued. "But I think I know what you are asking.

"Yes, we did successfully train Channelers to become Guides of the Astral. As part of that, a number of High Commandant's Poitch's vessels were refitted with Astral Mechanisms instead of Engines of Sacred Sacrifice."

"And where are these ships?" Rantala asked.

"They are in the Fourth Shield," Poitch replied. "Where, unfortunately, Forward Commandant Ulthor Adzha chose to commit his irreplaceable and unique strike force to a battle he could not win. What remains of the Shield is now in retreat from Orandar, fleeing to Shozhat."

"Forward Commandant Adzha did not have Mages aboard his ships," Naizha noted. "He still lost nine starships with Astral Mechanisms, ships we cannot easily replace."

"And where are those Guides you mentioned?" Connor asked.

There was a long silence.

"On my personal ship," Naizha finally said. "Eighty-six minutes from rendezvous with the Fourth Shield."

Connor shared a look with Rantala.

"How many ships is that?" he asked. "Will it make a difference, Commodore?"

"The Fourth Shield has nine starships left," Rantala said slowly, looking at Poitch to confirm his numbers. "No sublight ships. They're still led by a dreadnought, but my impression is that they lost their fight at Orandar."

"They did," Poitch confirmed. She sounded somewhat uncertain, and Connor suspected that the High Commandant was far less able to follow English than the other two reezh.

"My apologies," he interjected at the thought. "Ambassador Komarazhi, would you be able to translate for us? I learned that Troth and Naizha could understand English, but I am realizing I did not confirm with High Commandant Poitch."

His reezh companion swiftly translated the question to Poitch, who closed all four of her eyes in clear relief.

"I am a more recent recruit to the Society than the Director or the Academician," she admitted. "While I have worked with some of the Mars Expedition files in the original tongue, I have a very limited grasp of the language."

"Thank you, Adazh," Connor murmured to the Chimeran Ambassador. "I'm also curious as to your assessment of the situation here," he continued to her. "You have a different perspective from most of us."

He wasn't going to admit that a lot of the military situation was at least partially above his head. He could see a few mind games that could be played to even out the odds, but all he really understood was that the Kadak had a lot more firepower in play than the loyalists.

"I am a diplomat," Komarazhi replied, choosing her words carefully as she spoke in reezh. Not that Connor believed the Ordin would be surprised to discover she was a translator with a crash course in negotiations. "This talk of positions and velocities and fleets is difficult for me to follow, but I believe that even with the Fourth Shield, we are badly outnumbered?"

"In numbers, it is not as bad as it could be," Poitch said. "But where we have frigates and destroyers, they have monitors. We are outmassed and outgunned, for all that we expect them to only have a few dozen more ships."

"Which is why we must take a risk," Naizha told them all. "There are methods that could open a corridor through the debris cascade. As Poitch warns, they are dangerous and unwise, but the greatest difficulty will be getting to Orandar without being intercepted by the Kadak dreadnoughts. *They* will have Astral Mechanisms and Mages."

"*If* we put our stealth ship at your disposal," Connor said carefully, "what else would you need?"

"A small number of antimatter weapons, a radio that can send our frequencies and modulation, and space for a landing team of Mages and Paladins," the Director said. "And the best pilot we can find."

Connor thought about Captain Mike Kelzin and began to grin.

"Conveniently, our stealth ship should have all of those except space," he told her. "I believe her Captain might be the best pilot our task group has."

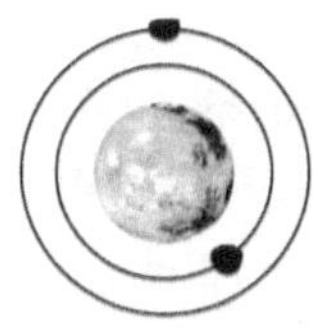

CHAPTER 40

"WE'RE DOING *what?"*

Xi and Mike were alone in the room when O'Hannagain told them the mission.

"We will be bringing the Cadatch's heir to Orandar and getting her to the amplifier, Captain," the Ambassador answered Mike's snapped question. "She is trained to use the amplifier matrix in a way none of the Kadak are. According to her, everybody else with the training is dead and she has the only copy of the training curriculum left."

"And we trust her?" Xi asked.

"Not one hundred percent," O'Hannagain admitted. "But everything she has told us has fit the pattern we're seeing, and there are definitely Mage trainees in the Academy who aren't part of the reezh's priestly families, so..."

The man had an absolutely massive shrug, Mike observed. It probably helped in negotiating when you looked like you could break anyone else in the room in half with one hand.

"I'm absolutely certain she's not telling us everything, but it's quite clear that the loyalists are in a bind and need us. They don't think they can get a ship to Orandar without being spotted and intercepted by the rebel Type Ones."

Mike had a momentary vision of what it would look like if the three seventy-five-megaton behemoths leading the rebel fleet intercepted *Rhapsody in Bohemia*. The vision didn't last long—because any attempt to fight those monsters wouldn't last long either.

"What do you need from MISS, Ambassador?" he finally asked.

"I need you to get here as fast as you can," O'Hannagain told them. "Stealthily if you can, but so long as all they have are questions, I'll prefer speed. Then you need to pick up myself and Naizha and her team and head for Orandar at your best stealthy speed."

Mike looked over at Xi.

"We're enough ahead of the enemy fleet that we can push fifteen gees all the way back to Dahnvangan," he said after she nodded. "I'll have an exact ETA for you once I've sat down with my people, but figure around twelve to thirteen hours.

"The problem is getting to Orandar from there, Ambassador," he warned. "I'm not sure we can pull fifteen gees along a line the bad guys are going to be watching without getting spotted. We might have to keep to twelve or even ten, which could put us getting to Orandar, well."

He wasn't sure of the exact numbers, beyond that if they had to stick to ten gravities, the enemy fleet *would* be in range of Dahnvangan before *Rhapsody* reached Orandar.

"We will have to choose our risks," O'Hannagain said grimly. "I have faith in your judgment, Captain. We can talk over the exact level of risk-reward ratio we're prepared to chance once I'm aboard."

"You're coming with us?" Xi asked.

"I'm the one who negotiated this deal and this plan," the Ambassador told them. "I'm going to see this through to its end, one way or another."

With engines burning at full power, Mike spent several minutes watching the distant reezh fleet. They'd never come closer than a light-minute to the rebel force, but they still weren't entirely sure how hard they could push their magitech stealth against reezh sensors.

After five minutes, he was certain that no one had seen them, which gave him hope for the next stage of the mission. There were almost certainly sensor platforms around Orandar, left behind by the Flotilla there—not to mention some kind of watch on Dahnvangan itself—but if he could push fifteen gees at this distance, he believed they could pull twelve across the course to Orandar.

Probably.

"Prinz, take over the simulacrum," he ordered aloud. "Xi, Fischer, meet me in the main briefing room. I'll ping Rennel and Zhao."

He did that silently while waiting for his wife to pass their magical stealth over to her senior subordinate. Mike had occasional moments of concern over the amount of augmentation he'd accepted, but if he was going to be honest, he'd had the work done to make sure Kelly didn't feel isolated.

His augments had been more voluntary than hers—though he knew that she tried very hard to forget the accident that had broken her back and both arms. It had been just that: an accident, one of those things that happened sometimes. A car crash when she'd been on her way to a meeting without her spouses.

She'd have recovered without the cybernetics, but accepting the hardware had cut her recovery time in half. Mike had chosen to undergo the surgery alongside her, with the excuse of needing to keep up with his wives. After all, Kelly's cybernetics would have left him the only non-superhuman in their marriage.

He doubted he'd fooled either woman for an entire second, but he had the hardware, and it meant he didn't have to speak aloud to tell Britta Rennell and Akari Zhao he was calling an all-officers meeting.

It still distracted him enough that he didn't realize Xi was standing over his chair until his wife pulled him to his feet and into a deep kiss.

"You're cute when you're all scheming and thoughtful, my love," she told him with a chuckle when they came up for air. "And sometimes, we need to scandalize the Navy types so they remember this is a *spy* ship!"

He was still grinning and blushing by the time he left the bridge.

Mike cleared his throat as his officers took their seats. Fischer still had a bemused look on their face, though he knew they were hardly bothered by PDA between the married Captain and XO on the ship.

He also knew that he was still a touch flushed. Xi was still very able to take his breath and brain away when she chose to.

"I see someone got the Captain's tongue," Rennell said with a cheery grin as he blinked back to reality.

"That's my job, yes," Xi said smugly, managing to shock the other three into chuckles.

"What's going on, boss?" Zhao asked. The Asian-featured engineer rarely left her domain of engines and power plants, leaving running the ship to Mike and Fischer so long as they didn't break *her* ship.

Unlike the other officers, Akari Zhao was the subject of several criminal world bounties—and while the charges were in abeyance while she worked for MISS, had a rap sheet as long as the woman was tall.

Mike would be more bothered if even one of those crimes had involved violence against another human being. Theft and hacking and illegal machinery work weren't crimes he was going to cry a river over—if nothing else, they were all things that he and Kelly had done both in and out of the service of the Protectorate.

Plus, the criminal bounties suggested that at least some of those crimes had been against people who very much deserved them.

"We have been asked to achieve the impossible," Mike finally answered her question. He placed his hands on the table, as utilitarian and plain as the furniture in his office. Nothing inside *Rhapsody in Bohemia* looked unusual in the slightest. If he needed to, he could bring an inspector aboard and, with only the slightest guidance of their tour, have them sign off on her as a regular courier with no real effort.

"The impossible is our stock-in-trade, but I have the distinct feeling you're talking something new and even more dangerous," Rennell said. The big commando looked like she might either crush or fall out of her chair, but she was clearly used to it.

"You have all been briefed on the status of Orandar, I know," Mike said. "Severe Kessler cascade situation caused by the orbital forts shooting each other to pieces. Civilian space infrastructure was either caught in the crossfire or in the debris shower.

"Debris density is dangerous at all latitudes. It's not a full sphere of rock, but it's fast enough and hard enough to track that even warships are going to get ripped to shreds if they try to breach it. Orandar is cut off."

"You can't..." Zhao trailed off, shaking her head. "Finish up, boss."

"Thanks for the vote of confidence, Cheng," he told her, using the old nickname for a civilian chief engineer. "Because yes. We've been asked to breach the cascade and get a landing party down to the surface.

"There is a planetary amplifier in Ushola, the capital city on Orandar," he reminded them. "And it turns out that our lead ally here is the only person in the system who knows how to use it. Lock, meet key—but there's an enemy fleet that knows what she can do positioned to intercept any move *she* makes toward the planet, and the cascade itself creates a near-impenetrable barrier."

"We're the solution to the enemy fleet," Fischer said slowly. "Though I'll want to run some analysis on what thrust we'll be able to pull, especially at the end. They *will* have sensor platforms at Orandar."

"Agreed. And they'll be watching the route between, because they know that getting Naizha into the amplifier is the win condition for this damn civil war," Mike replied. "I think we can pull some twists and tricks, average twelve gees across the whole trip and get into orbit in about fourteen hours.

"That, unfortunately, only gives an hour or so to get through the cascade and put Naizha on her brother's throne," he said grimly. "Because after that hour, Flotilla Charlie will be putting missiles into the Dahnvangan defense forces like there's no refunds on antimatter."

His people considered that situation.

"Now. Our reezh friend apparently says there is a way through the cascade, some plan she's cooked up," he told them. "No one has told me what that plan *is*, only that her people think it's suicide.

"But she doesn't know this ship or this crew. She's going to bring some Mages and troops with her, but *we*, my friends, are a covert-operations ship of the Mage-Queen of Mars. Her people are going to be the bodyguards assigned to the Cadatch's sister.

"So. Ignoring the resources our friends are bringing to the party, how would *we* breach the most expensive accidental fortification we've ever seen?"

A holographic projection of Orandar appeared above the table. The planet was a pretty one, though it was dry and cold for human tastes. Heavily populated, with over half of its surface being land instead of water, it was a blue-and-white marble, gleaming with the gemstones of reezh cities.

That marble vanished behind the datacodes of the cascade. Everything they'd been able to establish about it in days of scanning. *Rhapsody* had some of, if not *the*, best scanners in the galaxy, but they hadn't flown particularly close to Orandar since arriving.

"It's a mess," Fischer said. "We're talking a danger zone almost five thousand kilometers deep. Even one of our *dreadnoughts* would get beaten to crap on her way down, no matter what her Mages and point defense could do."

"You're talking armor that can absorb a gigaton-range antimatter explosion," Rennell countered. "A couple of them, in the case of a dreadnought. I'm sure one of the big girls would be just fine."

"You'd be surprised," Fischer warned grimly. "There are some distinct weaknesses to the energy-dispersal nets we use for handling antimatter explosions. Our armor is very specifically built to handle very large explosions and high energy transfers. Even the reezh ion cannons are enough outside the design paradigm for it to give us a headache.

"Even for *Rhapsody*, we'd be better off getting hit with a dreadnought's laser broadside than a reezh cruiser's ion-cannon battery."

"The difference would only be whether the parts left were millimeter-sized or nanometer-sized," Mike pointed out. "But yes, for anyone trying to come up with something scary to do to a Martian warship, one of their largest weaknesses is medium-sized bits of metal moving at speeds under thirty percent of light. Good luck *hitting* one of them with that, except..."

He gestured at the debris field.

"We, of course, sacrifice much of the energy-dispersal networks and armor of a true warship for inversions of those systems that we use to sink heat," he reminded everyone. "There are civilian ships out there more able to handle a meteorite impact, though not many of them.

"That cascade will chew us up and spit us out. If we could clear the little pieces, I'm confident that our Mages and I can get us through the big pieces, but we can't detect pebble-sized debris quickly enough."

"So, why try?" Zhao asked. "We can jump a light-year at a time. What's stopping us from jumping from Dahnvangan orbit directly to underneath the cascade?"

"Data," Xi replied before Mike could say anything. "Jumping out of a planetary orbit is a headache. So is jumping *into* one, which is why even Navy ships like to get at least a light-second clear before they jump.

"We need information on the gravity well, moving objects, anything we might hit on the way in or out. Jumping out of Dahnvangan's asteroid cluster would be a pain, but we could do it. But if we're not jumping into perfectly clear space, I'd want to be jumping somewhere with a clearly defined zone and information on everything in the area."

She gestured at the hologram of Orandar.

"*That* is anything but. We don't know how thick the debris zone is, and we definitely don't have solid data on where everything is. We can't jump there from a distance."

"So, jumping through is hardly an option," Mike told his people.

"I didn't say that, Mike," Xi countered. "I said we can't jump there *from a distance.*"

He'd heard the modifier, but he hadn't thought about it. It simply wasn't something they did.

"How far?" he asked, possibilities suddenly alive in his mind.

"It depends on how deep the debris field is," she said. "If it's only five, maybe even ten, thousand klicks deep? We'll need to get within about ten thousand klicks, and have safe space to work with on the other side."

"That depends on how messy Orandar's exosphere is," Mike noted. "On Mars, we'd have *lots* of space, because Mars's exosphere only reaches about two thousand klicks. Earth, on the other hand, we'd be in trouble up to ten thousand."

That was, he understood, one of several key signs as to the artificial and literally magical nature of the Martian atmosphere. He had been a *lot* more comfortable visiting the capital planet before he'd discovered that the atmosphere required regular magical maintenance.

"The layer is anchored on the geostationary-orbit level, which is lower for Orandar than for most of our inhabited worlds," Fischer warned. "Call it twenty-five thousand from the surface, only thirty thousand-ish from the gravitational center."

"We'll ping the Ambassador and see if we can get orbital and exospheric data for Orandar from the locals," Mike said, the note as much for himself as anyone else. "So, if there's space between the atmosphere and the debris field, we get as close to the field as we can and just hop past, huh?"

He knew damn well it wasn't that easy, but he wanted Xi to lay it out.

"That kind of short jump with the amplifier is hard," she warned. "We can do it, but I'm not sure many Mages could. It's more important that we avoid any physical debris than that we stay out of the exosphere, assuming we can burn up to an active orbit once we're in place."

"That would take a good pilot with a maneuverable ship," Mike said with a grin. "Fortunately, we have both of those."

"Then, what, I load this Naizha and her people on my shuttles and drop when we pass over the capital?" Rennell asked. "That sounds like it could get ugly. Do we know what kinds of defenses the city has?"

"No, but we'll get that from the locals before we kick this off," Mike promised. "Naizha has no desire to die in this attempt, any more than we do. The more data we have, the better we can plan—though I'm liking this plan better than the unknown but apparently terrifying plan *Naizha* is bringing.

"We'll see what her plan is, of course," he said virtuously. "But I'm liking this one. The timing is going to be tight. By the time we get into position to deploy Rennell's shuttles, the battle over Dahnvangan will probably have started."

"We do have flexibility that will give us some options," Zhao said, the engineer looking at the holographic globe. "This ship is more capable than anyone gives her credit for. The first thought that comes to mind, of course, is that flying a salvo of missiles through the debris and using them to clear an emergence zone for the jump would be simple enough, right, Commander?"

Fischer raised an eyebrow at Zhao but then shook their head.

"With the speed of the debris, it wouldn't clear it for long enough. We'd need to detonate the warheads and jump in practically the same moment, close enough that we'd suffer as much from the antimatter warheads as we would from the debris hits. Or worse."

"Darn," Zhao said mildly. "I also have to warn that we will lose our stealth once we're in any kind of atmosphere. The heat-sinking systems simply can't handle the extra heat from atmosphere. Magic should be able to make us difficult to track, but we'll still glow as we fly through any kind of air."

Mike nodded, then paused.

"Wait, how deep *can* we go into the atmosphere?" he asked. Flying ships into an atmosphere was generally regarded as *a bad idea*. Theoretically, RMN destroyers *could* land, but that was a brute-force effort. Once they landed, they made lovely pyramids for a while, because they couldn't use antimatter engines to lift off and would probably need to rebuild their secondary engines after the landing process.

"We're rated to land and lift off, though I'd want to make sure we had full hydrogen tanks before trying it unless I didn't like the planet," she told him. "It was theoretically always part of the *Rhapsody* fit-out, but my understanding is that the second-generation ships have actually tested it."

"I'm not going to say I don't trust the tests, because I apparently missed them," Mike admitted. "But I think I'd rather stick to Rennell's plan of sending everyone down in our assault shuttles. We'll bring *Bohemia* in close enough to help suppress the city defenses and clear a path to the amplifier, but landing the ship seems like it might be a step too far!"

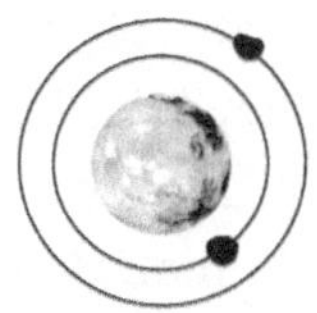

CHAPTER 41

"EVERYTHING IS IN PLAY, AMBASSADOR," Rantala told Connor, walking by his side as they approached the shuttle up to *Rhapsody in Bohemia*. "I won't say we can win this—but I will say we might not lose, which I'm not sure I'd have believed when we first arrived."

"If you can hold off this attack, even just convince them to bail, that buys time," Connor replied. "I'm going down there with Naizha; I'd prefer we weren't rushing."

"I still think that's foolish, Connor," the Commodore warned. "You're a civilian, not a soldier."

"So is Naizha," he said. "And I think that wherever our Cadatch-to-be goes, I want to be there for the next little bit. There are promises we need her to keep, after all."

"It'll be some time before Ordin will have ships to spare to fight for us," Rantala reminded him. "They're shielded by the amplifier, but when the dust settles on this mess, Naizha isn't going to have much of a Shield left."

"It's going to be a year, *maybe* less a month or so, before we have any significant numbers of new heavy ships ready to fight," Connor said grimly. "And you know as well as I do the problem with expanding the fleet."

His companion nodded. The Protectorate's industry could build as many warships as they could possibly want, at least in theory, but even if the Mage-Queen conjured dreadnoughts from thin air, they would still need crews to operate them and Mages to carry them to battle.

Navy Mages were the choke point, the limiting factor that would limit the Royal Martian Navy's strength. There were enough already-trained Mages for a larger fleet than they had, but Connor didn't know exactly how large that number was.

Only that it was measured in thousands. Single-digit thousands, and not with a particularly high number at the front. Prior to the current crisis, Parliament had authorized the Navy to expand to four hundred ships and to replace every ship built prior to the war with the Republic.

That would have required two thousand Navy Mages, so Connor presumed they had *those* Mages. How many more would be needed as old ships didn't get decommissioned and construction ramped up?

Connor didn't know. He hoped that the people at the top of the Navy did and that there was a plan. His old job had been economic negotiation, which meant he had a better sense of the industrial might of the Protectorate than most.

No matter how optimistic the projections, he knew they'd run out of qualified Mages before they stopped being able to build ships for them.

"Our delay allows them to get restarted as well," he told Rantala. "And for us to exchange knowledge, both magical and technological. We have an open promise in repayment for this stunt, Ketil. Naizha will owe us her throne and her system, and she strikes me as the type to respect that debt."

"And if she isn't?"

"That's why I'm going with her," Connor admitted. "Because if she takes control of that amplifier and turns on us, someone will have to do something—and I'm the one who decided to trust her."

Something was mostly going to be *order everyone to jump to safety and face his own fate*, but having someone at Naizha's side would give them that option.

"Any of the commandos going down with you could do that, you know."

"I have the grim suspicion that our bionic friends are going to be very, *very* busy in the Mountain of Astral Might, Ketil.

"Plus, I don't trust anyone else's judgment when the stakes are this high. It was my call to make this alliance. It'll be my call that decides whether it lives or dies."

There was an arrogance to that, Connor knew, and he didn't care. If there was also a tiny piece of survivor's guilt, of *not* being able to do anything when Chimera's fate was sealed?

That wasn't something he needed to tell anyone.

"I can't talk you out of it and we both know I've no authority over you," Rantala said with a sigh as they reached the underground hangers. He offered Connor his hand.

"Good luck, Ambassador. We'll hold the line."

"Good luck to you too, Mage-Commodore," Connor replied, taking Rantala's hand in his. His grip dwarfed the darker Mage's, but he was never one to crush bone unless someone tried to do it to him.

"I'll see you when this is done," he promised.

"Or I'll see you in hell," Rantala replied. "Either way, Ordin will remember we were here!"

Naizha joined Connor on the shuttle a few minutes later, bringing Troth and a trio of white-armored Paladins with her. One of the Academy's own shuttles was bringing the rest of her force—two more Academicians with combat training and another dozen Paladins.

"Do you have any forces here other than the Paladins?" Connor asked her quietly as she belted herself in next to him. It was strange how smooth the cross-language conversations had become. Thanks to his earbud, he could understand her reezh, and she had a far-better understanding of English than she'd wanted him to think originally.

"Yes, but they are the best equipped and know the Mountain better than anyone else," she replied. "And I trust their loyalty."

Connor wasn't going to argue with her, but he had to wonder. The Mountain of Astral Might and Orandar City had fallen, according to her, because the clans that produced the Paladins had betrayed them.

"You worry," she guessed.

"We aren't going to be able to take many people down," he replied. "I hope we have the right people; that's all."

"We must have faith," Naizha told him. The word she used, *orlo*, didn't really translate as *faith*, of course. It was less fatalistic than *faith* was often used for in Connor's experience, but more determined and solid than the softer *optimism* that it might be used for.

"Poitch and Rantala have put a lot of moving pieces into play," Connor said. "I trust them, but I can recognize the odds we're facing."

"But no magic can bring starships from across the galaxy to here." Naizha raised her hands palms-up as the shuttle left the deck, the engines pushing them into their seats.

"Even if you were prepared to commit the resources of your Protectorate to save us, they could not get here in time. If anyone was going to intervene in this war, they already would have."

Connor took a moment to consider that. The Primes were spread across a cluster of stars denser than the neighborhood of Sol. Eleven star systems with a habitable planet within twenty light-years of the Nine had given them a solid head start on colonization—enough of one that he wondered if some of the Primes had been colonized before the reezh mastered amplifiers and jump magic.

But it also meant that even the farthest of the other Primes was only fourteen light-years from Ordin. Presuming they had Jump Mages, they should have been able to reach Ordin in five days.

"Why has no one intervened?" he asked. "Are you in contact with the other Primes?"

"Singers of the Astral are difficult to train," Naizha told him. "And they can only sing to places they have been."

That wasn't an answer to his question, he realized, but he let that hang in the air.

"The Kadak are followers of the Kazh, the Church of the Nine?" he asked. "Would they reach out to them for support?"

Naizha was silent for a few moments, and it was Troth who finally answered the question.

"The Kazh has always endured among the Ordin, but it has been fully separate from the Kazh in the Nine for lifetimes. The Kadak and the others they have recruited share a faith with the Kazh, but they will not surrender power to them without reason."

"So long as our rebels think they can win, they will not surrender our system to the remnants of the Ida," Naizha confirmed. "Once they lose, they may grow more desperate, but for this moment, we only face the monster of our own creation."

That was bad enough, but Connor could sense a self-justifying explanation across species boundaries. If the Kazh intervened, Naizha's cause was truly hopeless, so there had to be a reason for the rebels *not* to call them in.

The reason made sense, but he had to wonder.

Connor let Naizha unbuckle herself first once the shuttle had settled on *Rhapsody in Bohemia*'s decks, watching to see whether she expected magical gravity. The Academy had used a similar magic to shield the Observatory, but he hadn't seen gravity runes anywhere in the school—and reezh warships were clearly built to rotate for gravity.

Rhapsody in Bohemia, a clean and even half-ellipsoid that resembled a beetle to human eyes, was visibly not designed to rotate. A ship like her either had magical gravity or none—and while Connor knew she had gravity runes throughout, he had wondered what Naizha had been expecting.

From the way she tried to launch off, stumbled and nearly fell flat on her armored face, she had not expected the field of magic providing a steady sense of down throughout the stealth ship.

"What... what *is* this?" she asked, her voice soft.

"A standard Terran gravity," Connor told her, rising from his seat and offering a hand to Troth as the other reezh Mage unbelted himself. "It's a bit heavier than you are used to, about eighteen percent higher than your standard and eleven percent stronger than Ordin's gravity."

Naizha looked around her.

"The shuttle isn't doing this. The ship?" she asked. "That is an extraordinary investment of magic. Is having the shuttle bay so enchanted worth it?"

"The shuttle bay, Naizha?" Connor countered.

"To lay such runes across a space is a great effort, as is keeping them maintained. Many Mages would feel charging such was beneath them."

He smiled.

"The entire ship has gravity runes, Naizha," he pointed out. "As I understand it, it's part of our military Mages' training to charge the gravity runes of any space they enter. I doubt it's even conscious for most of them now."

He led the way toward the exit, the ramp descending as he stepped up.

The second shuttle wouldn't be able to land until they'd left the shuttle and Kelzin's people had moved it into its storage niche. The bay wasn't big enough to have two shuttles in operation at once, but the MISS crew had still managed an honor guard.

Eight troopers, plain-looking in simple black uniforms with minimal insignia, outlined a path out to where Mike Kelzin and Xi Wu waited for them. Connor didn't know much about what kind of soldiers were assigned to an MISS scout ship, but he doubted that the quiet competence the troops radiated was understated.

"Captain Kelzin," Connor greeted their host, offering his hand. "It's a pleasure to see you in person again. It's been a worrying few days."

"That it has, Ambassador," Kelzin agreed as he shook Connor's hand. His hand disappeared in Connor's grip, but he noted an unusual strength to the Captain's fingers.

"This is Naizha," Connor continued, gesturing toward his companion. "Director of the Academy—I never did get a longer name. She's been responsible for training Channelers to be full Mages.

"Her companions are Academician Troth, a Mage by Right as we would label him, and her personal detail of Paladins."

It was Wu who stepped forward and bowed her head slightly to Naizha before speaking—in reezh!

"Welcome aboard our vessel, honored one."

Out of the corner of his eyes, Connor saw both Naizha and Troth blink all four eyes. Apparently, it hadn't occurred to them that the shared population of Chimera had resulted in humans who spoke the reezh language.

Though Connor hadn't realized that Xi Wu had put the effort into learning the alien language. She was more fluent than he was, but there had never seemed to be enough time for proper lessons or practice.

"This is Mage Xi Wu, senior Ship's Mage and second-in-command of this vessel," Connor said, indicating the Mage with a small bow of his own.

"I honor you, Mage Xi Wu," Naizha told Wu. "I did not realize that anyone aboard this vessel would speak our tongue. Thankfully, Academician Troth and I understand your English sufficiently to handle affairs, we hope."

"I have been tutoring our ground team in reezh Korazhi for some time," Wu said in English. "That should help with coordinating on the ground, though only Major Rennell is fluent enough to truly speak it."

"That will indeed help," one of the Paladins said. "I had expected to need to keep the Academician or the Aha Cadatch with our teams to coordinate, which seemed not wise."

Naizha—presumably the *Aha Cadatch*, or Voice of the Primary, in question—indicated the speaker with a wave.

"This is Paladin Commandant Sheel," she introduced the soldier. "Senior officer of my personal bodyguard. My cousin."

Sheel bowed, their armor flexing to allow them to bend nearly in half.

That at least explained why Naizha trusted her bodyguard detachment despite other Paladins betraying her brother. It made sense, Connor supposed, for the Mage families to make certain the clans responsible for the securing and maintaining the Mountain of Astral Might were bound to them by blood.

"We need to clear the bay to allow your next shuttle to land," Kelzin warned. "Once they're aboard, we will be leaving immediately. We will be accelerating at twelve gravities and should reach high orbit of Orandar in fourteen hours and ten minutes."

Naizha clearly understood enough of that to show a moment of concern.

"That is... an extraordinary acceleration," she said. "Is it safe?"

"This vessel is equipped with powerful gravity runes," Kelzin promised. "We have complete control over internal gravity up to fifteen gravities and can keep subjective gravity to safe levels up to twenty.

"We currently calculate that we can conceal this ship from our enemy for our entire journey while sustaining twelve gees. As we increase acceleration, it becomes more difficult to conceal our maneuvering."

What Kelzin did not note, Connor realized, was that it *was* possible to conceal *Rhapsody in Bohemia* at fifteen gravities of acceleration. They just couldn't do it for very long without wearing out their Mages.

"Please, we need to clear the shuttle bay," Kelzin repeated. "Every moment we delay is a moment we won't have above Orandar."

That was an argument that couldn't be countered. There were no more questions as Connor waved his alien companions forward.

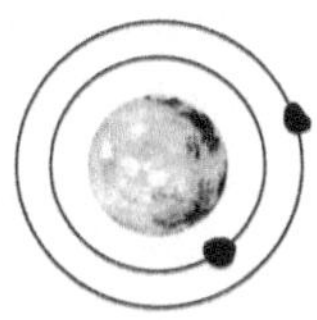

CHAPTER 42

"SHE SEEMS NICE ENOUGH for the descendant of the people responsible for Project Olympus," Xi told Mike as they settled back into the bridge.

Vitaliy David was at the simulacrum, his magic weaving around *Bohemia* to shield her as she began the long burn toward her destination.

"Or an aristocrat, for that matter," Mike agreed. "I keep being surprised that *our* aristocrats that I meet are surprisingly sane and down to earth."

"That is because I am careful what Mages by Blood you meet," his wife told him sweetly. "You are impulsively protective, my dear. Valued trait in a husband, but if you met some of the assholes who wear the medallion... well, I'd have to stop you punching them, and I wouldn't *want* to."

Mike chuckled. She wasn't wrong, though he was far more self-controlled now than he had once been—and he found the reputation for impulsivity he had in the Agency useful at times.

And his protective urge toward his wives was all too real, though he was fully conscious of the fact that he was the least dangerous of the three of them.

"We're committed to putting her on a throne that's just as directly powerful as the one in Olympus Mons." He looked at Xi, who met his eyes levelly and nodded her understanding. "I'm glad that she and her 'Society' seem to be on what we'd call the right side of history *now*, but I'm not sure I can forgive them for what they did to our ancestors."

"A large reason that I believe Naizha can be trusted is that she does not *expect* us to forgive her for what was done to our ancestors. She recognizes that her ancestors committed a great crime in enabling the Eugenicists. Whatever came of that and whatever her Society has done since, Project Olympus remains."

And so did the Fields of Sorrow. They had been there once, with Kelly and Damien Montgomery, visiting the grave of Hand Alaura Stealey—the woman who'd saved all three of them from a crime lord and recruited Damien Montgomery.

After they'd paid their respects at the Black Mausoleum, the sepulcher that held the graves of Hands and Mage-Kings, all four of them had felt drawn farther up the mountain, to stand at the edge of the silent fields of markers with no names. Thousands upon thousands of children and youths, many forced to have children of their own at grotesquely young ages, and all of them lethally discarded when they were no longer useful.

That was what had shaped Mages in the Protectorate—and that was what Naizha's "Mars Expedition" had enabled.

"All for a lie," Mike admitted. "That's almost worse, you know? That they committed this grand atrocity because of a *lie*. I don't know what the Reezh Ida might have become if they'd respected and trained their Mages by Right like we do. They might still exist."

"We might not." Xi sounded vaguely sick at the thought. "Without their interference, who knows what it would have taken for any level of magic to be found in humanity again."

Mike chuckled as the answer struck him and he grinned at Xi.

"It would have taken *Damien*, my love," he told her. "Everything I've seen suggests that most of our magical myths in the past were groups created because a Rune Wright was born and couldn't *not* use their powers. They trained other Mages, but without any way to *find* new Mages without the Rune Wright, magic became ritual and tradition within a few generations.

"But if the Rune Wright was someone like Damien Montgomery, in a world with modern communications... I think he'd have found a way to share what he was. The man doesn't have it in him to do anything else!"

"Maybe." Xi sighed. "I certainly don't want to say that this Mars Expedition did us any favors, not at the price it cost, but I like being a Mage."

"I know. We don't have to like what happened in the past to recognize that we benefit from where we are," he told her. "We recognize the horror of what was and move forward to make sure it never happens again.

"We're not going to forgive what happened. But that doesn't mean you have to stop being happy you're a Mage, just because horrifying things were done to give your ancestors that gift!"

An hour and a half passed in quiet calm on *Rhapsody in Bohemia's* bridge, the assorted icons on Mike's displays slowly creeping toward each other. The rebels had combined their forces now, assembling a giant hammer of metal and magic now heading toward Dahnvangan like the inevitability of time.

Over a hundred and thirty ships and two billion tons of warships. It was a mind-blowing amount of firepower, and Mike wasn't entirely convinced their clever plans could really even the odds.

"There they go," Fischer suddenly announced. "*Andrew Lloyd Webber* just broke Dahnvangan orbit at sixteen gees. They're on a direct course for Orandar, and I think the whole star system is going to see them in short order."

Rhapsody had seen the destroyer move sooner than anyone else would, via a Link connection to *Last Stand at Alamo's* scanners. It would be a few minutes before the Kadak fleet saw her, but Mike was curious as to just what Forward Commandant Sujam—or whoever was in command of them, he supposed—did about it.

"What is *Webber's* ETA?" Mike asked.

"Seven hundred thirty minutes," Fischer replied. "If nothing gets in her way, she'll make Orandar orbit twenty minutes before we do."

Well before the battle over Dahnvangan was joined, even at extreme range. If Naizha had been aboard that ship, she'd be in position to take control of the Mountain before the Kadak could even engage her base of support.

"You're the Navy officer, Fischer. What do you think they'll do?"

"I'm not sure any of my tactical scenarios included a planetary amplifier except as a black box of *your ship enters this area around the designated planet, you lose*," Fischer pointed out. "But treating it as a *we win* button to get Naizha into the amplifier, means that I'd be putting a *lot* of force into making sure a ship I thought she was on didn't make it."

Mike grinned.

"That's what I was thinking, too. And so was the Commodore."

There wouldn't be an immediate reaction. The rebels would want to let the destroyer get out of mutual-support range of Dahnvangan's defenses, if nothing else.

"Given the lecture my dear wife gave me all too recently, I'm going to go take a nap," he told Fischer with a smile at Xi. "Call up your relief, Commander. We both need to be rested when this well and truly starts coming apart."

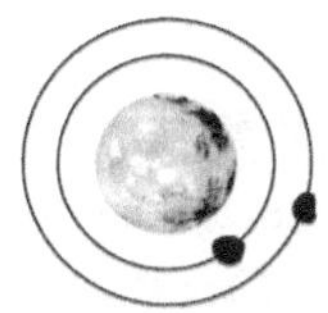

CHAPTER 43

DESPITE THE AMOUNT OF SILICON built into his body, Mike still needed an alarm clock to make sure he only slept four hours. He groggily tried to turn it off, to find that his arms were pleasantly weighted down by Xi.

"Can you grab that—"

There was a small tearing sound, and the alarm clock stopped. Still mostly pinned under his wife, Mike managed to rise enough to see that the utilitarian black box on the side table was now in four pieces.

"And that is why we don't use the alarm on our wrist-comps." He chuckled, then ordered the room to turn the lights on.

Xi's skin was far darker than his own, a contrast and juxtaposition he never tired of. He'd never tire of seeing her naked, though he didn't remember her joining him in their quarters.

"Should I be waking you up or letting you get back to sleep?" he asked.

"I'm getting up with you." She shifted and stretched. "But I wasn't on the schedule until after you were planning on being back on the bridge, so I figured I would take advantage."

She looked him up and down appreciatively, and Mike grinned.

"If you wanted to take *advantage*, you should have woken me up," he suggested. "As it is, I have to shower and get right back to work."

"Oh, I know. I need to do the same. But before I do, I believe I'm getting a *show*," his wife said brightly.

Despite the clear temptations, both of them made it back into ship-suits and onto the bridge before Mike's mental target of four hours and twenty minutes after *Webber* broke orbit.

It was a somewhat-arbitrary figure that put the destroyer just under a light-minute away from Dahnvangan and still over fifty million kilometers from her destination.

Rhapsody in Bohemia was twenty light-seconds ahead of *Webber*, hopefully even more invisible in comparison to the destroyer's blazing energy signature. Their course had an arc to it that the destroyer's didn't, hopefully putting them out of any intercept course someone plotted for *Webber*.

"Captain."

"Lieutenant," he greeted Katré Grant, one of Fischer's two junior officers. Including Mage-Lieutenant Prinz, there were only four RMN officers on the ship to manage the twelve techs and analysts aboard for her tactical department and weapons. "Any updates?"

"Everyone has held to their course since you left the bridge, sir," Grant told him. "Which stinks, looking at the main Kadak fleet."

"The Ninth Shield, apparently," Xi noted. She took the support seat next to where Mage Maiella was busy using the simulacrum. "Or at least that's what our local allies have tagged it, based on the most important pre-rebellion formation involved."

"Fair enough," Grant said. "The Ninth Shield hasn't deviated from their course toward Dahnvangan. Either they've decided *Webber* is a decoy or they're planning something."

"Oh, I'm sure they're planning something." Mike ran his gaze across the displays. Four and a half hours, and nothing had changed that couldn't have been predicted when he went for his nap. Xi wasn't wrong about his needing to get more rest.

"Fischer will be back on duty in thirty minutes," Grant offered. "Should I wake them early?"

"No. I don't think we've been exposed, and there isn't much we can do about the next few steps." *Andrew Lloyd Webber*'s fate depended on just what the Kadak did—and on how quickly Mage-Commander Mwenya Šulcová, her Captain, reacted when the Kadak acted.

"We don't have a Link with *Webber*," Xi noted. "I would have expected us to, honestly. Should I try to set one up?"

"No, *Webber* is running with her Links disabled," Mike replied. "It's not likely to make an immense difference, especially as we have seen no evidence that the reezh can detect a Link in operation, but I understand the Mage-Commodore wanted to remove any possible failure point."

The back of Mike's neck was itching, and he took his seat to make sure he could act. He could easily see ways that everything working out exactly as they'd hoped would put *Rhapsody in Bohemia* in danger. At least he had both the Ambassador and the Cadatch's heir aboard.

They could extricate *Bohemia* from almost anything, after all, and his orders were to keep O'Hannagain safe. He figured extracting the loyalist heir to a deposed head of state would be a good thing too, even if there wouldn't be much more they could do for Ordin than they could for Chimera if this didn't work.

"Jump flare!" Grant snapped into the calm silence of the bridge. "Multiple jump flares at *five million kilometers!*"

"Show me," Mike barked. "Parvati, make us disappear as hard as you can!"

He cut the drive as he gave the order. They *should* be able to hide from reezh sensors if the Mage at the simulacrum put everything they had into it, even with the drives running, but five million klicks was the accepted useful range of Navy lasers—and, in the absence of detailed contrary information, they were assuming it was at least that for reezh ion cannon.

Six massive reezh starships had placed themselves directly across *Andrew Lloyd Webber*'s course, their bulk outmassing the Martian destroyer hundreds of times to one. Three Type Ones and three matching Type Threes, just in case a single destroyer had enough missile launchers to get through the dreadnoughts' massed defenses.

"Designate targets Bandit Two," Grant said, her voice calm and level. "Total mass two hundred seventy megatons; estimate armament three thousand three hundred missile launchers and an unknown number of ion cannons.

"Range to us, five million kilometers, increasing at just over seventeen hundred klicks per second with the geometry. Range to *Andrew Lloyd Webber* is six million kilometers, dropping at twenty-five hundred klicks per second.

"Bandit Two has fired."

There wasn't even a pause for breath in Grant's report.

"Three thousand four hundred missiles inbound on *Webber*," she continued after a moment. "Number is approximate, plus/minus seventy. Flight time is five minutes, twenty seconds from *now*. Adjusted for light-speed lag, that is."

"Let Fischer sleep," Mike ordered again, before Grant even asked. "You're doing fine."

The range was increasing, but every second *Bohemia* wasn't accelerating was about a second and a half longer it would take them to reach Orandar.

Grant didn't even announce when *Webber* returned fire, the *Bard of Winter*–class destroyer's twenty missiles barely a speck against the titanic overkill pointed at her.

A cough behind him announced O'Hannagain's arrival. He waved the Ambassador forward without even looking back at the man. The BCR wouldn't have let anyone on the bridge who wasn't authorized, and Mike recognized the sound of O'Hannagain's attempt to get his attention.

"I see the decoy has worked beyond our hopes," Connor noted, stepping up next to Mike's chair. "I presume Captain Šulcová has an exit strategy?"

"So do I," Mike agreed. "Our large new friends out there emerged from their jump closer than I'd like. We don't have any real chance to get around them; I have to let the range play out."

"How long will that take?"

"Almost forty minutes at this drift. Half a light-minute before we can bring the cold thrust up, a full light-minute before I'd risk the main drive."

"Unless something happens to our large friends," O'Hannagain pointed out.

The missile storm was still creeping in on *Webber*. Mike wasn't particularly *concerned* about the destroyer, if he was honest. The only real question was where they were going to jump and whether Bandit Two could follow them.

"If Bandit Two jumps away, I have to assume they've left sensor drones behind. My parameters don't change much. If the Commodore had a superweapon to hide aboard *Webber*, I doubt we would be playing nearly this many games."

"How much time is this going to cost?" O'Hannagain sounded concerned, and Mike couldn't blame him.

He was running the numbers as the Ambassador asked, and grimaced as the final figures fell out.

"Eighty minutes," he told O'Hannagain. "Which means we'll arrive after the battle at Dahnvangan starts. They're going to have to hold out against the enemy fire for over half an hour."

"At extreme missile range," Fischer pointed out. "It could be worse."

"It might *be* worse," Mike countered. His attention turned back to the plot marking *Andrew Lloyd Webber*'s fate. "We don't know that those are the only ships they have that can jump. Hell, from the information we had from the locals, those cruisers *shouldn't* have been able to jump."

"That's not quite what Naizha told us," O'Hannagain noted. There was something in his voice that made Mike turn to look at him.

"What do you mean?" he asked.

"She said that no one had been willing to murder to fill an Engine of Sacred Sacrifice in generations—but everything I saw suggested the ships still have the *equipment*. They kept records of Channelers so that in an emergency, they could be 'drafted.'"

"And the revolt was weeks ago." Mike swallowed. "And while the loyalists haven't regarded an in-system war as worth sacrificing innocents for, the rebels may have a different opinion."

He wanted to swear. That meant they had *no* idea how many of the starships in the enemy order of battle could jump—only that every one of the twenty-three lighter ships, the battleships on down, that could jump had required the murder of an innocent.

"*Webber* has jumped," Fischer reported. "I presume the Commodore knows where she's going, but no one told us."

"Keep an eye out for where she appears," Mike ordered. "If the big guys put themselves near our path again, this trip could get even longer."

His hands itched to grab the controls and fire up the engines, to take control of his ship's fate and push for Orandar at fifteen gravities. That might—*might*—be safe if the dreadnoughts on his screen jumped away after *Webber*, except that if anything else in the Kadak fleet could jump...

Rhapsody in Bohemia couldn't take even a reezh Type Five, a destroyer-equivalent, in a clean fight.

"It's more important that we get there undetected than that we get there in any time limit," O'Hannagain told him, his voice barely above a whisper. "If Naizha takes control of the amplifier, she can protect Dahnvangan from there, even if the fleet is lost."

Even at a whisper in a room without the locals, no one was going to say that the locals might be prepared to sacrifice even Dahnvangan to get Naizha to the amplifier. Or to mention that the RMN couldn't afford for TG 28 to fight to the last ship to defend *anything* in this system.

Mike's fingers twitched toward the controls. He could manage patience and waiting—he commanded a spy ship, after all.

But that didn't mean he was ever going to *like* it.

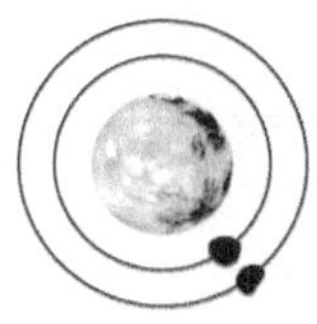

CHAPTER 44

CONNOR NODDED TO THE PALADIN outside the guest quarters. The armored reezh made no attempt to stop him entering Naizha's space, so he presumed he was welcome. He still knocked so she knew he was coming.

"Ambassador."

The reezh Mage was seated on the floor in the middle of the room. The guest quarters aboard *Rhapsody in Bohemia* were cramped at best, but everything could fold back into the walls, leaving enough room for Naizha to sit on the floor and for Connor to enter the room without stepping on her.

"Naizha," he greeted her. "Is there a title I should use for you? Aha Cadatch?"

"That title does not officially exist," she replied. "It is only used for the period between a Cadatch dying and another taking up the burden, for the person the previous Cadatch wished to take their place.

"It only marks the previous Cadatch's desire, though, and the Cadatch *should* be selected by the Ahadan. I am sure this will not be the first time the Ahadan has assembled after the burden has been assumed, but we have a tradition."

"Possession is nine-tenths of the law," he said with a grim chuckle.

"Intriguing. I recognize the meaning of the statement, but we rarely phrase things so bluntly," Naizha replied. "The closest we come is... *sometimes, the will of the Nine is made manifest before the law can see.*"

With the bed folded up, that wall became a full screen. The imagery on it was unfamiliar to Connor, with text in reezh, though he recognized enough to know that it was a map of the Ordin System.

"You are watching the battle."

"It is not yet a battle, but yes," she confirmed. "Commander Fischer was able to set up an interface that provided the data in a format I was used to. I am sure they also are censoring anything I should not see."

Connor didn't pretend they wouldn't be. He studied the display in silence.

"Our engines remain silent," Naizha told him. "The Kadak lurk, all too close—but well beyond a distance where they can threaten Dahnvangan. As a decoy, the plan worked."

"They haven't moved." That worried him. It suggested that the enemy were planning something clever—the downside of clever plans was that no one had a monopoly on them.

"No. They are preparing for another jump. They do not know where your destroyer has gone, but they judge her flight to suggest I am aboard. They prioritize that."

"The cruisers... for them to have jumped, their Engines must have been... filled." Connor couldn't think of a clean way to phrase it, especially with the language barrier.

"Yes. The Aha Kadak would have had access to the list of registered Channelers." She stared blankly at the screen, none of her eyes blinking for several long seconds.

"They may have even found volunteers among those who follow the old faith. I cannot pretend that is unlikely—but I also cannot pretend they would not have taken what they needed regardless.

"What I do believe is that there were not enough Channelers in the Star Home cluster for them to equip all of their ships with the minds and powers of the murdered. So, it will be telling, Ambassador, if the smaller ships—that *must* have Engines of Sacred Sacrifice—leave with the dreadnoughts, who have Priest-Mages aboard."

"First, they will need somewhere to go," Connor replied, looking back at the chart. The Star Home cluster had to be the primary habitat zone in the asteroid belt, where Flotilla Charlie had started. Even as he tried to math out how many people and, presumably, Channelers, were at Star Home, a new gold icon appeared on the display.

Six light-minutes distant, on the far side of Orandar. Only slightly farther from the planet, in fact, than *Rhapsody in Bohemia*. They'd have shed most of their velocity in the jump, but Connor also knew that they could have jumped right into orbit.

Webber was still playing bait.

"Or someone to chase," Naizha said quietly. "They will assess quickly. I assume Sujam will not have abandoned his flagship, so he has taken personal responsibility for this."

"I hope he enjoys endless chases," Connor told her. "*Webber* has five Mages aboard. How many is Sujam likely to have on his dreadnoughts?"

Naizha chuckled, the gravel-clacking sound still strange to him despite his growing exposure to the reezh.

"Not five," she agreed.

"Does Sujam command the Kadak forces?" he asked. "I would have expected them to promote someone to High Commandant."

"They will, but the Forward Commandants they have kept are maneuvering for the role. We have spent four lifetimes in this standoff with the Kazh, Ambassador. Why would an active war slow the politics and deals?

"We only had three Commandants-of-Forces, Poitch's chosen subordinates. One commands the Second Shield at Shozhat in my brother's name, though we have tried to inform Commandant-of-Forces Allo Hozh that Izhom is dead."

Naizha shook her head.

"I know that news will harm Allo," she said quietly. "He and my brother were close. Had Izhom not known his duty to sire a new generation of Mages, he may have chosen differently."

"Your brother had a partner? Children?" Connor hadn't realized that.

"Yes and yes." Naizha stared at the display, watching the force that thought they were pursuing her. "But given that I know Izhom killed his mate's father on the steps of the Mountain of Astral Might, I fear for her and their children."

Connor winced. *Civil war*, right. It made sense that the Cadatch had married a member of another important lineage, one entwined with the leadership of the Aha Kadak and now the rebellion.

"And there Sujam goes, in pursuit of a title that will mean nothing," Naizha noted.

Connor could tell that there were fewer of the bright red icons marking the enemy fleet, but he couldn't tell who had jumped and who had remained.

"The dreadnoughts have jumped," Naizha said, either thinking aloud or recognizing his failure to read the reezh symbols. "The cruisers remained, though I believe they have set their course for Orandar. In case they have missed something... except that they are not nearly as swift as this vessel you have loaned us."

As they had half-expected, then, the cruisers had only a single victim in their Engines of Sacred Sacrifice. That meant those ships couldn't jump again for almost half a day—but the dreadnoughts clearly had at least two Mages aboard.

But if they were going to keep chasing *Webber*, they were as out of the fight for Dahnvangan as if they had been obliterated.

"Captain Kelzin will get us to Orandar, Naizha," he promised. "Your people at the Academy just have to hold out."

"I have faith in Poitch. She has faith in me. Neither of us will fail the other."

Connor smiled and nodded—but he had to wonder just what that kind of unbreakable faith felt like.

The odds were, after all, impossible.

"I can ask Captain Kelzin if you can join us on the bridge when the battle is joined," he offered. "That way, we will all know what we are facing."

"I do not wish to interfere with the Captain's ship." Naizha looked at the wallscreen and then closed all four eyes. "But I would be among comrades when I watch the fate of my friends. If he invites me, I will join you."

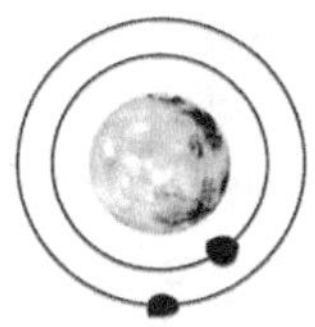

CHAPTER 45

"RANGE TO ORANDAR is four hundred twenty thousand kilometers," Fischer reported. "ETA is forty-eight minutes. Enemy range to Dahnvangan is fourteen-point-six million kilometers. ETA to extreme missile range, ten minutes."

Mike nodded.

"Xi?"

"We are as shielded as we can be," his wife and Executive Officer confirmed, her hands on the simulacrum. "If we suddenly need to jump, I'm on it, but I'm prepping for the short-range jump through the debris field."

Mage-Lieutenant Prinz sat behind her in the seat for the backup Mage, and for once, Mike knew that the other two Ship's Mages wouldn't be far away. Running the cloaking spell was difficult and draining, but only over extended periods. It wasn't as bad as the jump spell for rendering his Mages drooling hunks of exhaustion.

There was still a trio of reezh cruisers on his screens, left long behind now. They were clearly not taking their mission with any particular urgency, pushing along at a single reezh gravity, almost a full day and a half behind him.

The dreadnoughts were away and gone, a quarter of the way across the star system, as their pursuit of *Webber* had proven exactly the wild goose chase it had been meant to. The downside was that they were now accelerating toward Shozhat, but that was a problem for later.

"She's here," the Ambassador told Mike. He heard the big man rise from his seat and turn, presumably saluting or bowing to the *foreign head of state* Mike had allowed on his bridge.

Concealing his sigh, Mike rose in turn. He offered his hand to Naizha.

"Welcome to the bridge, ma'am," he told her in slow but coherent reezh. He had been taking the same lessons as Xi, after all, though she was far faster learning it than he was.

"Thank you for being willing to share space with me, Captain," Naizha told him, her lower eyes blinking at his use of her language. "I will take an observer seat and remain out of the way. I do not wish to cause distraction."

"Thank you for your understanding," Mike said in reezh, before turning to O'Hannagain and switching to English. "Get her secured safely, please. We'll be steady enough for now, but when we make the jump…"

The Navy jumped into and out of planetary orbits on a regular basis, but it was rare for someone to jump from one planetary orbit into the same planetary orbit. They were talking about a range more normally suited to a personal teleport spell, but Xi couldn't bring someone along with her on that.

"Captain, *Last Stand* just started transmitting a timer on the broad tactical network," Fischer said. "Counting down from one hundred eighty seconds."

"Please, Director, take your seat," Mike told the reezh leader in her language. "It sounds like the show may begin sooner than we were expecting."

The counter hit zero.

The entire region of space around Dahnvangan *flickered* on the scanners, as if the universe let out a sigh of relief, and Mike very nearly swallowed his tongue as *Rhapsody in Bohemia* updated to show the reality.

The First Shield had left orbit of the asteroid at least an hour earlier, burning out into space at twenty-five meters per second squared—three standard reezh gravities. Yet an immense spell had been woven across that region of space, showing them still in orbit of Dahnvangan.

That spell had now dropped, the Mages behind it probably utterly exhausted from the scale of their working, but they had done what they needed to: the First Shield was over a hundred and fifty thousand kilometers closer than the Kadak had expected and was launching missiles.

"The Observatory is more than a tool to see your surroundings, I take it," Mike heard O'Hannagain note to Naizha.

"It is not an amplifier," the reezh Mage said. "But it *does* permit one to see at a scale that would normally be beyond us. And so, a spell that requires sight can be done on a scale that could not otherwise *be* done."

"Your people did well," Mike said, watching the missiles blaze out. More than just the launchers on the reezh ships, too. They had clearly stacked salvos from the orbital launchers, using the same magical shield to conceal initial burns before shutting them down and letting them drift to rendezvous with the eighty-odd ships of High Commandant Poitch's fleet.

Twenty thousand missiles lit up their drives, an opening salvo that matched the firepower the attackers could bring to bear—and the attackers met it in kind.

"That's a sucker punch, but at this range, it won't make the difference you'd think," Fischer warned.

"That depends on how close to real-time Poitch's data is," Mike countered, comparing the position of the hostile fleet to the sensor buoys they'd dropped earlier. "Our buoys are only a million kilometers from that fleet."

"The buoys don't have FTL coms!"

"No, but *Sondheim* does, and she's not in the Commodore's battle line."

Mike's people hadn't noticed that. The First Shield had charged out, but TG 28 had remained in orbit of Dahnvangan with the defensive platforms. Except only *nine* ships were in orbit. *Webber* had lost her pursuers but so far hadn't returned, *Barracuda* was flying with the First Shield—and *Sondheim* was also missing.

And unless Mike missed his guess, the *Bard of Winter*–class destroyer's Mages were working the same magic Xi Wu was, only without the support of a ship designed to make that work easier.

"*Sondheim* is adrift, probably at a very low relative velocity, with her Mages cloaking her," he explained, knowing that Naizha might not be familiar enough with the components to put it together. "She'll be at ten, maybe twelve light-seconds. At that range, she'd provide decent data on her own, but the passive sensor buoys are even closer—and they can be set to send data back via a laser-com system.

"So, while the data she's relaying into the tactical network is ten to twelve seconds old, it's at a level of detail a ship couldn't provide without being seen, magic or no magic," Mike continued. "And she's feeding it through the Link, which means that *Barracuda* and *Webber* are both getting it as soon as she does."

"Remind me, if I ever start having the foolish concept that I understand this, that I am in the presence of professionals," O'Hannagain replied. "What does all of that even *mean?*"

"It means our friends have been very clever." Mike was unsurprised to see a second countdown pop up on the Link feed. "And, I suspect, that whoever Sujam left in charge of his main force is about to have a very bad day."

At first glance, the timer could have been mistaken for "time to impact" for the massive alpha strike, but Mike checked the math and realized it wasn't *quite*. The timer would hit zero six seconds before the missiles impacted.

He checked his safety straps, almost unconsciously. Whatever happened was going to be... dramatic. The first stage, after all, had used an illusion so powerful that his data feed from a cruiser *in Dahnvangan orbit* had been deceived.

Missiles began to die in the cataclysmic detonations of antimatter warheads. The reezh weapons were driven by fusion drives, but they used the same matter-antimatter reaction as RMN weapons. Lighter warheads, but at a scale where *lighter* could only be relative.

Antimatter explosions made a hash of the sensors. Whatever data feed *Last Stand* was getting from *Sondheim* and the sensor buoys wasn't going into the tactical-network level that *Bohemia* was picking up.

The performance of the missiles was evidence of the buoys' existence, though. Some missiles always wandered off, but this time, the First Shield's salvo bore straight and true.

And then the timer hit zero. The feed from *Last Stand at Alamo* stopped completely for a whole second, and Mike knew *exactly* what reckless trick Rantala had pulled out of his hat.

When the data feed returned, twenty starships were positioned *behind* the enemy fleet, barely two million kilometers away. The Kadak fleet's velocity was carrying them away from their ambushers, but at that range, it didn't matter.

Ten Martian—including the missing *Andrew Lloyd Webber*, done acting as a coms relay to the Fourth Shield—nine Ordin, and one Chimeran warship opened up on the enemy with everything they had. Amplifiers tore through battleships while heavy lasers smashed into asteroid monitors and missiles blazed toward lesser warships.

By the time *Rhapsody in Bohemia*'s data feed was fully back online, every battleship and cruiser in the enemy fleet was gone, along with over half of the monitors—and *then* the missile salvos began to arrive.

This wasn't, Mike realized, the hit-and-run attacks of the Horatio strikes carried out in Chimera. The Ordin starships didn't have the training or the Mages for that. Instead, it was a close-in slugfest, with the metronome of missiles from the First Shield continuing to even odds already tipped by the surprise and the brutal strike.

Even from a distance, it was clear that the reezh ships had no idea how to fight against an amplifier. Lasers and ion cannons hammered ships on both sides, but the devastation unleashed every few seconds by the RMN Mages had no counter or counterpart.

It took two minutes for Mage-Commodore Rantala and his allies to utterly dismantle the largest rebel force in the Ordin System.

There were too many damage codes on the display for Mike to think it had been done cheaply, but it had been done. Over a hundred warships had been reduced to scrap and escape pods, and as he watched, the survivors of Task Group Twenty-Eight began to match velocity to retrieve the rebel survivors.

Eleven Martian and Chimeran warships had joined nine Ordin ships in the ambush. Only eight RMN ships remained, and Mike judged that *Barracuda* was in serious trouble, for all that she had survived where *Eye of Newt* had not.

He heard Naizha's sharp inhale as the reezh leader managed to read enough of their displays to guess how badly the Fourth Shield had been handled. Her students had put their lives on the line for their star system... and the bill had been called.

"How many of my starships were lost?" she asked carefully.

"The First Shield is still under fire, but... seven in the Fourth Shield, ma'am," Mike told her gently. "The dreadnought and one of the cruisers remain. The rest are missing from the scans. There are almost certainly escape pods, and *Pride of Liberty* is remaining in position to sweep for them."

As well as their own, of course. *Eye of Newt* had carried seventeen hundred souls. Mike didn't even know how many reezh had been aboard the seven ships that had just been lost.

There was a long silence on *Rhapsody in Bohemia*'s bridge as everyone considered the new situation. The First Shield would probably survive the remaining enemy fire without significant damage, but their losses were already heavier in total than the Fourth's.

Still, the combination of the First and Fourth Shields would rival the remaining rebel force at Shozhat. The three dreadnoughts under Sujam were a problem, but the balance of power in the system had just changed dramatically.

"Our mission remains critical," Naizha said, as if she read his mind. He didn't think that was in the realm of the powers reezh Mages had learned that humans lacked, though, which meant she was just a very smart lady.

"With control of the Mountain of Astral Might, we can convince the remaining rebel forces to lay down their arms without further bloodshed." That was probably too optimistic, but even she seemed to realize it. "Even if they will not yield, the Mountain will permit me to remove them from anywhere they can harm others before they are neutralized.

"If we can avoid more battles like this, we must," Naizha declared. "We must end this violence so my people can heal. Safely."

The speech wasn't really necessary, Mike knew. O'Hannagain had committed *Bohemia* to this mission, and he wasn't planning on doing anything *else* today, but he knew why she had to say it.

The speech was for herself, not for the humans around her. Maybe even for Troth and the Paladins, if they were listening.

Mike's focus remained on the ship's controls and sensors. There wasn't a lot of point in bringing the ship's engines up to full power at this point, he judged. There was no reason *not* to, either, with the only nearby threat being the three Type Threes whose commanders had to be really thinking about their life choices.

"Captain." Fischer's voice was calm, but there was an urgency to it that Mike hadn't heard often. "Sujam and his dreadnoughts just diverted away from Shozhat."

"I guess they saw the battle results," Mike said with a chuckle, then fell silent, realizing the timing wasn't right. Sujam was almost eight light-minutes away. The reezh was only seeing the light from the ambush right then—and *Bohemia* wouldn't see their response for another eight minutes.

"They can't have; they diverted before it even started," Fischer said. "They seem to be heading for deep space, but I don't see anything out there— Wait, the Kadak task force at Shozhat just moved as well. They're pulling twenty-five MPS-squared, though I think that's more about keeping the planet between them and the loyalists."

"Are they heading for the same point?" Xi's question was the obvious one. A rendezvous made sense, but Mike's spine was starting to prickle.

"I think so; there's definitely an intersect. Checking in on Flotilla Kappa—they are also moving."

"Project all three courses and give me the intercept," Mike ordered. Thankfully, both O'Hannagain and Naizha seemed to know when to watch professionals work.

Three vectors gave a very clear point in space. Several light-minutes from Shozhat, at least a dozen from *Rhapsody in Bohemia*.

Lightspeed lag wasn't the problem. Anything their hostiles had seen, they would have seen before they saw the hostiles move. At over two hundred million kilometers, though...

"Would we pick up a jump flare at that range?" Mike asked slowly.

"No." There was no hesitation. Fischer had clearly thought the same thing as their boss.

"I'm hijacking the tactical network," the Navy officer continued. "I need your override codes, boss."

Mike didn't hesitate either. They could work with *Last Stand*'s people—they inevitably *would* once they knew what was out there—but *Rhapsody in Bohemia* had the best software and hardware for this kind of haystack search.

"Link under my control," Fischer confirmed. "Downloading new instructions to all sensor buoys, using *Sondheim* and *Last Stand* as relays. Pulling sensor data from everybody— Oh. That's helpful; remind me I owe Bourgeois and her people a beer."

"Commander?" Mike asked.

"Someone saw what I was doing and attached their feed from the Ordin Shields to it. I have every friendly eye in the system, and I am interpolating. Give me... *Fuck*."

The Tactical Officer threw their discovery onto the display. Scarlet red icons gleamed in the dark, row after row of them filling out and adding new datacodes as the massive virtual telescope Fischer had assembled fed them data.

"I count four Type Ones, with the Shining Shields' two-three ratio all the way down the classes," they reported grimly.

The codes were calm and simple depictions of the new factor in the star system. Fifty-three starships—and these, Mike knew, were unquestionably *starships* that had made the journey from elsewhere.

"They are accelerating at roughly one MPS-squared," Fischer continued. "Low enough not to be picked up at a distance without effort, but enough for me to identify masses. I mark the types as seventy, fifty, fifteen, five, and one megatons. Masses and what other signatures I can see align with Shining Shield forces out of the Nine."

"But why?" Naizha finally asked. "If they were going to intervene, the Kadak would have sent a ship weeks ago, and the Kazh would have already returned."

"It's small enough to be a ready reaction force, even with everything they've sent at us in Chimera," Mike observed. "They've reliably made the crossing to Chimera in twenty-four to twenty-five days, so they could have made the trip in two, maybe three days, after someone here sent them an FTL message."

"The Kadak called them in when they saw us," O'Hannagain concluded, the Ambassador following the same math. "Presuming they had a... What did you call them, Director? A Singer of the Astral?"

"They must have," Naizha agreed. "With the damage the First Shield and your forces have taken, this turns the balance against us once more."

She straightened her back and lifted her head, looking around the bridge with her lower eyes.

"It seems, my friends, that is more important than ever that we do not fail."

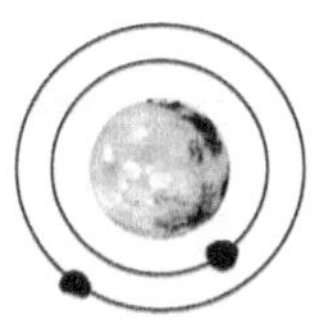

CHAPTER 46

CONNOR WAS NOT NEARLY AS SURPRISED by the arrival of Kazh forces as Naizha seemed to be. The only question in his mind had been whether the rebels would call in the church with all of its fleets and firepower themselves, or if the clearly ongoing scouting operations would reveal Ordin's weaknesses.

The clear redirection of all of the Kadak fleets toward the Shining Shield force answered that question, of course. The rebels had panicked at the arrival of a new player in the humans and called for help.

In theory, he supposed he should try to talk to the Kazh commander. While Mars was unquestionably at war with the Church, Ordin wasn't part of that war, and historical standards called for certain courtesies and communications to keep the neutrals uninvolved.

Except, of course, that Ordin was in the middle of a civil war, and it seemed quite clear that both the Kazh and the Protectorate had chosen their sides.

"If they're rendezvousing with the locals, they're taking the long way in," the senior Navy officer on the bridge reported. Lieutenant Commander Fischer seemed competent, though Connor didn't have much to go on there.

"They may change their minds if they realize what we're up to," Connor warned. "They'll be playing the game on multiple levels. They want the rebels to carry the majority of the fighting, but they also cannot afford for us to get Naizha to the Mountain of Astral Might."

"And that's why we're not going any faster," Captain Kelzin agreed. "The cruisers back there are already closer than I'd like. If we pushed to fifteen gees, it wouldn't make any real difference to our arrival time at this point, but it *would* make us more visible."

"How long?" Connor asked.

"We're already close enough to start resolving the debris cloud and see how deep we'll have to go," the Captain said. "I want to get into a steady orbit—zero to the planet in a Lagrange point if we can get into one safely."

"Unfortunately, there's no moon," Fischer pointed out. "Any Lagrange point is too far away."

"I know, but the thought struck me and fell out of my mouth before that caught up with me." Kelzin chuckled. "How bad is the cascade looking?"

A quiet fell over the bridge as *Bohemia*'s crew set to pulling together the information. Connor wasn't going to be any help in that task, so he stayed back, seated with Naizha.

"Are your people ready?" he murmured to her.

"As ready as you or me," she confirmed. "The time is coming to fix this mess. I thank you and your people for your help, Ambassador. Your intervention will not be forgotten."

"We share an enemy. Our efforts here are not selfless, Naizha."

"I know. Your price will be paid, Ambassador." She met his gaze with her lower eyes, the more-protected set. "We will share our magic and technology with you—and once we have rebuilt the Shield of Ordin, our warships will stand shoulder to shoulder with yours."

Connor's immediate reaction was to ask if he could get that in writing, but he restrained himself with a smile. If Naizha was playing them, this was going to be an expensive mistake on his part—but it would still keep Ordin out of the Kazh's circle.

Having one of the Primes as an ally would be a boon, but they *needed* to keep the Kazh contained.

"It's not good," Fischer finally declared as the crew completed their analysis. "How much metal did these people *put* in orbit?"

"Nothing about Orandar's orbitals was allowed to happen without organization and design," Naizha told them. "We had seen problems with debris above the Builder, and we had learned these lessons before we came here. We kept much of our industry in orbit, which required careful arrangements, especially when we added the fortifications."

"A lot," Connor summarized to the Tactical Officer. "They had a *lot* of asteroids and stations in orbit... and a lot of *people*, too."

"I'd say that when Naizha here gets her throne, her first course of action should be shooting the fucker who decided to pick a fight above Orandar, but I have the suspicion that the Kessler cascade already took care of that," Fischer said grimly. "The debris zone isn't quite as dense as we feared, but that's because it's significantly deeper than we feared."

"Show me," Kelzin ordered.

Every eye in the bridge was on the main display as Fischer zoomed in on the planet ahead of them. A red shell encased the world for a second before it split into quarters, allowing the highlighting of the layers making it up.

"Orandar is a lovely planet, average temperature eight degrees Celsius, forty-five percent surface water," Fischer noted. "Radius sixty-five hundred kilometers, surface gravity point-nine standard gravities.

"Fifty-four hour day. Unpleasant for both us and reezh, but I guess people adapt. Orandar is bigger than Earth but lighter on the heavy metals, hence the lower gravity.

"Key points of the day: the exosphere extends about eight thousand kilometers up from the surface, and geostationary orbit is at twenty-five thousand kilometers."

A translucent collection of images appeared on the display, marking the ring of stations and captured asteroids that had surrounded Orandar in the scan data from *Thorn*'s visit to Ordin.

"The orbital network was, as Naizha noted, extremely well organized. The primary ring was at exactly geostationary equatorial orbit, consisting of over four hundred captured asteroids averaging one kilometer in diameter." Fischer shook their head. "The scale of even that project boggles my mind, though I recognize most of our Core systems have a similar scale of orbital industry. It's just generally spread across most of the system.

"Anyways." They gestured back at the chart. "Our data from the locals doesn't actually have a figure on the number of platforms that were *smaller* than a kilometer across, only that it was large. The primary ring was generally assessed to be five thousand kilometers across, and while it wasn't dense enough to walk on, you could probably have jumped from station to station by visual navigation."

Connor presumed Fischer was exaggerating. But, from what he'd seen, probably not by as much as it felt like.

"The primary ring was, of course, just that: the primary. There were an untold number of *other* satellites in lower and higher orbits, providing everything from agricultural surveys to navigation. It was all classified, organized, and charted, allowing for a degree of easy mobility to and from the surface that some of our Core Worlds would envy."

There was an oppressive silence as everyone considered just how much time, money and effort had to have gone into that infrastructure—not to mention the millions of people who had lived and worked on it.

"All of that is gone," Fischer concluded quietly. "The firefight amongst the defensive forts and ships was catastrophic. A Kessler cascade was inevitable and devastating. The velocity added by the initial explosions has made things significantly worse.

"The red zone is the region I don't believe we could pass through without taking critical damage. The blue zone is the exosphere."

They didn't really need to explain further. Connor had only missed the problem because he'd been following along with Fischer's explanation of the background.

The blue zone extended, as they'd noted, eight thousand kilometers from the surface. The red zone started at *seven* thousand kilometers and extended up past thirty thousand, where it faded into an orange Connor assumed meant there was *some* chance of them surviving.

"The overlap between exosphere and danger zone is too much," Fischer said. "We can't make the jump. Either we go too deep and hit atmosphere that's too thick, or we come in too high and get struck by debris—or worse, we hit a point where we collide with *both*."

"There are potential options," Naizha said, her reezh voice a rough contrast to Fischer. "There are facilities on the surface I should be able to access by remote control. Last-ditch anti-orbital weapons. Combined with the properly sequenced deployment of high-yield antimatter weapons from this side, they should suffice to open a passageway large enough for a single ship.

"It will take an extraordinary pilot, but it should be doable."

"Mark the locations, please, Director," Kelzin asked. "And the location of the Mountain itself."

Naizha crossed to the display and pointed out several spots as the globe reassembled itself. Each of them acquired an odd square blue icon it took Connor a moment to identify as a bunker.

"And Ushola, with the Mountain, is here," she concluded. "The remote defenses are positioned to protect it, of course, which will make opening the passage easier and more direct."

"Of course, the people around the capital will notice that," Kelzin replied. "Even if we kept this ship invisible, the passage would make our approach obvious. Can you disable the other anti-orbital weapons? For that matter, are you certain you can control these ones?"

"The codes I have to access them do not officially exist." Naizha cast her lower eyes down, still looking at the display with her upper eyes. "I should be able to override any software they have put in place. I will order the shots necessary to clear our path and then shut down the systems.

"They will be able to restore function, but it will take some time. Thirty minutes, at least."

"Okay, that might not be the worst plan." Kelzin stepped up next to her. "We don't want to put antimatter weapons too close to a planet." He snorted. "Hell, our antimatter weapons will automatically self-destruct if they get within a certain distance of a large mass."

"The defense batteries are a wide-focus version of our ion cannon," Naizha said. "They will not have the same impact as detonating antimatter weapons, though they will have long-term weather effects in the region."

Connor remembered the sight of reezh ion cannon plunging down onto Garuda, seen on scanners from far too great a distance for Second Fleet to do anything, and shivered.

"Or we could *not* wave a giant flag across the entire star system by unleashing weapons of mass destruction and beams that are only slightly less destructive than said weapons," Xi Wu said pointedly. The Ship's Mage stepped up next to her husband and pointed at the southern pole of the planet, where Connor realized there was a patch of orange on the debris zone.

"The majority of the orbital structures were around the equator," she noted. "The debris zone is thinnest at the poles. Ushola is twenty-five hundred kilometers from the south pole, a distance we can cross with ease if we're coming in from the top of the exosphere."

"Those orange zones are not safe," Fischer objected. "That only means we aren't guaranteed to get hit inside the first thirty seconds. The chances are still over fifty percent every ten seconds!"

"We already established all of these plans are going to need a damn good pilot, some reckless maneuvers and a lot more risk than any of us would like," Xi replied. "I can put us here." She tapped the orange zone. "We can shield ourselves against the debris Mike can't dodge and drop out of the danger zone in a few seconds.

"Then it's an angled descent that will bring us above Ushola in, what, twenty minutes?"

"Twenty-five or so, depending on how much rotational velocity we have with the jump," the Captain murmured, clearly studying Xi's proposed path. "We'll break every sound barrier along the way and freak out a lot of people, but Ushola's defenses won't have line of sight until we're in the final approach, the last hundred kilometers or so."

"At which point Naizha can use her codes to shut the guns down *without* vaporizing a few cubic kilometers of the air," the Mage declared. "We fly right into the middle of downtown, dump the shuttles onto the entry plaza and hold *Bohemia* up to shoot the hell out of anybody who tries to follow you in."

"I believed *my* plan was reckless," Naizha finally said. "But if everything goes correctly, yours will avoid detection by the Kazh fleets."

"And if even the slightest thing goes *wrong*, we all die," Fischer countered. "Though, no offense, Director Naizha, that's true of your plan as well. We would need an *extremely* precise Mage and a pilot like none I've ever seen."

"We have both," Kelzin said, the determination in his voice perfectly clear to Connor. "Though I'm going to ask everyone who isn't absolutely essential to leave the bridge for this. I can't afford distractions."

"I am precise, yes, but for this... I do have a better plan," Xi Wu said, leaning over to press her forehead to her husband's. "I am as confident in my ability to make this jump as I am in your ability to fly through the maelstrom it will leave us in... but while no one can back you up on the flying, *Barracuda* is in the system with us, and few living Mages can match the precision of a Promethean at this sort of calculation.

"Lisa and I will see this ship through the debris field. Then it will be down to Mike to get us to Ushola."

"And then it will come down to me," Naizha concluded.

"To us," Connor corrected. "Our commandos and I are coming with you. We will see this through to the end, Naizha."

"Of course you will. You need our alliance." Even across languages and species, Connor knew she was gently mocking him.

He would get the support Mars needed from Ordin, but even Naizha wasn't fooled as to why they were helping. They were there because of the Channelers—and even Connor wasn't going to pretend that motivation was selfish.

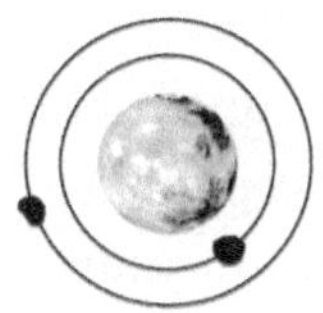

CHAPTER 47

MIKE HADN'T BEEN KIDDING about getting everyone off the bridge. As *Rhapsody in Bohemia* dropped into a high orbit of Orandar, there was only him, Fischer and Xi on the stealth ship's command deck.

Everyone else was hopefully preparing for the landing action that was going to follow. Mike wasn't entirely used to sending other people down in the assault shuttles, but that was part and parcel of his new job.

As Kelly's XO, he'd been able to make the argument that a landing operation was important enough to need his hand on the stick. As Captain, there was no way.

"Lisa has confirmed the jump numbers," Xi said aloud. "I'm adjusting for our final position."

"Thank you, Xi. Fischer?"

"Tactical is green. I've offloaded as much of the systems to the secondary center as I can," Fischer told him. "I can't promise we'll shoot down everything, but the RFLAMs are online and scanning in independent mode."

"Shut down the energy-concentration network and stand by to vent heat sinks," Mike ordered. "Let's not make this jump with molten metal inside the ship."

"Energy-management network now in dispersal mode," Fischer confirmed. "Heat sinks standing by for emergency dump."

"Vent it."

Normally, once they were out of stealth, they would open panels along *Bohemia*'s flanks that exposed the heat sinks to vacuum. It would take vastly longer for the heat sinks to cool down than it took to heat them up, but usually, they *had* time.

Now a camera feed popped up on Mike's repeater displays, showing those same panels opening, except instead of extending cooling loops to expose the heat sinks content to vacuum, a second set of interior panels opened. A blast of semi-molten metal—a tungsten-lead alloy selected for its high melting point—released into space.

The temperature indicators on the screens dropped precipitously at the same time. Hours of heat from silent running concentrated into tons of metal and now loosed into the existing debris field.

"Xi, ready on your mark," Mike told her as the panels resealed.

He took the ship's controls into his hands. A course had been programmed into the computer, but it would need to be adjusted for their exact emergence point—and there was a level of intuition to surviving the task ahead that few computers could match.

"Fischer?" Xi asked.

"Defenses online; scanners going active on your word," they confirmed.

"All right." She exhaled a long breath. "Mike?"

"Yeah?"

"I love you."

"I love you too."

He hoped that wouldn't be the last thing they said to each other.

"Mark."

Mike didn't normally perceive jumps. Once in his life, Xi had taken him as a ride-along on a personal teleport, an experience that he could only describe as nauseating, and he'd always assumed that a bad ship-jump would end up feeling much the same.

The jump into Orandar's atmosphere felt like repeatedly slamming his face into a brick wall he couldn't see. Everything *hurt*, and he found himself blinking against the shock as he tried to process how much force had been packed into an instant.

Some instinct he couldn't explain moved his hands, triggering the engines and spinning *Bohemia* off her planned course to starboard—only afterward did he even register the contact on the sensors.

"Sensors are active," Fischer said in a strained voice. "RFLAMs firing."

Beams of coherent light flickered around them, vaporizing any piece of debris large enough to threaten the ship. At the speed needed to maintain an orbit at this altitude, that was just about everything.

Mike dove. *Rhapsody in Bohemia*'s engines came to life at his command, accelerating her toward the planet surface as he pushed into Orandar's gravity, combining her engines with the planet's pull to get them down and out of the debris field.

They almost made it. They were at the edge of the zone, actually *out* of the orange zone Fischer had marked, when a chunk of debris smashed into the stealth ship. Red alerts flared across the displays, and Mike *felt* his ship start to change. Enough of a hole had been torn to change her flight profile, and he grimaced as he had to adjust.

His face *hurt* from the aftereffect of the jump, and he couldn't even spare the attention to make sure Xi was okay.

Bohemia was sliding sideways. One of the cold-thrust engines was offline, and she was bleeding air all along the starboard side. He adjusted the engines as best he could, trying to balance on the ship's almost-nonexistent aerodynamic surfaces.

They weren't landing. They were *falling*, and with one of the secondary engines gone, that was a problem. They couldn't use the antimatter engines in atmosphere, not without catastrophic results for both *Bohemia* and the planet.

For a moment, even Mike panicked—and then a hand settled softly on his shoulder.

"I'm fine," Xi Wu whispered in his ear. "And you've got this. I know you do."

He spent a second he hoped he could spare covering her hand with his—and then got to work.

They were still far enough up that he *could* fire up the antimatter engines. Not for very long and there'd be a spectacular southern-lights show across the planet for the next few days, but it wouldn't cause damage until he was much lower.

A few seconds at five gees was enough to counteract the thrust he'd created toward the planet, stabilizing his velocity back onto the line he needed. With only two cold-thrust engines, stability was going to be a problem... but *Bohemia* had more than primary and secondary engines.

Chemical-rocket maneuvering thrusters were for close-range delicate work, docking with space stations and cargo craft. Even the massed force of every maneuvering thruster *Bohemia* had couldn't counteract Orandar's gravitational pull.

But Mike didn't need it to. He just needed to make up for a missing cold-ion thruster—he wanted to delay and *control* his descent, not completely arrest it.

"We're going in faster than we planned," he warned over the ship PA. "The good news is that we're not going to need to worry about those assault shuttles." He paused. "I strongly suggest that everyone with access to one of them go strap yourselves in, though. This is going to get bumpy."

Warning icons blazed across his displays. He didn't have enough thrust. He was descending too quickly. He was off the planned line.

Xi reached over and muted them all for him. Her eyes were bloodshot, and she had a trace of dried blood under her nose. Mike wanted to grab her and hug her, tell her she was wonderful and that she was the only reason they had a chance at pulling this off.

Then a targeting radar painted *Rhapsody in Bohemia* and a threat detector pinged loudly.

They weren't in range of Ushola's defenses. This was something more remote, a ground position that could easily belong to either side in the civil war. It wasn't like Naizha was in reliable contact with loyalists on the ground—or that she could have told them they were coming even if she was!

Mike sensed as much as saw Fischer firing off decoys. They didn't have many of the anti-targeting systems that an aircraft would have—not least because their sheer size rendered them useless. At a hundred-plus meters long, *Bohemia* was larger than almost any pure airbreather built by humans or reezh.

He cut the engines entirely. For a few moments, only momentum and gravity carried them forward, as the decoy drones did everything they could to pretend to be the starship. They weren't designed for this environment or for ranges this short, but after a few seconds, the threat detector put the radar beam under the detection threshold.

Without a lock, nothing fired, and Mike brought the engines back online—just in time to drive *Bohemia* through Orandar's Kármán line, where the atmosphere grew thick enough to truly start to heat his hull.

Thin as the mesosphere was compared to the lower layers, the transition felt like belly-flopping into the ocean. Mike changed a dozen factors on his console with a thought, linking his implants into the control console.

He couldn't fly by the implants, but he could give secondary instructions.

A waypoint popped up in his vision, marking the direction of Ushola. He was lower than he'd wanted to be at this distance and moving far too fast. The atmosphere would help with the velocity, but the price was the terrifying increase in hull temperature on his displays.

The temperature stabilized before it should have, and Mike realized that Fischer was backing him up. The energy-dispersal network in *Bohemia*'s hull wasn't enough to stop antimatter warheads, but it was intended to handle anything short of that. Against sustained heat like this—of course.

Fischer was somehow forcing the dispersal web to work in a combination of *both* of its designed modes. It was dispersing the heat from the bottom of the ship across the entire hull—and then it was sinking as much of the heat as it could gather into *Bohemia*'s massive heat sinks.

Mike used that ruthlessly, keeping their air speed at a level that should have been suicidal at the atmospheric level they'd entered. If he didn't have the height he'd wanted, he'd use the speed he *hadn't* wanted.

Rhapsody in Bohemia's sonic boom probably echoed across the entire continent, but she reached Ushola well ahead of the sound of her approach.

He was less than five kilometers in the air and still moving *far* too fast when the Ordin capital came into view. More targeting radars locked on to his ship, and this time, Mike couldn't risk killing the engines.

Bohemia danced in the air, pointing up and away from her destination as Mike fired every non-antimatter engine he had to slow their headlong rush toward the ground. He barely noticed the targeting radars all shutting off in the same instant as Naizha sent out her codes.

He only had eyes for his destination and his vector. Even with gravity runes, he was starting to feel the pull of Orandar's mass, its gravity sharply different in both feel and angle from that produced by *Bohemia*'s magic.

No one on the bridge said a word, but the ship was far from silent now. With the atmosphere around them, the rumble of even the weaker engines shook the entire ship, and their push against the air only added to the sense of riding a bucking horse.

The angle was right. Mike had the approach line *perfect*, but they were still moving too fast. With a final twitch to the spy ship's angle, he took a risk he knew he shouldn't.

As *Rhapsody in Bohemia* descended into the plaza in front of Ordin's Mountain of Astral Might, her mighty antimatter engines woke once more. For less than a tenth of a second, they blazed with the fury of nature defied—and for that tenth of a second, everyone aboard the ship was stepped on by an angry god as five gravities punched through the power of the gravity runes.

It wasn't enough to stop them crashing.

It was enough to make the crash *survivable*...and to vaporize the armored regiment standing guard over their target.

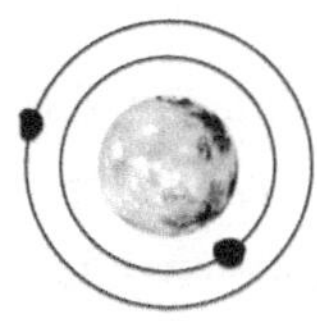

CHAPTER 48

CONNOR COULDN'T AVOID FEELING HELPLESS as *Rhapsody in Bohemia* started her run toward Ushola. The commandos had strapped black clamshell body armor over his shipsuit and handed him a weapon.

The armor wasn't something he was used to, though he appreciated that Rennell's people had assembled it around him with professional precision. It was surprisingly comfortable and had moved well with him in the twenty seconds or so before the universe punched him in the face and Kelzin ordered them to strap themselves in.

He wasn't entirely sure *what* the sensation they'd all just endured was. He'd never felt anything like it and tentatively moved the muscles in his face to test whether there was any bruising.

Just some tenderness, nothing to match the feeling of being repeatedly punched. As he was reaching that conclusion, he *felt* the starship drop in a way he'd never experienced aboard a ship with magical gravity.

He gripped the gun in his hands more tightly and looked down at it. The commandos had seemed unsure about handing him a weapon, so Rennell had told him to pick one. He suspected she knew that the Protectorate Secret Service had insisted the Arbitration Commissioners regularly qualify with a variety of weapons for their own self-defense.

The Martian Armament Caseless Rifle, Linear, Nine Millimeter, was the heaviest of the weapons Connor was comfortable using. Rejoicing in the nickname among the Marines of the Mackerel-Nine, it was the Corps' medium battle rifle, intended for targets with body armor much like what Connor was wearing.

Against the exosuits worn by the Paladins that lined one half of the shuttle, the Marines preferred a discarding-sabot penetrator round fired from a significantly heavier rifle. The most visible sign of the augmentation of the Bionic Commandos around Connor was that they were each carrying the standard penetrator rifle as a personal weapon—and the twenty-four-sixty model Martian Armaments Rifle, Sabot, Twenty Millimeter, was a weapon more commonly carried by exosuits or used on a mount.

The BCR troops wore heavier armor than Connor did. Their underlying shipsuit had integral armor his lacked, and where they'd only put a front-and-back plate and greaves on him, they wore interlinked series of plates over their own gear.

It still paled next to the exosuits he usually saw Marines wearing—like the ones the Paladins wore.

His focused attempt to catalog the gear available to the landing party hit the swords carried by the Paladins around the same time the world went crazy inside of ten minutes. A giant stood on his chest, and then everything around him tried to move as *Bohemia* very clearly hit the ground.

Even the elite soldiers around him weren't silent as the ship crashed. Curses and shouts in at least five languages—including a reezh dialect Connor didn't know—filled the shuttle bay before Rennell's voice cut across them all.

"Hang on; we're moving," she barked—then repeated the same thing in reezh.

Before Connor could question whether that meant the shuttle or the troops themselves, engines rumbled to life and the assault shuttle shot forward with enough speed to press him into his seat.

They were moving for less than ten seconds before Connor was subject to a second rough landing, the shuttle clearly having merely flown clear of *Bohemia* to expand options.

Even before the aircraft had finished moving, the back hatch was swinging open and Rennell was standing.

"Vanguard, go!"

Four of the commandos clearly knew that order referred to them. They were on their feet in the same moment as their commander and moving even as she gave the order. They were out of the shuttle before Connor had even finished unbuckling himself.

He found himself still held in his seat by an arm that might have been made of the same armored composites covering it.

"Stay with me, sir," the commando told him. "Sergeant Lebovitz. I'm to watch your back."

Connor nodded to the man as the Paladins and commandos stormed out of the shuttle.

"I appreciate that, Sergeant," he said. "I'll be good, I promise."

"The more you listen, the closer we can stick to the others," Lebovitz replied.

"Sergeant... I am here to stick with Naizha. No matter what. That's the mission."

Lebovitz's faceless helm regarded him silently for a moment, then the man nodded.

"All right, then. Let's go find ourselves an alien queen."

Naizha might be the woman the Paladins were all there to escort, but that hadn't slowed her down at all. She was already on the ground and moving forward when Sergeant Lebovitz led Connor out of his shuttle, forcing the Ambassador to pick up his pace to catch up to her.

There was no missing the Mountain of Astral Might. *Rhapsody in Bohemia* sat almost exactly in the center of a broad plaza paved with a white concrete that glittered in the morning light. The plaza had been a single smooth surface, without a single breaking line that Connor could see, though now that white was marred with wreckage and destruction in the aftermath of the starship's descent.

In three directions, broad avenues led off into the rest of Ushola, their size and sharp lines a clear sign of a preplanned city to Connor's mind. To the north was the reason they were there, an artificial mountain at least two kilometers across and just as high.

The same artificial white stone that floored the plaza in front of the Mountain covered the structure itself, somehow absorbing just enough light to prevent the pyramid being painful to look at with reflected sunlight.

"This way!" Naizha shouted, waving toward the Mountain. She wasn't even carrying a weapon, only a staff of a black wood that gleamed with silver inlay. A wave of that staff followed her words, and the debris blocking the path swept aside.

Connor followed her. It was what he was there for, after all. The three rose-robed Academicians were a few steps ahead of him, and the Paladins formed a moving phalanx of white armor around the Mages and the diplomatic add-on.

The commandos were already ahead of even Naizha, he realized, but it was hard to tell as their armor turned out to have active camouflage. The pattern-matching to the stones around them wasn't perfect, but it made the two dozen cyborg soldiers far harder to spot than Connor had expected.

"Main entrance is clear," Rennell's voice said in his helmet. "There were troops on the ground in the plaza, but our landing made a mess. Shuttles are going up to provide air support."

Connor caught up to the reezh leader as the sound of shuttle engines swept the plaza again. Naizha had hesitated at the foot of a set of broad steps leading up to a shadowed opening in the artificial mountain.

"Naizha?" he asked, stepping up beside her. Her accompanying Mages, even Troth, had hesitated.

"This is where Izhom died."

Connor realized why the others had hesitated. He hadn't taken *on the steps of the Mountain* to be quite so literal, but it seemed he'd been wrong.

"Here is where Okozhol Azhma breached his highest oath and where the men who should have guarded our world killed each other."

"And if you want your brother's death to mean anything, we have to keep moving," Connor told her. "Unless you think Azhma left this place without security?"

"No. We must move. But I…"

Connor shook his head. He understood—but there was no time.

The main doors into the mountain were easily twenty meters high—and Connor would have been stunned to learn they had *ever* closed. They were wide open, revealing a ceremonial entryway built on the same scale.

It resembled nothing so much as a royal court and was likely used for ceremonies and press conferences, to put the source of the Cadatch's power in the mind of everyone seeing him.

The space felt like it was never empty. It should have been full of bureaucrats and officials, members of the Ahadan and the Cadatch's staff, a bustling entryway marking where the arteries of power in Ordin met.

It was dead. Silent. The only noise was the sound of the Paladin's armored feet on the stone as they advanced.

"There should be someone here," Connor muttered.

"We scanned for snipers and ambushes," Rennell told him. "But we don't have a plan of this building. Naizha, you'll need to lead."

"This way," she replied, pointing with the runed staff.

The route she took them down was as deathly silent as the entry chamber. The Mountain had been evacuated, but Connor doubted that meant it was undefended.

The first trick was less than a minute into the pyramid, when Naizha turned a corner to find Rennell had disabled her active camo to meet them.

"There's no way forward," the BCR officer reported in reezh. "It's been filled in."

It was clear that the hallway had continued forward, but the defenders hadn't just set up a barricade or even bricked it up. Connor suspected they'd set up a cement truck and filled the entire hall, from floor to ceiling.

"How deep?" Naizha asked.

"We only had the time for quick soundings, but at least five meters, maybe more. Our explosives can't breach it. Could your magic?"

"No, whitecrete is used for this space because it resists magic. The only magic that flows in the structure of the Mountain is in its runes—and the stone that shapes that would resist my powers." Naizha still stepped forward to poke the plug with her staff.

"We need a new route." Rennell had reactivated her camo, but her voice was audible through Connor's helmet.

"They will not have sealed the central chamber," Naizha said firmly. "There are other ways."

Connor was no soldier... but he suspected there might only be *one* way, and it would be where all of the Kadak's fiercest soldiers and most powerful Mages awaited them.

They'd reached their destination, but it could still turn into a trap.

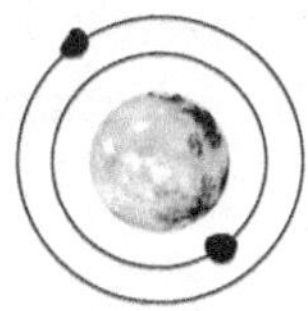

CHAPTER 49

TWICE MORE THEY FOUND corridors blocked by huge plugs of concrete—and as they were staring at the third plug, Kelzin's voice popped into Connor's headset.

"Okay, folks, *Bohemia* is not getting back into the air, let alone space, without major repair. I'm hoping you're close to finishing this too—because our shuttles are starting to pick up movement heading our way.

"I've got enough weapons clear that I'm going to give them a real bad day when they get here, but we can only blockade this side of the Mountain, and nothing that big only has one way in."

"Understood." Reezh was a growled and sharp language to begin with, but the way Naizha bit off those syllables said a lot.

"Contact," a commando snapped in the net. "I've got five reezh approaching down a corridor from the north. Four Paladins, one reezh female in... *a tunic* is the best description I've got, sorry."

Rennell's response was a series of clipped phrases Connor didn't even begin to follow. The commandos clearly did, though, as there was a subtle moving in the space, like that of ghosts, as the active-camoed troopers moved out.

"They may be scouting for us," Rennell warned. "This building has surprisingly little electronic surveillance."

"If the Cadatch is in residence, it is unnecessary," Naizha replied. "Even without, there are usually Mages to survey the corridors without cameras. That, of course, presumes the intruders are not shielded against that kind of spell.

"We are."

Connor hadn't asked. There were a lot of bits of the plan that he hadn't been filled in on, and he was starting to realize he really didn't belong there. If Naizha did betray them, he wasn't going to have much of a chance to put a bullet in her.

But he was going to be with her until she had her brother's throne. That was his promise, so he'd keep it. Leaving Chimera to occupation had been the only broken major promise his reputation could afford.

"Naizha, they've surrendered," Rennell reported unexpectedly. "I need at least one of your people up here to make sure we've handled their weapons and armor properly, and the lady is asking for you. By name."

There was a pause.

"What is *her* name?" Naizha asked.

"She says she's Lora Azhma and you need to talk to her now," Rennell replied. She paused again. "She also just dropped Ambassador Komarazhi's emergency code phrase."

Lora Azhma had the same smooth marble skin as Naizha, but past that, the two reezh women barely resembled each other. Azhma had a more-pronounced armored ridge and a narrower mouth, with all four of her eyes darker than Naizha's.

Where Naizha wore an ankle-length robe with careful stitching to provide freedom of movement, Azhma wore a long-sleeved green tunic belted under her arms and again at her waist, with what Connor could only describe as black leggings underneath it.

Both reezh women were tall, but Naizha's height was in her torso and Azhma's was in her legs—legs that were shown off to great effect by the outfit she wore, not that the multi-jointed limbs were of any interest to the humans.

What was of interest to Connor was the phrase Lora Azhma repeated when the commandos delivered her to Naizha and him. Her hands were cuffed behind her, and her Paladins were waiting out of sight, under guard by their cousins from Naizha's detail.

"Sister," Azhma greeted Naizha. Her gaze then fell on Connor. "And more humans. As I told your ghostly soldiers, the phrase is... *the sun dawns twice on two republics.*"

It was obvious that she'd learned the English phrase by sound, without knowing the meaning of it.

"Are you still my sister, then?" Naizha asked. She was staring at the newcomer like she was a snake, unsure if the woman was going to bite her or not. "Everything I have heard places you in the highest councils of the new Aha Kadak. The Aha that would make itself Iladaha."

One Voice. Given that the Ahadan were the elected part of Ordin's government, Connor could see the metaphorical translation of *Iladaha* without assistance.

"I have children, Naizha," Lora Azhma said quietly.

"And where is So Komarazhi?" Connor growled. He managed it in reezh, hopefully understandably.

Azhma looked at him—and, to his surprise, raised her head to study him with her lower eyes for a moment before saying anything.

"So Komarazhi is dead, of course," she told him. "Executed for her crimes against the true faith, along with her companions."

Naizha's staff slammed onto the stone. She didn't say a word, but Azhma didn't even look at her.

"Of course, there was a *lot* of confusion in the early days. My esteemed father, may the Night know its servant, told as few of his plans as he could. My husband had fears and took actions."

There was a long silence. Connor wasn't sure of many of the details of the actual religion behind the Kazh, but he somehow doubted that *may the Night know its servant* was a particularly nice thing to say about the deceased.

"We could not save them all, but we saved over half of Komarazhi's people," Azhma said. "Komarazhi is in a safe place—with my children. They are as safe as I could make them, but it took a great deal to remove the Cadatch's children from the eyes of his enemies."

Naizha was continuing to glare at her sister-in-law, whatever that relationship meant among the reezh. Connor glanced away from Azhma to meet his ally's gaze.

"That was an emergency phrase Komarazhi was given to summon assistance from Joto's people," he told Naizha. "I don't believe Komarazhi would have given it to someone she didn't believe was a friend."

"I do not understand the human's tongue," Azhma said. "But you know where we stand. I am not my father. I cannot be Cadatch. But there are those among the Kadak who could, though Izhom's plan robbed them of the knowledge they need."

"When did they call the Old Kazh?" Naizha demanded.

"When the humans arrived. It was the first time I even knew that a Singer from the Nine had come here to act as their voice. My Izhom was betrayed long before the Kadak raised hands against Ushola."

That... answered the question of how there had been a Singer of the Astral who could speak to the Kazh, given what Naizha had said about a Singer only being able to communicate to places they had been.

The Kazh had sent their own Singer, to infiltrate, spy and create trouble.

"You are in grave danger, even for surrendering without a fight," Naizha conceded. "What do you want, sister?"

"I cannot be Cadatch," Azhma repeated. "I am cursed, my father's broken daughter. But *you* can be, and I know you are trained to be. The Old Kazh are here. We must end this conflict, drive them from our voids and reunite our people.

"That can only be done by Izhom's blood on the Stone of Ordin. You must reach it."

"That is what I am trying to do, but I cannot pass through these walls by magic. Your friends have barred many of the ways."

"But not all. And not even all the ones they *think* they have," Azhma promised. "Follow me, sister. I will show you the way."

"And what do you want in return?" Naizha demanded.

"That my children be raised as the children of the Cadatch, trained to serve as their father did. I cannot be Cadatch—but *they* can."

Azhma knew the layout of the Mountain of Astral Might even better than Naizha, Connor judged, even without taking into account the new barriers that had been installed. She was far more certain of the path as she led them into a maze of secondary corridors.

Everything the woman was saying made sense and added up. Connor wasn't quite sure *why* she was so insistent that she was cursed and couldn't be Cadatch, but it made sense that she would then want to work with Naizha to lock down her children's future—and that she'd have been working with the rebels prior to Naizha's arrival to secure their safety.

And yet Connor couldn't quite trust her. He'd only been officially a diplomat for less than a year, but so much of his job beforehand had involved similar skills. He knew when everything someone said was true but still wasn't the whole story.

He tapped a few commands on his wrist-comp, locking down a channel back to *Bohemia*.

"Kelzin, it's Connor. This link is private," he told the Captain. "I need a favor."

"I'm currently doing you the favor of keeping people from coming up behind you with tanks," Kelzin replied. They were deep enough into the Mountain for there to be interference, but the transmission was still intelligible.

"I need your sensors and potentially your Mages," Connor said grimly. "I may be wrong, but if I'm not, we might be in real trouble.

"I need you to turn *Bohemia*'s sensors on the Mountain and dissect this hunk of rock like it's a bad contract," he told Kelzin. "I think there's a prison somewhere in here, almost certainly with Mages guarding it, and it's where So Komarazhi is held—along with some hostages that we absolutely *must* rescue."

There was a pregnant pause.

"I'm not sure Xi and the others can teleport into the Mountain. She said there was some kind of interference she'd never seen."

"If you find that prison, Captain, find a way past that interference," Connor ordered, aware he was quite possibly asking for the impossible.

"When the time comes, there's someone I need to be able to tell her children are safe."

"Kids. Right." Something in Kelzin's tone said Connor had landed the hit he'd meant to. "We will do what we must."

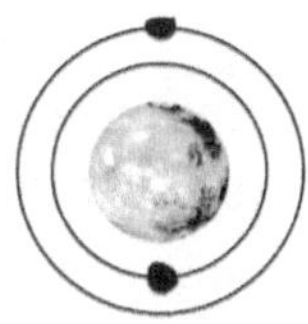

CHAPTER 50

EVEN CONNOR COULD FEEL it as they approached the Central Chamber of the Mountain of Astral Might. There was an ozone tang to the air, a sharpness he associated with recent lightning rather than anything else.

The corridors Azhma took them through seemed to be getting narrower and narrower. When she finally led them into a broader corridor, the scent of ozone and the tingling feeling on Connor's skin only grew clearer.

"We're almost there," Naizha said. "I know this corridor."

"Good. Stick with me, sister," Azhma replied. "It's time for us to make sure of our people's future."

A faint wrongness was the only sign that Connor had of things going amiss before a strange burning, crackling, sound snapped through the corridor. He had a vague sensation of a blaze of green light before Naizha and her Academician Mages collapsed like their strings had been cut.

More familiar-sounding weapons cracked in sequence as Paladins stepped out of the illusions shielding them. They had been waiting and prepared. Half of Naizha's own Paladins were down before the rest managed to surrender.

Connor barely even had time to try and raise his rifle before one of the Paladin's strange swords sliced through it. He let it fall and raised his hands.

"I yield," he said in reezh, hoping he was understandable enough. His hands were swiftly bound and he was shuffled forward next to where Naizha had fallen.

That was when he realized that Azhma had also been caught in whatever pulse had taken down Connor's friend—and the Paladins that had escorted her were definitely among the dead.

He was quite certain she'd betrayed them, but the people laying the trap hadn't set any value on the bait.

The point of a sword prodded him in the back, the force clearly not intended to pierce the armor.

"How many of your humans were there?" a voice demanded in reezh.

Connor tried to turn to look at the speaker, only to find another sword suddenly next to his face—but when the speaker repeated themselves, his earbud didn't translate. He could get the gist of what they were saying, but his translator was gone.

The sword poked harder, and the question was repeated.

"I don't understand," he said in English.

"Stupid," the voice snarled, still speaking reezh. He couldn't follow the next sentence in detail, but it was ordering the Paladins to bring him.

The only person who might have confirmed that there were camouflaged human soldiers to the reezh soldiers was Azhma, and they'd stunned her. Connor didn't think that the Paladins had actually taken down *any* of the commandos, which hopefully was going to bite his captors somewhere sensitive.

"Stay still; show no sign that you're receiving this," Rennell's voice instructed firmly in Connor's ear as he was dragged forward.

"I've disabled all of your outgoing systems remotely," she continued. "That took out your translator, sorry, but I wanted to be sure they didn't think you were talking to anybody else.

"I got my people out, because my job is to be paranoid, but I'm not seeing a way to necessarily turn this around at this point. I'm not sure Azhma expected them to blast her, but it won't make much difference. We've got eyes on the security now, and I'm not punching through that with two dozen bionics.

"We're not that sneaky, after all. I'm sweeping and we're picking positions. If the moment comes, we'll take it, but this just got really ugly."

Connor didn't say anything. Part of him had been hoping Rennell had a plan to save them, but the growing number of Paladins and what appeared to be regular exosuited soldiers—plus the distinctive Priest-Mages with their smooth, near-white, skin—that he was passing told him the odds.

Naizha's Paladins found themselves led away, but Connor was dragged forward with the five unarmored reezh. A Paladin sniffed down at him and demanded to know if he was armed.

"I don't understand your language," Connor retorted.

The sharp response from the reezh warrior was beyond his ability to follow their language, but the pommel of a sword to the stomach was an unfortunately universal form of communication. The armor kept it from being injurious, but Connor still let it push him back.

A rapid-fire exchange of more words, too fast and complex for him to understand, followed between the questioner and the one who'd been behind him with a sword.

Finally, armored gauntlets grabbed his shoulders and yanked him forward. The armor plates were prodded and examined, the Paladins looking for concealed weapons—or potentially just the latches to take the gear off.

Connor could probably have figured it out, but the commandos had armored him up. He certainly wasn't going to *help* his reezh captors.

They managed to detach the arm plates and chest plate, but the backplate appeared to defeat them. It was more integrated with his shipsuit than the other pieces, he supposed.

The sword at his throat nearly stopped his heart, until he realized they were using it to *saw* at the connections for his helmet. He couldn't even take the headpiece off himself with his hands behind his back, so he just held very, *very* still.

Finally, the Paladins had him stripped of his helmet and most of his armor. They either didn't recognize his earpiece for what it was or didn't care since it wasn't actively transmitting.

And despite their caution and the several high-tech-seeming sensors they'd swept over him, they didn't appear to have noticed the hand cannon strapped to the small of his back. He wasn't sure which part of the backplate, the suit jacket he was still wearing under it or the concealing fibers in the hidden holster itself had prevented the revolver from being detected, but he wasn't complaining.

Not that it mattered. His hands were still bound behind him, after all.

Once they thought he was secure, the Paladins dragged him forward again. His reezh companions had been taken somewhere he hadn't seen, leaving him alone with a seemingly endless number of white-armored enemy soldiers.

Two dragged him while another four surrounded them, bringing him toward a door unlike any he'd seen so far in the Mountain. He'd lost track of where he was in the rough handling by the Paladins, but he could guess.

The door was made of a single slab of black stone, constructed to pivot on a single point of contact. Every part of the door, including that pivot point, was covered in silver runes. They spread out into the walls from there, vanishing inside the white stone of the rest of the structure.

From what Connor could see, the Mountain's runic constructs had been built and then covered in the strange white rock that Naizha had said contained magic. A magical assemblage of immense power surrounded them, but there was only one point at which the runes could be seen.

The center.

The door pivoted and the Paladins moved with it, the ease of long practice showing in their sure-footed steps, even dragging him.

The Central Chamber of the Ordin Mountain of Astral Might seemed to be a lightless cavern for a moment, but then Connor's eyes began to adjust. Dim light reflected in the silver runes that covered every surface, but the black rock around the silver seemed to drink in light that fell across it.

There were a few pools of light on the floor, one of them around what he judged to be the equivalent of the throne on Mars: an elevated hexagonal dais carved from the same black stone as everything else. The rune chains on the dais seemed both bulkier and more complex than the ones coating the walls, creating a point where six lines converged into a space just large enough for a single person to stand.

A female reezh stood on that spot. She wore stark white robes that seemed to glow with an inner light as she stood there, but even Connor could tell the Mountain wasn't answering to her call.

Then she turned to face him, and he stumbled, forcing the Paladins to drag him forward more forcefully for several steps. It *wasn't* Naizha, he decided after about ten seconds, but the woman could have passed for the Director's sister.

She barked an order for the Paladins to put him with the others, waving peremptorily toward where Connor saw Naizha and the others, still slumped on the ground. Whatever pulse had taken them down seemed to have left them all unconscious.

Except that Lora Azhma was up. She was standing watch over the prisoners, looking the worse the wear for her own encounter with the stun weapon, but upright and unbound.

"Boss, do not react," Rennell's voice said in his ear. "I have eyes on you again. If you can hear me, look down at the floor for a few seconds."

That was easy to justify. With his hands tied and his shoulders held by armored gauntlets, the only reason he hadn't been watching his feet was because he needed to take in as much of what was going on as he could.

He looked down as requested, getting his feet sorted out as the Paladins delivered him to the pool of light serving as a prison.

"Okay. Good to know that. Without your helmet, Captain Kelzin can't reach your earbud through the Mountain's rock," the commando officer told him. "We think we've located the prisoners. Not just Azhma's kids, either. Fischer's best guess is that we've got at least two hundred, maybe more, juvenile reezh in close quarters.

"That's more than a few Mages can handle, so half of my commandos are moving to support. I really hope we don't have a time limit here, boss, because I'm not seeing options that aren't going to take time."

Connor couldn't reply and wasn't sure there was anything for him to say. They'd made it to their destination—he and Naizha stood at the heart of the Mountain of Astral Might, exactly as planned.

But he suspected he recognized the manacles that had been clapped on them all. There wasn't much of a point in putting antimagic cuffs on him, but with Naizha's access to her magic blocked, even putting her on the dais might not be enough.

They weren't going to get out of this by violence. Only by being clever... and by talking to people.

Those, at least, were things Connor O'Hannagain was good at.

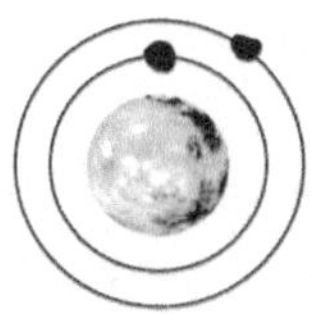

CHAPTER 51

CONNOR TOOK A LONG LOOK at the four reezh Mages he'd arrived with. For all of the sturdiness that reezh normally radiated, they all looked so fragile and helpless, unconscious on the ground like that. Naizha was a powerful Mage, though he suspected she paled against even Roslyn Chambers with the Mage-Captain's secret Rune of Power, but the reezh could do nothing with Mage-cuffs on her wrists.

His gaze turned to Lora Azhma. She was studying him with her dark upper eyes, her face turned down to conceal her lower eyes.

The Paladins shoved him, releasing his shoulders and sending him stumbling over to where Naizha lay.

A barked order to stay there was probably as much habit as anything else, since Connor had done everything he could to convince them he didn't understand their language.

He fell to one knee and was surprised to find Azhma there, taking his shoulder and helping him back up.

"I..."

She didn't finish the sentence. She didn't need to.

"They have your children," Connor whispered. His voice was very quiet. He was going to give up the illusion he couldn't speak Korazhi in a moment or two, but he needed this conversation first.

"Yes. And without a mate, I am expendable. I am no Mage."

She wasn't any louder than he had been, but her words explained a lot. If Azhma's father had been the leader of the whole rebellion, she had to be from the purest and most powerful bloodlines of Priest-Mages. But those families would always throw up a few who had the wrong genes come up dominant in the biological lottery.

Her value to her family was that her children would almost certainly be Mages, but he couldn't imagine what it would have been like to grow up among reezh, knowing that all too many of those around you only saw you as a source of the next generation of actually *useful* family members.

"You should have trusted us," Connor told her. "We could have saved them."

"They are here. Inside everything the Aha Kadak can muster. You couldn't have changed anything."

"Picking this convo up on shotgun mike," Rennel said in his ear. "If she knows any details of what's guarding the kids, now would be the time."

Connor wanted to roll his eyes at the cyborg officer, but instead, he held Azhma's gaze. Long enough and hard enough that she finally lifted her head to look at him with her lower eyes—shorter-sighted but more capable of making out detail.

"What kind of guards, Lora?" he muttered. "It may matter."

He held her lower eyes for a moment more, then turned away from her to survey the room, intentionally ignoring her as she considered whether to trust him.

"It's an old prison block, from the early days," he heard her say behind him. "On the eleventh and twelfth floors, north side. Only two ways in or out. Both have at least six Paladins on them at all times, with dozens of regular soldiers throughout the prison.

"They're all networked to the Mountain's security system. They promised me, as if it was *protective*, that any danger would have a response in two minutes or less."

"Bingo," Rennell said. "I got all of it, boss. Passing it on to Mage Wu. That gal knows her covert ops, O'Hannagain. I can't say how *fast* we'll have the kids, but soon."

"Thank you, Lora," Connor told his captor, then stepped toward the central dais and raised his voice.

"Hey!" he bellowed in reezh. "Someone around here is in charge of this shit show, right? I am the Ambassador for the Protectorate, and I will be heard."

His voice garnered confusion. He doubted he was particularly intelligible at that volume, but like his own understanding of the reezh speaking to him, they would get the gist of it.

A pair of Paladins seemed to appear from nowhere, their swords raised to shoot him, when a new voice sounded in the space.

Another reezh stepped forward, conjuring a light around themselves as they did. They were dressed completely differently from anyone else he'd seen in Ordin, a form-fitting dark red jumpsuit with short sleeves and legs that ended at the first joint on all four limbs.

Their skin was the same white marble as the Ordin Mages, but their features were a touch more angular, accentuated by a small number of silver piercings that drew attention to the sharp edges.

Unlike the Ordin, the stranger wore something that closely resembled a Protectorate-style wrist-comp. They finished entering a command into it and waved the Paladins back.

"Who are you?" they asked—and their wrist-comp repeated the words in passable English, as good as any machine translation Connor had heard.

"I am Ambassador Connor O'Hannagain, charged by Her Majesty Kiera Alexander, Mage-Queen of Mars, to negotiate with the people of Ordin on her behalf," he replied.

The wrist-comp started speaking in reezh as soon as Connor stopped. The software might have been better than what the Protectorate had for a Korazhi-English translator, he realized—especially if it was all running on the Mage's portable computer.

"Greetings, O'Hannagain," the Mage told him through the translator. "I am Atraj Koban, Singer of the Astral, and Farsent Speaker for Those-Who-Speak for the Nine."

"You are in charge here?" Connor asked with a laugh.

The device had barely finished translating before the woman who looked like Naizha had her hand on Koban's arm, snapping at them in rapid-fire reezh—reezh that the translator happily picked up, though Connor was probably the only one who heard or cared.

"You do not rule here, Farsent Speaker," the Ordin Mage snapped. "You overstep the lines of our agreement."

"You cannot even understand the words the beast says without my aid," Koban replied, their words utterly calm in either language. "I will translate for you if you wish, Speaker for the Ordin Kadak.

"I remind you, though, we all share the same Light of the Nine. Those-Who-Speak will guide your people as their own lost children, as is only proper. We have done all that you asked, Speaker. Remember the Light. Remember the words of the Nine."

That seemed to go down like a ton of lead bricks, Connor judged, but the Ordin woman wasn't ready to tear anyone's head *literally* off yet.

"Translate," she ordered—and only then did she seem to realize that the device had been translating her argument with Koban.

Even across species and cultures, he could recognize the death glare she gave the Kazh's representative.

"I am Ovaizh, Speaker of the Aha Kadak," she introduced herself. "You demand a right to speak in this most sacred of spaces, but you are known to us only as an enemy, one who lured our shield into a trap and then attacked this place in the company of my treasonous cousin.

"I am tasked to protect this system against all danger, and you seem to be merely one more danger."

Connor tried to spread his hands, then remembered he was still manacled, wincing at the pull.

"I was sent here to make allies for my people," he told her. "We seek to open trade and cultural exchange, and we judged it best to work with the people our allies of Chimera had already been working with.

"That may have been an error, but we are still open to making friendships here in Ordin, Speaker Ovaizh. I am tasked to speak on behalf of Mars.

"Will you listen?"

If he was being honest, Connor was playing for time. If Ovaizh was the new leader of a rebellion launched, so far as he could tell, over whether they should be killing kids to put their brains in starships, there was no conversation possible with Mars.

But he still drew satisfaction from the fact that she was taking him surprisingly seriously. She waved the Paladins moving up on him away, though she didn't go so far as to have his manacles removed.

"You have not made a great impression here, Ambassador," she told him through Koban's translation program. The Kazh Singer had found a fascinating way to make sure that the Ordin didn't talk to Connor without including them, he noted.

"Captain Joto and Ambassador Komarazhi had made contact with Cadatch Izhom's government," he reminded her. "Chimera is our ally, and we trusted their judgment. With no knowledge of who was in control of the Mountain of Astral Might, we followed on our existing connection."

"Chimera," Koban echoed. "You mean *Allosch*, do you not, Ambassador? I must advise you, Speaker of the Kadak, that the people of Allosch have returned to the Light of the Nine. We have heard stories from them of the aliens who tried to conquer their world by lies and force of arms—and if this Ambassador speaks for the same, then they have shed the blood of the Shining Shield."

Connor smiled, though he doubted these reezh would pick up the meaning of the expression. He didn't bare his teeth, at least. Even among human cultures, a closed-lipped smile was safer.

"Our ally was attacked by the Shining Shield, yes," he confirmed. "Our warships fought to defend Chimera before she was overrun.

"The Protectorate of the Mage-Queen of Mars is at war with the Kazh. We seek allies against them. So, perhaps this conversation should take place without the Farsent Speaker?"

Koban drew themselves up straight and glared at him with all four eyes.

"You admit to shedding the blood of our holy warriors, join arms with the faithless here in Ordin, and expect the Speaker to talk in private?" they demanded. "You overstate your position."

"So do you, Farsent Speaker," Ovaizh noted. "We share your faith, but we have not yet decided if we shall reintegrate into the Ida. We listen to the Nine in the voices we know them by."

Connor expected Koban to snap back at that, but the Farsent Speaker said nothing. They simply tapped their wrist-comp with one finger and waited silently.

"As the Farsent Speaker has the only translator for now, we will endeavor to include them," Ovaizh told Connor. "We have nothing to hide from the Kazh. We do not seek allies against our shared blood and faith."

"Of course not."

"As followers of the Nine who are not yet involved in this conflict, we may be able to act as mediators," she continued. "That is a matter for later, once we have dealt with my traitor cousin and her supporters."

The dismissal was clear, and Koban cut off the translator. A Paladin was suddenly looming over his shoulder and Connor allowed himself to be guided back to Naizha and her watcher.

"Got a second shotgun mike on the Speaker," Rennell said in his ear. "She and the Kazh bugger are arguing. Koban is refusing to give her a copy of the translation software, making veiled threats and... Oh, *fuck*."

Connor had no way to demand explanations from Rennell. He waited for her to explain, reaching the guarded cluster of prisoners and taking a cross-legged seat on the floor, just within whispering distance of where Azhma stood guard.

"Connor, the Farsent Speaker is High Chosen. They're trained to use the amplifier—and the only thing holding them back is that Ovaizh is refusing to let them. I'm moving one of my guys to get a line of fire on them, but that's a suicide shot that may not even work against a Mage."

Years of self-control kept his face from showing his reaction to that. The Kadak had held the *I win* button in their hand the entire time, and only their refusal to surrender to the Kazh was keeping them from pressing it.

Because there was no way they were putting a Kazh Priest-Mage on the Mountain of Astral Might's control dais and *not* surrendering. Once Koban had that power, the system would fall in line or be broken into line.

He spared a glance at Lora Azhma. The reezh woman stood stiffly, her upper eyes sweeping the prisoners and an unfamiliar weapon in her hands.

"Step carefully," she told him in reezh. "This weapon is not intended for humans."

He didn't follow her next words, but he could guess: it was supposed to be nonlethal, but she had no idea what would happen if she fired it at him.

"Did you know Koban was High Chosen?" he asked her.

Azhma was a politician's daughter and wife. There was no sign of surprise, not even a twitch. She did slowly turn to look at the Kazh Singer where they were patiently waiting.

Connor suspected Koban thought they had all the cards. The balance of power in the system, even with the arrival of the Shining Shield formation, hung by a razor-thin margin. If Rantala brought in his logistics ships and resupplied the loyalists along with his own ships, the odds were narrower than anyone might think.

And the Martian formation had demonstrated their ability to jump faster and more accurately than the locals could. Connor couldn't see how, but he believed that Rantala could probably find a way to turn the battle against the rebels and the Kazh.

Which would give Koban the argument they needed to take the dais and control of the star system with it.

"I did not," Azhma whispered to him. "It changes nothing."

Naizha grunted awake before he could say anything more. Connor knelt by her side.

"You were stunned by the enemy," he told her swiftly in English. "We are prisoners, and they have a High Chosen from the Kazh. Ovaizh is in charge and not letting them take the Mountain, but the situation is bad."

She remained lying down for a few moments, then closed all of her eyes for a moment before rising to a seated position.

"Lora," she greeted the woman guarding her. "What have you done?"

"Protected my children," Azhma said. "It was difficult to find a way. I am sorry."

Ovaizh had seen that Naizha was awake and walked over to them.

"Cousin. You have, once again, chosen poorly."

"Not as poorly as you."

Connor wasn't entirely sure that *cousin* meant the same thing to the reezh as he translated it. The relationship between the two women was obvious to the eye, though, even with Naizha tied up.

"There is still an answer here," Ovaizh declared. "Tell me how to use the Mountain of Astral Might, and I will weave a tale to protect you."

Troth groaned, the first of the Academicians to wake. Ovaizh gave him a disgusted look.

"Or would you rather continue to play with mongrels?" she demanded. "Our blood raises us up, as ordained by the Nine, and you would throw that away."

"There is a reason no one ever told you the truth. Even as a child, you were—"

Connor couldn't follow the stream of words after that, but Ovaizh clearly could. She slapped Naizha across the face, throwing her back onto the ground.

"Our people are trapped while the wreckage of this stupid war blockades us. Your *mistake* of a brother killed the Speaker, and *you* have betrayed all blood and honor. I would share a faith with the Nine without bowing to them, but to protect our people, I find I have no choice."

"There is a choice," Naizha said, muffled enough by the ground that Connor had trouble making out the words. "There is *always* a choice."

Ovaizh spat on the ground next to her cousin, then turned on her heel, striding back toward Koban.

Connor had the grim suspicion they were out of time.

"We've got them," Rennell suddenly snapped in his ear. "Mage Wu and the others are in the prison. We've jammed coms and taken down the guards.

"Wu has found Komarazhi, and there are three reezh children in the cell with her. Toddler through preteen, she figures."

Connor closed his eyes and shifted closer to Azhma.

"You have three children," he whispered in Korazhi. "Young, very young. They are, as you told us, with Komarazhi."

"How..."

"They're safe," he promised her. "Trust me now as you didn't trust us before. Martian Mages have your children. *They are safe.*"

Across the central chamber, Koban and Ovaizh were talking. He couldn't tell what they were saying, but while they were as animated as before, it didn't look like an argument this time.

"What does it change? We can do nothing."

The two reezh Mages were walking toward the dais. They were out of time. Connor was out of ideas.

"Untie me, Lora. I can end this—then you get Naizha to the dais and she can end *all* of this."

Everything they had done. Every piece of luck, good or bad, that Connor had been hit with in this system, had put them all there. Less than five meters from victory.

With everything riding on whether Connor O'Hannagain had convinced an alien mother her children were safe and that he held the key to the future of the Ordin System and her people.

"Which is more dangerous, the Mother or the Warrior?"

Naizha's phrasing and words were reezh, but Connor understood the meaning. Kipling had once summarized it terrifyingly well: *For the female of the species is more deadly than the male.*

For a moment, he thought Azhma was going to be frozen until it was too late, unable to decide even in the face of the surrender of her people to the empire they'd bled to escape.

Then he felt long-fingered hands on his wrists, and the manacles fell away.

In the same instant that Koban stepped onto the dais and raised their hands. Magic filled the room with a spark of barely sensed electricity, and the silver dust the darkness had concealed flared with brilliant light.

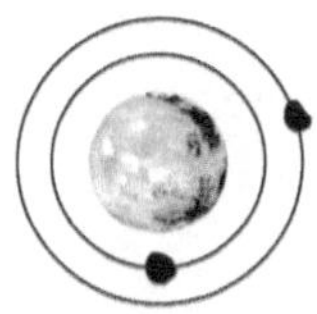

CHAPTER 52

THE DARK AND SHROUDED Central Chamber of the Mountain of Astral Might came to life under Koban's magic, a liquid silver orrery forming above the High Chosen's head that perfectly mirrored the star system surrounding them.

Victory or defeat hung between breaths as Connor plunged his hand under his armor and suit jacket, through a space between straps that his reezh captors had failed to find. The massive five-cylinder revolver slid into his hand like it had been custom-smithed for him—because it had.

"Look to the sky and the magic of our people," Koban proclaimed. "This is the gift of the Nine, my friends. Through their power, we can shape the galaxy."

The silver swirled, sections of it expanding. The asteroid cluster around the Academy was recognizable after a moment as Koban located their enemy and expanded them so everyone could see.

The combined force of Ordin and Martian ships above the Academy were little more than silver chips, even at the increased size, but Connor knew it was enough for Koban to act.

"Through the power we have been given, we can find our enemies, wherever they hide. We can bring them within our reach and we can strike. Them. Down!"

Koban raised their hands and Connor fired.

He'd never fired a weapon at another living being before. Roslyn Chambers had once warned him it was a burden he didn't want to take onto his soul, but at that moment, the lives of thousands of friends and colleagues and the freedom of *billions* of innocents was at stake.

He'd practiced with the weapon religiously. It held five shots, each a high-velocity discarding-sabot tungsten penetrator designed to punch through exosuit armor.

Two hammered into Koban while a third buried itself in the wall of the chamber somewhere. Almost perfect center-mass shots, the penetrators tore the reezh Mage's torso apart, collapsing them to the dais in pieces and spraying the space behind them with gore.

For a moment, everything was still, the entire space at the heart of the Mountain deadly silent in pure shock.

And then a lot more shooting started.

Connor's revolver had almost as much power as a proper penetrator rifle at close range but lost that kinetic energy swiftly over any distance. It was still able to put both of the remaining rounds through the first Paladin to come at him, their sword glowing with energy that blazed toward the ceiling as the reezh crumpled.

The *second* Paladin to charge at him with a raised sword went down like his strings had been cut as a round fired by one of those full-sized penetrator rifles struck him. Others were going down all across the room as Rennell's commandos took ruthless advantage of surprise.

Then Connor saw Ovaizh coming at him, light flaring around her hands, and remembered the speedloaders for his revolver had been tucked behind the chestplate of his armor. He didn't have a reload, and even if he did, he didn't have time.

Ovaizh's rage-fueled magic hammered toward him in spikes of blazing white fire that helped replace the swiftly dimming illumination from the silver simulacrum above them—especially as those spikes froze in the air, suspended a full meter from Connor as he and the reezh Mage glared at each other.

"It's over, cousin," Naizha said flatly, her own hands glowing with power as she stepped up beside Connor. "For the sake of our people, stand down. I will end this *stupid* civil war and drive the Kazh *you invited* from our star."

The glow of the conjured fire vanished as Ovaizh released her spell. Suddenly, Connor wasn't the focus of her attention, and the two reezh woman stared at each other, a moment of constrained quiet in the chaos of the firefight.

"No." A new blaze of fire hammered toward Naizha, who blocked it with a gesture—but Ovaizh clearly knew exactly how her power stacked up against her cousin. Connor didn't see her draw the gun before she fired it.

Troth had. The Academician was still Mage-cuffed, his hands manacled behind him to prevent him from using his magic, but neither Connor nor Naizha had gone far from where they'd been prisoners.

He flung himself forward, knocking Naizha out of the way as a blaze of green light accompanied by a crackling hiss filled the room. *Something* struck Troth in the chest, flinging the Mage backward—and then the sound and light repeated itself and *Ovaizh* fell.

Lora Azhma strode forward, her weapon in her hand, and pulled Naizha to her feet.

"You have to get to the dais," she growled, pushing her mate's sister toward the center of the chamber.

"Troth!" Naizha exclaimed, trying to push past Azhma to reach the fallen reezh Mage.

"He'll still be there after you've saved everyone," Connor told Naizha. "I've got him."

He wasn't sure how his first-aid training was going to handle an alien species and an energy weapon unlike anything he'd ever seen, but he *was* sure how ugly things might get if Naizha didn't reach the central dais.

She hesitated for one more moment, then was moving again. A Paladin tried to intercept her and was smashed aside by a blow of magic Connor didn't even see. Another was shot down by one of Rennell's commandos before they even got close.

The entire simulacrum chamber seemed to freeze as Naizha stepped onto the dais. Whatever trick was needed to activate the Mountain of Astral Might, it took moments, nothing more. The simulacrum lit up above their heads, the silver swirling around the star in a surprisingly simple yet extraordinary gesture of power.

The shooting stopped. A fence of Paladin swords appeared around Naizha, standing still for only a moment before they toppled to the ground. She'd just, Connor guessed, disarmed every hostile Paladin in the entire *Mountain*.

Silver chips appeared on the simulacrum, flashing with light as Naizha turned her attention to them. As each spark representing a ship flashed, it grew large enough to be judged as to its position and type.

Connor knew roughly where the Kadak and Kazh formations were and could tell when Naizha found rebel ships. They vanished—reappearing elsewhere in the system, he realized with a mental sigh of relief.

He turned his attention to Troth, checking the reezh's pulse. Thankfully, he knew enough first aid for the aliens to manage that, finding a weak but present beat.

"What did she shoot him with?" he asked Lora.

Her answer meant nothing to him. He didn't know the words. Before he could say more, Rennell was suddenly there, her armor turned a pale gray that was clearly visible in the room as she offered Azhma a medical kit.

"My reezh first aid is rusty," she told the woman calmly. "Can you help him?"

Azhma replied, still using reezh too complex for Connor to follow—only for his earbud to suddenly start translating again.

"The neural disruptor is supposed to be nonlethal, but I believe Ovaizh overcharged it. His responses are wrong. I don't know what to do with this. He needs a hospital!"

"Then we get a stretcher," Rennell said. "My people are on it. We'll get him the help he needs, Lora Azhma."

The reezh nodded, taking the medkit and going through its supplies like it might have an answer for her. Finally, she looked up at Rennell.

"My children?" she asked.

"I judged it best to keep the prisoners where they were," the commando replied. "They're protected by five of our Mages and half a dozen of my best people. You have the word of the Mage-Queen of Mars, your children are safe."

Lora Azhma would not know how rarely officers of the Protectorate pledged the word of their Queen, but she seemed to pick up some of the weight.

Connor joined her in going through the medkit. He judged Troth was going to live, but a neural weapon could have terrifying side effects. Humans had never succeeded in building a safe one.

By the time the stretcher arrived, though, the simulacrum above them was calmly clear: Naizha, Cadatch of the Ordin System, had moved all of her enemies to an isolated spot well inside the orbit of the asteroid belt.

They wouldn't be able to jump out from there. The negotiations, Connor suspected, were going to be very short.

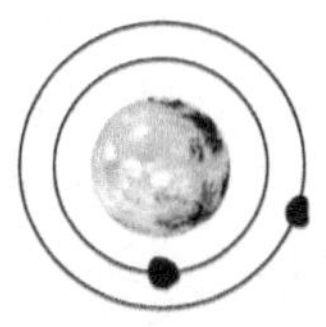

CHAPTER 53

"ORDIN SYSTEM, ARRIVING!"

Last Stand at Alamo's Marines had formed a perfect honor guard. They snapped to attention as the shuttle ramp hit the deck, disgorging Cadatch Naizha and her personal escort.

Mike Kelzin stood off to one side with Xi, watching the alien head of state nod respectfully to the Marines before walking between them to reach her destination and her hosts. Rose-robed reezh walked with her, their eyes ever-watchful, even here.

"Those rose robes now mark graduates of the Academy," Xi murmured in his ear. "All three of her escorts would never have been Mages without her and her brother."

"Sending a message," he replied. "To us, and to her people."

The reezh media had sent reporters up earlier and were positioned with cameras and drones to pick up this historic moment, the formal meeting between the Ordin Cadatch and the aliens who had helped her system stay free.

Those recorders were picking up the three rose-robed Mages making up Naizha's escort. They would also pick up that Naizha knew exactly how to respond to Connor and Rantala's extended hands, shaking them in a manner no Ordin reezh should have known a few weeks earlier.

Rantala led the way for the first group to head deeper into the ship, but Mike was there for a reason. There were a few people he needed to be sure left the shuttle safely—not that he'd gone quite so far as to offer to fly it.

If only because Xi had told him that would be stupid.

The two Komarazhis and Captain Joto were next. The Kessler cascade above Orandar had been clear for less than twenty-four hours, but Joto and Adazh Komarazhi had been on the first shuttle down to check on So Komarazhi.

The same shuttle that had brought Mike and Xi up to the cruiser, in fact. His own shuttles had burned their fuel flying air cover over the Mountain of Astral Might. He'd done enough damage with his burst of the main engines that the locals hadn't managed to find real anti-aircraft gear before it was all over, but the shuttles had taken more than scratches along the way.

Like *Rhapsody in Bohemia* herself, the shuttles couldn't safely make orbit. Mike had been forced to order his crew to destroy the classified sections of his ship and leave her to the Ordin.

"I think we're up," Xi told him as a message chimed on both of their wrist-comps. "Are we waiting for anyone else?"

"Our Chimeran friends are safe aboard and our crew came up an hour ago," he replied. "Let's go to the party."

It wasn't really a party, but Mike was more willing to go to a party than a diplomatic meeting. Telling himself that it was a party helped him walk into a room where he was the official representative of the Protectorate's intelligence services, strange as that concept was.

It wasn't like he and Xi could even wallflower, as she might have done at an actual party. There were less than a dozen people in the room including them. There were designated seats with name tags!

"I believe this is everyone," O'Hannagain said as Mike and Xi sat down. "I appreciate your willingness to come aboard our vessel, Cadatch Naizha. We recognize that separating you from the Mountain does create a vulnerability for your people."

"The last of the rebel and Kazh crews were removed from their ships fourteen hours ago, Ambassador," the new reezh ruler replied. "Those vessels will be examined and repaired, as necessary, before being refitted for service in the Shield of Ordin."

Her English was surprisingly good. Mike had been briefed on the strange source of the language proficiency of key members of the Ordin government, but he was still impressed by Naizha's ability to speak it.

"We will not have the strength we had before this nightmare, but we will be more capable than I had dared hope while the conflict was ongoing," she continued. "I do not believe we will be able to commit warships to our mutual cause immediately. There is much work and reconstruction to be done—not least, refitting our warships to remove the mark of the Lie present in the Engines of Sacred Sacrifice."

"Will there be problems training the Channelers now?" Xi asked, leaning forward next to Mike. "Not all of them may be capable of serving as Jump Mages, but even so, training them all will be a massive undertaking."

"It will," Naizha agreed. "And if our connection prospers, I may, in time, ask your Protectorate for teachers."

"We may be sending you students first, Cadatch," Rantala said drily. "It seems there is much of magic we have not yet seen."

"The starship we sit within, Mage-Commodore, suggests that your people have done far more with the tools my ancestors left you than we could have," she replied. "Without your aid, we would once again bow to the Reezh Ida.

"You have come far further than my ancestors could have imagined when their work with your people exposed our own lies. We owe a debt against our parents' crimes that could not be easily paid—and yet your aid is the only reason we are still free.

"The debt I, as Cadatch, owe to your nation is beyond accounting. I do not believe it can ever be paid, but we will begin as we have already acted: as friends and allies against the dark.

"I will take the time I need to prepare my fleets and educate my Mages, but when Mars calls for the aid of Ordin, know that the Cadatch ozh Ahadan will be waiting to answer."

"The price has been too high," O'Hannagain said grimly. "But that is why we came, to build alliances." He paused. "How is Academician Troth?"

For the first time since Mike had entered the meeting, Naizha lost some of her perfect composure. She closed her eyes and looked down at the table.

"Our doctors assure me that he is… *in there,* I believe is the best translation. But he has lost his speech and much of the control of his body. We will do all we can, but in the best case, it will be some time before he is himself again.

"His sacrifice will not be forgotten."

The thought of being in that kind of state was frankly terrifying to Mike. To be conscious and aware but unable to speak or even interact with the world around him? He shivered—and then had a thought.

In *his* particular case, the situation they'd described would be easily circumvented.

"Cadatch, I am not certain how advanced your own neuro-electronic systems are," he said slowly, "but we have several different types of high-complexity cybernetics capable of interacting with the brain.

"I have a short-range radio communicator inside my skull, for example," he said. "While I imagine interfacing these kinds of systems with reezh neurology wouldn't be simple, it might be easier than starting from scratch."

"We… do not generally allow such technologies to directly interface with the brain," Naizha replied after a moment. "The only technology of that type that we use is the Engine of Sacred Sacrifice, and I believe that may have tainted the area in my people's minds."

"The existence of both the Prometheus Interface and the Engine of Sacred Sacrifice may make transferal of the technology Captain Kelzin mentions easier than you may think," Lisa's voice said from thin air.

"If you would be prepared to share the Engine's schematics with me, I would be able to compare them against my own Interface. With that comparison, I believe it would be simpler for *Last Stand*'s doctors to fabricate an implantable cybernetic interface for Academician Troth."

Naizha was silent, as if stunned, for at least twenty seconds before she finally spoke again.

"You are… one of the Prometheans?" she asked.

"I am Lisa, senior Promethean aboard *Barracuda*," Lisa confirmed. "I apologize; I was invited to this meeting, and I presumed you had been informed."

"I did not realize what that meant," Naizha admitted. Mike was pretty sure he heard awe in her voice. "Please, I would be delighted to provide you the schematics for the Engine—on one condition, Promethean Lisa."

"Your condition, Cadatch?" O'Hannagain asked.

"That in addition to seeing if the cybernetics Captain Kelzin mentions can be adapted for reezh neurology... I ask that you decipher what would be required to allow the victims in our engines to speak as Promethean Lisa does.

"Our sacrifices are lost; they never speak again. I did not realize that was different for your Prometheans. Between the Kadak and the Kazh ships we have captured, Ordin now possesses over a hundred Engines of Sacred Sacrifice with victims inside.

"Please. If you can find me a way to give them some form of life, I will..." She sighed. "I will owe an even greater debt than the one I already do."

"I know my Mage-Queen," O'Hannagain said. Something in his voice drew Mike's gaze to focus on the big Ambassador. "Not as well as perhaps I should, but I do know her.

"There will be no debt for anything we can do to help the victims of this monstrous technology. The life we have given our Prometheans is a shadow of what we would *like* to provide, but it is something.

"If we can provide that to the victims of your own monsters, we will. This is not a negotiating point. It will happen."

Naizha nodded, then gestured to one of her aides. The Mage passed her a chip case and she laid it on the table.

"This, too, is not a negotiating point, Ambassador O'Hannagain."

She slid the case over to O'Hannagain.

"That contains a complete copy of every record my ancestors brought back from Mars. Every record, every video, every report that was assembled in the years our expedition was there. Everything we learned about your species and magic while we worked with yours."

Everyone stared at the chip case like it held live snakes.

"I hope you find answers to your question inside, Ambassador, but these files do my ancestors no favors. We did great harm to your people, and these records explain it all. Providing the information is the tiniest beginning of the recompense I intend to make."

"The full records of the reezh side of Project Olympus."

Kiera's words hung in the room like a falling sword.

"Not full," Mike cautioned, glancing at his other wife on the holoconference. "I haven't had time to go through it all yet, but my impression is that we've got about fifty years. Maybe sixty. We're not sure of the exact start date of Project Olympus, but the last of our dates in the files is twenty-two-twenty-five."

"Before we know of any Mages in the Eugenicist families," Montgomery said grimly. "But not before magic started showing up in the Olympus subjects. Those records alone might just make the whole mission to Ordin worth it, Captain."

"We also got the alliance we were after," O'Hannagain pointed out.

There were only four people physically in Mage-Commodore Rantala's office. It was the plain room next to the Flag Deck, not the gorgeously decorated space next to the bridge, but it could conference with the Link systems and kept him from interfering with Mage-Captain Bourgeois.

"Nine Type Ones and a slew of escorts," Rantala agreed. "Once they've been refitted and cleaned up, that's not a small fleet. How much Naizha might be prepared to send to liberate Chimera is an open question, of course."

"She owes us," the Ambassador said grimly. "I would suggest we allow that to act as a passive lever rather than actively calling in the debt. It will be more effective that way."

Sometimes, Mike was starting to think that Connor O'Hannagain was an all-right guy. And then he said something like that.

"What about continuing the survey?" he said. "My other ships are at Azha right now, confirming what Mage-Captain Chambers reported. The occupation force there doesn't seem to have been reduced by the new conflict, which suggests they may be concerned about their ability to hold on to the system with fewer ships."

"That suggests options," the Queen conceded. "But until we believe we can *hold* any system we take from the Kazh, I refuse to paint a target on any other populace's collective head.

"We couldn't avoid making Chimera a target, and Ordin was drawn into this before we really had enough information, but we have to be careful.

"Scouting the Primes continues to be our starting point, Captain Kelzin. I wish we could replace your ship more readily than we can."

"I'm not sure another ship or crew could have done what Mike did, Kiera," Kelly finally said. "Not that I'm particularly *happy* with my spouses deciding to take that risk, but I honestly don't think anyone else could have done it."

Kiera laughed, the Queen's amusement a relief from a momentary spike of concern on Mike's part.

"No, Mike, you did what you had to do, and you did it well," she told him. "We lost more than I had hoped Ordin would cost us, but you achieved the mission. I'm sure we'll find something for you to do while you're on *Last Stand*."

The conference fell quiet. Mike was studying Kelly and trying not to show it. She looked tired, her hair marked with the beginnings of the faded tones he recognized as her not having dyed it recently.

"What's our status with Chimera?" O'Hannagain finally asked. "It's been two months; we have to have heard something by now."

Kiera shook her head, any humor fading from her face and eyes.

"Second Fleet has been scouting the system with destroyers from a great distance," she noted. "Their force there is remaining constant, and we *think* they've stopped orbital bombardments, but we've had no contact from Garuda or anywhere except the surveillance outpost.

"Thanks to your mission in Ordin, we now know that the Kazh have no way to detect the Links, which means that we should be able to reestablish contact with the stay-behind force safely, but..."

"But someone has to get in to tell them they can turn the Links back on," O'Hannagain finished for the Queen. "And until then, we know nothing?"

"Unfortunately." Kiera fell silent.

"That's not your mission, my friends," Montgomery finally said, the Prince-Chancellor audibly forcing a touch of cheer into his voice. "You're to continue your sweep of the Primes.

"Hand Shea Riley has taken responsibility for making contact with our forces on Garuda," he told them. "If anyone can find a way to breach an orbiting armada and connect with an army told to hide until further notice, it's one of Her Majesty's Hands."

ABOUT THE AUTHOR

 **GLYNN STEWART** is the author of Starship's Mage, a bestselling science fiction and fantasy series where faster-than-light travel is possible–but only because of magic. His other works include science fiction series Duchy of Terra, Castle Federation and Vigilante, as well as the urban fantasy series ONSET and Changeling Blood.

Writing managed to liberate Glynn from a bleak future as an accountant. With his personality and hope for a high-tech future intact, he lives in Canada with his partner, their cats, and an unstoppable writing habit.

CREDITS

The following people were involved in making this book:
Copyeditor: Richard Shealy
Cover Artist: Roman Chalyi
Faolan's Pen Publishing:
Jack Giesen

And a sincere thank you to Glynn's Patreon subscribers!

OTHER BOOKS BY GLYNN STEWART

For release announcements join the mailing list
or visit **GlynnStewart.com**

STARSHIP'S MAGE
Starship's Mage
Hand of Mars
Voice of Mars
Alien Arcana
Judgment of Mars
UnArcana Stars
Sword of Mars
Mountain of Mars
The Service of Mars
A Darker Magic
Mage-Commander
Beyond the Eyes of Mars
Nemesis of Mars
Chimera's Star
Ambassador for Mars
Chimera's Fall
The Lies Arcana
Shadow of Mars (upcoming)

Starship's Mage: Red Falcon
Interstellar Mage
Mage-Provocateur
Agents of Mars

Starship's Mage Novellas
Pulsar Race
Mage-Queen's Thief

HOUSE ADAMANT

The Exodus Gambit
The Old Guard
The Valkyrie Stratagem
Regent's Mate (*upcoming*)

EXILE

Exile
Refuge
Crusade
Ashen Stars: An Exile Novella

CASTLE FEDERATION

Space Carrier Avalon
Stellar Fox
Battle Group Avalon
Q-Ship Chameleon
Rimward Stars
Operation Medusa
A Question of Faith: A Castle Federation Novella

Dakotan Confederacy

Admiral's Oath
To Stand Defiant
Unbroken Faith

VIGILANTE

(WITH TERRY MIXON))
Heart of Vengeance
Oath of Vengeance

Bound By Stars: A Vigilante Series
(With Terry Mixon)

Bound By Law
Bound by Honor
Bound by Blood

AETHER SPHERES

Nine Sailed Star
Void Spheres (*upcoming*)

TEER AND KARD

Wardtown
Blood Ward
Blood Adept
Adept's Path (*upcoming*)

CHANGELING BLOOD

Changeling's Fealty
Hunter's Oath
Noble's Honor
Fae, Flames & Fedoras: A Changeling Blood Novella

ONSET

ONSET: To Serve and Protect
ONSET: My Enemy's Enemy
ONSET: Blood of the Innocent
ONSET: Stay of Execution
Murder by Magic: An ONSET Novella

STANDALONE NOVELS & NOVELLAS

Children of Prophecy
City in the Sky
Excalibur Lost: A Space Opera Novella
Balefire: A Dark Fantasy Novella
Icebreaker: A Fantasy Naval Thriller
Seekers in the Void: A Space Opera Adventure

www.ingramcontent.com/pod-product-compliance
Lightning Source LLC
Chambersburg PA
CBHW031201310726
48969CB00001B/165